PRAISE FOR *ALL THE*

"A heady and haunting mix of historical fiction, polar survival horror, and a meditation on gender, identity, and the enduring mysteries of the self. You won't soon forget Jonathan Morgan and his trial by ice."

—Paul Tremblay, author of *A Head Full of Ghosts*
and *Survivor Song*

"Deeply haunting and full of dread, *All the White Spaces* beautifully balances grief and loss with concepts of family honor and self-determination, in the midst of frozen survival horror, with echoes of Dan Simmons and John Carpenter. Highly recommended."

—Christopher Golden, *New York Times*
bestselling author of *Road of Bones*

"Frozen into the desolation and isolation of Antarctica, this stunning debut delivers a thrilling tale of survival, terror, and strength that will chill you to the core."

—Tim Lebbon, *New York Times* bestselling
author of *Eden* and *The Silence*

"A sly and unsettling gem of a book that makes for an immersive read. The storytelling is as taut as the setting is stark, and rife with creeping dread. . . . I was chilled to the bone while reading it, and could not put it down. I loved every frostbitten word!"

—Camilla Bruce, author of *You Let Me In*

"A journey into winter, a growing sense of isolation, a battle with the elements, and facing down the ghosts of the past—Ally Wilkes has taken some of my very favorite ingredients and bound them into a deliciously spooky and compulsive tale."

—Alison Littlewood, author of *A Cold Season*
and *The Hidden People*

"A masterpiece. A journey of discovery that left me breathless and emotional for all the right reasons. With this powerful debut, Ally Wilkes has not arrived quietly on the horror scene; she has scaled a towering iceberg and roared."

—Rio Youers, critically acclaimed
author of *Lola on Fire*

"An intricately described story of loss, self-discovery, and belonging . . . Wonderfully immersive; I heard every creak and was bitten by the freezing fog. *All the White Spaces* is a ghost story of the heart that becomes a harrowing battle for survival in malicious barrens."

—Louis Greenberg, author of *Exposure*

"A gripping narrative that is at once explorer's yarn, a trans man's coming-of-age story, and a tale of a survivor grappling with horrors that defy definition . . . from gritty seafaring challenges to a desperate struggle with demons that blur the line between the supernatural and the subconscious."

—*Publishers Weekly*

"A vivid, immersive tale about a fictional British expedition to the Antarctic in 1919–20—classic territory, but with a transgender perspective . . . A gripping read. On top of that . . . is the element of supernatural horror. Here, too, the author excels, creating a new sort of ghost story in the empty, icy wastes."

—*The Guardian*

"The desolation of the Arctic and human desperation . . . might intrigue fans of *The Terror* or *The Thing*."

—Den of Geek

"A great debut . . . If you're into supernatural, psychological thrillers, this is perfect for you. This book will keep you on the edge of your seat and you won't want to put it down."

—Red Carpet Crash

ALL
THE
WHITE
SPACES

A NOVEL

ALLY WILKES

EMILY BESTLER BOOKS
—
ATRIA

New York   London   Toronto   Sydney   New Delhi

An Imprint of Simon & Schuster, Inc.
1230 Avenue of the Americas
New York, NY 10020

First Emily Bestler Books/Atria Paperback edition January 2023

EMILY BESTLER BOOKS / ATRIA PAPERBACK and colophon are trademarks of Simon & Schuster, Inc.

For information about special discounts for bulk purchases, please contact Simon & Schuster Special Sales at 1-866-506-1949 or business@simonandschuster.com.

The Simon & Schuster Speakers Bureau can bring authors to your live event. For more information or to book an event, contact the Simon & Schuster Speakers Bureau at 1-866-248-3049 or visit our website at www.simonspeakers.com.

Interior design by Hope Herr-Cardillo
Photograph p. iii by Elisabeth Ansley/Arcangel and Getty Images.
All other images courtesy of Shutterstock.

Manufactured in the United States of America

1 3 5 7 9 10 8 6 4 2

The Library of Congress has cataloged the hardcover edition as follows:

Names: Wilkes, Ally, author.
Title: All the white spaces : a novel / Ally Wilkes.
Description: First Emily Bestler Books/Atria Books hardcover edition. |
New York : Emily Bestler Books/Atria, 2022.
Identifiers: LCCN 2021042630 (print) | LCCN 2021042631 (ebook) |
ISBN 9781982182700 (hardcover) | ISBN 9781982182724 (ebook)
Subjects: LCGFT: Horror fiction.
Classification: LCC PR6123.I5363 A79 2022 (print) | LCC PR6123.I5363 (ebook)
| DDC 823/.92—dc23/eng/20211006
LC record available at https://lccn.loc.gov/2021042630
LC ebook record available at https://lccn.loc.gov/2021042631

ISBN 978-1-9821-8270-0
ISBN 978-1-9821-8271-7 (pbk)
ISBN 978-1-9821-8272-4 (ebook)

For anyone who's survived a Winter Journey

Men go out into the void spaces of the world for various reasons. Some are actuated simply by a love of adventure, some have the keen thirst for scientific knowledge, and others again are drawn away from the trodden paths by the "lure of little voices," the mysterious fascination of the unknown.

—Ernest Shackleton, *The Heart of the Antarctic*

THE 1920 BRITISH COATS LAND EXPEDITION

James "Australis" Randall...*leader*

Liam Clarke...*second-in-command*

Christian Mortimer ....*captain*

Jonny Wild...*sailing master*

Richard Boyd ....*first officer*

Mark Nicholls...*navigator*

Dr. Alexander Staunton ....*surgeon*

James Tarlington....................................*chief scientific officer*

David Laurence ....*first engineer/motor expert*

Reginald Ollivar.........................*second engineer/mountaineer*

Howard Holmes ....*mountaineer*

Bert Rees..*carpenter*

A. K. Duncan ....*dog master*

Harry Cooper ....*dog master's assistant/"dogsbody"*

Robert Macready..*cook*

Antonio "Tony" Perry...*able seaman*

Ted Smith ....*able seaman*

Martin Benham ....*able seaman*

Louis Archer..*able seaman*

Bill Jones...*able seaman*

Victor Bedloe..*storekeeper/seaman*

George Ellis...*stoker*

Phil Parker ....*stoker*

Jonathan Morgan......................................*stowaway/"spare"*

The War had ended.

My mother had opened the Christmas jam, as if conscious she had been keeping it in reserve for nothing; the breakfast room smelled of quinces, damsons, and pine needles. Our maid, Chloe, turned the house into a perfect bower, bending branches over the mantelpieces, garlanding the stairs with ivy, and bunching wreaths of holly around the photograph of my brothers. A sort of shrine had grown up in the front hall, where they stood resplendent in their brand-new uniforms. The patch of carpet in front of it was thready and uncertain from my mother's constant pacing, echoed in the burnish to the sides of the photograph frame, too often picked up and set down.

The telegram—the telegram that changed everything—had arrived early, the boy ringing the doorbell and cycling away without waiting for a reply.

My mother summoned me to her too-hot, too-fussy, floral-scented sanctuary in the morning room. I stood awkwardly at the door in my long, scuffed boots as she flitted around a table heaving with poinsettia. She didn't look at me.

"I know I'm being silly—Jo," she said, slender fingers wrapped around the little envelope. "It's probably just news—they must be well on their way to the coast by now. We'll have them back for Christmas!"

The shortened name sounded wrong in her mouth; she was using it to jolly me along. Unlike my brothers, my mother normally insisted on my full name, which I hated.

I swallowed, and didn't trust myself to reply. The War had ended, but Rufus and Francis were still in France, incapacitated by their wounds. Their best friend, Harry, had already sent me a letter—uncensored—about the horrors of the Casualty Clearing Station. I'd hidden it from my parents in the biscuit tin under my bed. Partly because they didn't like Harry writing to me, it wasn't appropriate; but mostly because it was so stark and unflinching. Harry had never learned to dissemble.

A week ago my brothers should have been fit for repatriation, put on an ambulance train for the long journey to the coast, Blighty beyond. I'd worried, of course, but small worries, tame ones. Whether they'd have enough blankets, or if Rufus was being rude to the nurses. He had a temper on him.

We were unlikely to get them back as we'd known them, although that hadn't quite sunk in yet. Their wounds were terrible—*septic*, Harry had written, badly septic, from the thick mud of the battlefield.

"It's probably just their arrival date." Hovering, she still didn't open the envelope. It wasn't a thick envelope—contained only a single sheet of paper. But a horrible clawing sensation rose up in my throat as I considered what news that single sheet might hold.

"Sit down," I said, and she did so with a little sigh. I would do no such thing myself—not on the satin chaise, nor the dainty antique armchair—but I crossed the room, boots muffled by the thick carpet, to stand over her writing desk. Her lily-of-the-valley scent was stronger there, making my breakfast turn in my stomach. A short glance to the clock above the mantelpiece. The sun was still struggling to come over the rosebushes, and Father, as usual, was absent: he wouldn't be back until long after winter dark.

We looked at the envelope together for a long, long time.

She reached behind and crept her hand into mine. It was the first time she'd done so without remarking how blunt my fingers were, how I bit my nails savagely. *Unbecoming*.

I thought of Harry's description of their last engagement: the long quiet stealing over the battlefield when the guns stopped. The smoke billowing over the riverbanks, Harry lying in the mud with his binoculars, not daring to breathe, making terrible bargains. A man could suffer a dreadful wound—it could blow clean through him, painting his insides onto the dirt—and stay silent. He might not even notice how badly he was wounded.

"Here." My voice sounded rough. "If you won't." I took the envelope. Her shoulders sagged, and I realized she'd been waiting all along for me to do it: for one of us to be brave.

I didn't want to open it, but set my jaw and fumbled with her delicate little letter opener as though my hands were icy cold. I saw the familiar form, my eyes jumping ahead without me, picking out the handwritten words and sentences:

Deeply regret to inform you that—

I felt a wave crashing over me. The ordinary sounds of the household were suddenly far away: Chloe, humming to herself as she swept the back hallway; the birds scratching in the chimneys; the faint growl of a motorcar going by. The ice had spread to my face and mouth, and I could no more speak than I could breathe underwater.

"Oh," my mother said. "Not the boys, not them—"

The Army Council expresses their sympathy—

I dropped the piece of paper—so few words, so many blank spaces—onto her desk.

Although I'd lain sleepless for several weeks with my eyes fixed on the ceiling, imagining maps of the Hindenburg Line marching across the plasterwork, I hadn't understood how very far away Rufus and Francis really were. They always felt just around the corner, as if they'd stepped into the next room. But they had been miles and miles away, dying of their wounds.

I had been at home, when I'd so desperately wished to go with them. I'd been at home, while they—

Both always did their duty—

With some difficulty, I realized I was starting to cry. I scrubbed my eyes furiously with the back of my hand. My mother was still looking at me: I had refused to cry in front of her—or Father—since I was very little.

"I'm sorry," I said, and my voice was so thick and deep I barely recognized it. "I'm sorry, I'm so sorry."

I put my hand on her shoulder. She was warm, and I could feel her birdlike bones through the fabric. She slapped me away with such force it rang across the room. The telegram lay on the floor.

Died of their wounds without suffering—

They had died together. That is to say—they'd died the same night. They would have wanted it that way. Together in all things. Their bedroom had been cleaned and aired for their homecoming, and in my long nights of half-waking sometimes I thought I heard familiar sounds: the creak of mattress springs as they told ghost stories by moonlight or traced expedition routes on the atlas. On clear summer nights they would sneak out into town, leaving the windows open and bodies made of empty clothing in their beds, coming back for breakfast with tales of adventure, dragging Harry apologetically in their wake.

They would not come back again. The vicious hurt of it grabbed me around the chest and made me stagger away from the desk like a drunk.

"I should go—" I said, my voice finally breaking. "I should fetch Father—"

"No." Tight, quivering, almost another slap. "Go to your room."

She didn't look at me.

I reeled out into the dark hallway, grabbing at the door handles, levering myself down the corridor until I was in the water closet, throwing up my eggs and bacon into the sink. I braced myself against the porcelain and shuddered, wiping the sweat off my face and loosening the stiff fabric of my day dress around my neck. It was normally my favorite, the plainest and most masculine one I had: it did up tight like a shirt collar, revealing no expanse of pale skin.

Our house was large enough that I could wander in a daze through carpeted corridors and narrow tiled passageways. I passed Chloe, peeping out of the kitchen door like an apparition, and it seemed to take an age to climb the back staircase, one step at a time; my boots dragging on the tread; my layers of flannel and velveteen weighing me down like lead. Everything once familiar was strange. I felt as if I were opening doors at random. But suddenly I was in my brothers' room.

They'd insisted on sharing: of course they had. Their room took up the entire length of the first floor; faced the harbor, across the blur of December fog and half-empty streets. They could look out and see the sea, the distance and the sea, while I had to be content with a small patch of garden wall and my mother's magnolia. I heaved the sash window up with a judder, the movement making the tight little buttons at my cuffs bite into my skin. I wasn't expected to raise my arms above my head—I was expected to be satisfied with convention, even when it pained me. I stared out. The wind whipped at my raw cheeks where unchecked tears had dried.

I took a long, shivering breath, bracing myself against the windowsill. *Not the boys.*

I tried not to think about my brothers lying under that stinking dirty foreign soil, the same soil that had stopped their hearts. They'd sent letters—at first I'd found them funny—about staying in dusty little French farmhouses, making friends with the locals. About long marches through blasted fields, and the terrible food in the trenches. They'd continued to joke affectionately: telling us it was all a game, and one they intended to win. But when Harry's letters started arriving on my doorstep in their green envelopes, apologizing for the presumption—he needed to tell *someone*—they had a very different tone.

Duty, and sacrifice. And horrors.

I turned slowly. Dark wallpaper, gray and burgundy, a stark contrast to my own room: chintz and lace and all the things I hated; all the things that had been chosen for me. My brothers' bedroom was as neat and businesslike as a hospital ward. Blankets tucked in at perfect right angles, unfilled water carafes on the nightstand, sparkling in the pale sunlight like cut ice. Combs and brilliantine lined up on the dressing table, programs for social dances tucked into the corners of the mirror. The long north wall was covered entirely with maps. Sea charts. Newspaper cuttings.

I wiped my mouth, and stared across at the perfect jagged ball of Antarctica. Its unfinished edges and tints of pale blue dominated the room entirely: for as long as I could remember, the South Pole had been the center of everything. I could almost see fingerprints on the glass, ghostly traces, where fingers had slid their way down from the Weddell Sea. Of course Chloe would have wiped it clean by now.

"That's where we'll land," Rufus had said, tapping a finger against his lips. "Vahsel Bay. Base camp. Then the sledging parties—off the maps and straight to the center."

"You'd better hope there's nothing in the way," Harry said from behind him—Harry's allotted place—and Rufus raised an eyebrow.

"There won't be. Old Australis knows what he's doing."

From the newspaper clippings, James "Australis" Randall stared down at me, handsome and commanding. He was broke—nearly bankrupt—but insisted he *had* to try, again and again, for the South Pole, despite the accident that had swooped him off the deck of his ship, crushed him in the freezing water against the hidden terrible faces of an iceberg, left him battling for his life on a floe in thirty degrees of frost. I wondered what it would be like to die from such intense cold. "I imagine it'd be rather like falling asleep," Francis had replied, and squeezed my shoulder. "Not so bad."

Randall's accident had been in the Weddell Sea, that treacherous and deadly expanse of water, churning with pack ice, which blocked the route from the islands of South Georgia down to the Antarctic continent. When he'd returned, he'd tried the ice from another angle, where Liam Clarke had lost his fingers on the pitiless Great Ice Barrier—had refused point-blank to speak to the papers about it—saying that a man was entitled to leave the past behind.

I knew their stories so well.

And I could see traces of my brothers in the impatient choppy edges of each clipping—my mother's dressmaking scissors, borrowed and blunted and never returned. I could see them in each pin jammed into the wallpaper—my mother's violent disapproval, and Rufus's smile behind her back. "Maybe we'll take you with us," he'd say to me, half serious, half joking, eyes fixed keenly on mine to observe my reaction. "Would you like that?"

"Don't tease," Francis would whisper in reply.

I'd loved him for it, and longed to follow them—but knew I never would. My war-hero brothers, off on their adventure to the great white continent: I could almost see them now. Invincible; laughing; triumphant. Leaving me behind again.

A half-sob. I buried my face in my hands, stretching my fingers wide, pressing into my flesh, trying to mold myself into someone different; someone who wasn't about to cry. Someone more like my brothers.

More like the man I knew I should have been.

I couldn't bear the thought of returning to my own room: cloying, stifling, as rigid as the tock-tock-tock of the metronome beating time during my endless piano lessons. The only thing in there which was mine—really mine—was shoved under the bed, hidden from Chloe and my mother as if it contained a hand grenade. But it was just a Crawford's digestive biscuit tin; a nude, tautly muscled Grecian discus thrower was stamped on the front. The tin guarded my greatest treasures: the fat bundle of letters from Harry—serving as my lifeline to the Front—and a gray woolen armband with a crudely stitched crown. Someone had dropped it on the street outside the recruiting station, in the early days of the big Derby enlistment drive. The army posters had stared down at me as I'd picked it up, slipped it into my pocket. It was given in return for pledging to serve: I couldn't believe anyone would treat something so precious so slightly.

Sometimes I'd try that armband on, see how it looked on me. I'd prop the biscuit tin in front of my mirror and stare at it. Then bury it back under my bed, with all its contents, shoving it out of sight.

I swallowed another sob. *Not the boys.*

A rustling. The wind came sneaking in like a thief, fluttering the curtains, toying with the newspaper clippings. The movement sent an unexpected shiver from the nape of my neck right down my spine. The fog made it dark for a December morning, so dark, and for a moment I could feel myself being watched by someone—something—just out of reach.

It was so quiet in the house I could have heard a hairpin drop.

I felt sure that if I removed my hands from my eyes, I would find someone else in the room. No—two someones, standing tall and straight with their backs to me. Hair neatly combed, uniforms pressed. Handsome faces still turned up towards Antarctica.

But Harry had been straightforward, hadn't spared me the details. While the shrapnel had mostly spared their faces (*mostly*), it was clear no one would be calling them handsome anymore. I thought about the ragged tearing of barbed wire, razor sharp on their tender skin, the mud, the mud, a chaos of shouts and screams and falling rain, the agonies of the men, and in the sudden darkness of the morning—

I opened my fingers, looked around the room. Breathed out. No one was there.

I gulped. I would have done anything to see them again, and it yawned beneath me like a crevasse in that quiet room. It opened up and swallowed me whole.

I knew where I'd find them.

My shoulders shaking, I heaved the window wider. I hung half out of it, a strand of stray hair plastering itself to my face in the pale, wet air. The fog was so thick I could hardly see the street, let alone the harbor, but I could hear the tide in the distance. The long, quiet pull of the sea, breathing itself back and forth against the shore, regular and composed as a sleeping giant.

It seemed wrong—fatally wrong—for it to be so calm. There should have been a storm. Wind lashing at my hair. Waves rushing forwards like dark battalions. The room seemed to lurch around me, like a gale in southern waters, and I clung on.

My brothers had left me behind. I'd hug their memories to my chest; I'd fix them forever in that photograph in our hallway. Rufus, looking straight at the camera with his tiger smile; Francis, a little more reserved, standing to one side. The studio walls were creamy white, and the frame gilded, but they didn't belong in it—no more than I belonged in this polite little floral world. They belonged outside, with a wider prospect, the sea stretching off into the distance. The endless washy horizon.

But now my brothers would never see Antarctica. Never know a clear day on the South Atlantic, or the jeweled ice of the floes. Their dreams had come to nothing, but I was the last Morgan sibling, and I knew where I'd find them.

I knew where I had to go.

The sea should have risen up. There should have been a tempest, a typhoon, a tidal wave. Crashing over the quay, breaking over me— making me anew.

Because I heard it then: the call of the South. I could hear my brothers. *Maybe we'll take you with us.*

ONE

THE *FORTITUDE*

THE *FORTITUDE*, AUSTRAL SPRING 1919

I

The storage locker was cramped and noisy.

When my candle guttered to its end, smoke curling inside the blackened panes of the trench lantern, I felt I'd been nailed into my own coffin. Rattling and shaking, the expedition's provisions strained at their lashings and tried to pry themselves loose. With sickening lurches, my stomach plummeting, the *Fortitude* made her way through the South Atlantic Ocean. It was more than I could bear: the all-consuming dark, the confinement, the need to hide. It felt like I'd hidden too long altogether.

I slept under a pile of blankets and tarpaulins: if the crew looked in, I'd be another sack of flour in the flickering light. The blankets were coarse, shot through with little knots and burrs, probably dirty—but I hardly cared. My jumper, a sober burnt green with two polished buttons at the collar, had been picked up on shore in South America; it already made me look like a vagabond. Nothing would be "kept for best" ever again. All the clothing Harry had bought for me, piece by piece until I had an entirely masculine wardrobe—it would be worn to destruction.

My pillows were sacks of dog food, making my cropped hair smell like a rendering house, but at least that dog food gave Harry an excuse to visit. Without him, there was nothing but crushing black, under the weight of all the decks and staircases: no food, no water, no candle. I was as dependent as a newborn child.

I drank in, greedily, glimpses of the *Fortitude* whenever he opened the locker door: I'd seen her only in the dark, head down and face covered. Stowing away, my heart in my throat. We'd paid the Argentine nightwatchman all the money we had left, and there wasn't a soul to be seen as we came aboard at Buenos Aires, rain seething off the deck like water coming to the boil.

It felt like an age ago, a dark frustrating age, and I longed to see the *Fortitude* properly. I'd whiled away long, lonely hours with nothing but my own thoughts; sometimes listening to the men clattering around in the galley, learning scandalous things—things I'd never even imagined, making my cheeks hot—about the women they'd left behind. I'd wished powerfully instead for the easy, idle chatter of Rufus and Francis, talking between themselves. But no matter how hard I longed for them, they weren't there.

Harry was my only companion. Just turned twenty-one, he seemed infinitely older than when we'd left England; although he'd kept his smart officer's mustache, his curly hair was becoming wild. He was a long way from the young man I'd met at Portsmouth harbor on that dull January day of the new peace; my mother shut away in her morning room, the house dimmed and shadowy. In the pinprick rain, I'd found Harry Cooper, unexpected—stepping out from behind a lamppost as if he'd been there all along. His face was unfamiliar; it had blurred in my memory, while my brothers' faces stayed fresh—although they might as well have been side by side in the same photograph frame. Despite the fact that we'd never passed a minute alone together, I knew Harry well, all his half-articulated doubts and fears. *I just need to tell someone.* Duty, and sacrifice—and men hanging on the barbed wire, worried by crows.

He'd said: "I wasn't sure if you'd want to see me"—as if we'd quarreled and he thought I might hold a grudge. I'd embraced him in the street, where anyone might see, and for a moment he'd gone limp in my arms.

I'd known, then, that I could talk him into anything.

But the farther we sailed, the more reluctant he seemed. We argued, quietly, by candlelight.

"Can you believe we've got away with it?" I almost forgot to keep my voice down—it burst out of me. Harry smiled, an overcast smile that made his eyes seem warm and steadfast.

"Not quite—not yet." He twisted his shirt around his wrists. "Look, Jo—"

"Jonathan," I said. "You need to get used to it—"

"Jonathan," he said, giving me an unhappy glance. "I don't know. We'll be at South Georgia soon. What if there's a telegram—what if they've found us?"

I scoffed, although the prospect made my heart beat faster. We'd been lucky to get to Dover and then to the Continent without being stopped. A daring scribble on Harry's passport had served to admit me—posing uncomfortably as his wife—as if I were only half a person. I'd *known* where I could find my brothers, felt it in my bones: if my parents had also put the pieces together, the two of us disappearing while the *Fortitude* sailed for the South Pole—a line from them could still spell disaster.

"What if Randall decides to throw you off? Then you'd be in trouble, stuck on a whaling station, with—with old soldiers and Norwegian criminals, until you could arrange passage home. It's not a place for you—not without me—"

It would still be southern waters. And if I'd stowed away on one ship, I thought recklessly, then what was another? It must have showed on my face, because he grabbed my arm. "Jonathan, *please*. You don't understand what kind of men they are. It's too dangerous!"

"What, then? I stay locked up in here until we make the Weddell Sea?"

"No, but—"

"Until we drop anchor? Until the sledging parties set out for the Pole, and we can be *sure* no one's after us? Harry—we're in this together. You promised." My voice sounded shrill, and I hated it.

He sighed. "I know, I know. But they'd have wanted me to look out for you." He sat wedged between two packing crates, long legs drawn up to his chin. In the shadows cast by the trench lantern, his brown eyes were almost black. I knew I must look ghostly by comparison: short straw-colored hair and pale eyes, pale skin grimy from the locker floor. A pause. He clasped his arms around his knees, allowing me to see a fresh scar on his hand, curled around the base of his thumb like a comma. I nodded at it.

"Oh—the dogs." He smiled a little. "They're brutes. They don't like me, or their kennels, or the motion of the ship. They fight constantly. Duncan has a technique for separating them—"

I felt I could guess what it was, but raised my eyebrows anyway.

"An absolute haymaker to the jaw of the bigger dog." Harry's laugh appeared to startle him. "Can you imagine? Shouting, 'Come on, you bastard.' He says we need to show them who's boss—or else they'll walk all over us."

I couldn't imagine Harry doing anything similar. Seeing my skeptical look, he shook his head. "Don't worry. I couldn't stomach it. So when Lurcher and Biter were fighting, I threw a whole bucket of water over them—they let each other go pretty quickly. And not a peep out of them for the next few minutes, they looked so *affronted*."

I snorted. I could picture it: the sun on deck, glimmering off the freezing water; two stunned and bedraggled dogs fixing Harry with looks of canine hate.

"The men thought it was hilarious. But the bucket was meant to be holding scientific specimens, so I got it in the neck. Plankton, apparently!"

There was a happy lightness to his voice. Harry had been an outsider to the ship's crew, having not sailed with her from England: how could he, when I'd needed him so much on the way down. I should be glad he was finding his feet—should be grateful, because so much still depended on it. But as I looked at him in the flickering light, my hands and knees all dusty, my limbs cramped, it couldn't help feeling like a slap in the face. I didn't want to hear about his daily life on the ship, not while I was confined. His eyes lighting up as he told me about mugs of hot cocoa on the fo'c'sle, trading nods with the officer of the watch. Beating his disagreeable bunkmate—the guardian of that bucket of plankton—in the chess tournament. Restraining the sledge dogs as they strained madly at their leashes, trying with enthusiasm and effort to pitch themselves off the ship. I bit my lip and drummed my fingers, trying to resist the urge to lash out at him. It wasn't Harry's fault, I told myself. He was just doing what we'd agreed.

But it felt like I'd already been left behind. "Honestly, you're safer down here for now," he added, as if he could tell what I was thinking. "The sea's getting much worse. That big squall at dawn? We were taken aback, and I nearly went overboard—some of the dogs, too." The smile slid off his face. "We might have been swept straight over the railings."

His horror was plain—and justified. Even if the *Fortitude* hadn't been scudding along at nine knots under sail, I still didn't think Harry could swim, despite growing up beside the sea. My brothers had summers of leisure and idleness, trailing saltwater and sand into the house; the Morgans weren't expected to concern themselves with how the majority earned a living. But Harry was different: even though the Coopers had come up in the world, their fortune was still newly minted. He was encouraged to spend his holidays learning about warehouses and shipping and stevedores—Rufus and Francis were impossibly glamorous by comparison. *Trade*, Rufus had teased him—and later, when Harry had earned his commission, *temporary gentleman*—bowing and scraping and tipping an imaginary cap. Harry, though, had always laughed; had always given as good as he got.

He started to explain, seeing that he'd successfully distracted me from whatever complaint I'd been about to make. The sub-Antarctic Ocean was home to the roughest seas known to man; they had champed their jaws around the *Fortitude*, and forced her nearly over on her beam ends. Down in the locker, I'd had to wedge myself, breathless, between the splintery shelves, fighting nausea as everything swung around me. Up on deck, though, the rigging had shimmered with movement; Randall had openly cursed the ship's captain, roared loud enough to be heard over the weather; it had nearly come to blows.

"What is he like?" I asked for the hundredth time. I could hardly bear the thought that I was aboard the expeditionary ship of "Australis" Randall, more legend than man. Harry, too, had been overawed to meet him; attending his appointment at the expedition office in London, the men from my brothers' newspaper cuttings had come vividly and aggressively to life. But he needn't have worried: Randall had taken his cash—given him a careless once-over, asked a few searching questions about his service history—and said: "Well, if you can get yourself to Buenos Aires by December, meet me there—I might well find a place for you."

"Fearsome, I suppose." I could see in the set of Harry's shoulders, the way he tried to straighten his cuffs, that Randall wasn't quite as he'd expected him to be.

"Harry." I put a hand on his shoulder, trying to choke down my impatience. "You know I'll be found, sooner or later. We need to go to him before that happens!"

He sighed. "I know. It's just—" He waved his hands, as if to convey the ship: the whole vast world of it outside my prison. From mast to mast, all the rooms and cabins and decks and kennels and dogs and boats that I'd barely seen—and then only in darkness. He had another bite mark on his left hand, surrounded by sickly green bruising. I envied him even that.

He didn't want to admit he was frightened of Randall. But I didn't fear him, or his infamous rages. He could have me flogged, or confined, or turn me off at South Georgia, leave me to the whalers. After three days of darkness, I didn't care—as long as I could stand on deck and take a breath of good clean air. See the horizon. Close my eyes and feel the rain on my face. Free.

The South Atlantic; my brothers would have liked that.

II

Harry was delivered by the ship's bell: he scrambled gratefully out of the locker, leaving me alone with my thoughts and the luxury of a new candle for the lantern. I stared at my shadow, thrown against the shelves and boxes. HP sauce; Keiller's orange marmalade; Tate and Lyle. Just like our pantry at home—if our pantry frequently turned itself upside down. But my shadow was different here.

The sea grew rougher and rougher over the course of the morning, until—with queasy stomach—I could hear a great commotion above me, the sound of countless men on deck. Muffled shouting. A moment later the ship shuddered, as if it had been stabbed, the ground dropping away.

It was a bad fall: too sudden to brace myself, and the bulkhead smacked the wind out of me. I was sure I'd cried out. A small, shameful noise, making familiar bitterness rush through me. I paused on the floor, panting slightly. Listening.

A creaking sound from the deck above. Life went on. It would be a whole day of darkness until Harry returned. I heard the pounding of my heartbeat in my ears, felt the sweat gathering at the nape of my neck. I was locked in the bowels of a ship crossing the most unsettled seas on the globe, only one person aware of my presence. If I was thrown too hard to the floor—knocked out—I knew people could die unattended from such an injury. And should the lantern turn over: "We're at the bottom of a three-mast tinder pile," Harry had warned. "Be *careful*."

I loosened the scarf from around my neck, telling myself this was my great adventure: the last Morgan sibling was heading South. My face was far too young for my liking, but I was tall for my age, carried some weight to my limbs; thought I might pass for a boy of eighteen. On our journey down, Harry had got hold of a pair of scissors and hacked my hair down to my scalp—then laughed with me as I'd scrabbled for the mirror to admire myself from all angles. "I don't think I'd be recognized," I'd said, hushed. "Even if they'd worked it out, wired the British Embassy—" and the thought had clanged around in my head like a stone in a tin can as I stared at the discarded locks on the floor. I could feel the packet ship surging and heaving against the waves, and pressed my hands into fists by my side, willing it to go faster: willing it to fly down the coast of South America to meet the *Fortitude*, before anything could overtake us.

That night, he'd agreed to finally start using *Jo*, which was what my brothers had always called me; could possibly be mistaken for *Joe* if overheard. But that was strictly for when we were alone. Elsewhere, I'd be *Jonathan*, and I turned it around in my mouth, liking the sound of it, the way something fell into place within me—resounding, deep—with those three syllables.

Somehow it described me perfectly.

The last Morgan sibling.

I crawled over to the locker door, hung up my sweaty scarf on a loose nail, and sat back on my haunches to stare at it—this one small bit of home. A bright crimson fabric, soft and bold together, it had once belonged to Francis. I remembered that day at the beach—a blustery April day, before the War had torn them away from me. Francis had been sitting in a deck chair, struggling to read a paperback, trying to ignore Rufus— nearly a year his senior—gently harassing girls on the promenade. The breeze had plucked at my parasol as if it wanted to lift me up and carry me away; Francis's scarf unraveled itself, scudding away along the sand.

Laughing, I'd kicked off my shoes and chased it along the shoreline in damp stockings.

Rufus hadn't looked up; my mother had pursed her lips. I was five years younger than the boys, but already expected to *behave myself*. Francis, though, had pressed the scarf back into my hands with a smile so wide his dimples showed. "Here, Jo. You'd better look after this for me."

But in the shadows the crimson fabric looked like blood; the hours of darkness wore on, every movement on the deck above me like a gunshot.

I was alone. But I wouldn't be forgotten or left behind. I wouldn't.

I sat up when the ship's bell rang for Sunday service, prompting a stampede of a great many boots on a great many stairs; I was surprised what a relief it was to hear these outside sounds, and the faint melody of hymns. Eternal Father, Strong to Save. *Whose arm does bind the restless wave?*

Afterwards, voices in the galley gave me a small measure of company—and nerves, as I held my breath. From their way of speaking, I guessed these were Randall's officers. I could hear the scrape of wood, a muffled curse as the ship moved suddenly. A clattering of metal utensils.

Someone let out a low whistle. "Old Australis on fine form today?" An Australian accent, all upturned sentences. I'd heard him berating Harry for dawdling. Duncan, our dog handler: determined to find fault with everything, particularly a soft English boy with more money than sense.

A snort. A deeper voice. "It's been doom and gloom with Randall recently, hasn't it? If it's not Job it's Psalms. *In their peril their courage melted away*, indeed."

"He must have been quite a peril in the lines—a peril to his own men, too, from what I've heard. I'm sure you could tell a few tales, Nicholls?"

"Not really my thing," a third voice said, rather absently. "Do you know where Macready keeps—"

"Don't see why the cook should get an afternoon off," Duncan said snidely. "And we all have to muck in, when we've got jobs to do." To emphasize the point, the deck rocked, causing another crash of falling pots and pans.

The mention of Randall had drawn me in like a fish on a hook, and I'd crept closer to the locker door, pressing my ear against it. I thought about

Harry's reluctance to face him, to own up to what he'd done, sneaking me aboard: a reluctance that couldn't help seem unmanly. I was sure—so sure—Randall would understand.

"I don't know what he's trying to do," said the doom-and-gloom man. "Having a fucking conchie—pardon my language, Nicholls—doing the reading. It's a smack in the face even having one of those cowards on board. Equality of sacrifice means nothing. The men don't like it—"

"He did his time," Nicholls said, a little sharper, in a way that conveyed he was uninterested in hearing anything further. "Same as the rest of us."

"Should've shot that lot at dawn, if you ask me, rather than giving them nice cozy cells—"

"Oh, shut up, Boyd—"

There was another crash, the sound of the galley door swinging wide on its hinges, and the Scottish tones of the ship's cook saying, "Made a meal of it, have we, lads?"

The voices died away.

But much later, at a time not determined by bell or dinner or Harry, the galley door opened again, making me freeze under my blankets. I thought those officers had returned to continue debating the Sunday service in private—although why the crew should contain a conchie, a conscientious objector, was beyond me. The very lowest of the low. *Should've shot that lot at dawn*; I'd heard Boyd's opinion, brutal as it was, so often from my brothers that I barely even questioned it. But there was absolute silence, and I let out a long and shuddering breath.

Then the bolts rattled on the locker door.

I extinguished the lantern, pulled the blankets entirely over me, backing away; tried to breathe quietly, but my breath wanted to escape in great gasps, heart jumping around in my chest.

The locker door creaked open. There was a breeze, faint and steam-scented, blowing in from the world beyond. A soft thudding of floorboards as someone stood in the doorway. I put my hand over my mouth, stifling the childish instinct to call out "Who's there?"

Whoever it was, they stayed very quiet. I could see the faint glow of a light being held up this way and that. I closed my eyes, willing it to go away. Not like this. I wasn't ready. Not like this.

The ship stopped swaying for a moment, as if holding its breath.

Then the light vanished, and I was alone again.

III

My candle burned down; the darkness was infinite, like being buried alive. I strained my eyes trying to make out shapes in the gloom. From my corner, the sacks and barrels and crates loomed—seemed to have grown bigger. Three sacks piled on top of one another made a crouching, rounded figure. The ends of barrels, stacked side-by-side on an upper shelf, were a pale row of moonlike faces, flat and expressionless save for their scribbled-ink mouths.

Shapes in the darkness. Somehow watchful. I shuddered.

The Antarctic night would be far worse. In April the sun would set for the last time, and we would spend months in a freezing dark unlike anything else on earth; the ice would be a desolate place, ruled by shadows. I'd read descriptions of the *overwinter*, which I'd once childishly interpreted as the *worst winter possible*. I hadn't been far off. Men went mad under the weight of that relentless dark. Melancholy and paranoia. Hoarding guns, before turning them on their companions—or themselves. It could happen to anyone; man wasn't adapted to deal with the total absence of light.

The faces looked down on me, and I shuddered, thinking of the ceaseless moaning of winds over the ice.

I pressed myself against the far wall, finding my eyes drawn to the nail where Francis's scarf still hung. But it wasn't comforting—its half-glimpsed shape seemed to creep away into the gloom, as if it didn't want to be seen. Not a speck of that bright crimson color survived. I swallowed.

Five days alone: maybe I'd started imagining things. It was impossible to believe that there were men out there, and daylight. Maybe I hadn't seen someone opening the locker door.

Maybe this inky blackness was all there was.

I stared into the darkness, fascinated by the long shape suggested by the scarf, and my heart thudded painfully. We'd lived in a coastal town, under lighting restrictions, the shadow of airship raids along the South Downs. My brothers would only ever have two days—three days—of leave, and be gone again; I'd been so embarrassed to show my childish fear of the pitch-dark house. But when they were home on nights with bad weather, the boom of thunder like guns in the distance, Francis would come to check on me; would linger half-seen, half-sensed, in my open doorway. "It's all right, Jo." Only by moonlight might I make out a glimmer of red hair, his shadow thrown over the floorboards. He knew how I hated the dark.

The faint swish of the scarf; a chill breath of air. I pressed my hands to my face, feeling the bones under the skin. I thought how I must have appeared to Harry when he'd opened the door—someone composed of flickers of light and shadow. Half-made. And the locker not a tomb, but an in-between place. Like my brothers, forgotten while others came home. Not quite alive—and not quite dead.

"The other country," the clergyman had said at their funeral. I felt myself in it now.

In a scuffle of shaky movement, I grabbed the scarf and wound it around my neck; that tall half-glimpsed shape disappeared. I put my head under the blankets. My breath steamed up the thick fabric, making it sodden and unpleasant.

I must have fallen into slumber, because I dreamed Francis was standing in the doorway, bringing me a candle: my room didn't face the sea, I was (technically) allowed the light, but Father had better not find out. I could almost hear my father's voice, distant and authoritarian: "In this house we all play our part." There could be no accommodation made. My brother, though, was trying to tell me something, his voice muddled with the sounds of the Antarctic wind.

A whistling. A howling. Getting louder, louder—

Louder—

The locker door was open again. Clear golden light streamed in, washed over my face. My blankets were off. I screwed up my eyes. A kettle on the galley stove, coming up to the boil, made a low trumpeting sound like hunting horns in the distance.

There wasn't enough air: I was drowning. I'd been discovered.

Someone was holding my arms, speaking to me in a low harsh voice. I caught a confusing impression of sharp dark blue eyes and neatly parted fox-red hair. There was a strange white patch in my vision, exploding outwards. Then darkness spun towards me.

IV

I came to my senses with my head resting on a tea towel that smelled of dish soap. The galley was crowded and steamy. Sweat trickled down my spine; I was still wearing my layers of woolen clothing, and my collar remained buttoned, hadn't been loosened to give me air—to display my smooth and narrow neck. Good. Harry must have seen to that.

Raising my eyes slowly, I could see that the cook—Macready, a small, compact man—had rolled up his jumper sleeves in the fierce heat of the stove. His hair was shaved close enough to expose scars on his scalp.

"You were a terrible liar," he said to Harry, without malice. "Next time you pretend your lantern and dinner have fallen overboard, remember that Randall could and would throw you overboard too, the mood he's been in."

Harry flushed, bending his head.

"But him, though? Childhood friend or not, Cooper—"

"He's nearly nineteen," Harry said. I blinked, knowing I looked younger. I could see we'd got this far on luck rather than Harry's judgment.

"Randall wanted *men*," Macready said. "Aged twenty to thirty-five. With experience, and you squeaked on board with little of that yourself." His gaze settled on me, and he frowned: I attempted a watery smile. "We haven't met," he said, not exactly unkindly. "But I understand you're Jonathan Morgan."

It rang in my ears, *Jonathan Morgan*, the enormity of it hitting me.

"Yes," I said, and stumbled through my how-do-you-dos.

He narrowed his eyes, turning back to the stove. A cast-iron monster, it took up one entire wall; the rest of the room was filled to heaving with buckets and pans and shelves and swinging lanterns. Hatches in the ceiling let in a beautiful pale light.

"I shouldn't have left you in there." Harry's fingers twitched; it looked like he wanted to take my hand.

"You'd better eat something proper, after all that," Macready said, putting a bowl of porridge on the table before me. I stared as if I'd never seen food before, taken aback by the rich burnt-sugar smell of Golden Syrup, the condensed milk pooling around the sides. The bowl was chipped enamel. Sweat dripped down my back. The food looked like something from a million miles away.

Suddenly, I was all the way awake. I knew—fully—where I was. The *Fortitude*.

I tried to stand, pushing the bowl aside. Randall. I'd expected to be hauled in front of him by the scruff of my neck, like a disobedient child. My knees caught the table and I looked around, wildly, as I steadied myself. It was surely time. But the galley door, up a flight of steps, was shut firmly against the outside world. The pot on the stove made a slurping sound as it simmered. The oven let off an uncompromising dry heat. Garlands of onions bobbed from the beams. An oddly domestic scene.

Perched on the other chair, the fourth—and silent—member of our little group made a steeple with his fingertips in front of his wide, sarcastic-looking mouth. His fingerless gloves were pulled all the way up to his elbows, despite the heat, and I could see now that his waxed hair was more ginger than red. He looked at me as if I were a perplexing natural phenomenon.

"Easy." Macready pushed me back with one hand, gentling me like a skittish animal. "You want to get something down you. Randall will send for you shortly, and you'll need to be in the pink. I don't ever think I've seen him so furious—like a bear who's stepped on a hornet's nest. And as for this one"—he indicated Harry—"well, no one has had the sheer nerve to surprise him like this before. Cash or not. There'll be hell to pay."

"That's not particularly helpful," Harry said quietly, but I could see he was stung at the prospect, and Macready's casually ominous tone. He was used to being liked by his superiors.

It all felt like a terrible ill omen: my first encounter with the rest of the expedition had me *swooning*, like in a railway paperback. I needed to stand up from now on. I started shoveling porridge into my mouth: it was immeasurably good. The redhead turned up his nose.

Macready shrugged expressively at Harry. "It doesn't do Morgan here"—*Morgan*, just my last name, like I was another one of the men, making me swallow too fast and cough into the back of my hand—"any good to sugarcoat it. There's a great many you've made look like fools—anyone so much as breathes in Randall's general direction, Clarke knows about it, and Boyd's been itching to take our poor progress out on someone. Randall, though—this is his ship, his expedition, and we're almost too late to make our landing, and now you pop up? Like a bloody *bear*, indeed."

Randall. He'd designed the *Fortitude* himself, down to the last rivet: named for his family motto, built in Norway for ice endurance. The crushing pack and the terrible swell. We'd all devoured the accounts of his previous expeditions. He would insist on staying at the wheel, without a waterproof, in the highest seas—soaked quite through, as if listening to the ocean with his skin. This was his world, and I'd stepped through the newspaper pages and dropped headfirst into it.

"I don't mind," I said quickly, *Morgan* still ringing around my head, clear as a bell. "The shouting. He has every right to be furious. What I've done is—"

"Pretty bold," Macready said, with a little quirk of his mouth.

"Absolutely ridiculous," said the stranger with the ginger hair. His raspy voice belonged to someone who smoked feverishly, and he gave me a long, cool look. "Stark raving madness, that you should think you could just hop aboard a Pole-bound vessel, like some sort of preposterous *Boy's Own* adventure. You know you could mean the difference between success and failure for us now? Randall doesn't carry *spares*, and we're short enough as it is. If you take another man's rations, or fall ill—which doesn't look out of the question on your showing so far—you'll be risking all our lives."

Macready shook his head, gave my shoulder a brief squeeze. I noticed he didn't rush to disagree.

"I doubt you'd care," Harry muttered. "On *your* showing so far. What were you doing in the locker, anyway?"

The stranger snorted. "Cooper. Mind your own business."

Harry flushed. The redhead gave him a look of great disgust, pushing his chair back from the table. "I hope you enjoy your porridge, Morgan," he said, taking the stairs two at a time. "Get a hot meal in you. Randall shall be putting you off on the first rock he sees."

"Oh, come on—" Harry said.

While the galley door was open I had a brief impression of the outside world above: blue light in the sky, people loitering nearby. I craned my neck to see, and it slammed shut with a shudder. The cooler air prickled on my sweaty face.

"He's always like that," Harry said. "Tarlington. We're sharing quarters, and why he can't just sleep in his precious laboratory, instead of coming in and out at all hours—"

"Our biologist," Macready said to me. "Chief scientific officer, if you please, even if it's because he's the *only* scientific officer. He gets a nice cozy little lab all to himself, when the rest of us are crammed in nose to nose. Some aren't too happy."

I fanned myself. Randall was our last great explorer, heading South for glory. Of course—it went without saying—any Antarctic expedition would have scientists. Meteorologists, to measure the polar winds; physicists, to chart the magnetic fields; geologists, to dig up what lay under the ice. But my brothers would have seen them as an irrelevance: would have focused on the brilliant expanse of the horizon. The fox-haired man—Tarlington—was also an irrelevance.

Taking up space, perhaps, meant for someone else. Someone bolder.

"It doesn't surprise me that *he's* taken against you," Macready said. "He doesn't exactly seem pleased to be with us—Randall practically had to beg him. But the others—well."

A prickle of unease. The idea of Randall begging anyone seemed preposterous. And I'd hoped the men of the expedition would see me as daring. Audacious. An adventurer. But a skinny scientist only a few years my senior had just looked me up and down like a specimen ready for dissection. It was a poor start.

The galley door swung open again, and my breath caught in my throat.

The man in the doorway was bigger than the frame. Six feet tall and broad in the shoulders, I knew him immediately: Liam Clarke, Randall's most loyal second-in-command. He'd survived a night on the ice with no tent, just a cave burrowed out with his hands and a tin-can shovel, keeping up his strength by gnawing raw frozen meat. I could hardly believe I was seeing him in person. I found my eyes drawn to the tan leather glove on his right hand. Neat little stumps, where frostbite had gnawed away at him; the armed forces had turned him down, and Randall had been criticized for taking a man missing his fingers.

"Get up," he said. "Randall will have you now."

A sudden sickening sensation, as though the ship had plunged beneath me.

Macready gave me a sympathetic look as I stumbled to my feet. I pulled Francis's scarf tighter around my neck; partly to give my hands something to do, partly for reassurance. After my first steps away from home—taking what I could carry, leaving no explanations—this would be my most terrible test.

"Jonathan," Harry whispered. It sounded an awful lot like he wanted to apologize. I shot him a scathing look.

I watched myself on the steps, dreading the spectacle if I fell over again. At the top, a scattering of men dispersed at some speed when Clarke looked their way. It was a curious time of day—nearly ten o'clock at night, with the southern sun still shining—and the sky was a deep cyan blue, untroubled by clouds. I felt like a prisoner on his way to the gallows.

Conscious it might be my only chance, I drank in the *Fortitude*. After so long below, she had a feeling of openness, endless possibility, although she was a small three-masted ship, one hundred and seventy feet long, carrying half sail. At her bow end was the galley. At the stern, the large black funnel of the engine. And in between, the bridge—the ship's wheel, the bell I'd heard so many times—raised up on steps with fine brass banisters. The forbidding doors of the wardroom ahead. Hatches disappeared into the deck, and fist-sized glass illuminators, wearing brass hats like toadstools, caught the sun and filtered it down to her secret layers below. Boats hung over the side; ropes; winches; items I scarcely recognized.

She was beautiful, full of harmonies in her shape, her gilding and burnished timbers glimmering in the light.

There were men, too, crowding the decks everywhere I turned. The ship's carpenter, wearing a beaten tool belt, was braiding rope into something that looked like a hammock, and winked at me as I walked past. A remarkably dashing-looking man—presumably Duncan—pulled dog harnesses from a locker, swore at the tangles, then glared at us.

Behind, perched above the galley stove vents, was Harry's domain: the dog deck. They must have caught our scent as the wind shifted, because there was an explosion of furious barking, and Harry shouted "Quiet, there—" before remembering his place in our gallows procession. Someone chuckled. It had a mean sound to it.

V

The wardroom door was so low that Clarke had to stoop. Down a flight of stairs, it wasn't a large room: the officers' cabins crammed the walls, names neatly stenciled in navy on their sliding doors. Those illuminators let in shafts of light from the deck above, shining off the rich polished woodwork. On a different ship I'd have expected a piano; here, everything was functional, right down to the laundry drying in front of the stove, fogging up the great gold-framed mirror.

This informality extended to the scene itself. When I'd imagined it, I'd always pictured Randall behind a desk, as if holding a court-martial, but the long table was pushed to the far end of the room, covered in charts: he was sitting on it instead. A man in his late thirties, salt-and-pepper curls escaping a knitted cap, was sketching something energetically in lurid red ink. Randall nodded, rubbed his chin. Two other officers fell silent at my entrance.

The ship rocked from side to side, making me feel sick. My first impulse was to go to my knees. To look down. To take up less space. I quashed it.

Randall cleared his throat, then looked at me with a steady, unblinking gaze. He was far less handsome than in the papers, and a little shorter. Frostbite had left its mark: much of his left eyebrow was missing, and that side of his face looked roughly sanded down. His nose was slightly out of joint, wide jaw set askew. His waistcoat was a few inches too small, his sleeves dirty.

The whole country knew him. I opened my mouth and closed it again. Zero hour.

"Ah," Randall said. "Fresh eyes, just what we need." His voice was low, with a growl to it. "Nicholls here, our navigator—" he indicated the man with the knitted cap—"plots an easterly course. Says we should aim to make an early landfall to the northeast—Coats Land."

The room fell silent. A clock ticked. The chairs squeaked as they rocked absently on their bearings. My breathing sounded terribly loud.

Nicholls glanced at Clarke behind me. "I'm only saying we should avoid the worst of the Weddell Sea pack. They'd tell you the same in Grytviken. Whalers don't risk damage to company boats."

Randall raised his eyebrows. One of them lifted, the other—on the frozen side of his face—seemed to deepen into a scowl. "And waste time we could use getting farther south?"

"We don't know the condition of the coast down there. If we end up having to overwinter in the ice—"

"She's sheathed in three foot of greenheart, and won't be breached," another man said. He wore a smart naval cap and epaulettes, stood perfectly straight: I knew he must be Mortimer, the ship's captain. "But if we can't find safe harbor south, we would certainly be frozen into the pack. No; February is our only window of opportunity to penetrate the Weddell Sea."

"There's no knowing when we'd ever get out again—why would you risk it—"

Randall silenced them, making a chopping motion with his hand.

"What do our new crew members think?" He heaved himself off the table and walked towards us with a rolling gait, as if he, too, were under sail. "Eh? You two? Slow and cautious or full steam into the pack?"

Harry shuffled his feet behind me. I crossed my arms—realized how confrontational this looked—uncrossed them again.

Randall paused. "Of course, you'll have an opinion," he said. "Bright young—*adventurers*—like you."

The ship dipped a little, and my stomach lurched. I caught a hiss of breath from the assembled officers; Randall's dark blue eyes on me were too bright, fever-keen.

The worst of it was, I did have an opinion. I'd listened to my brothers, up in their tree house, using the atlas to trace the route down from Buenos Aires. Francis, luxuriating in the sun, would make suggestions about the ocean currents and drift. The roundabout way, that was his nature. Rufus, of course, always favored the direct assault. And Harry had to pick a side—usually ended up pleasing no one.

"Well?" Randall growled, pushing me in the chest with one large hand just above my breastbone. The force of it made me stumble, my breath catch—Randall, Australis Randall, was *touching* me. Up close, he smelled of salt and tobacco, and I found myself wanting to take a step back. I stared at the ruined side of his face. No other man had fallen into the Weddell Sea and lived. All appearance of jovial interest had now gone.

I thought of Rufus. So bold. Always so direct. My brothers would have fought for this: I would do the same.

Randall pushed me again. I planted my feet. It was like being pawed by a large vengeful animal.

"Sir," I said, meeting his terrible eye, and deepening my voice. "Jonathan Morgan. I think—"

"You think," Randall said. "You think. You don't *know*, though, do you? You know nothing about these waters, or the pack. Might as well have looked at a bloody map. You've never been South. You've never been out of the nursery, to look at you, eh?"

A large hand closed around my jaw. I forced myself not to flinch. Bones ground under his grip, and I was grateful for the scarf pulled tight around my neck.

"Tall enough," he said, as if looking at an uninspiring racecourse prospect. "Well-fed, at least—useful for a *spare*. You lot?"

Clarke snorted. The men around us suddenly looked like explorers: the sort of faces I'd seen in the papers. Bright, sharp eyes, a brutal set to the jaw. Capable hands. Scars. Beards. I fell short in every possible way.

"Cooper's the one to blame," said a man with the largest arms I'd ever seen. I recognized his voice from the galley—angry, informal. Boyd.

He was nothing like I'd imagined, scowl lines on his forehead so pronounced they looked like tide patterns in sand. "He joined up—under false pretenses—to land us with *this*."

"They should both be turned off at South Georgia." Mortimer stroked the smooth wood of the mainmast, which ran through the wardroom from ceiling to floor, as if soothing the ship against our offense.

Nicholls shrugged. His voice—the voice I'd heard through my prison walls—was mild, pleasant. "We're more than a man short already. There's room."

Randall barked with laughter. "A *man short*, eh?"

He pressed the heel of his hand to my collarbone, and released me. I could barely feel it. There was a ringing in my ears, like an air-raid siren. "We had some like you," he said conversationally. "In my battalion. Young lads, thought they'd be heroes."

Boyd smirked. "So young they barely made a mouthful for the Boche."

My stomach turned. I thought I was going to be sick. The room was suddenly too crowded, too dark, too enclosed. As if I were being put back in my box; something found wanting, and discarded.

"Well?" Randall looked at me expectantly. I surprised myself by putting my hands up to fend him off: I wouldn't be shoved again. Surprised him, too—a flash of interest lit up those blue searchlight eyes.

Harry saved me from making a fool of myself. "Sir, I take full responsibility."

"Really?" Randall said, rocking back on his heels. "He was unwilling, was he? You tied him up and bundled him aboard, and he's been in our galley locker for days trying to—what—gnaw his way out?"

Harry flushed. "I'm the one you accepted—"

"And that was a mistake," Boyd muttered.

"Boyd is right," Harry said, perfectly wretched. "I've—misled you. It was my decision to bring him on board, and if anyone should be punished—"

"I should punish both of you."

"I know that," Harry said. "I only ask that you consider—"

Randall looked at him, face darkening. Storm clouds moving across the water.

"I will consider, Cooper," he said, voice coming to a roar, "what I damn well like!" He shoved past me and advanced on Harry. "This is my ship! My men! Who have entrusted me with their lives, at sea and on the ice and in all the *bloody* spaces in between! We're provisioned for twenty-three of us to survive eighteen months, right down to the last allowance of biscuits. Every step of the way I'll be charged with your lives and ends—decisions you couldn't possibly understand! If I misjudge the pack, we'll be crushed to smithereens and drown. If I take too long, we'll starve. And you presume—"

Harry shook his head, his throat bobbing. "No."

"Don't interrupt me, damn you! And as for *you* . . ."

Randall's gaze swept to me, and this time I did take a step back.

"D'you know," he said, "I won't have it! We'll split you up—confine you separately. Well? If this were wartime, with the threat of *sabotage*, someone sneaking aboard like a common criminal or a spy—by God— you're lucky you weren't shot! Boyd—search the stowaway, thoroughly. Strip him on deck if you like. Deal with him as you think fit, until South Georgia, when we'll throw them both out."

The wardroom danced about in my vision. The door seemed a long way above me. Clarke put a large hand on my shoulder.

"Don't touch him!" Harry wheeled around, throwing a punch that went mercifully wide. A small, choked sound as he realized what he'd done. For Harry, discipline was something sacred.

"Do *not*—" Randall growled; Clarke caught Harry's arm and twisted it up against his back, pulling him away from me like a rag doll.

"I'll deal with this," Clarke said grimly.

"Let him go," Randall said. Clarke shook his head. Randall repeated it, low and dangerous. Behind us, a squeaking of chairs as the other officers got up. I could hear Harry's unsteady breathing. I stood frozen. My mind stuttered, reeled, at *strip him on deck*.

Randall seized Harry by his collar; Clarke let go. Then Randall was dragging Harry up the stairs and onto deck. We were separated. The wardroom door slammed resoundingly behind them, and I was left in the dim light inside.

The moment stretched out. A shout outside made me jump, nearly overturning the hanging laundry, and my heart thudded. It was Harry, in fear or pain or surprise. Nicholls said, urgently, "Well?"

I bolted for the door.

Outside, clouds were scudding across the sky, canvas billowing. I looked around wildly, seeing immediately that none of the crew would help us. Clarke held Randall, fighting to keep his weight on deck, the muscles in his neck standing taut. Randall, in turn, was holding Harry over the side of the ship: over the railings, facedown, so far over that a single slip would have been his last. We were making a good pace under sail, and the crash of waves against the hull was loud as thunder.

I made two strides before someone grabbed me tightly around the waist, saying "No" into my ear. I clamped my hands to my mouth to stop myself screaming.

"My *crew*," Randall shouted, booming up and down deck. "My *men*, Cooper, not that it means anything to you. Their lives—your worthless little life! Good God, if I see you raise so much as a finger—if I hear another goddamn—out of you, when it's not wanted—I'll tear it up, you hear me. I won't take a penny, I'll go bankrupt, and *throw* you to the whalers, you little—"

"Australis," Clarke said.

The wind was picking up, whipping Harry's curls, plucking at his shirt. He wasn't fighting back. It would be like expecting him to strike God himself.

The ship creaked ominously, as if Randall had commanded the turn in the weather. A small gesture from Mortimer sent men into the rigging. I pulled away from my captor—slipped, going to my knees—scrambled to right myself like an overturned beetle.

My mouth was dry. I wanted to call out to Harry; something wordless, bubbling up inside me with guilt and fear. I wanted to say I was sorry—for all the secret meetings and pleading that had brought us here. Walks on the quayside, trading anecdotes like particularly prized cigarette cards; matching his pace, trying to keep up with him. His hair was plastered damp against his neck, and I swallowed thickly, thinking of the long drop over the side, the plummeting horror before he hit the water, the green swell of it smacking him in the face. How he'd thrash. How he'd scream. How he would slip into the deep, leaving me behind.

Not Harry, too. I couldn't bear it.

The wind crackled and popped in the sails. My breath hitched. "It was my idea!" I shouted. Then, lower: "Randall—sir—"

Randall half-turned, keeping Harry pinned against the railings, all that violent attention now fixed on me. "Well?"

"It was my idea," I said. "I made him bring me."

"Australis!" Clarke said again. Randall—grudgingly—hauled Harry back on deck, boots first, and let him go, limp as a fish pulled from water.

Randall wiped his hands on his trousers. Took two large paces to come to me, so close I could feel his breath on my face. I bit the inside of my cheek until I tasted blood.

"Well—*Morgan*. You and me."

I felt the air reenter my lungs.

Clarke held up his hand, giving Randall a warning look. "Not a democracy," Randall said, and pulled me down into the wardroom by my collar, my legs stuttering beneath me on the stairs.

When the door slammed shut, leaving us alone in the sudden warmth, Randall took up all the space in the room. Looming over me, swaying with the ship. "You've got one chance. By God, I'd throw you both overboard now."

I put my quivering hands behind my back; pressed torn nails into my palms; took a deep breath. "A chance is all I want—sir. I've put the rest of your crew in danger. I know that now. I'll be punished, just—please keep me on. Let me see Antarctica. Let me see the shores—just the pack—and you can do what you like with me."

It wasn't enough. The clock ticked away, the mirror winked behind him; Randall continued to stare at me, utterly impassive. I hadn't prepared a speech, like Harry. I'd been so sure I'd know what to say when the time came.

"Sir," I said desperately. "My brothers." It stuck in my throat, like a solid lump. "They were a little older than me—twenty-one and twenty-two, when they died. They'd applied for their commissions straight off, the moment it all started, because they thought it'd be an adventure. And they meant to join your next expedition, too. It was all they talked about. The South Pole was all they wanted. And then—when they didn't come back—I knew I had to come instead."

There was a long, terrible silence, and I tried to moisten my dry lips under the weight of that stare. Randall turned his signet ring around and around on his finger. His family motto: *Fortitude or Devastation*.

"And Cooper? Where does he come in?"

"He was over there with them. At the Front." My chest tightened. "Their best friend—a family friend. I knew he wouldn't—leave me behind."

My voice was trembling. As the ring gleamed in the dying light, I hoped I wasn't overdoing it. Randall had nearly thrown Harry over the side—he wouldn't hesitate to punch me, and one blow from those bearlike hands would knock me out. But I'd staked a great deal on the notion that he wouldn't stand someone being *left behind*—like Charlie Randall, abandoned by his regiment, missing presumed dead. Perhaps he'd ended up trapped in a shell hole, showers of earth and stone until the mud buried him alive. Perhaps he'd been left by the side of a dusty winding road, begging for water, waiting for a stretcher-bearer that would never come. Harry would never have abandoned a Morgan, and I was the last one left.

Some said the loss at the Somme of his only son had broken Randall; others muttered you wouldn't know the difference. He seemed to have frozen, one hand steadying himself against a beam, his reflection looming in the mirror.

"How'd you do it?"

I jumped. Clarke had perched himself at the top of the stairs.

"We bribed the nightwatchman." A pause, in which he clearly expected more details. "Sneaked away from—from our houses—in England, then crossed the Channel, took a liner to Madeira." That was the last time we'd really had to worry about names and documentation: it had felt like we were moving in leaps and bounds, each one getting a little bigger, a little farther, picking up pace. "Then packet ship—fast packet—to Buenos Aires." I glanced uneasily at Randall. "You'd said Harry would have a place. So we used his funds. All of them."

Clarke nodded, slowly. I could see him assessing me. I had the distinct impression he could tell I must have run away from home—that I'd left without giving my parents even the slightest hint where I was going. Doubtless they would guess Harry and I were together. When the War had broken out, our social circle had seen a flurry of hasty engagements—elopements. They could draw whatever misguided conclusions they liked, if only they didn't try to *stop* me.

"You said it was your idea?"

I nodded. It had taken time and patience, but I could remember the first sign of Harry's surrender. It felt incongruous—in the heart of the *Fortitude*—to recall that seaside tearoom. The owner had found excuses to adjust our tablecloth every few moments, looking as though she were chewing on a bee: it was *inappropriate* for Harry and I to be out together, no matter how people's views might be changing since the War. I remembered Harry's large hands wrapped around a china teacup; how he'd reached across the table when I told him I'd have traded myself for my brothers, if I could.

The *Fortitude* creaked. I flinched when Randall moved suddenly, releasing the beam above my head, shifting his weight back with a rocking motion to fix me again with that terrible gaze.

"Let me stay." I shivered, feeling Clarke's eyes on the back of my neck. "Please. I'll prove to you that I'm worth it. That I'd be—as good as my brothers."

"Well." It sounded dredged up from somewhere deep. "I don't like being kept in the dark. But that boy would throw a punch for you—and at Liam Clarke, no less! I suppose you come as a pair, eh?"

I knew what I was meant to say, the sort of thing he'd like to hear: that we'd promised to stick together, like boys in a public-school story. But a traitorous part of me could almost taste my success. One Morgan, at least, would see the ice, and damn the consequences: it was the sort of thing Rufus would say. A shiver ran down my spine. I'd seen how utterly *lost* Harry had looked. How small, without them.

Randall stared at me for a moment, then turned away. "Well, we'll see how you stack up by South Georgia," he said over his shoulder. "The two of you together barely add up to one expedition man. No complaining, d'you hear me? Not a peep. We'll enter you into the ship's book as a stowaway, or *spare*—I suppose you know what happens to *spares* when times get hard?"

I didn't ask. There was a cruel look about him.

I nearly ran out of the wardroom. The crew were going about their business on deck, turning in for the night as if nothing had happened; as if Randall threatened to murder someone every day.

"Harry," I whispered, an uncertain smile starting to pull at my mouth. "Harry!"

"Wait!" Standing in the doorway, Randall was a bulky shape in the shadows: some rough thing, shoved into man's clothing. "Your brothers heard the call of the South. They're dead and gone, you'll not see them again—it's your own life at stake. Is this what *you* want, Morgan?"

I'd spent hours staring at that map of Antarctica, at the white space in its center. Uncharted. Unconfined. As wholly perfect as a blank page.

I wanted so much. To take their place, on the ship and on the ice. To follow where they led. And on the deck of the *Fortitude*, the wind in her sails, as I faced Australis Randall—they might as well have been beside me.

I nodded. "It's all I want," I said truthfully. "Sir."

VI

"Another one for the Nursery," Nicholls said cheerfully, ducking through the maze of beams and compartments that made up the *Fortitude*'s main deck. Although he had both hands full, he navigated it with ease, pushing through a succession of doors far into the depths of the ship: down into the galley, then the mess hall, then another corridor. With each compartment, the sound of the wind receded further.

I was tripping over my feet, trying to look at everything at once, urgently hoping I'd learn the path to the latrines through this warren. We passed a row of communal basins, surrounded by curtains, a man lathering up his chin with an enormous badger brush; shelves of leather-bound books, storm lanterns and galoshes hanging below, every square inch of space in use. A cabin marked "The Coal Hole," where a short man perched on an upper bunk and polished his boots. Finally, a small cubbyhole with bottles on the walls and a microscope on the table, Tarlington staring into it with a tightness to his back that made me utterly sure he was aware of our passage behind him.

"Oh, stop it—" Harry said when I stumbled, and grabbed my shoulder to march me into a small room marked "The Nursery." The walls were curved where wood paneling covered her bones; despite the *Fortitude* being double-walled Norwegian fir and greenheart, I found myself listening for the sea outside. There were only two bunks. One was made up neatly. The other, with a bunched blanket and a pair of abandoned waterproofs, I knew at once to be Harry's.

"You'll be sick at first," Nicholls said, beginning to string up a hammock—the hammock, I now understood, I'd seen the ship's carpenter making for me. I fought down a smile. "You think you've got used to it—but now you'll be going in the opposite direction when she rolls, and you'll be sicker than you ever thought possible."

I looked around. The cabin was barely six feet across, a small latch on the door. When Tarlington stood in the connecting door to his laboratory, fiddling with a handkerchief and wearing a scowl, it felt even smaller. It was perfect. I imagined my brothers heaving their packs onto the bunks, shouldering off their coats.

"I don't mind," I said quickly.

"You'll have to look after him," Nicholls said.

Harry bristled. "Of course I will."

Nicholls chuckled, lines crinkling around his eyes. "All right, then. Get settled in. Best show yourself for cocoa, once you've changed those clothes."

He was right, of course: that night I leant over the side of the hammock, retching into a pail. The room was claustrophobic and dark, and I could hear men snoring down the corridor in the mess hall. Harry made restless noises in his sleep; Tarlington hissed, "*Will* you be quiet!" It was nothing like my bed at home, fresh linen and silk-smooth sheets. I lay with my eyes half-open, dozing, as the ship swayed around me. I couldn't help smiling until my face hurt.

It was a start.

VII

I had never needed much sleep, but the days that followed were designed, with brutal efficiency, to push me to my limits. The sun shone relentlessly, casting me into a strange world in which time held no meaning. The ship rolled, pitched, took me off balance. "Get Morgan a bucket" became a joke—at least, I hoped it was a joke—amongst the seamen who clattered up and down the decks teasing Harry about his reluctant charges; dog-skin mittens; dog-meat sandwiches. The work was constant, broken only by meals snatched on deck with Harry perched beside me like a sentry; I loitered outside the mess hall sometimes, but didn't quite dare go in.

On the second day Harry lent me a hand scrubbing the crew WC—a small closet next to that row of basins, it thankfully had a latch on the door—until Clarke strode in and pulled him up by his collar. "What do you think you're doing?"

Harry squirmed, looking around for support. "I was only—"

"You've got work of your own to worry about," Clarke said, his voice soft. "He needs to earn his own way, or he'll remain just a *spare*."

"I am—" I started hotly, but Clarke had already gone. After that, Clarke did his best to break us up, although he said little. He wouldn't easily forgive my intrusion onto his—Randall's—expedition. I was certain he knew I'd run away; it was dizzying to think that this was the first time I'd even left home. I'd been meant for boarding school, around the time my brothers were finally being sent to the Front: another way in which my parents hoped to make me different, more *appropriate*. I'd dreaded the very thought of it, some entirely foreign and female country, from which—somehow—I'd never expected to return. Francis had sat on the end of my bed, on the lavender chintz I'd always hated, and put his arm around me. "Some prissy boarding school—I'm not going to let them. Don't you worry, my dear Jo."

He'd kept his promise—but failed to return himself.

On the *Fortitude*, I'd expected to wear his scarf like armor, like a signal flag, but when I'd first reported to the sailing master for duty in the rigging, Wild had taken one look at me and said cheerfully: "D'you want to strangle, then?"

And later—"Like a monkey, that Morgan!"

I'd always loved climbing—the tree house, my brothers' tree house, was my favorite place in the world. Back in Portsmouth those pin-tucked blouses had welded my arms to my sides—long, dull day dresses had to be kept clean—and worse than that, climbing was another thing that was *inappropriate*, and Rufus would always shout at me to get back down. Then in the next moment I'd be expected to hide his own boyish transgressions, whenever my mother was in a flap over bootprints on carpet, or my father thundered at an evening spent somewhere out of bounds to young *gentlemen*. A finger pressed to Rufus's Cupid's bow lips, his gaze lingering, would thrill me with its complicity—its promise that we were on the same side. The same team.

Here in my new trousers, however, I was finally free. Standing as I'd been meant to, taking wider strides as I'd been meant to—climbing as I'd been meant to. No one would tell me to get down, not anymore. From up on the yards—the spars of the ship's three masts—the *Fortitude* was small, and I was a giant, laughing at the motion of the waves, the speed of our swooping progress.

But by my third day out of the locker, every muscle in my body ached. My armpits felt tight, and I'd grown iron wings on my shoulder blades. Letting out a deep sigh when I came down from the rigging for the final time, I hugged the mast, sinking my weight into it. I longed to lie down, or soak my sore hands and feet in warmish water, but Clarke—as usual, refusing to look directly at me—said, "You're wanted back on deck, so snatch something to eat and report."

It was a little after eleven o'clock, but the perpetual twilight still shone white and gray. The ship was settling down for the night: galley stove cooling in a series of muffled bangs, lights coming on in the ward-room and glimmering up onto deck. We'd been making good progress through an uncharacteristically calm sea, but freezing mist had rolled in, and all sails had been reefed. The air wrapped me up in a wet cloak; I could barely see from port to starboard. The ship hung suspended in dark water.

The nightwatchman on the bridge was Boyd: big arms, no-nonsense mustache. He was Randall's first officer, and would gladly have flogged or caned me if Randall had ordered him to do so, regulations be damned. His knotted knuckles popped as he took the steaming mug of coffee.

"Dog deck," he said, having a gulp then scowling. "Needs a scrub."

"Yes, sir." It came out automatically: I never needed to think about saying "yes" to everything. But the dog deck had been scrubbed by Harry that morning. Boyd had been about, barking orders at the seamen, getting in their way—or so it appeared to my untrained eye—and must surely have seen so.

Boyd shrugged, giving me a look that might—just—pass for a smile. "There's no use shirking," he said, mistaking my pause for reluctance. "Clarke's compliments. The fog will make the bastards sleep, at least." His language spoke of the Front—it seemed to cling to him. Sugar and condensed milk were in ample supply, but he insisted on taking his coffee black: *Good enough in the lines,* he said proudly, *and good enough here.*

I'd tried it a few times; it tasted like mud to me. If I'd thought to appeal to Boyd, I didn't have the slightest notion how to go about it.

Although the dog deck had a clear line of sight to the bridge, once I went up the steps the fog engulfed him entirely. I recognized that it was the first time I'd been so alone on deck. The *Fortitude* was small, and I was forever turning a corner headfirst into someone, being barged and shoved as I made my way below. I exhaled a long, deep breath, feeling my chest expanding. It was clearly the first time I'd been trusted: I tried to recall how Clarke had looked, but only came up with the impression of his size, and silence. If this were progress, it hadn't shown.

I smiled as I turned to work. The dogs seemed to be obeying Boyd in their stillness, and I was glad, thinking of all the scars and torn sleeves I'd seen on Harry. "Brutes," he'd say, with a rueful sigh. It was true he had no real experience with dogs: with my encouragement, he'd told some absolute rot about hunting, implied he spent weekends in the country, which was good enough for Randall, who'd said jovially, "Well, I suppose you'll be a *dogsbody* then, eh?" That lie, and nearly a thousand pounds in funds, had bought Harry his place. We hadn't been able to believe our luck.

But I'd egged him on only because I'd known he would come good: Harry had a knack for picking things up, and there'd be plenty of time before the dog teams were needed on the ice.

For now, our dogs slept or quarreled in an unpredictable rota, largely housed in a horseshoe of kennels between the dog-deck steps and the prow. The smallest mongrel—Jamieson—made a few groaning whimpers as I knelt outside his hutch, fingers already numb around the scrubbing brush. The night had a bite to it, and the fog settling on my face seemed to beckon from the frozen Weddell Sea.

I worked silently and diligently, determined not to shirk: if Boyd came up to check, he would find me hard at it. Shuffling on my knees down the deck, the rest of the ship became invisible. The fog simply cut it off at the steps, where I could have walked down into nothingness. The angular crosses of the foremast yards, naked of sail, loomed at the very limits of sight. The sun—bobbing low along the horizon—had been taken up, and the world was white.

I started to hum; fell silent after the first few notes, telling myself I didn't want to wake the dogs. When one turned over in its sleep—tail thumping against the kennel—the sound sent a shiver right through me. I paused, listening hard.

Muffled by the fog: Boyd ringing the ship's bell. It sounded like it had come from the dark water outside, a drowned city still ringing its church bells. I straightened up, rolling my aching shoulders back, telling myself it was nothing.

I didn't look around until the deck was fresh and glistening, prevented from freezing over by the faint warmth of the galley below. My lantern was a small pool of light, ending at the railings, the barriers between the ship and the vastness of the sea around us. The foremast was gone.

The fog was advancing on me.

I sat on my heels, listening again for the sounds of the ship. Timber creaked. The long steady breathing of the dogs was absurdly comforting. I tugged my hat down lower, jammed my hands under my armpits.

Jamieson made that whining sound again, high-pitched and mournful. It made all the hairs lift on the back of my neck. The visible world around me was small, and I had a sudden dread of leaving the dog deck, fumbling down the steps into the unknown. I stayed silent. I told myself not to be afraid: this was simply the first in a succession of even stranger nights to come.

A slow scraping noise just below me. The dogs stirred. One growled, drawn-out and watchful.

Boyd couldn't possibly have left the bridge; we were the only ones on deck. My heart hammered, and I crept forward on hands and knees, still clutching my brush.

The steps were solid in all that nothingness. True visibility ended at the third step down. A lantern glimmered below me, Jamieson continuing to make small warning sounds. In the half-light I could see my breaths, small and erratic, blending with the fog.

Then, on the deck beneath me, almost floating in the whiteness: a tall red-haired figure, wearing a long coat, hands thrust deep into his pockets.

My throat closed up. The figure seemed in the act of dissolving, and I dropped the brush. Opened my mouth to speak to him. He'd come back. He'd returned to me.

Francis.

He was floating, like the uniforms my mother had hung up in the hallway, looming over the sour-smelling cut flowers. They'd come back to us in linen drawstring bags, neatly pressed: my brothers' personal effects. Little nicks and holes, ragged sleeves, and one horrible area of tearing on each tunic, as though savaged by a wild animal. I'd dared to put my fingers into the holes, reaching through to *absence*.

The scraping noise came again; I saw the shallow door of the foredeck locker open. A broad shadow came out, moving with confidence on the slippery deck, and walked away swiftly, footsteps muffled.

The ghostly figure that remained suddenly became Tarlington, standing in the fog, his greatcoat undone despite the night's chill. He didn't turn around. I ducked behind the railings, pressing my hands to my chest, feeling dizzy.

When I could breathe again, I retrieved my bucket. It clanked and jangled as I hauled it down the steps, but the spell—whatever it was—had been broken. The water from the pump was like pure burning fire on my fingertips, and I flexed them hastily to restore circulation. "Again," Boyd said, coming up to cast a jaundiced eye over my handiwork, when I'd thought I was more than done. He didn't give the slightest sign that I'd impressed him.

I had the rest of the watch, surrounded by the quiet warm sounds of dogs in sleep, to wonder what two people would want in the foredeck locker, when the rest of the crew was below. All was in order: I'd held my breath as I opened the locker door, almost expecting—something—to come out. But it was low-ceilinged and unremarkable, filled with coiled ropes and washy with rainwater. No dredging nets, no part-dissected seabirds, nothing at all to do with science. It was after midnight, the foggy sky starting to reveal a gray morning, and Tarlington had no possible business there.

Tarlington was described as our biologist, but I'd picked up how very young he was: barely older than Harry, he could have no experience, couldn't even have finished his undergraduate degree. If Randall needed a bone to toss to the old men of the Royal Geographical Society, for funding or forbearance, Tarlington was surely the skinniest bone he could find—an interested amateur at best. But he was still entitled to order the men around, and had the run of the ship. Which, now I thought of it, had extended to my own hiding place, the darkness of the storage locker.

I shivered, closing the door with a muffled bang.

When Harry came to relieve me, yawning and waking the dogs with his clumsy footing on the steps, I didn't mention any of it. I resented the way my childish heart had pounded, the fact that my imagination had made Francis from thin air. The fog and isolation had spooked me. *They're dead and gone, you'll not see them again.*

VIII

"Must you?"

Harry pressed his knuckles into his eyes, exasperated.

Five in the morning on my fifth day of freedom. I'd lit the Nursery's safety lamp on my first attempt, and warm golden light penetrated every inch of the room. The soft glow, the smell of blankets and sleep, reminded me of the last night in Portsmouth, waiting for the appointed hour to climb down the ivy—the same route my brothers had always taken—and cycle away to meet Harry at the station. Sometimes it felt I had simply snuffed out my bedroom lamp and lit this one, and all the time in between had been a dream.

But Harry—it was becoming harder and harder to remember his eyes, bright with excitement, as he took my hand and watched the white cliffs of Dover fall away. As we'd bounced up and down on our heels against the chill of autumn passing over the Channel, too tightly wound to sleep, certain that every small boat in the water—every ship blowing its whistle as it passed—was someone coming for us.

Harry waited while I pulled my jumper over my head. Taking advantage of Tarlington's absence, I'd stripped down to my linen shirt in front of our small folding washstand, scrubbing under my armpits with a damp cloth and a bit of soap. Over my combinations, a closely fitted vest; over that I wore my shirt baggy, my jumper with boxy shoulders. It was fortunate that I was flat-chested: "A late bloomer," my mother used to say wistfully, looking at her own narrow frame. "It must run in the family." She meant the bloom of a flower unfurling, but it made me think of mold creeping over old bread, making my body one I would increasingly fail to recognize.

Here on the *Fortitude*, I wore almost as many layers as I had back home, but it was different. The colder seas had not yet arrived, and the ship was perfectly warm below; some in the mess hall slept topless, or worse. It made my cheeks burn—made me look away hastily, not wanting to be caught staring.

"Jonathan!"

Harry was glowering at me. He wore absurd striped pajamas, his binoculars—neat little chrome-plated ones, a gift from the men in his battalion—dangling around his neck, even when he slept. He'd joined up as a private, been commissioned from the ranks, and the binoculars marked the occasion. "They think me a steady hand," he'd written. "I feel almost a hundred years old."

I ignored him, smoothing my scalp with a bit of wax, delighting in its curves.

"Stop . . . grinning like that," he said with feeling. "Look, you need to slow down—"

"This is what we wanted," I said. "*Both* of us. And now we're here!"

"You've slept for barely a few hours."

"So?"

He sighed. "Just—look, this isn't a game. I know you think you can pull it off, but Randall—"

"I'm not pulling anything off," I hissed, reflexively running a hand over the back of my head, still relishing the feel of it. The first time I'd seen myself with short hair, it had been—not a surprise, exactly. If the person looking back at me would have been unrecognizable to my parents, he'd been instantly recognizable to me. Utterly familiar. As if I'd always known he was there.

Harry tried another tack. "You're running yourself ragged. You need to be careful. You're not—used to this." He had an irritatingly grown-up air; as if I didn't know all this was foreign to both of us. The *Fortitude* was hardly the Front.

"We're not all as cautious as you, Harry," I said, crossing my arms. "Act the accountant if you must." I knew that would hit home—the idea of this being a *game* had stung. I left the lamp flickering.

It was a cool rainy day. Harry reappeared halfway through the morning, smelling of wet dog, to bring me tea by way of apology. I pretended I didn't care about the apology, or the earlier fight: I took my tea out on deck, where the rain was inconveniencing Nicholls in the crow's nest. Randall was on the bridge, accompanied by Mortimer and the sailing master, and I squinted at him swaggering about, shouting something disparaging about the bearings from the magnetic compass. Nicholls suggested that perhaps if the ship had been outfitted in months, not *weeks*—and I snorted quietly, thinking he was taking his life in his hands.

"All right!" Randall bellowed, rolling his eyes in good humor. "And watch yourself up there—I've no desire to explain to your wife and sweethearts—"

"May they never meet!" Nicholls laughed, popping out from below the crow's nest and shimmying down the shrouds. He would not hold on to the rat-lines; it made me feel very uneasy.

Randall's gaze fell on me. I straightened up, putting down my mug. "Morgan," he said. "Take a brush and bucket to the laboratory. I understand our chief scientific officer needs assistance clearing up a—mess."

I scrambled to my feet. I had to appear instantly willing, though I'd been enjoying the spattering rain on my face, and my vantage point to soak up all the ship's goings-on. Being a *spare* on the expedition, I'd quickly learned, meant I belonged nowhere but might be required anywhere.

It also meant—according to polar lore, and Randall's threat—if it came to it, I'd be eaten first.

Tarlington's laboratory was little more than a storage cupboard with shelving and a desk. The daylight from the illuminator didn't quite penetrate, but glimmered dismally off the row of small, sharp scissors pinned to the wall. The smell was strange and dusty; the shapes in the specimen bottles murky and lumpen. Everything about it made my skin crawl. I paused in the doorway to let my eyes adjust to the gloom.

Tarlington could barely stand up inside, which seemed like a cruel joke. He looked annoyed to see me, and I scowled back naturally; it took me a few moments to realize that his annoyance was directed elsewhere. Books and bottles lay in disarray. There were pools of yellow liquid on the floor, and the microscope dangled from the ceiling on a rope, spinning crazily as the ship moved.

"Oh." I remembered the previous evening. There had been singing in the wardroom and mess hall; Clarke had got out his trumpet, and Randall led the men in a rendition of "Pack Up Your Troubles," his growling baritone lending the song a threatening air. I'd hovered—been pulled in by the laughing seamen—just as if I belonged there. A rowdy night I'd treasure for the rest of my life.

"Yes," Tarlington said. "Oh. Can you clean up the iodine, and I'll have to hope I can get more." His fingerless gloves were stained faintly yellow, as were his long, thin fingers.

"I'm sure they didn't mean anything by it," I said, shifting the bucket from hand to hand. "It was just a joke."

He stared at me. "Shut up, Morgan."

I knelt, fighting back a retort, and started to scrub the floor. He was—even by default—still an officer. I was only a *spare*.

"Childish nonsense," he said faintly. "Good Lord, it's just like being back at school. I daresay I should be used to it by now."

I gave him a sidelong glance. If he wanted to complain—well, he'd get no sympathy from me. Even Harry had joined in, his singing voice clear and pleasant, if tentative; with a bit of encouragement from the men, he'd turned out some shockingly bawdy songs. But while we'd all been packed into the mess hall, Tarlington had hidden away somewhere, hadn't condescended to join us. He'd brought this on himself.

"The CSO should be someone with more—standing. Experience. Then this sort of nonsense wouldn't—" Quieter: "They don't respect me." He rubbed his eyes, appearing to gather himself. "But as Randall hardly had his pick of candidates—none of his scientific staff would return—"

"Why not?" I found myself asking.

"Pay." He sighed. "Priorities—theirs and his. Do you imagine Randall cares much about anything, except the Pole?"

There was something slimy in the shadows under the desk that I didn't think I could bear to touch. Tarlington looked so downcast I said, "Well, he took *you* on, didn't he? So that counts for something."

He laughed. "Lord, yes. I've all the benefits of an *intensive* correspondence course—a summer with a veterinarian. The product of a rigorous recruitment process! When really it came down to whoever turned up at the expedition office in the right trousers. Or could afford to lose a great deal of money, like your friend Cooper—Randall wasn't going to find it elsewhere. This'll be his last expedition, you know."

"That's not true," I said shortly, applying myself vigorously to the decking. Randall had led two previous expeditions, was barely into his mid-forties. He'd been going South before I was born.

Tarlington shrugged. "England has stopped believing in this sort of—vainglorious pursuit. We're the tail end. Believe me, Morgan, this *will* be his last expedition."

"As if you'd know!"

I worked the brush harder, until my knuckles scraped the wooden floor.

"Only examine the evidence," he said in his hoarse voice. "You think these are the men he wanted? No. We're simply all he could get—and then there's *you*."

I stood so fast I whacked my knee on the table. In the cramped room we were nearly face-to-face—and although he towered a head above me, he took a gratifying step away. I clenched my fists, heard my aching joints crack.

"Careful, Morgan." His skin was so milky pale he looked like something from his own specimen jars. "It's not far to Grytviken."

My thoughts flew—I didn't know what came next. I'd never punched anyone before. Something so simple had been left out of my life, like a painting omitting a vital color: the possibility of violence. It thrilled me a little, though. I could abruptly see, in my mind's eye, Tarlington staggering backward, holding his pointed nose. Blood gushing. It was an image I liked. I wanted to wipe that look off his face: as if he were simply *too good* for the rest of us.

Tarlington's eyes widened briefly, as if I had indeed thrown a punch. "Come on." He deliberately presented me with his back. "I doubt someone in your—position—fancies brawling belowdecks to prove what an asset you are."

"Try me," I said, deepening my voice to conceal the sudden thudding of my heart. The flush rising across my face. Squaring up to him—it was like my body was beating a tune, telling me violence would feel right; natural; just. "Or *you* don't want to fight—is that it?"

He turned, the light flashing on his microscope. An incongruous and delicate sight at the heart of a ship so weather-beaten and rough. White sleeves. A pocket handkerchief. He sighed, and it sounded like he'd done so a hundred times. "I suppose you're like the rest of them. You must think I'm a coward—"

"I don't care *what* you are, but—"

"Lord, Morgan." He flexed his fingers in those long gloves. "You can start this with me, if you like—I'm very used to it. There are no secrets on the *Fortitude*, and I'm sorry, I really am, about your brothers. I can't imagine how you must miss them. Particularly when you didn't go yourself."

"I was underage," I snapped automatically. My mouth was dry. He had no right to bring them into this. *No one* knew how I missed them—what shape that took for me. The men would naturally assume I was missing football games, bicycle rides, wrestling; the idle joshing among brothers. Shared experiences, shared adventures, a shared boyhood. The way it should have been. Not what I'd actually had: the moments of indulgence then denial, chasing after Rufus, trying too hard to impress him, as if I could—by sheer force of will—make him see me as another Francis.

No one knew how I missed my brothers, except Harry.

He shrugged. "Cooper, well—I can do basic arithmetic. No one would be too fussy about nice boys who could handle a gun—warm bodies in a shell hole waiting their turn." His tone was sardonic. "He must have been tall for his age—am I right? Sixteen. Seventeen, maybe."

The Coopers had called my father every name under the sun. Accusing him of whipping up Harry against them, encouraging their son—their *underage* son—to lie to the recruiting sergeant. To fake his papers and run away to fight. My father had borne their accusations remarkably well: he knew that was exactly what Rufus had done. Father had been so very proud of the country going to war, as if he'd had some part in it. I could almost see him standing with his back to the fireplace, straight as a sentry, telling the Coopers—Harry's mother staring at her handkerchief—that it would be *the making of him.*

"But you, Morgan—you either didn't try—or didn't make it past scrutiny," Tarlington said, with a small upwards quirk of his mouth. I looked quickly around, but the door was shut. He continued, carefully, to wipe the specimen bottles. I couldn't tell what he'd meant: what sort of scrutiny. The physical examination, maybe. The chest-measuring, the casual assessment of my age, that crowned recruitment armband—*I fully understand the consequences of issue and wearing*—I'd never be given. "So you needn't be—like that—with me. You don't seem the sort. Not the sort to play dirty tricks on a man just because he thought it was all rot—"

"Not the sort," I said hotly. The suggestion struck me in the chest like a fist. "You're implying that *I'm* a coward? You're older than Harry." I shoved the bucket hard against the table. "You're older than me." My voice shook, and the iodine water slopped onto the floor. I wouldn't take this, not from him. "Where were you?"

He didn't look up. "Princetown."

"Where did you serve?"

He sighed, his face becoming pinched. "I did not submit myself to military service," he said slowly. "My education was interrupted. I was meant to be at Oxford, but I was sent to the work camps instead—somewhere vile, to do useless labor in the cold and wet. I'm here, like everyone else, because I was all Randall could get. An afterthought. So we have something in common."

This was what I'd overheard them talking about: the conscientious objector—*conchie*—on our ship. We had nothing at all in common—

worse, he seemed to think he was better than me. Better than all of us. I thought about pushing him up against his own neat shelving. But if he wouldn't fight back—

"Go on," Tarlington said sharply. "Call me names."

"I think very little of—"

"No, no one does. Go on, then. Call me a coward for not wishing to die for some stupid notion of glory. I wouldn't do it."

"It wasn't stupid—"

"It's not even a question of cowardice," he said, suddenly sounding very weary. "Good God. Heroism, patriotism, all of it—thousands of young men wasted. All because they wished to be heroes."

"They *were* heroes," I said. "They fought and died as heroes." I was horrified to find my voice shaking, sounding shrill, moving up a range. "Harry, too. He's worth two of you—two hundred of you. He didn't have to go when he did—and he was there when—"

He was there when my brothers died. It stuck in my throat, as if I'd swallowed a rock.

"It's a ridiculous sham," Tarlington said, his nostrils flaring. "The whole idea that being willing to die makes you more a man—"

"You were afraid to die, is that it—"

"Nonsense," he hissed. "I'm *not* afraid to die."

The connecting door opened. Harry looked wildly in. "For God's sake. They can hear you in the wardroom! Shut up with that sort of talk."

I glared at Tarlington, who was relabeling bottles, very deliberately, in his green ink. His hand shook a little.

"At least I've done something with my life," I snarled, finishing the last few inches of floor with a flourish, throwing the scrubbing brush back into the bucket. "I ran halfway across the world and smuggled myself on board. I'm not afraid to die. If you don't even want to be here—that just shows what sort of a man you are."

Harry took the bucket, and I could see his jaw clench as he silently shut the door behind us. I'd been asked to wield the scrubbing brush; I'd done exactly that. Normally I'd linger, find something else. But Tarlington could finish righting his own laboratory; the men could turn it upside down nightly for all I cared. His words echoed horribly in my ears. *Thousands of young men wasted.* Passing the row of swaying galoshes, I swallowed hard, seeing again those orderly, pressed uniforms hanging by my mother's flower arrangements, all gold buttons and khaki stitching. The dreadful chaos of holes and tears showing what my brothers must have become.

There was no door to slam as we came out into the mess hall, where men were gathered around the stove. It was impossible to quarrel in private on the *Fortitude*: everyone knew everyone's business, the crew tightly knitted with allegiances.

And I was becoming one of them. Over my close-cropped hair, I wore a woolen hat: doubtless crafted by someone's wife or daughter, it had found its way onto my hammock when I'd been out on deck. There'd been no message left with it, nor to accompany the pair of oversized wolfskin mitts that arrived the next day. I liked the way the hat made my roundish face more angular, accentuating the lines of my nose and brow, sharpening my features.

A few low whistles. "Our pipsqueak's got a temper," said Rees, the ship's carpenter—his combed-back hair as jet-black and shiny as any hat—and winked at me.

"Quite right," Boyd muttered, bringing in sails to be mended. A jagged scar from a German bayonet ran right the way up one of his arms: he'd seen close-quarters fighting. He gave me a warm look, and I flushed with pleasure. "It's a bloody disgrace—"

Nicholls shushed him, catching my eye. "He'll calm down. It's only some of the men having a laugh. You'd think they'd done worse, from the flap he was in."

I rubbed my brow, wanting to request another cabin, a hammock in the mess hall with the sailors, anything. I couldn't sleep next to someone who could say those things, call the foundations of my world a *sham*. He was a coward. He was a traitor. And I wanted nothing more to do with him.

IX

It was simple to avoid Tarlington after that: he seemed to keep his bunk neat as a pin without ever actually being there. Sometimes I saw him on deck, the dogs gazing with slavering jaws as he expertly wielded a knife to break the wings off a tern, or slit a fish open to its glistening belly. His notebook weighted down against the fresh easterly breeze, hair blowing into his face as he bent down to sketch with quick careful fingers. I supposed this was another type of *intensive course*, and wondered whether his university place had evaporated on Armistice Day with the coiling smoke of the guns. He'd look up and meet my look of fascinated horror, then nod, scowl, and turn away.

The other men seemed to share my contempt, and were similarly content to leave him alone. By ten days' sail, I was on speaking terms with most of the expedition, the men missing fingers and toes and marriages and prudence, who talked about the South like it was a living thing—beguiling and hostile by turns.

Clarke had decided, with a prohibitionist air, that if there was time for drinking and games, there was certainly time for education, and we'd had our first round of wardroom lectures. A projector cast flickering shadows over a suspended sheet as we listened raptly. Holmes had spoken at length on ice-climbing, showing us haughty indifferent white-cloaked mountains, peaks obscured by cloud; little dark figures at their base, as if drawn on simply for scale. There had been a lively debate on tactics in the Hundred Days Offensive, although Harry steadfastly refused to weigh in. Poor Harry: he hadn't talked about his service since that dreadful day in our parlor—Rufus and Francis staring down at him from the mantelpiece, their cuff badges and bright eyes dulled by the camera to an ominous black-and-white.

On the day we reached South Georgia, however, I was brought back down to earth. Reminded of my place: the *spare*.

My hands were red and sore from unaccustomed hard labor with the ship's tarry ropes, and I'd sought out Macready. He gave me oil for the cracks on my palms, and a long, fiery drink of whisky. I'd let out a hissing breath through my teeth as I replaced my gloves. "They think you've got some nerve," he said. "Randall, too—standing up to him like that."

I scoffed. Randall had showed no sign that I was anything other than a convenient tool, to be picked up and set down at will. But Macready, who was an old Randall hand—had been out with him each time—shrugged.

"It's the sort of thing he'd have done as a lad—stowing away, seeking adventure. Wouldn't have succeeded on any other ship."

I flexed my hands gingerly, a warm feeling deep in my chest. Perhaps it was the whisky—perhaps it was the thought of being like Randall as a *lad*. Macready knuckled my shoulder, and I thanked him awkwardly, wished him good night. Back in the Nursery, I'd fallen asleep immediately, sleeping deeply—too deeply, straight through four bells in the morning watch.

I'd expected to be roused by one of the stokers. Miners from the grubbier parts of the British Isles, they normally shook me ungently awake. But instead, someone said, "What's this, skiving off?" and I found myself snapping awake as my hammock was roughly upended, sending me crashing to the floor.

I cringed. I'd hit my head hard on the way down, and stared at the timbers, my vision careening into focus. I put my hand to my forehead as a sharp pain rang through me, temple to temple.

"Coaling." It was Duncan, Harry's dog-deck boss, his Anzac tang coming from a long way above me. I could see Harry's pajamas discarded on the floor, the rich grain on the decking, a small pile of Tarlington's books.

Duncan pulled me up, and I bit off a curse as the pressure in my head settled behind my right eye. He looked at me appraisingly. "You're not injured," he said, although I detected a hint of embarrassment. Lights flashed in the corner of my vision. I focused on his face, goggling at him and his clean, harsh jaw. He was handsome as a Greek god, up close: I thought crazily that my hand might reach up and touch him of its own accord.

"Get up on deck."

I did as I was told. The morning was cool. Clarke saw how I clutched my head, and appeared—for a moment—about to say something. Duncan marched me straight down the long stair into the bunkers. Ellis and Parker, the two stokers—equally short, equally stooped, equally caked in coal dust—leaned on their ladders. The air smelled like wet tar and brimstone.

"I'm not sure the pipsqueak will help," Ellis said in his Northern drawl, as I swallowed repeatedly. "Are you going to puke again?"

"He'll help." Duncan gave me a pointed glare before swaggering off.

I was sick twice during the watch, my head growing heavier and heavier. Worse than useless where brute strength was required, my arms were exhausted, from my bruised palms right up to my abused shoulders, which seemed about to pop out of their sockets. I understood this wasn't just work: this was a message. I shouldn't have got ideas. I cursed myself silently, Ellis saying, "They'd better hope you're never needed for man-hauling, eh? Last ten minutes."

Back on deck, I was black with coal dust. It had smeared across my face when I'd wiped away the sweat, stuck to the short fuzz of my hair when I'd held my throbbing head. I didn't mind being dirty—liked it, even—but I could hear every pulse of the blood in my veins. Harry brought me hot milk, looking at me with a kind of resignation. "You could wash," he said, clearly resisting the urge to examine my head himself. His hands were dirty and bitten, his eyes tired: he looked like the *hundred years* he'd once felt. "I'd watch the door."

I shrugged.

"I could ask them to stop it," he said, quietly so Duncan wouldn't hear. "It might work."

I pulled a face.

"It won't be forever. Just to South Georgia, and then—"

I gave another half-hearted shrug. My entire body ached, and if he'd told me we were in the Weddell Sea, a troop of Emperor penguins dancing a can-can off the starboard bow, I wouldn't have cared enough to get up and look.

"Morgan," Duncan called. "Dog deck, come on."

I put down my mug and went to stand up, but Harry placed his hand on my shoulder, holding me down. "Don't," he said. "I'll go, you've surely done enough—"

I pushed him off, hissing. I was terribly conscious that I was under observation. I'd been so careful to be up early, to bed late; always ready to lend a hand in any spare moment. I worked hard. I could almost feel the terrible weight of Randall's gaze on me.

I had to become more than a *spare*.

I wobbled to standing on my heavy legs. "I don't think this was a good idea," Harry muttered, shading his eyes to look up at me.

I suppose I gave him a pitying look, thinking of his letters: "The thing to do is stick it out, of course, and just do one's best—then right will follow." He'd never asked his parents to write to the War Office and pull him out, despite being too young for the Front. He'd seen it through; wasn't the sort to jump for an easy life.

He flushed, the pink going only as far as the bruise-dark circles under his eyes. "We'll be there soon," he said. "And the dog deck gets scrubbed twice a day, they're doing this to show us—"

I shrugged, and regretted it. I didn't have time for Harry's troubles as well as my own—walked off, my head spinning, to put some distance between us.

Duncan raised an eyebrow at me. Then his attention fell on Harry, and he shouted, "Cooper—this isn't a fucking Sunday school trip, let's go," and strode off.

I knelt beside the kennels. Sanchez strained at his leash to lick the coal dust off my hands, a wide canine smile on his face. The sun turned his fur golden, tracing his eyelashes. Struggling to form a fist, I took up the shovel, knowing what was expected.

Another day.

But there was a shout from the crow's nest—"Land ho!"—the ship's bell ringing, and cheering from the men. We went to the railings in a hurry, Mortimer handing Randall the binoculars.

"South Georgia," Randall said with satisfaction. "Well, not a day too soon."

X

The islands were not much to look at: they crept up from the horizon like a lump of sugar floating in the dregs of a cup of tea, then resolved themselves into gray mountain ranges and stiff peaks marching steadily away.

The wind, though, made its own impression. Persistent and dogged, it battered us towards the shore, and I saw why South Georgia was famously hard to approach. The *Fortitude* creaked and groaned, the sailing master called up the next watch early, and Nicholls pulled himself up into the rigging with easy confidence to join them.

I struggled to lift a crate, groaning inside when Duncan took the other corner. "End of the line for you, eh?" he said, inclining his chin towards the salt-and-pepper shore. I stared at him.

"He'll put you down in Grytviken, at least. The whalers send transports every few months, so I'm sure you could be packed off home before the weather turns?"

I bit my lip hard, resisting the urge to argue. I had to believe Randall hadn't yet made up his mind about me.

"I daresay the Coopers'll make good the bill." I hadn't realized everyone would know that Harry had practically bought his way on board. But a lot of the men also assumed Harry and I were related, which made me bristle—I didn't want us to be lumped together.

I put the crate down, flexed my numb fingers. Duncan laughed. "What's the matter? Scared of the mean old whalers?"

I thought of what Harry had said—they were *criminals*. To be feared, if I had to overwinter there alone.

"As if they would—" I'd said to him hotly.

"They *might*," Harry had insisted.

"You're wanted below," Macready said, appearing between us and giving Duncan a very sharp look. "I heard about your head," he said, once Duncan was gone. "Are you—"

I shrugged, put on my bravest of smiles. Wanting him to call me *lad*, and ruffle my short hair. "It's nothing."

But I found myself staring at Randall, standing on the bridge with the ship's captain, leaning against the railings as the wind pitched the ship in a horrible roll. I wished desperately that he'd look at me.

Boyd took Duncan's place, shifting his own crate single-handed. If he'd wanted to balance one on his broad shoulders, he could have; he wore a baggy blue jumper with the sleeves rolled up, although the wind on deck was freezing. I still hadn't got used to the cold—or developed the art of pretending. It crept into my bones, making me grateful for every single layer. I'd already been issued some winter clothing from the ship's stores, including a thigh-length Burberry windproof jacket, tightly woven and dense. My silhouette on deck—I noticed with satisfaction—was nearly square.

"Look," Boyd said. "Randall's overstretched himself. I know you two think this was a joke, but things are going to turn serious—there's only so much help we'll get from the whalers. We can't afford surprises, or make exceptions."

A matter-of-fact tone; he thought he was being helpful.

I rubbed my knuckles, feeling my abused hands ache, half-hoping to draw Boyd's attention to my hard work. But it was no use, and when I turned to look at Macready, I found that—for once—he refused to meet my eye.

As the *Fortitude* raced towards that pale shoreline, I hauled crates and was pushed past and ignored. I wearied Harry, whenever we crossed paths, by asking if he'd heard anything; if the whalers would really lock me up. Eventually he said, "Just shut up," and stalked away, trench coat billowing behind him. I was replaceable. We both were. When the seas grew rougher towards the coast, I was sent down to the galley, peeling sprouting potatoes with grim determination until, finally, I slammed the knife into the table blade-first.

I watched it quiver. "God," I said tonelessly. "God."

I had come so very, very far, and thought I'd found a home. I wished—for a few moments—to be back in my bed in Portsmouth, and this all a dream. I wished I'd never started South. I'd done my best, and it hadn't been enough.

I hadn't been enough.

I rubbed at my eyes with my rough damp sleeves, staring fiercely at the wall, trying not to see my brothers. Disappointed. Turning away.

The pan clattered off the table and crashed to the floor. The ship was rocking in earnest. She was built to rise above the ice, and the wind was sending her shallow hull careening up one wave and smacking down the next. The galley danced around me. I fought to quell my lurching stomach as I went to my knees to rescue the potatoes.

"All hands to take in sail!" Clarke shouted. I stayed on the floor a moment longer, feeling the ache right down to my bones.

The door to the galley opened, and Macready threw himself in. "Now, Morgan—get up there." His eyes searched my face, eyebrows two large gray signal flags. I picked myself up reluctantly, limb by limb.

It was sleeting cold sheets on deck, the shuddering getting worse. I shielded my face and held on to the rails as the *Fortitude* lunged forward in fits and jumps, sails tearing at the rigging, every inch of canvas billowing taut.

Randall, Mortimer, and Nicholls were crammed behind the wheel; our sailing master clung to the foremast, shouting down, and Randall was shaking his head. It was impossible to hear what was being said. Nicholls threw up his hands, taking several sure strides across the moving deck to hoist himself back aloft.

A crash. The ship moved suddenly sideways, and the wheel spun crazily, nearly a full revolution, before Randall put his weight against it.

"This is fucking stupid—"

"If His Nibs would listen for once—"

Now Randall was shouting over Mortimer, not even a sou'wester or waterproof on, just his plain gray trousers and cable-knit jumper, soaked to the bone. The air smelled expectant: salt and secret places.

"Come up!" Wild yelled from the rigging, seeing me staring. "All hands!"

"Not you." Clarke pushed me aside roughly, and there was another terrible crash as the ship dipped.

But I found myself climbing up hand over numb hand. The horrible jumping-through-hoops, scrubbing decks, fetching buckets, day in, day out—it hardly mattered. None of it mattered, if I'd be abandoned at South Georgia. If I wanted this—the pounding of my heart, the wind smacking me in the face, spray in the air—I'd have to take it while I could.

When the sail was tightly tucked the *Fortitude* slowed, still pressing and pitching, treacherously unstable. Land was coming up close, jagged mountains reaching into the pale sky. I couldn't drag myself back down to deck; a familiar knot had formed in my stomach, and my eyes were drawn to Clarke, far beneath me: "Not *you*." He wasn't yet looking my way, but I knew I'd be punished, and it was all for nothing.

I stayed where I was, sitting out on one of the foremast's great waist-thick yards, hugging it with my knees, barely able to comprehend I might have had my last time aloft. A hollow lurch. The sense of a door slamming.

No—the sudden sound of something falling from above.

Beneath me, Nicholls dangled in thin air. He'd grabbed onto a line to save himself, but the momentum of his fall—a slide—had taken him out along one of the braces running between masts, away from the spider's web of rigging. Although the braces were taut and sturdy, could support him easily, he'd have to haul himself back up hand over hand, and with everything wet and slick—

I saw his legs kicking, windmilling.

Shouts on deck. I looked around desperately, saw men some distance beneath us. Randall had abandoned the wheel. Time seemed to stretch out.

There was nothing beneath Nicholls but a long drop. Two stories or more; the deck would break his spine, smash his skull. A quick death. Better than the alternative—falling into the cold, churning sea. The sudden chill would open his mouth: he'd gulp water, then choke, and his treacherous arms would refuse to fight it.

I knew how people drowned.

Randall's gaze landed on me. My chest felt tight. A split-second decision.

"Hold on!" I shouted, then ran one-two out along my own yard, arms spread wide, lurching and off-balancing, light-headed and breathless— ("Jesus, Morgan!")—until I reached the end of the yardarm. From there, I could monkey down the line leading below to the next one. There were no rat-lines leading out to Nicholls, none at all. But it would take everyone else too long—I had to trust myself.

"Morgan!" Clarke shouted. "Damn it, come *down*—"

Nicholls flung an exhausted arm over the brace. I could see his eyes as he looked at it in despair. "Hold on!" I called again. I could be punished for disobeying orders—*stripped on deck*—put off at the whaling station to meet my fate. The expedition might go on without me. But Randall was watching—

Putting all my weight onto the footrope beneath the yardarm, I felt it strain beneath me. I'd grown heavier—I hadn't noticed. The wind plucked at me. I panicked; looked down, for a moment. I wished I hadn't. The deck was so small, and the men looked tiny. Sleet blew sideways, making my eyes sting, my vision blur. The sea readied itself to swallow me up.

Shouting below. Movement. Nicholls didn't look like he could hold on much longer. I tried not to think of the awful percussive *snap* of my own footrope reaching its limit—the lurching sensation of the fall.

I took a deep breath. Holding on as tight as I could with one hand, I squeezed my eyes closed for a second, then opened them to reach out to him. The moment of truth. "I can't hold your weight."

Nicholls nodded, and unhooked an elbow. Reached for me.

A lurch. For a very short moment, it felt as if I did have his full weight: a fully grown man, clothes sodden with spray. I could feel myself losing balance, losing my grip on the line, and opened my mouth to scream. I was over the deck. I was over the side. It didn't matter; either way, this fall was my end.

Then Nicholls was swinging himself up onto the safety of the yard.

"All well?" Clarke bellowed. My head was ringing. I watched my hands scrabble. I suddenly thought I would fall. "All well? Morgan? Morgan?"

The world tilted, Nicholls putting his arm around me. "I've got you. Don't you *dare* fall. But if you're going to be sick, be a good fellow and do it that way." He smiled, the crow's-feet around his eyes deepening. I could feel him shaking.

He didn't let go of me until we reached the deck. The moment my boots touched wood, my legs collapsed underneath me, and I sat down hard, watching with surprise as I started to shiver. The shock of it all. I put my hand to my head again.

"Staunton!" Clarke shouted, and the ship's surgeon ran up, tripping over his own feet. His sea legs were awful.

Harry hugged me and hissed, "You idiot, you *idiot*—"

In the small lull that followed, I'm ashamed to say I was sick again. When I'd finished wiping my mouth and spitting, I could finally feel the weight of Randall's regard. He'd come down from the bridge, and we were making a steady course, rocking slightly, the air wet and metallic. "Nicholls?" Nicholls gave an uncertain wave, still looking a little light-headed. "Well, we couldn't go on without you, eh!" A small laugh from the assembled men.

Randall sat down next to me on the deck. His jumper was drenched, hanging off him, although he seemed to neither notice nor care. He stared at me, and I stared back. "We couldn't. Just think, Morgan, the middle of a blizzard: snow screaming around you, so thick it's darkness itself. No horizon, sky, stars, or moon—not even your own feet! The map's a big blank thing, and there are crevasses lurking. Moving is deadly—stopping might be worse. Nicholls here—he knows the white spaces."

Both sides of Randall's face curved upwards in a large, wolfish grin, and my heart stopped beating.

"And this is why we have *spares*," he said to the men around us. "No one else'd be crazy enough to do that." He put a large hand on my back. "Morgan—I don't think we could in good conscience eat you. No matter how low the supplies. We'd boil our boots first. Well—you've made me proud."

XI

Grytviken whaling station could be smelled from the water. Gliding into King Edward Cove, the reddish sea placid under the *Fortitude*'s bow, the odor was impossible to escape. Blubber, blood, sickly sweetness underneath. Small red-roofed buildings gathered around the water's edge, a small white church where the ground swelled up into mountains, and the flag of the Argentine Fishing Company fluttered in the steady breeze.

The stick-figure men on shore waved with great energy. Randall wiped his hands on his grubby trousers and rang the ship's bell himself.

When we dropped anchor, I sighed heavily to find myself left to the last boat, despite the "Three cheers!" that still echoed in my ears. No one wanted to travel with our sullen scientist: Boyd's mutterings about *conchies* had filtered through the whole crew. Tarlington was not a bad oarsman, though, his long arms freckled and bare. Glowering at each other, we had a silent journey to shore.

The tide was in, the waves lapping against the corrugated iron jetty, seaweed trailing like the hair of a drowned girl. I stepped off carefully, trying out the novelty of steady ground. Randall was clasping the hand of an enormous man with a large waxed mustache: Captain Hvalfangeri, a good friend to explorers. "So late! Australis! We did not think you would come," he roared.

"Any word from the South? What of Karlmann?" Randall asked urgently. He furrowed his dark eyebrows at the captain's reply—he appeared disquieted. A group of men surrounded them: pale-skinned, blond-haired Norwegians, and darker-skinned Cape Verde islanders. I listened with interest, catching snatches of what I thought I recognized as Portuguese from our journey down. One of the Norwegians broke away to put an arm around Nicholls, who started talking animatedly, gesturing over to me.

The whalers seemed perfectly friendly; I couldn't see why Harry had been so afraid.

I was presented to the captain, who nearly crushed my hand when he shook it. I blushed, and looked at Harry, battling to hold Biter down for inspection by the station's veterinarian. Harry's right arm was bandaged, and he was heavily favoring his left. I caught his eye and smiled, but the look of misery on his face stopped me. It suddenly occurred to me he'd seemed miserable for some time.

Tarlington bent to Harry's assistance, catching and holding the dog's paws as it struggled and yelped. He gave me a long, cool look, his gaze lingering on Nicholls for a moment, then turned away.

I was taken to the stores by a whaler who was so dark-skinned it made his neck muscles gleam in the sun like beaten metal. Though Harry had told me about the Commonwealth soldiers on the battlefields—terrified white and black and brown faces pressed into the mud side-by-side—this was all entirely new to me. A long way from Portsmouth. I was shy, and didn't want to stare; but the whaler helped me pick out clothing that might fit, clapped me on the back, then left me to try it on.

Outside, a slanted plane led down to the sea, and a whale was beached upon it, skin sloughing off as if from a rotten fruit, the whalers wielding their large, straight flensing knives. The windlass at the end of the jetty spun, squeaking repetitively, and I was struck by how cheerful and stark it seemed here at the end of the world. Things were declining gradually into ruin: rust on the gantries; windows smashed, facing the water. But there was also hot tea, served black and very strong. Geraniums in the window boxes. Randall sitting enthroned in the foreman's office, studying our further course south.

XII

That night, the whalers threw us a party. A large bonfire wafted acrid smoke into our faces. It was a balmy four degrees, quite clear and bright until after ten o'clock, when the sky was punctured by the black teeth of the mountains behind us. We sat on pallets around the fire; potatoes baked in its ashes were served with a deliciously rich brown cheese that Smith—his mouth full—immediately pronounced "A-one." "You think everything's A-one, you ruffian," Benham said, punching him. Barely older than Harry, they'd both been at sea since boyhood, and seemed much younger with it—restless, energetic, kicking their football around deck to Clarke's displeasure. I still wasn't sure where I stood with the crew, and of course—when we reached the shores of Antarctica—we'd be parting ways. I would be part of the land party. Part of Randall's expedition.

Grytviken looked like a stony English beach out of season; devoid of tourists, home instead to a group of vagrants. I wore brand-new long johns, pressed on me as a gift by the tall Viking-like man who'd embraced Nicholls. Once we got to the ice, the men would put on their long johns and vests and Jaeger combinations and not take them off till Michaelmas. And I would be the same.

We were waiting for a whaling ship to tell us the condition of the Weddell Sea ice. A steamer in the harbor had brought correspondence in turn—for the rest of the expedition, at least. No letters had awaited our arrival; the Morgans had flung no threats and denunciations at Randall, and we seemed to have—finally—got away with it. I'd thought it would cheer Harry up; but he'd turned away from Boyd ("No mail, you two") as if he'd been denied a last-minute appeal. Maybe he pitied his family: their only son had vanished, for the second time in his life. Maybe they'd finally given up on him.

And if my parents had guessed where I'd gone—maybe they'd done the same. I could see my own father saying, sternly: "You've made your bed, and now you must lie in it."

Clarke was delighted to receive new sheet music, and puzzled out the songs on his trumpet, working around those missing fingers, making us whoop loudly. Across the fire, the stokers were telling a sort of ghost story, half-heard, about what had happened to another party in these waters. I tried to listen without being obvious.

"Vanished without a trace—like the ice just swallowed them up."

"Oh, rot. It was mutiny, surely—the Krauts went mad and killed each other." Ellis sucked his teeth.

"Their ship must have sunk—"

"Then they're as good as—"

Macready put his hand on my shoulder, softly shared his news from home: a baby daughter called Roberta, who looked unsmiling and dark-haired, apparently the image of his wife. I stopped eavesdropping on the men, and enjoyed the glow of the fire; even more so, the glow of Randall, sure and certain and larger than life, raising his glass to me across the flames. Boyd was pouring whisky like water. I was warmer than I'd been in months, and it radiated through my body like a small sun. I felt I might reach up and touch the dark overturned bowl of the sky.

A hand on my shoulder from behind. I jumped, nearly lashing out. Smith laughed, asked if I'd been heroic enough for one day; I said I hoped to be a great deal more heroic still. But it was just Harry, bundled up until only his earnest brown eyes were visible. I shifted myself over. He didn't sit.

"Jonathan, can I have a word?"

I sighed a little, and stood up.

Harry walked silently away. I followed him between buildings into a small alleyway ending at the harbor. Rubbish drifted up against a scrap-iron door, and stones crunched underfoot. Away from the fire, it was darker than I expected, a row of flickering lanterns on the jetty lending their assistance to the small chunk of moon.

Harry leaned against the wall, exhaling softly. His face was in shadow. I opened my mouth to speak, then followed his gaze. The steamer was a silhouette on the water, a few pinpricks of light aboard: the crew was German, and they hadn't been invited to the whalers' party. I'd seen Boyd's face when the letters were handed over. He'd pulled them roughly out of the messenger's grasp, and walked away without saying a word.

I knew what he would have said, though: Krauts. The Hun. The *Boche*.

"They're taking some of the whalers back to South America," Harry said. "Those who've served out their contracts."

I shrugged. The steamer was of no concern to me. Not now. It was all coming into focus. The wind changed: smoke from the bonfire drifted thickly in the air, smelling of Norwegian cheese and paraffin lamps.

He looked down. "Harry," I said, awkwardly. I wanted to ask what was wrong. But I didn't want to hear how dreadfully unhappy he was: I knew he couldn't lie to me.

"Where to start?" His voice was hard-edged. "I've been bitten to the bone. What I'd do for a proper bath, you can hardly imagine. I've been awake for weeks. I sleep—for an hour or so, before someone shouts at me or I wake myself up falling out of that bloody bunk. And if I do get any sleep, all I can dream of is—*them*—"

I noticed I was shaking my head. He stopped abruptly. "I'm sorry. I know you don't want to hear it." He looked out over the water. "She'll sail within the week, Jo."

"Jonathan," I said, my hands curling, my spine stiffening.

"There's no one else here."

"Harry—" I exhaled in frustration. "That doesn't matter."

I'd thought he'd grown accustomed to it, would come to call me *Jonathan* automatically. Our compromise was nearly two months ago, and in my mind it was still tied to our lurching six-by-two cabin aboard the ship to Buenos Aires, where I'd tried things on in front of the mirror wedged against Harry's sea chest, starting to recognize this person as he took shape before me. My new clothing—trousers, unremarkable and beige, except for the fact that they were mine, and they were trousers— had made me stand a good few inches taller.

"We could be home by Easter."

I stared at him, not understanding.

"We could—I do not wish to go on."

I bit my lip; fought back my first reaction. Harry wasn't a coward— my brothers would never have been friends with a coward, even though Rufus joked about the battery's position behind the lines. Harry would laugh, as if it didn't bother him; I thought that anyone within five miles of those thundering, earsplitting guns was brave enough. But as I looked at him now, all I could see was an overgrown boy. The shabby bandage. The dark rings under his eyes. The crusted salt in his curls. His constant complaining, where anyone could hear.

I didn't trust myself to speak. I gripped his shoulders instead, and he set his jaw. "Don't think you can tell me—"

"Tell you what? This was *your* idea, as much as mine? This was what you wanted?"

He shook his head.

"But it was. Harry, you know it. We both wanted this. I know I—might have twisted your arm a little." I wouldn't apologize for it. "But you were sure, too. Making things right, you said. Doing what they would have wanted. And when you talked about them, you were so—"

He shoved me away from him, hard.

"You were so—"

"I haven't forgotten," he hissed. "I'd do *anything* to see them again—"

I caught his shoulder as he turned to walk away. He wheeled around. "It's all right for you!" He was nearly shouting. "You're enjoying this, aren't you? Jonathan Morgan and his bloody—adventure. The early mornings and bullying and getting knocked around. *Honestly.* It's like a game for you—all the things you never had. It's different for me."

My fingers tightened on his jumper. We were both breathing loudly. "It's not a game!"

Harry had once called my baggy woolen clothing a *disguise*—with a lurch, I remembered loitering outside a shop in Funchal, the sort of place they sold hard-wearing gear for men going out on the ships. The windowsills were rimmed with ocher dust, through which I'd run my fingertip while peering at Harry inside. He'd been making himself understood, carefully and sensibly, with gestures indicating he was buying clothing for someone shorter. "My brother," I'd heard him say, and clutched my fist to my chest.

"Harry—none of it's a game. Not to me."

I let him go.

I heard Clarke striking up "On Patrol in No-Man's-Land." Laughter and voices carried on the breeze. South Georgia and the men and the expedition, and all I'd found on the *Fortitude*: I loved it. I'd fight to the death to keep it—the place I'd won by the fire, in that circle of men.

"I don't know how you can just act like—like none of this ever happened." Though I didn't say it—like my brothers had never happened. "You want to go home, is that it?" I knew this would needle him. "Back to England and—what? Say sorry to your parents? Step into the *family business* and get *married* and become the good obedient son?"

I sounded like Rufus. The keen sense of one's standing in the world; our family's sense of its own importance. Harry, the Coopers—they were a bit beneath us. Not a great deal. But enough to matter.

Harry looked at me, and I didn't recognize him. "Yes," he said, his shoulders set. "Yes, I would. I'm not like you."

And he wasn't. I understood that, understood—painfully, with a rising sense of panic—how he might hold me back. I let go of him like I was scalded. "You can do—all of that." I rubbed my aching neck. "I won't stop you. Just—afterwards."

He laughed harshly. "Afterwards?" He raised his arms out wide, and slowly turned around, indicating the night, the island. The water beyond. "After this? If we even return. People come through here—and they don't all come back. The whalers know." He gestured at the German-crewed steamer. "What about Karlmann and his men? They were off to Coats Land too—and two years now they've been gone. They were here, just like us, and they spoke to the whalers, just like us, and they sailed out south-southeast past the Sandwich Islands—just like we're going to—and *disappeared*."

"Come on. That's nothing to do with us. Plenty of things could have happened to them—you've been listening to the stokers." The summer sailing season wasn't yet over: there was still some small possibility that Karlmann might turn up in his *Drygalski*—a year later than expected, but safe and well. I'd heard Randall arguing with Captain Hvalfangeri and the steamer's bosun over the possibility of the German nation sending a relief ship now the War was over. There was an unfamiliar concern in Randall's voice, and I'd felt a strange sense of betrayal. It wasn't our responsibility, to worry over the fate of foreign men—and Randall had never once organized relief for his own expeditions. Of course he wouldn't.

The word *disappeared* stuck in my head for a moment.

He stared at me, his face coming back out of shadow, and he was suddenly Harry Cooper again, who'd written me all those letters, who'd walked with me on the rain-slicked quayside. I *knew* him. "What scares me," he said, slowly, wearily, "is you don't realize how bad those things could be. That the same things might happen to us, and I won't be able to keep you safe."

"It's not your job!"

"It has to be someone's job," he shot back.

"You're being paranoid—"

"And you're being naïve!" he shouted. "We could *die*."

Silence.

"I promised myself I'd keep you safe. I'm doing that now. If I leave, if I—desert—you must come with me. It won't be safe for you alone, Jo."

"*Jonathan*," I hissed, taking a step forward, my fists curling. "My name's Jonathan. And you won't do anything." My voice rose. "Harry, you won't *say* anything."

I hated him then. Tall; handsome; he had everything I'd ever wanted, but seemed determined not to value it. Maybe he'd secretly wanted his parents to take him out of the lines. Maybe he'd wanted there to be a letter spilling out my old name, my old life, making it *unsuitable* for me to go any farther. He could shrug his shoulders and say he'd tried: he'd done his best, that was all anyone could expect of him.

But he was all I had left. I took a deep breath, squared my shoulders—tried not to believe it. Tried to take some of the venom out of my voice, as he looked at me with his big, sad, coppery eyes. "I can't go home," I said. "I could never go home, not now. You can turn back, if you must. Harry—"

My voice broke a little. I stuffed it down, because I could hear people approaching, boots crunching on gravel. "I'd be sorry to see you go," I said plainly. "I really would. But I have to do this—for them."

He rubbed his hands over his face, and I could see that faint tremor was back. His grief for them was raw and devouring; impossible to sate.

Whispering, in the alleyway; the sound of Nicholls saying "Shh, shh!"; Randall in the distance, a terrible singer. On the *Fortitude*, a single dog howled when the steamer blew its whistle. The moonlight glinted off Harry's binoculars as he turned them over and over in his hands, caught up in his own thoughts, then ducked his head and walked off towards the jetty.

I took two steps after him, then stopped. I wanted this, I wanted it all. For my brothers. For myself.

I turned, and went to take my place amongst the men.

TWO

THE ICE

THE *FORTITUDE*, AUSTRAL SUMMER 1920

I

The sea changed from green to deep indigo as the floes started to drift past: the first signs of the winter country approaching, with its long night ahead.

Randall took to the bridge when the Antarctic pack ice finally swelled to surround us. He'd been caught in the middle of his bath: hair plastered thick to his skull, beard wet and dripping, sparse on the frostbitten side of his face. Grasping at the railings with large bare hands, he looked like a sea leopard. I remembered his roaring confrontations with Captain Hvalfangeri, who'd told him it was foolish, madness, to go south that late in the season.

"Well, this is it, eh?" Randall said. "The pack! We know the Weddell Sea has a stern face—she may well turn that face against us. The start of February already, but God—by God, we're up to the challenge, and will win our glory."

I took ice watch, eager to see some of that *stern face* for myself. But the sea had exploded into life instead: birds crying over our masts, the dark, glistening fins of right whales taking refuge from Grytviken's slaughter. Harry joined me as I sat wide-legged and careless on the kennels. Wrapped up in his gold-buttoned trench coat, scarf wound around his face, he was all eyes.

Cherry—named for the bisected black patch on his nose—curled up at our feet, panting clouds of steam into the cold air. I'd grown fond of the dogs: highly strung huskies and mongrels of dubious origin, they wolfed down their dinners and howled constantly for more. The smell of Macready's "miscellaneous stew" tempted them from the galley beneath:

seal with cloves and cinnamon, to be dished up with tinned peas—custard for dessert. Perhaps I'd sneak a few scraps for Cherry later.

"It's so lovely," I said, feeling the inadequacy of words. The pack was crackling and washing around us, as though we floated on a sea of diamonds. Harry's eyes creased into a smile.

"I'm glad—" I didn't really know what I was going to say.

He came a little closer, putting his arm in a protective circle around my back. "And I'm sorry. For trying to make you leave."

"No," I said. "No, I'm glad you stayed."

"I had to." He pulled the scarf from his mouth, looking serious. "I couldn't have left you, Jo, not after—everything."

It caught me by surprise; I winced, looking down at my callused hands. It had been two weeks since we'd set sail from South Georgia; I thought I'd been very clear that I was *Jonathan* from now on. I'd thought Harry would have understood with time, would have seen—football on the beach, cards in the mess hall—none of it was a disguise or a game to me.

"I'd never leave you behind," he insisted before I could correct him, voice low and earnest. "If I didn't keep you safe—they'd never have forgiven me."

I flinched, sending up a silent apology: the mention of my brothers was jarring, and I realized—with a creeping sense of guilt—that I hadn't thought of them in a while. "And—you'd have missed this," I said out loud, indicating the terns dive-bombing our wake, screaming their delight to one another as they startled the fish out of the open water. The frost-smoke of the sea trying to freeze around us. The faint vibration of the *Fortitude* under steam. I didn't want to be the only reason he'd stayed. "Tell me you wouldn't have missed it for the world."

On the bridge, Nicholls sounded the ship's bell, raising a hand to me in silent salute. I grinned back. Harry's gaze followed mine, and his mouth twisted. "You're the dashing stowaway," he said. "I'm the *spare*, now."

I raised my eyebrows, trying to stop a traitorous swell of pleasure at how our roles had changed; turn and turn about, for all the time I'd sat in the locker and had to listen to his stories. "It's not like that."

"It's exactly like that."

We watched the ice in silence. "They'd have loved to see this," he said eventually, giving me a half-smile. "Francis, especially—I suppose we'll have to make the best of it now."

I nodded, not trusting myself to reply.

Another hour must have passed; Harry started yawning, and I fetched us both tea from the galley, ducking into the small copper-plated chart room to offer a mug to Nicholls, bent over his maps. He followed me out on deck, rolling back his shoulders, flashing Harry one of his bright smiles. "Stop skiving, Cooper—eyes on the water!"

Harry snorted. He was famously farsighted—the best on the ship, in fact—and had great success spying the local wildlife even in the worst weather. Seals and seabirds marched their unhappy way into Macready's pot, to lukewarm thanks: Clarke only ever said, "A larger one next time, if you please," with the slightest of nods.

A tall figure in a greatcoat appeared behind Nicholls: Tarlington. It seemed absurd I'd ever mistaken him for Francis, even for a moment. My wish to see my brothers again had got the better of me. He looked out of place in the light of the ice sky; I'd last seen him down below, examining one of our huskies—with his dubious experience, he was the closest thing to a veterinarian we had. Staunton, our surgeon, had been heard to blow his nose loudly, saying: "I draw the line at having to chop up *animals*." Pale light filtering through the laboratory illuminators, the dog had been limp and unresponsive, tail lolling off the table like a bit of rope, pink paw-pads splayed wide. I'd noticed a number of bites and scratches to Tarlington's bare arms as he thumbed open an eyelid to shine light into a dark pupil. He'd run a hand, distracted, through his hair—looking for a moment strangely pleased with himself—then scowled at me, as if from habit.

I made a great show of looking through an imaginary telescope, and Nicholls laughed. "You're right," he called. "This isn't ice. When we get into the Weddell Sea proper—then you'll see ice. Packed around us like quicklime, wind squeezing it against our hull. The pressure trying to tear open our seams, pop our rivets—smash us into splinters."

"You don't seem concerned," I said, thinking of the warnings I'd heard him give Randall in the wardroom—so long ago it seemed like a hazy dream.

"I'm one of nature's optimists." He paced back and forth, as if he had too much energy to be contained. "Soon we'll see the face of the South. The very heart of *ice*."

I swallowed. The knocking of the pack against our hull suddenly seemed very loud; the ship herself very flimsy. I couldn't imagine what it would be like to wait—with bated breath—an entire winter listening to that sound.

"Shh—look at them." Harry put his hand on my arm.

I tried not to be obvious about it. Over by the chart room, Tarlington was fidgeting with his long gloves as he spoke quietly to Nicholls. I saw a grin come over the older man's face. They sometimes worked together: with no meteorologist on board, it was natural that Nicholls should split the role with the only scientist; Tarlington seemed to keep himself as busy as possible, speaking to no one. Although Nicholls was pleasant, fond of practical jokes, it struck me that their relationship ought to be strictly brass tacks: he should have little time for a *conchie*.

"What do you suppose they've got to chat about?" Harry said, hardness entering his voice. I shrugged. But I crept over nonetheless, loitering with the ice watch's pair of binoculars, until I was leaning around the corner of the pumps, one of the brass handles digging into me as I tried to make out their hushed conversation. The crack and pop of the pack made it difficult, and the pealing cry of a skua overhead startled me.

"I suppose you'll show him," Nicholls said, then laughed suddenly—an uneasy laugh, I thought. "Not before time."

A pause. "Meet me on the dog deck. Later. We need to talk."

I shifted my weight, and the creak must have carried: when I looked back, both Nicholls and Tarlington had disappeared. Neither appeared on deck again that night, although once or twice—the sun bobbing along the horizon like a pitiless gas flame—I had the sense of someone watching me. The unpleasant feeling that I'd stumbled on something I shouldn't have. And although I couldn't say why—perhaps everything on the *Fortitude* led back to him—I was certain they'd been talking about Randall himself.

When I finally turned in, my eyes had become overaccustomed to the daylight, and I couldn't sleep. I leafed through a book from Clarke's polar library as my hammock swung from side to side with the motion of the ship. Harry insisted on wedging his broad and bony shoulders in beside me. In the lamplight his nose was too large for his face, his brown eyes dull like the water in a well. It did him a disservice: sometimes, in the sunlight, Harry was capable of taking my breath away.

I half-shut my eyes, tried to stop seeing that pale wavering light. *Terrible winds*, the book said. *The madness of storms.* Together with Nicholls's words—the image of our ship under attack—it made me shiver. I hadn't quite been able to put out of mind the stories of Karlmann and his lost crew—our stokers egging each other on to come up with the most gruesome accounts. The Germans were the only other expedition who'd ever attempted to land on that coast. And they had disappeared two years ago into the dark of an Antarctic winter. Their ship; their leader; all twenty-nine men. Their post was still uncollected at South Georgia. *Vanished without a trace.*

Eventually the southern sun would start setting on us, too.

Harry paused. "Is this all right?" He was warm against me, and I wished I didn't find it a comfort. For a moment—a fleeting moment—I was back in my own bed, listening to the rise and fall of voices in the next room over, the sound of my brothers telling their own ghost stories. Harry's laugh, carrying down the corridor; his weight in my hammock now. How I missed them.

The door opened. "Excuse me," said Tarlington hoarsely. He stopped in the doorway, letting in a breeze, and Harry frowned at him in irritation.

My heart pounded, although I couldn't tell why. I struggled to sit upright, to put my feet out of the hammock and to the ground, but only succeeded in ending up even closer against Harry, my knee hooked around his thigh. I tried not to feel how hot he was through his clothes. There was nothing unusual about what we were doing—nothing at all. I could feel Tarlington examining us nonetheless.

"Do you want something?"

Tarlington, silhouetted against the light from the mess hall corridor, seemed to shake himself, as if dispelling some fancy. "Hell, I—no." And he left, shutting the door behind him. I stared at it. *I suppose you'll show him.* Show him—what or how, I had no idea. But something about it made me desperately uneasy.

Once Harry was back in his bunk and the lamp put out, the boiler knocking away on the other side of the bulkhead seemed louder—more distinct and regular—like the heartbeat of a giant creature. I fell into shallow sleep with the book still propped open on my chest. Harry half-woke me several times in the early part of the night, with a rap or a thud as he flung out his hand and connected with the wall. He'd have bruised knuckles in the morning. When I finally cracked an eye open, I saw him swimming in his blankets. His movements worming and stilted, as if something were pressing down on him; a pale inch of wrist visible at the cuff of his pajamas; his face screwed into his pillow.

Then I heard him speak—barely a murmur, and slurred. As if his mouth were too heavy to move.

"Rufus . . ."

The *sss* sound seemed to linger in the air for a moment, louder—by far—than he had said it. The boiler knocked.

"Harry." My voice came out in a croak. "You're dreaming."

But he pushed his face into the pillow as if trying to smother himself. As if he were in a waterlogged gun pit, sandbags leaking, trying to dig himself into the walls as the shells came screaming overhead.

"Francis," he whispered. Again, the sound of that *sss*. All the hairs rose on the back of my neck. I couldn't move.

A pause. He groaned, then said something muffled and indistinct. It sounded like "must"—or perhaps "must go." I turned over in a single jerky movement, putting the blankets over my head, trying to block it out. *Must go.*

He meant that he had to go to war, that it was his duty. He'd repeated it time and again in his letters, as if trying to convince himself. That was all. Or maybe he was simply repeating the last thing he'd said before turning in, glaring after Tarlington's retreating back: "Must he come and go like that? Like some sort of . . . spy?"

II

"Oh, you poor little bugger." Duncan hauled Crippen out onto the snow-covered deck. "I've never seen anything like it." He was just skin and bones. In their long confinement, our dogs were losing condition rapidly: becoming quarrelsome and weary, refusing food.

It was barely above freezing. Ice-crammed seas; dark sky, clouds scudding over the sun, flurries from the invisible shores to our southeast. The open water had got sparser and sparser, until we were sailing through a vast snowfield, the *Fortitude* edging through the pack like a killer whale nosing for prey.

"Morgan!" Duncan called.

I gestured wordlessly at the awful sea of ice. We'd already been two weeks in the pack—two weeks, when I'd heard so much about our four-week *window of opportunity* with the Weddell Sea—and I'd started skipping sleep to do extra duty on deck, watching the tortuous maze shifting around us. The ship's engines whined—a sudden jump forward made me clutch the railings—Randall roared, "Hold her steady!" and there was an answering shout, in explanation or apology, through the speaking trumpet from the engine room.

"Get some rest," Duncan said roughly. "You've been on deck the whole night." I scowled at him, not wanting to tear my gritty eyes away. Razor-sharp, jagged ice. Dark water.

The hull screamed; the *Fortitude* tipped. "What the hell, Laurence—" Boyd came running past, throwing himself against the shuddering prow railings, where her timbers slid away smooth and clear to the churn below. Her smokestacks seemed to quiver as they spit steam into the sky. We came to an abrupt halt. "Watch her bow!"

"No lead!" Boyd shouted to the bridge, rubbing his palm over the scars on his left arm, making his muscles bulge alarmingly. I tried to stop my envious stare; I was proud of the way my shirts had started to tighten around my wider shoulders and back. He looked around, eyes narrowed, searching, and shoved Benham—who objected with a half-hearted "Hey!"—although it hadn't been his fault. "Keep a better bloody lookout."

Our weeks in the pack had worn all patience thin. Harry had suggested to Clarke—who was drinking coffee straight from the flask—that we might exercise the weakening dogs on a floe, give them fresher air and more space. "He won't stop." A sigh. "Not with this open-water sky." Clarke nodded at the dark undersides of the clouds: the tantalizing promise of unobstructed sea ahead. Harry had smacked the deck in frustration, and turned in.

"Morgan." Duncan softened his voice a little. "Report back when you can, hey? And if you see Tarlington, tell him to get himself up here."

I could tell he disliked Tarlington's examinations of our sick dogs as much as I did—worse, his dissection the previous day of the first one to succumb. The seamen, too, sucked their teeth and thought it bad luck—accused Tarlington of being a Jonah, although not in so many words. "No wonder we're going nowhere," they'd said. "Unnatural."

Blinking, I pushed through the throng on deck and went below. The Nursery door was shut; it was just after five o'clock in the morning, but artificial light was spilling through the cracks. Another nightmare, perhaps. They were getting worse. I often woke to find Harry staring at the roof of his bunk, his breathing shallow.

"Close the door," Harry said immediately. He leaned in the connecting doorway, head against the crossbeam, looking very tired. "Come over here."

"You should be asleep." I started to hook up my hammock. "And have you seen Tarlington?"

"It doesn't matter. Come *here*."

The laboratory was somber; the illuminators had clouded over with condensation, the door to the corridor was shut, and the dark wood seemed to weigh down on us. Harry reached over to the shelf of leather-bound books, pulled one out. "Look at this." He thrust it into my hands.

"Harry—" I said wearily. "Where's Tarlington?"

He shrugged. "No idea. And that's my point. Just look at this."

I leafed through it, until Harry sighed and grabbed it back, forced it open at the frontispiece.

I blinked. As my hands closed over his, it came into focus. Where there'd obviously been a bookplate—the ornate scrollwork still visible—it had been torn out with violence, leaving jagged edges. The book looked wounded. I couldn't imagine Tarlington owning something so scruffy.

"Now look at this one," he said. He turned to the contents page of another; flipped it over to show the bookplate on the other side. This one was intact. Below *EX LIBRIS*, someone had written a name in faded black; then it had been scribbled out. Vehemently, in Tarlington's fresher emerald-green ink, as if the person holding the pen had been in a terrible temper. I could just make out "James." The rest was a mystery.

I crossed my arms, feeling a knot enter my stomach. "Just listen, Jonathan." Harry spoke quickly. "I don't think Tarlington is his real name. He didn't get any post at South Georgia. I don't think he's who he says he is."

I shook my head. "Harry—"

"Trust me, Jonathan. I've been watching him." A rather bitter laugh. "It's not as if I've had much else—look, why is he here? He obviously doesn't *want* to be."

I chewed my lip, thinking of my earlier conversation with Tarlington, the phrase he'd used. "Maybe this was—all he could get."

Harry brushed this aside. "That's my point. The only thing we really know about him is that he was locked up—with the rest of those rotters. Saboteurs and spies and criminals. Dartmoor Prison, wasn't it?"

Harry was stealing the light from the Nursery, a tall curly-haired shadow. His eyes gleamed in the darkness like coal—as if a spark had been kindled. "He's up to no good."

"What sort of no good?"

"He might mean to . . . sabotage the expedition."

I glanced around at the chrome-plated microscope, the neatly labeled specimen jars, as if I'd find some evidence of wrongdoing laid out. Tarlington had pickled a gull, crammed it in with its wings splayed against the glass, screaming to get free. Thinking of Tarlington made me angry; like a stone in my shoe, or a piece of grit in Macready's rather lumpy mashed potato. He wouldn't take ice watch. He wouldn't help with the ship's tasks. Just stared at his notebooks, treating our poor dying dogs like some sort of scientific conundrum.

We were meant to be here—Tarlington wasn't.

"But—what on earth for?"

"You know what Randall did."

I took a sharp breath. Randall had threatened to sue the papers, saying the insinuation was unfounded and scandalous, un-British. But I'd cut out the article and posted it anyway, knowing it was the sort of thing that would delight Rufus. A deserter from Randall's unit had been mysteriously shot, left in a ditch—on the way to his own court-martial.

The rough justice of the trenches. It had Randall's bearlike hands all over it.

"I don't see what that has to do with Tarlington." I kept my voice even, although what Nicholls had said was rattling around in my head like a ping-pong ball. *You'll show him.*

Harry clenched his fists, staring past me. "No," he said. "I don't suppose you do. But this is important. We have to look out for ourselves, and that sort—well. They must hate Randall."

I knew what they called COs: *a friend of the common enemy.* "Harry," I said tightly. "He makes no secret of it. If he was a—spy, surely he'd try to hide it a bit better." It was an effort to stay quiet, though: I bristled at the thought of someone choosing to dig holes, break stones, stay safe rather than serve. Tarlington's talk of the physical examination—he was tall and capable. Born fortunate. Would have been taken on the nod, whatever name or age he chose to give.

"Randall must—" I paused, thinking how easy it had been for Harry to enlist; how I'd slipped from country to country with a scribble on a piece of paper, like a ghost.

"Randall—" A curt laugh. "You know what he's like. And Tarlington's what—an assistant zoologist at best? We have no idea what's making the dogs so sick. What if it's . . . poison?"

"Harry—"

I thought of Tarlington's hands cupped gently on the curve of Prancer's skull, turning his neck with infinite care, a stark contrast to the dogs' usual manhandling. He was easily better qualified to deal with them than Harry.

"It'd destroy our sledging capacity—might put the kibosh on the whole bid for the Pole. I told you, I've been watching him. One of those . . . bloody conchies." Harry rarely swore. His voice was unsettled, fervent. Utterly unlike I'd ever heard it. "Sneaking around on *our* ship."

I squeezed the back of my neck, trying to work some of the tension out.

"He found *you* in that locker, didn't he? Come on, Jonathan. We could take it in turns—"

"Oh, shut up," I snapped. "As if there's time for that. We've both got work to—"

He snorted. "Well, I've been keeping an eye on him. And Nicholls. They're thick as thieves."

"Nicholls was a cavalry officer—"

"And plenty of those officers came to regret it, over there," he shot back. "You don't understand."

I had nothing to say to that. The silence stretched out; I listened for footsteps in the corridor. The ship was creaking around us like a living thing. I thought of my desire to wipe that superior look off Tarlington's face—a violence that both surprised me and felt utterly right. I tapped my fingertips against my bruised lips. Perhaps I should trust those instincts now.

You'll show him. Not before time.

"He said this would be Randall's last expedition," I said eventually.

And he'd sounded like he knew—was utterly certain—that would be the case.

The little desk looked so ordinary. Light flashed off the rows of scissors, and I thought of them being used to snip fur; skin; flesh. So harmless-looking—but so sharp. It didn't seem possible that someone could be on the expedition to destroy it.

"Bloody hell, Jonathan. He actually *said* that?"

Harry's eyes glinted in the dim light. I felt light-headed, already starting to have second thoughts. In these confined spaces—it was easy to see how this kind of talk could take on a life of its own. The seamen half-laughed when they implied that Tarlington was responsible for the narrowing leads, the encroaching ice, but it was the sort of laughter that had a blunt and ominous edge.

"Go to sleep," I whispered. I knew he wouldn't: the dark circles around his eyes were cavernous. He would turn it over and over in his head, and it would worm its way out in nightmares. "Just—go to sleep. We'll talk about it tomorrow." And I struggled to get past him, sending my shadow dancing around the walls of the laboratory, like a puppet show.

III

The next day I refused to talk about it; just worked harder and harder, as if through enthusiasm I could avert all danger. When we gave up for the night, when most of the men had retired to the wardroom for Laurence's mining talk ("No slides," he'd said, to a general uproar, "but you can sit here in the dark, if you like—"), I'd stolen away.

Meet me on the dog deck, later.

The ship was quiet. The muffled boom of pressure in the distance. Every step I took was echoed, magnified; the chart room and foredeck locker were empty. I waited for the creak of a hatch, the swish of a coat. Wind flapping in the furled sails startled me, and the sound of one of the dogs sobbing away in its kennel was uncomfortably human.

But no one came. It was nothing, I told myself. Nothing.

I went down to the Nursery and slept like the dead.

The next few days were all the same. South Georgia felt a hundred years ago, although it was just over a month. We tried the ice, threw ourselves at it—testing Mortimer's proud assurance that the *Fortitude* wouldn't be breached, even by the worst of the Weddell Sea pack. Randall had said we'd penetrate that pack in February: get through, make landfall, and put the ship to safe harbor—or back to Grytviken.

But February was ending fast. Autumn had come creeping into these waters, and our progress had ceased. An unmapped coast now loomed enticingly off the port bow, with darkly glittering cliffs and a persistent breeze. Winter in the pack beckoned, the ice clutching at our hull, making me count down the days with a feeling that we were running out of time.

A rainy morning woke me, the ship moving not an inch; the two bunks in the Nursery were empty. When I went up to the dog deck, the chains over the stairs rattled like Marley's ghost, but Harry didn't bother looking around. A handful of huskies, lying on the slippery wet decking, barely had energy to pant. Time was running out for them, too, although I didn't say it.

"Another one," Harry said bitterly. "Crippen will never haul—now Isaiah. I bet *he's* enjoying this."

"You're tired." I could see Isaiah's ribs through grayish fur, but I could also see every bone in Harry's face. His hair stuck up as if he'd been pulling at it.

The sound of hesitant footsteps on the stairs; I had a horrible intuition it would be Tarlington. "I heard Clarke arguing with Randall earlier," I blurted out, trying to distract Harry. "He thinks we should—retreat. Try to leave the pack before we get completely frozen in."

Harry looked up, his eyes flashing. "The farther we go, the worse the dogs get. *Something* down here is getting to them." He paused. "Or—"

I hushed him. The sleeves of Tarlington's greatcoat were pushed up, dark smears of blood on the fabric. His breath steamed in the freezing air. He glanced at me, then Harry. He'd obviously overheard.

"Cooper."

"What?"

"I can't be sure what's wrong with them. I'm sorry."

"They weren't sick before you started—"

"Oh, accuse me," Tarlington said, and exhaled a long, deep breath, looking around rather helplessly. "I said I was sorry."

"I'd rather they were put out of their misery," Harry said tightly, "than you conduct your filthy—experiments. Stay away from them, do you hear me? We don't need your sort—"

Tarlington's mouth twisted. "And what *sort* is that? Just what do you think is wrong with the dogs, Cooper? Enlighten me."

"I don't know!" It came out as a howl of despair, Harry fisting his hands into his hair again. "I don't—"

He bit it off. I thought of how blithe we'd been, Harry and I, how sure that we would *get away with it.* But our dogs were collapsing before even reaching land, and—an unpleasant feeling in my chest—I thought we might have done the expedition a terrible disservice in coming. I stared at the two of them, standing very close together. Two tall figures—one with bloody hands, a long green parody of a trench coat, his shadow sharp on the deck. Tarlington's ginger hair. Harry's dark and troubled eyes.

Francis came suddenly to mind.

"What a surprise," Tarlington said, sardonic. Then, lower and less biting: "That makes two of us, doesn't it?"

"Enough," Harry snapped. "Just go and do—whatever it is you do."

The wind was starting to shift—blowing from the shore, across the ice, smelling fresh and clean like thunderstorms. I felt goose bumps rising on the back of my neck; the strange feeling that I was being watched.

I could hear excited shouts, the sound of ice splintering under the *Fortitude*'s bow. My heart tried to lift in my chest. A lead at last. Maybe the lead we needed.

Isaiah suddenly gave a growl, backing into a crouch at Harry's feet; those languid huskies were standing on unsteady legs, lifting their noses into the air to howl. Even the mongrels joined in, scrabbling at their kennels, as if some silent signal had been given.

"Cooper!" Randall roared. "Get them under control! Mortimer! Press it, damn you! There's a lead!"

"Get out of here," I hissed at Tarlington, with his bloody sleeves and perplexed face. "Just go—"

"Cooper!" Randall shouted again.

"It's not my fault!" Harry shouted. "Something's getting to them!"

Randall surged down from the bridge, men leaping aside as he crossed the short distance to the dog deck, taking the steps two at a time.

"Cooper," he said, grasping the chains. "We'll need those dogs when we reach the shore. They can't be bothered by a good polar blow! Duncan says you're doing your best—but it's obviously not good enough."

"You won't let us exercise them, we've hardly got any medication," Harry shouted. "Your naturalist doesn't seem to know what he's doing— *mysteriously* can't help—"

"That's enough," Randall snapped. "I'm not going to argue the toss with you." He turned and made a gesture to Clarke, standing silently at the wheel.

I remembered Clarke lowering his voice, saying: "You asked me to give you advice you don't want to hear—well, now I am."

And Randall's harsh laugh in response. "She won't be breached, Liam. We must go on. We must be ready to start for the Pole in spring—think of our sponsors. Think of the press! There's no turning back."

"If you're just going to let them weaken," Harry called, over the cacophony of howling, "we might as well *shoot* the ones that fall sick. Letting them get picked off like this—one by one—"

Randall cast his narrowed eye over the dog deck, where the exhausted huskies were raising grubby muzzles into the air. Where the mongrels had flattened themselves against the backs of their kennels, hackles raised. "No," he said. "We'll need them, damn it. Come what may. Just keep 'em alive, Cooper."

I swallowed, my stomach roiling.

"And when we get frozen in?" Harry said, urgently. "Maybe it'll start affecting humans, too. You can't just—"

Randall stared at him, unblinking. Then grabbed a bucket—wheeled it up and around and over his head, like a shot-putter—and slammed it down on deck with an almighty clang that started the dogs clamoring again. "Don't *presume*, Cooper," he snarled, "Remember your place."

His lopsided gaze turned on Tarlington. "As for you—waving the white flag, eh? You're *meant* to be a scientist."

"There are limits," Tarlington said coolly.

Randall's mouth twisted, and for a moment I thought he would surge across the deck and drown us in his rage like an unwanted litter of pups. "Learn," he snapped, "by *doing*. I'll have your—report—on the state of the dogs in my cabin."

The ice groaned around our hull.

"Now!"

Harry was about to say something to Randall's back: he always did wear his heart on his sleeve. I threw myself against him, feeling the quivering tension in every muscle from his clenched fists to his ramrod-straight spine. "Don't," I said, my heart thudding. "For God's sake, Harry. Don't."

Tarlington wiped his mouth on his coat, a long, shaky gesture that smeared blood on his face like a barbarian. "I suppose the master awaits," he said. "Sorry, Cooper."

"I'm right," Harry whispered. "I know I'm right." I gripped his forearms, steering him away. On the bridge, the officers surveyed the ice; Nicholls leaned into the covered chart table, scarf billowing out behind him in a long green banner. The pack was heaving and popping in the breeze, and I could sense the slow clench of the ice around us, squeezing and crushing and searching for our weaknesses. Randall had once seemed so confident, so sure we wouldn't get frozen in.

But—dark eyes flashing, unguarded—he'd just said we'd *need* all the dogs. Even the ones too weak to pull a sledge. It was the last week of February, and my heart beat rat-tat-tat in my chest as I looked at the gemmy waters, seeing the *Fortitude* captured and held fast. No way out, perhaps not even with spring. I could see it in the ice—a second dark winter, trapped off this coast, and the dogs butchered, one by one.

Harry shook his head, his expression anguished. "No one ever listens to me, Jonathan. We have to say something. If there's the slightest chance he's—"

I squinted against the sunlight, screwing up my face. It made my jaw ache. Tarlington had no business being summoned to Randall's cabin, the inner heart of the *Fortitude*, a room I'd only ever see with bucket in hand. Macready had said Randall begged Tarlington to come—but that couldn't be right. The tale must have got warped in the telling. Far more likely, I thought, that it was the other way around. He'd *begged* to come, for his own inscrutable purposes.

My brothers might have thrown Tarlington overboard. Or beaten him, to find out his secrets—Rufus had always been bloodthirsty. But they weren't here, and I was. I'd fought for this; I wouldn't see it destroyed.

"All right."

Harry looked surprised.

I followed his gaze across to the bridge, wondering who we could approach. Macready was passing out mugs of tea to the men lining the railings. I thought back—longingly—to those first days aboard. The warmth of the galley, the slow slurp of porridge simmering, Macready jostling me for space at the stove. But that was a long time ago, and he was just the cook. *Things are going to turn serious.* Boyd took his tea without looking at Macready, his weathered face reflecting the ice.

With a sudden flash of spite, I knew exactly who would take this seriously. Very seriously indeed.

IV

"You should marry her," Nicholls was saying to Ellis, a companionable hand on his shoulder. "Trust me—she's a real looker. Snap her up or someone else will."

Ellis rolled his eyes and pushed Nicholls off. "I suppose you'd be a contender, old man?" His accent was deeper, broader, down here in his own territory. I could hear the mines right the way through.

The other men in the mess hall looked up as the door slammed shut behind me, bouncing violently against the frame. The warm air made my waterproofs steam and hiss as I hung them above the stove. It was blowing a fury outside, the *Fortitude* rolling despite her ice anchor; although the season had threatened to end abruptly, this late February gale was raising the temperature, smashing the ice to smithereens. The pack ground and pounded, and Mortimer had begged Randall not to press on into the new black water, not to risk her against bergs more than twenty feet high: Clarke had looked ready to break up a fight.

I pulled up a seat shyly at the long table, where Archer was mending his socks and Jones was playing solitaire. The gramophone was bolted down, but the constant tilting made the needle waver, and the music skipped several beats every time the ship lurched. I ran my hand over the soft blankets on the swaying hammocks. It was a friendly scene; even Harry was there, perched knees up to his ears on one of the common bunks.

I raised an eyebrow at him. We hadn't spoken properly in nearly a week—not since we'd taken our concerns to Boyd. Who'd snorted, shaking his head, first saying: "That lanky piece of bad news—what could he do—" then, more thoughtfully, forehead deeply furrowed: "I wouldn't worry about Randall. That man's survived everything possible—I hardly think he'll be brought low by bloody no-fight Tarlington. And he'd never get away with it. We're all in the same boat, so to speak."

I'd been reassured at that obvious point; but Harry had been entirely unable to let it go. Fingers wrapped tightly around the spine, he was frowning into one of Nicholls's weather books as if it held the answers he sought. "I hope that's the Ladybird guide to dogs, Cooper?" Duncan drawled, raising a few smirks from the stokers. "For the next time you tell Randall—"

Harry ignored him.

"Don't make me start on *you*, Duncan, and that sending-off at Cowes," Nicholls said, magnificently, drawing him off. "Twelve single girls and not one dance, despite that handsome mug." I liked Nicholls, quick to laughter, who never appeared to care whether his comments were welcomed. I didn't believe—couldn't possibly believe—he was part of any plot against Randall. Boyd had been certain: "Randall would throw you overboard for even suggesting—*no*. Nicholls has been with him from the start. There's no better navigator. We trust him."

"We can't all have your way with the ladies," Duncan retorted, wrinkling his nose. "And you're meant to be married."

Nicholls gave him an easy smile and drummed his fingers on the table, looking around for his next victim. I hadn't the skill for easy banter; I didn't know if I'd have wanted to dance with the girls—if such a thing would even be possible for me. My cheeks felt hot. I kept my head down, pulling my scarf up around my neck, and his gaze passed.

The gramophone music was tinny and warm, the sound of the rain distant: it reminded me of autumn evenings in Portsmouth, sitting on a window seat in one of the living rooms while Rufus and Francis bickered around me. Rufus in particular hated feeling *cooped up*—always looked for someone to take it out on. "Here." He offered me his hand, his eyes gleaming at the idea of this diversion. "I'll teach you to dance. You might as well learn—"

Francis, pinching the bridge of his nose, said faintly: "My eyes are tired. Jo, can you read aloud?" And passed me his latest adventure novel, as if I were doing him a favor. I looked down and pretended not to smile—he was so transparent—as the rain came down in buckets outside, and the fox-and-hound paintings in their mahogany frames looked on.

The door thudded open, and I jumped. The waterproofs swayed, the stairs creaked. Tarlington stalked down, wiping his face; he was soaked through, from his long riding boots to his trousers, from his gray-greenish coat to the scarf around his pale neck. Someone swore at him to take off those filthy wet clothes. He sat on the bottom step and peeled off his fingerless gloves with shaking hands, glaring at Nicholls, who didn't look up.

"The dogs are fighting again," he said in his raspy voice. It occurred to me I'd never seen him smoke; I'd never seen him on deck with pipe or cigarettes, or bartering tobacco. But his voice sounded like it had been ruined by the stuff.

I felt the prickle of a stray misgiving moving up my spine. At the end of our conversation—after Harry had stormed off in a huff—Boyd and I had been left alone. "And you'll say nothing to Randall about Tarlington, d'you hear? Leave it with me. You just leave it with me."

Boyd had looked as though he were chewing over something vile. I stared at Tarlington, soaking wet and out of place.

"Go on, then." Duncan unfolded his legs off the table and poked Harry with the toe of his boot. The gramophone skipped another few beats.

Harry pulled himself up with a sigh, scooping his jacket off the hook. Falling droplets sizzled on the stove. "You don't need to come," he said to me, putting his hood up to barge past Tarlington, still sitting on the bottom step.

"Excuse me—" Tarlington said.

"Don't." I pushed past him with an armful of waterproofs.

Out on deck, the rain was coming down in vast relentless sheets, sweeping from port to starboard and pattering at the hatches. I was immediately soaked.

"Harry?"

No answer. The rain fizzed at my feet.

"Harry?" I called again, holding up my arm to shield my eyes. The ship slid sideways, and I saw him—silhouetted against the clouds, standing on one of the deck lockers and looking out at the water. In the distance the dogs were barking.

I struggled over, and he caught my arm, helping me up beside him. It was the start of the polar autumn at last: civil twilight, sun just below the horizon, the clouds backlit as if by camera flashes.

"What are you looking at?"

Harry shook his head, gripping my shoulder, turning me to face the shore. Dark cliffs, the faintest suggestion of a red glow southward. I'd been eagerly awaiting the longer, darker nights when the aurora australis—the Southern Lights—might reveal themselves. While the sun shone, the South teasingly kept on its mask.

"It's lovely," I said very softly. And it was. But the rain was turning to sleet, finding its way down the back of my hood, funneling itself into the secret places under my waterproofs. "Harry, the dogs—"

"Yes." There was a faraway look on his face. "Of course *he* comes in, and the dogs are worse."

"Give it a rest—"

"Then what was he doing on deck?"

I shrugged off Harry's arm. The air sizzled around us. "You probably can't see," he said, putting his binoculars to his face. "But there are mountains in the distance—large black mountains."

If there were, we might be the first people on earth to see them. Whalers wouldn't come this far into the pack, and Karlmann—doomed Karlmann—had left no signs of his passing. No one knew what was waiting over that horizon. I thought how excited my brothers would have been to travel off the edge of the map, and shivered from my thighs to my shoulders with delight.

Harry, too, gave a sudden twitch, grabbing for the ropes to steady himself.

"What?"

"Nothing—I didn't say anything." He was leaning too far over the side for my liking. I was getting stronger, could climb the rigging almost one-handed. But I didn't think I could catch him if he fell.

"Come down."

Indistinct, far-off barking.

"What does it matter?" Harry said. His eyes were dark, ringed with shadows. "We'll probably end up shooting them all." He made a chopping motion with his hand—so completely unlike the boy I'd watched growing up, all long limbs and games and easy smiles, that the hairs rose on the back of my neck. "Some of them are getting worse—it'd be kinder to make sure they don't suffer. We'll all probably suffer enough if we go on, you know. We're going to be trapped in the ice. Our coal is running low. And if we lose the ship—"

It was like he'd heard my own fears, was speaking them aloud, giving them life. He held himself rigid and tall, as if looking over a battlefield; the Harry my brothers must have known. I wondered if they'd respected him. In the end.

"We're not there yet," I said fiercely. "This won't help! For God's sake, come down."

I let go of the rigging, but the *Fortitude* was battered from the shore—a large gust of wind, cold enough to flash-freeze my ears through my woolen hat and waxed hood. The deck revolved underneath me, and I hung suspended for a moment, Harry's arm across my collarbone the only thing pinning me in place. Suddenly winded, I stared down, my breath hitching. I'd have bounced to deck—then hit the mast—before the starboard railings snapped my legs. Perhaps Staunton could have set them cleanly; perhaps not, down here. There might be gangrene, amputations. There would certainly be screaming.

I thought—just for an instant—that the wind was trying to tell me something.

The dogs stopped abruptly, with a lone *awoo* I recognized immediately as belonging to Sanchez. The ship righted herself, and I let out a deep breath. I told myself it'd just be ten minutes, ten freezing minutes that would test my fingers and my patience. Ice-cold latches and dripping wet fur, snarling, then I'd be back in the mess hall again. The gramophone; cards; tea.

"Thanks," I said, rubbing my breastbone hard. "What?"

Harry was staring at me, at the small, pale strip of skin where my eyes and nose were exposed to the elements. I noticed I was smiling, lightheaded with relief, and it must have shown in my eyes: Harry knew me better than anyone.

"Why aren't you afraid?"

"Why should I be?" The storm would pass; I was where I was meant to be.

The wind sang.

"Jo."

"I've told you," I snapped, and pushed him, rather harder than I intended. He looked down for a moment, worrying at his bottom lip with his teeth.

"I wish I could love it here," he said. "Like you do." Slowly, very deliberately, he unwound Francis's scarf from my neck.

I didn't know what to do. It felt as if everything around us were holding its breath.

"Harry—"

I turned my cheek, thinking he'd understand: this wasn't how things were between us. But he moved closer, his hand on my face. Everything was languid, dreamlike. His lips were against my neck, breath hot on my chilled skin. His hood fell down; rainwater clung to his curls, I could see the worn leather straps of his binoculars, a small cut on his neck where he'd been careless in shaving. The ship was still.

I shoved him away.

"That shouldn't have happened." I was horrified to find my voice weak and shaking. High. *"Harry."*

He dropped his full weight onto the deck with a thud and walked off. The wind screamed. I was frozen in place, face and fingertips prickling as blood rushed back into them.

It shouldn't have happened. My head whirled. He still didn't understand. After our journey across the Atlantic, after our months on the expedition, our time at South Georgia—he still didn't understand who I was. Or perhaps he'd just shut his eyes. I was stuck in Portsmouth to him, stuck in that smart red-and-white town house. He'd visited to formally extend his condolences, and the scene in our parlor had been excruciating, an infinity to be endured: the cloying smell of lilies; the chink of dainty silver sugar tongs; awkwardly crossing and uncrossing my legs. Afterwards, I'd caught him alone in the hallway, wanting to bridge the gap between all those letters and this orchestrated meeting. He'd been awkward, but met my eye readily. "I'm sorry," I'd said, gesturing towards the parlor door.

"It's all right," he'd replied, his voice hoarse. "I didn't expect it to be easy."

But that gap still existed in his own mind. He still expected me to be—someone different. Someone who belonged in that stifling parlor, would return to it in time.

Not me.

I swallowed thickly, feeling my heart going like a marching band. For a moment I thought I would scream—could feel it bubbling up in my chest. An awful desire to scream at the top of my lungs, and I knew if I started, I'd never stop.

But the dogs needed us. And Harry still needed me. I made my unsteady way to the dog deck. The wind was strong enough to blow me sideways, and the dogs barked madly, incessantly.

I felt if I could get him to look at me—*really* look at me—it would all make sense again. We could go on from this. But when I put my hand on his shoulder, he pushed me away with such force I fell onto the slippery deck, staring up at him. His eyes were wild dark pools, and behind him the shadows yawned. A long waterproof, hung up uselessly on a peg, became a tall shape peering over his shoulder—something seen and unseen in the scudding light of the storm. The movement of the ship made it sway, as if breathing in and out, silent and watchful. I thought, again, of my brothers—their long, ruined coats; their silhouettes in my dreams. Standing in a half-open doorway, their shadows spilling over the threshold.

I froze, feeling sure I'd see fingers creeping from those hanging sleeves; arms stiffening, elongating, lifting; that it would reach out towards me—towards Harry.

But it was nothing. Just some abandoned clothing. Harry's hair whipped in the wind from shore. My breath hitched, the phrase popping into my head: *the madness of storms.*

"I'll take care of it, Jonathan." He said my name as if slamming a door shut, wrapping his arms around himself and squeezing, trying to trap something inside. A long gap of decking opened up between us, the storm-light glimmering off it.

I told myself I was glad, and went down to the dim rocking Nursery, stared into that little shaving mirror. On the fold-down washstand were two shaving kits, which Harry scrupulously rotated in use: if anyone looked, mine would be as worn as his. I was grateful, I told myself. But my eyes were watery and bruised-looking, face sunburned from the southern daylight, my hair a dull sandy blond. I could see nothing to attract him there, few traces of softness. I looked like Jonathan; I looked like myself.

And when I tried to sleep, my thoughts raced. I wondered if I'd given him the wrong idea. I wondered if I'd misjudged the situation—I'd seen so little of this world—whether it had been all my fault. Half-seen images shaded into dreams: that swinging shape looking over his shoulder, a presence close at hand. My brothers, marching out the door, leaving Harry holding a bayonet, white-knuckled. "Jonathan!" I'd called him, from the foot of the stairs. Giving him my name in the confusion. The third Morgan brother, and who knew which one of us it might be? He didn't turn.

V

A gunshot woke me the next morning. Sitting bolt upright, hammock swinging all helter-skelter, I told myself it was just the ship trying the ice: the *Fortitude*'s engines were humming, and the illuminator showed a speckled blue sky. I was fully dressed and fully alone. The Nursery was empty.

I took the mess hall stairs two at a time, winding my scarf around my throat with emphasis—no bare skin, just sweaty fabric, the pleasant rasp of damp wool. Duncan was dragging something down from the dog deck, heavy and limp and wrapped in tarpaulin. I stopped in my tracks.

I stared. A small trail of blood glistened on the steps, making my stomach plummet.

"What—"

"It's kinder this way," Duncan said. "Randall finally changed his mind, it's been—well. Long enough. They're only running through their food if they'll be useless on the ice. And Clarke's a good clean shot, uses his left hand like he was born to it." His mouth lengthened, making him far less attractive, but a great deal more sympathetic. "Cooper will stay out on deck, keep an eye on the rest. See if he can stop whatever it is from spreading."

"How—how many are gone?"

"The worst." A pause. "The ones not fit for hauling. Cherry included. Sorry, Morgan." No sarcastic drawl, not now.

Staunton bent downwind over another lolling body, pushing up his little checkered scarf to cover his nose and mouth; I supposed he wouldn't be too good to *chop up animals* now. Tarlington joined him, hunched over like a grave robber. I swallowed, bile rising in my throat. Dogs were resources; I should be harder. I turned away.

A heavy hand landed on my shoulder, and I jumped. It was Clarke, bareheaded, sleeves rolled up. "All right, Morgan," he said, looking at me seriously. "Better not dwell on it. We've got enough to worry about."

I couldn't help glancing up to the dog deck. Harry sat against the kennels, stuck in the act of cleaning Clarke's revolver. He was doing it mechanically, no sense of relief on his face. I hadn't heard him come into the Nursery at all; he must have stayed up there the whole night. Pacing, perhaps. Staring overboard. Cut off from the rest of the expedition.

I looked around. Even with the sun out, the *Fortitude* gleamed with frost. We'd had heavy snowfall a few nights before, and winter would drop the mercury far below freezing. We were running out of time. "Is it really safe—"

Duncan shrugged. "It was his idea. It's warm enough by the stove vents. And the Norwegians sleep with their dogs—lets them know who's boss."

"It'll show us what Cooper is made of!" Randall appeared behind us, casting a long shadow. He was wearing a jumper so holey it was nearly a vest, and his breath plumed hot in the cold air. "It's good to see some initiative." He jabbed at a bowl of porridge with a silver spoon held in his fist. His scowling face said plainly that he'd had expectations; expectations Harry had failed to match.

I hesitated. Blood smeared on the deck. Harry stared straight ahead, the revolver loose in his hands, seeing none of it. The breeze ruffled his curls. Perhaps the time alone would be good for him.

"Well. No one will die of frostbite or exposure on my ship. You have my word, eh?"

Randall rubbed his thumb over his signet ring; took a bite of his breakfast, chewed it with open mouth. I thought—for a moment—to ask him his plans. Wanting more of his growling voice. Wanting to be told something comforting. But although the engines were running, the sailors hanging from the yards like Christmas decorations, the lack of wind might make any leads from last night's gale freeze too quickly to be penetrated. The coast lay teasingly out of reach; Randall would be concerned with the *onwards*, and the onwards alone.

"Yes, sir." I didn't know what else to say. Clarke clapped me on the back, told me to get on with it. I took a deep breath, rolled my shoulders back, and took hold of the rigging, shielding my eyes against the sharpness of the sunlight.

VI

Down in the bowels of the *Fortitude*, gleaming seams of coal ran through the bunkers, and the subterranean sloshing of water in the ballast tanks was like something laboring to draw breath. The air was thick with coal dust: I tasted sulfur when I spat. Our safety lanterns populated the space with looming shadows, and whenever I put my back to the fire doors, I had the impression they were sneaking open behind me. A thin surreptitious crack, just big enough to admit an eye, as if something were peering in at us. The feeling would grow and grow, making the hairs on the back of my neck prickle, but when I turned, just to check—the doors were firmly shut. Turning back, the reflection of light off pitted white metal made my vision hazy. Shadows rippled.

The coal sacks at our feet became a cluster of men bent over, hunched and stunted from the dark. They were hiding from something.

Ropes hung on a peg by the store became a loose body, swinging weightlessly at the edge of the lantern-light.

"Someone's coming."

I jumped. "Ease up there, Morgan." Laurence leaned on his shovel.

I listened, and heard the metronome sound of boots clanging on metal. We'd worked in silence, save for Laurence's colorful language—sometimes in Welsh, but I got the picture—about how low we were getting. There had been no more movement for days, the engine ticking uselessly over. A week of make-work and strained silences; with Harry absent from the Nursery, I had no one to share my sense of unease. Sometimes I woke, in the dark, sure that the *overwinter* had already arrived.

A light shone down the long stair from deck, and Tarlington appeared, ghostly and pale-faced, wrinkling his freckled nose at the filth. "Come up," he said. "There's a meeting."

"About time," Laurence said with feeling.

"Randall must know what he's doing," I said, instinctively looking around for something to wipe my grimy hands.

"Yes, trust Randall." There was a hint of sarcasm about Laurence's singsong valley vowels. "But even he can't make coal out of nothing."

Tarlington produced a handkerchief from his trouser pocket. "Here." I stared at it: white, neatly trimmed, "JWT" embroidered in the corner. James something Tarlington. Perhaps not his real name at all. A stage prop. I searched his pinched face, trying to imagine him toiling away in a prison camp, trying to imagine what he could possibly want with us. "Suit yourself," he said, snatching it back. I scrubbed at my face with the back of my sleeve, and hurried to follow.

The wardroom was full of barely repressed excitement, men talking over one another. The glass in the large mirror was clouded; smudged dark fingerprints on the clock face, thumb marks on the brass, and grit underfoot. The coal dust got everywhere belowdecks, Randall always saying, *We don't put on airs on this ship.* He sat now on the dresser at the end, turning his signet ring around on his finger. Clarke was stone-faced; beside him, Mortimer packed his pipe assiduously. I caught a glimpse of the charts laid out on the table. A sardonic question mark next to our intended route was underlined, vehemently, in Nicholls's red ink.

"Well," Randall said, and the room immediately quietened. "Settle down. We're at the point of no return." I felt my heart flutter in my chest.

"Or we've passed it, maybe." A few laughs. "March, by God—I didn't expect ice like this, whatever the whalers said. We've spent too long fighting it—autumn's upon us. We'll lose daylight soon, and the sea will freeze over."

He stared at us while he talked. One dark eye flashing, animated. The other—on the ruined side of his face—stayed fixed in front of him.

"Well. That leaves us to the pack. I won't pretend it isn't risky. But the *Fortitude* is solid." A small, unhappy expression crossed Mortimer's face, although he wiped it off almost immediately. "And there could still be a lead, any day now."

Randall paused. I noticed Clarke's gaze was fixed very determinedly on his reflection in the table's surface, eyebrows drawn. An expectant silence in the room.

"The alternative—I've heard the talk—is to try to retreat. Give up on southward progress. Save our coal, and look for somewhere to bunk down for winter." Randall paused. He didn't say—although we all knew it—that it might already be far too late to retrace our steps. He banged a fist on the table, an easy gesture reminding me powerfully of Rufus. "But—by God—you know my ship—I know my ship—and she'll hold, come what may. For the big push. We stay on course."

Nods and smiles, noises of agreement. A few whistles. This was the Randall from the papers, from the books; the Randall I'd expected. My eyes prickled.

"Bloody madness! Expecting her to open up now," someone muttered in a distinctive Northern accent.

Randall scanned the crowd, his face darkening. "By God," he growled. "Will whoever said that speak up?"

A dreadful silence. I loosened my scarf, feeling myself start to sweat in the confined space. The clock on the wall ticked like a heartbeat.

"We don't have the coal to press on like this," Laurence said finally, although he hadn't been the one to speak. "We're going through it like water. Heating the ship alone takes tons—whether we'd have enough to force our way out again—" He twisted his hands, giving Randall an agonized look. Laurence had made his way up through the mines, from pit worker to overman, and then—unthinkable, for a man born in the same room as four generations of his family—qualified as an engineer. After serving with Randall, he'd have work wherever he wanted. But not if we turned back.

Randall rubbed a hand over his beard. "Well, you tallied that coal, Laurence—we sketched it out on a napkin at the Dorchester!" Laughter. "They thought we were mad, didn't they? I trusted you then." He paused. "I trust your steadfastness now."

Laurence pressed his lips together, his mustache twitching, and said nothing more.

"He's making a mistake," another voice said, and I turned to see Harry behind me. He looked pale, and very drawn, from his week sleeping up on deck with the dogs; Rees had constructed him a little lean-to, and our cozy bedtime stories and his ridiculous pajamas were now just a memory. He looked at me almost pleadingly. "Jonathan—"

He wasn't close enough to kick. I hoped no one else had heard.

Randall was setting out his plan to storm the coast. Mortimer looked a little sick on the *Fortitude*'s behalf. Although a polar ship, she wasn't an icebreaker, and if the pack damaged her rudder—or her propeller—she'd be crippled, coal or no coal. She should have been safely in harbor by now.

"And if the ice stays shut?" Nicholls came into the light beside Clarke. His salt-and-pepper hair was growing untidy; he looked ready to snap with repressed energy. "The whalers have been right so far." He glanced around. No one smiled at him.

"Yes, thank you, Nicholls," Randall said. A pause. "You've been capital. But now—" He clenched his fists and looked at us. "Well—now."

I wanted to fix the moment in my mind: my place in that room, in that circle of upturned faces. The smell of tobacco and coal. The deliberate tick of the clock, and my own pulse loud in my neck. We were committed. Below us, the South waited to be discovered, with Randall leading the way.

"Don't give me that look," Randall growled. His good eye was fixed on Clarke, his mouth twisted. "Don't." Real steel behind it. The room was perfectly still. Clarke said nothing. I remembered him shouting at Randall, trying to be quiet, trying to hide it from the crew.

You asked me to give you advice you don't want to hear.

"We entered the pack far too late—" Duncan's upturned vowels. "February! This is crazy—"

"You think you'd know better?" Randall snarled, and slid his weight off the dresser to standing. Duncan shuffled backwards—men moved hastily out of his way. "You think it was that simple?" Randall's stooped frame looked more bearlike than ever. "Does anyone else have any *contributions*? Anyone who won't put their faith in me, by God—and the pack—"

"We could try to return to South Georgia," said a familiar voice. "Wait out the winter, return in September. Sir."

Harry, direct as always. His arms were folded, and his face looked ashen in the light of the illuminators. Randall turned. "We don't have to overwinter in the Weddell Sea," Harry said quickly. There was a murmuring around the room, low and dangerous. I bit my lip savagely, ducking my head, hoping no one would think I agreed. "We're already losing our dogs, who knows what'll happen if we get frozen in. We should turn back while we still can—"

"There's no turning back," Randall said, almost thoughtful. He wasn't a tall man, but his thickset shoulders and bullish neck made him seem like an ogre. "Another word from you, Cooper—I'll have you confined."

I could see a pale flush rising up Harry's neck, the muscles moving as he swallowed, the military mustache making him seem frozen in time. He was almost standing to attention. Earnest, hardworking Harry: it was obvious he would never really please someone like Randall.

"Try me!" said Randall. "There's no place for naysayers, day-trippers, *cowards*—not on my ship! We're in this together. We stay in the pack. And, well," he turned a slow circle, looking around the room, "the aurora will greet us soon."

Nods. Someone clapped, then someone else, loud and staccato in the close space, and it moved around the room like a wave. My hands came together by themselves, a great bursting lightness in my chest. It was bold. It was all I'd ever wanted.

The aurora will greet us soon.

Randall seemed to look straight at me—and like what he saw. "Now the real battle begins," he promised. "A glorious one!"

The room broke into excited discussions. Harry moved alone through the crowd, door slamming shut as he slipped out into the scudding clouds. I blew out a sharp breath, feeling the heady momentum. Setting foot on Antarctica. Taking my brothers' place in the great unknown. Macready patted me on the head. Benham, beaming widely through his gappy teeth, shook my hand with mock solemnity.

It was quite a while before I thought about Harry: what it must have cost him to be called a coward, in front of everyone.

VII

Returning to the dog deck the next morning took everything I had. I'd tried—honestly—several times since the night of the storm. Harry always refused to talk to me, stubbornly busying himself with the dogs, every line of his body tense and coiled as if freezing before a terrible blow. Watching from a safe distance, I couldn't help thinking of his hand, gentle on my face. It made me shudder, a curious piercing stab of sadness hitting somewhere in my throat. It wasn't really me he'd been seeing.

Carrying tea—a peace offering—I nearly fell on the stairs. The sun was nowhere to be seen, the temperature dropping like a stone, the ice endless. I was unhooking the chains when I heard the sound of his boots nearby, and my stomach swooped to see him standing close, hands shoved deep into his trench coat pockets, as though he didn't quite trust them to be loose.

"Tea." It came out unexpectedly gravelly.

"Thanks." He sighed. "I know people are talking about me. Voices carry, up here. I made a fool of myself yesterday—with Randall. I should've known he'd never listen to me. Or turn back."

I took a long hot mouthful of tea. "He's not the sort to change his plans," I said, feeling rather defensive. "Or take advice." Even from Clarke. "Harry—why don't you just trust him? He's Australis Randall. There was a time you'd have followed him anywhere."

"I know," he said distantly. "I know. He'd have listened to—well. It doesn't matter."

Up on the dog deck, that freezing wind blew constantly. The remaining dogs quarreled with it, fur glimmering in the salty air. They seemed uneasy, as if they could smell some sort of large animal encroaching on their territory, and were trying to see it off. Harry insisted something was getting to them—for all that Randall had shouted him down. Watching them stare at the horizon with pale eyes, I half-believed it myself.

He unlooped his binoculars and held them out to me formally. "Just look. Over there. And—listen."

I obeyed, trying not to flinch when our hands touched. The sea was flat, the ice sparkling around us like deadly cold cut crystal. The shore lumbered into view, unlovely and dirty white beyond those vast cliffs, resolving into a long, flat, featureless plateau.

"Look for the mountains," he said, pointing. A gust of wind smacked me straight in the face as I did, and I thought—for a single confused moment—I could see the auroral lights, just beneath the horizon, and smell thunderstorms. The effect was uncanny.

Something just out of sight, waiting for us.

I took a step back. Lowered the binoculars, suddenly not really wanting to see what was there. The dogs continued to scrabble and bark at the wind. "We shouldn't be here—shouldn't be so far south!" he said. "I thought—I thought I could *make* him change his plans." Then, quieter, "I wish I knew what to do. If only they—I wish they were—"

His hands shook slightly as he spoke, his fingernails bitten right down. I couldn't imagine it was easy to sleep on deck; nakedly exposed to the gray sky, sea, and shore. And he *missed* them. Missed them painfully. No one else could come close.

Max—a rangy black-and-brown dog—padded over, and Harry briefly ruffled his ears, snapped his fingers. Max raised his paw to shake, and I smiled a little.

"You don't have to throw buckets of water on them anymore?"

"No." A corner of his mouth turned up, then twitched. He stared into the distance. "I've had time on my hands." I understood this was the closest we'd get to talking about what had happened between us. I'd chewed my lip until the skin was sore and reddened, and I worried it with my teeth, watching Harry carefully. He didn't move.

"Have you seen the aurora?"

Tea slopped over the side of Harry's mug. "It's not dark enough. Not yet. Soon." Silence. He passed his hand over Max's head. Max dropped like a puppet: paws limp, lying flat out, eyes closed. Playing dead.

I glared at Harry. "That's not funny."

I thought, for no reason at all, of that night in the fog. My mind playing tricks. Conjuring memories, shapes on deck. *Francis.* And that time I'd seen a tall figure in the darkness behind Harry, watching over him. Close enough to touch. Even if it was an illusion, if the dogs disliked the wind so much—if we were going to be frozen in over winter, to await our fates in the pack . . . The thought making my voice strained, I said recklessly, "Come back to the Nursery. You shouldn't be up here alone."

Harry turned away, tucking the binoculars back under his jacket. "Someone needs to keep an eye on things." He looked like he was going to say more. But he attempted a smile, and drained his mug before thrusting it into my hands still steaming, as if there were something very important he needed to be getting on with. "I'll see you at tea, Jonathan."

When I went below that night to change out of my sooty clothes, Tarlington was humming to himself, low and tuneless. He'd started wedging open the connecting door between the Nursery and his laboratory, and I'd fall asleep with light burning at his desk, the methodical scratching of his pen. Sometimes his presence kept me awake—morbid thoughts about his bloodstained coat, his little gleaming anatomy scissors. But at least his nighttime hauntings seemed to have ceased.

"The dogs, Morgan, are they well?" The unexpected question made me stop and stare. "I did my best. Whatever people think."

I shrugged. "They seem in good shape now Harry's up there." I didn't mention the foul wind. The momentary feeling of something reaching out to us over the ice. The way it made my skin crawl, made me suddenly reluctant to see what lay beyond that glimmering white horizon. I pitched my voice low. "So *you* can leave them alone."

He half-smiled. "Oh, I'm sure I will. And at least it'll be quieter down here, won't it? All those—denials."

I opened my mouth. Shut it again. It hadn't occurred to me that he'd have paid attention to Harry's nightmares.

The wind creaked the ice up against the *Fortitude*, trying to get in.

VIII

It was the wind—that terrible wind—which undid us.

The next day dawned bright and clear; sharp, crystalline, perfect. I popped my head up on deck and shivered at the biting breeze; the mercury had been plummeting for days. Our boiler was ticking over to heat the ship, and the crew deck was full of snoring men.

I was sent into the creaking spirit room below the galley to puzzle out Clarke's crabby handwriting on our winter inventory. The close air of the belowdecks smelled of vinegar and molasses. And—just a whiff—of something burning.

I called to Macready through the hatch, "Did you leave a light down here?"

He called back—"You've mistaken me for your servant, lad." An exasperated Scottish tone. *Lad.* Right from the beginning, he'd put me at ease. But the cropped hair at the nape of my neck prickled at that faint singed smell. It seemed like it came from the other side of the bulkhead, packed with lumber to build our winter quarters, the line of starboard coal bunkers beyond.

I took another deep breath. I was still sure I could smell it.

The growing sense of unease bore down on me like a weight. The ship's silence became sinister. I squinted to make out a glimmer of light coming through the cracks, when all should have been dark in the ship's midsection. I stared at it, unable to move.

Fire.

I recoiled. "Macready!" My voice broke. "Macready! Fire! Fire in the bunkers!"

His boots thundered across the galley. "All hands! All hands! Fire aboard!"

The bell started to sound, and the ship thundered awake. Shouting. Cursing. Something closed the spirit-room hatch on me, and I was alone down there in the dark. Trapped. I made a small, terrified sound as I scrabbled to the top of the ladder: I didn't know whether anyone would come for me. My fingers found wood, and I threw myself against the hatch. There was no handle on the inside.

It stuck on its hinges.

I opened my mouth to scream for help. But it burst open with another blow from my shoulder, and I hauled myself up headfirst, arms screaming at me.

The sky outside was an impossible blue. The bell rang continually, deep and dolorous, and the mongrels drove themselves into a frenzy on the dog deck: Harry was nowhere to be seen. Seams of smoke were starting to steal up from the crew deck below. I looked around at the stairs, the bridge, the lockers, the railings. All that painted, varnished, old wood.

Fire at sea—on a wooden ship—unimaginably dangerous.

"To your stations—" Clarke shouted. He'd timed us at our drills:

I knew what I should do. But I couldn't seem to make my legs move, and fell back against the railings as if the ship were plummeting. From below—very close—the ice boomed.

Randall appeared. "Report!"

"Starboard bunkers—coming up the shaft!" Boyd hauled himself up half-dressed.

"Contain it," Clarke shot back. "Seamen to the fire doors—"

"No!" Randall shouted, staring wildly at the smoking decks. "By God, don't just stand there—"

Boyd was armed with a fire extinguisher: a heavy metal Minimax cone. He eyed the door to the subdeck shaft. It led to the coal bunkers through the mess hall, and—from the way Duncan and the others stared at it—I could tell it would be red-hot to the touch. Those extinguishers looked tiny. And the smoke was spreading, spreading—

"Your orders, sir?" Duncan, as it swirled around his feet.

"Don't be a fool!" Mortimer yelled from the bridge. The sound of boots as the able seamen reported: they lined up smartly, even in the chaos. Wide eyes. The younger sailors looked as frightened as I felt.

Randall snarled, "Good God, man, *put her out!*"

"Don't—" someone shouted. My throat ached, and I grabbed at it.

Duncan braced himself—pulled open the door. It slammed back on its hinges. An answering hollow slam came from the fire door at the bottom. That terrible, unearthly wind.

The fire burst onto the deck, rushing over Duncan like a wave.

A choked scream.

"Your *stations!*" Clarke shoved Duncan to the ground, covering the flames with his own body. Duncan's face was a rictus—a ruin. His left arm moved fitfully against the deck, trying to beat itself out.

Stillness erupted into movement. The thud of a Minimax cone on deck, then the violent spurt of compressed liquid, like a thimbleful to a furnace—the fire that spiraled out of the shaft was six feet high, twelve feet high, whipped up by the wind. I cast around—picked up another extinguisher, my heart stuttering like a wind-up toy. I ran towards the flames, the acrid heat beating against my face.

I would have reached it if Boyd hadn't shouted, "Like hell you will," and knocked me off my feet. I hit the deck hard. Rolled over. Gasped. Another scream—this time from the wind, picking up, making the ship rock and creak around us. The fire *roared*.

"To your stations!" Randall shouted.

A frantic avalanche of boots and grasping hands; the clank and thud of the pumps. A sloshing bucket was thrust at me, and I passed it on blindly in turn.

"There won't be enough coal left," Parker shouted. "For South Georgia—"

"There won't be enough bloody *ship* left," Laurence hissed.

I looked around wildly. Smoke was now billowing from the bridge. The *Fortitude* had shafts and hatches in the same way a human body had veins and a windpipe, and the fire must have been racing through them. There was no way of knowing how long it had been simmering down there, undetected, while the rest of the ship slept.

Another bucket—Clarke was shouting something in the distance, the whole deck filled with frantic activity. I could hear Duncan somewhere out of sight, hidden by the smoke, saying: "Oh God, oh Christ, oh Jesus," in a high slurred voice that made my skin crawl.

A sudden crack, high-pitched and blunt: I ducked as the chart room windows shattered. The bridge was going up.

"It'll blow." Laurence's face was white. I turned towards him in mute horror, pausing, holding up the whole bucket chain. "Coal dust," he insisted, "coal dust, it'll blow, I've seen it before—" and Boyd shouted, "Shut *up*!"

More men hurried past, heaving crates; the wind *howled* across the deck at them. Black spots floated across my vision. I reeled—"Morgan," Ellis shouted, shoving another bucket of water my way, "keep yourself together"—and then there was a solid wall of smoke cutting the deck in two.

Nothingness. I bit my lip to stop myself crying out, swallowed blood.

"The boats—"

For a moment, a patch cleared, and I could see through the haze. The wind was whipping the fire across the *Fortitude*, bow to stern. The flames were licking over her pale birch decking, picking their way nimbly up the tarry rigging, the sails going up like beacons; worse, I could feel the planks starting to grow hot under my feet. The ship was built of timber, but more than that—the expedition ran on coal. The bunkers stretching the length of her midsection, the dust saturating her decks and clouding her brasses. The heat down there must have been unimaginable, and the wind beat us back across the deck, the chain straggling, threatening to break up.

"Just a bit longer—" Clarke coughed from somewhere in the billowing whiteness, and I understood we were only buying time.

We were nothing but fuel.

Another bucket. Then another. How quickly it spread—as if Duncan had fired a starter's pistol, and we were racing down the track. The bucket chain paused as a dull *boom* came from deep in the hold, the whole ship shuddering. The hiss of water.

It'll blow.

"Where are your orders?" Mortimer shouted at Randall, cap askew. "The water's no use—we can release the inlet valves, flood the subdeck, try to get ahead of it—"

"It'll *sink* her," Boyd yelled from the pumps.

Randall passed his hand over his face, shakily, and didn't answer.

Nicholls thrust a muzzle at me. "Get to the dogs," he said. "We need them harnessed. Now."

I stared at him, not understanding.

"It's your order," Clarke said urgently. "Australis!"

A deep bellowing from the wind.

"Preserve the stores!" Randall roared. "Keep fighting—"

Clarke swore. Above him, I saw the mainmast rigging go up.

I looked at the dog deck, which appeared to be floating in space.

"It'll get up there soon," Nicholls said. "Go and see where the *devil* Cooper is—"

The dogs were tearing themselves into a frenzy, throwing themselves against their cages with rolling eyes and snapping jaws. I skittered down the stairs to the mess hall, where thick black smoke was billowing from the wardroom, flames starting to lick into the crew area. A scene of desperate activity as men fought to salvage their gear; on the ice, a sleeping bag could make the difference between life and death. I put my face into my elbow, taking shallow and rapid breaths through my shirt.

In the Nursery, Harry had his back to me; he was hurrying to pull on a large woolen jumper. I clutched at his arm. "The dogs—"

He scooped up his kit bag, shoving in his waterproofs. "This is for you," he said roughly, and thrust another pack at me. My hands were trembling, and I dropped it immediately, going to my knees on a pile of blackened and sooty clothing.

I scrabbled to my feet, looking around desperately: I hadn't thought the fire had found us yet. The Nursery walls were still intact, but heat was blazing from the other side, smoke creeping across the floor like a cat burglar. I could hear the wind even here, and it was *screaming*.

"Come on!" I yelled into the laboratory, where Tarlington was a tall shadow. "Just leave it—"

"Damned if I will—" he said tightly, and strained to gather up his notebooks. I crawled to help him, panting hard; Harry pulled away from us with a look of disgust, and was gone.

Out on deck, the wind was a slap to the face. Shapes whirled in the smoke. Pockets of sky gleamed through, blue as a berg, as Nicholls helped us muzzle the terrified dogs. Howling, whimpering, it was desperate work: my world narrowed down to teeth and claws. "Down, down, steady," Harry muttered in a foreign and choked voice.

"Cooper, damn you!" Randall yelled. "We'll leave them!"

A wordless yell. I looked up to see Wild—the sailing master, who loved this ship like a sweetheart—grabbing Perry by the hand. They vanished into that wall of smoke. Nicholls paused for a moment, then continued, his mouth twisting. They were heading to the engine room.

A low, sickening creaking came from the mainmast above.

"It's going!" Clarke shouted. "Get to the sides—"

The lowest spar swung. The ceaseless, angry wind seemed to worry at it—shake it—pull it from side to side. A destructive child playing with a toy-sized ship. The rigging was disappearing. The sails shed burning chunks of canvas like fireworks. We dragged the dogs down the stairs, Harry shielding them behind his outstretched arms, as the yard shuddered and cracked and finally fell.

Smash.

The decking splintered under its weight. Fire licked up through the gaping hole, urged on by the shrieking wind. Looking down, I could see that the crew deck was alight, glimmering against the pale morning. It was surely the end. We couldn't fight this. Clarke looked desperately at Randall.

"Off!" Randall bellowed. "Everyone off! Abandon ship!"

A scream. I turned to see Smith and Benham stumble under the weight of their supplies—then disappear. Straight through the deck with a crash, into the glowing heart of the furnace. A pause. Then I dropped the leashes and ran to the stairs, thinking—wildly—that I could climb down to them. I could climb down into the burning belly of it. If anyone could, it would be me.

"Smith!" I yelled. "I'm coming—"

Nicholls shouted, "Morgan, *stop*, it's no use!"

I skidded to a halt.

"We have to leave them!" Clarke held Mortimer as he teetered on the edge of the deck, his eyes full of horror.

"We should—the valves—Wild—we can still fight this—"

"They'll follow later," Clarke said grimly. "Now abandon ship."

"Fucking get to the *boats*!" Boyd bellowed, and Mortimer reeled away like a drunk.

The dogs cowered in the lifeboats, making deep whimpering noises. For once, there was no room for fighting. I made myself small against the side. Harry heaved his pack in next to me, gave my clammy hand a brief squeeze.

Then the boats were on the winches, beginning the long way down to the Antarctic waters, and the fire and winds were given full possession of the *Fortitude*.

IX

Three small boats. Twenty men, our necessities, and a roiling mass of dogs. This we had saved from the fire.

The wind smacked the boats against the side of the stricken *Fortitude*. Each sudden drop made my teeth chatter, and when the curve of the ship's hull fell away, the strength of the wind told in earnest. The dogs barked, their weight swinging us to and fro. Nicholls cast a desperate look at Harry, who was coughing too hard to control them. I was sure the winches would fail, and we would plummet into the icy water. Another lurch, and I instinctively reached for Harry, then bunched my hands up tightly in my coat instead.

From the waterline, the *Fortitude* looked both unimaginably huge and terribly small. I wanted to peel off my gloves and touch her glowing side as she dropped away from us, the last heat for a long time.

Maybe the last ever.

We landed too low, in a tiny, snaking channel of hissing water; it had started snowing ferociously. The current tried to suck us back under the ship or smash us against the nearest floe. Dogs scrabbled and strained, panicking. They couldn't bite, but their claws were sharp. "Cooper," Boyd yelled across from his own boat. "How do we keep them still?"

Harry looked despairing, doubled over again. His cough sounded dry and painful, like he'd taken in a good lungful of smoke, and I wondered if he'd been much closer to the fire than I'd thought.

"Here—" someone said, and an oar was thrust into my hands. I took it automatically. I'd never rowed before. Beside me, Tarlington set to grimly, elbowing me hard with each stroke. The open water seemed to be shrinking around us. We'd been lucky to find our narrow lead—the ice was solid around the *Fortitude*, vaster and thicker and more brutal than I'd ever imagined. I'd believed Randall when he'd said we should head straight into the pack. I'd believed Randall when he'd said we would find a way. I'd been concentrating on the parts I could see; but down here, the underwater ice was already clutching the *Fortitude*, holding her fast. We'd been trapped by something invisible and deadly.

I noticed my mouth was open. I sucked in wet air; swallowed; my hands stuttered on the oar. "Row!" Randall shouted from the lead boat. "*Row!*"

One dog team made a break for it in the confusion, launching themselves over the side, flailing as their harnesses caught them. They were pulling us over, a dead weight of fur and jaws—even Boyd wouldn't have been able to haul them back. Harry worked quickly, his fingers trembling, to unleash them. They paddled away from us into the dark water, still joined together; they scrabbled and lurched onto a nearby berg, watching us leave. My chest constricted as I thought of killer whales cruising through the pack, searching for prey, making short work of anything that entered the water.

Our remaining dogs had the fight knocked out of them. They curled up under the tarpaulin, keening.

We pulled away, water pitching and sloshing over the sides, and I relinquished my oar for a bucket. I lost one of my gloves in the first few minutes, and wanted to sob aloud, my knuckles cramping painfully into a claw as I bailed. I tried not to feel it. I couldn't afford to feel it.

The sun made its stately pace towards the horizon. Months of darkness, creeping closer. Months of darkness, without a ship. Nicholls caught me staring; my eyes felt like they'd been open a million years. "It's later than you think, Morgan. We won't see true dark for a while. Don't dwell on it."

I felt dizzy when I turned back to look at the *Fortitude*. Randall hadn't ordered us to stop, but many hung on their oars to take in the scale of the disaster before the ship passed from sight. The flames through the flurries gave the air a nightmarish quality, making the bergs around us into fiery castles. Harry wouldn't look, and I nudged him hard. It seemed blasphemous not to look at the *Fortitude* in her death throes.

A commotion in one of the boats. Duncan, who ought to have been unconscious, was trying to stand up—the side of his face a ruined frenzy of bandages and gore—Staunton wrestling him down. "There's someone on deck!" He struggled with the words, his lips contorting. He pointed: "Tall—so tall!"

We looked in vain for those we'd left behind. It was impossible. Clarke had said they would follow later, but he'd lied. There would be no returning from the belowdecks.

Staunton shouted, "Shell shock—ignore him—" to Randall, who looked ready to swing the boats around. Duncan was given more morphine, and subsided.

Someone on deck.

I stared at the burning ship, at the eddying swirls of smoke. For an instant—just an instant—I thought I could see it. There was something on the dog deck, a blot of darkness against the graying sky. Unmoving, when everything else was chaos. In the shape of a man, standing beneath the foremast, it appeared to be watching our little flotilla. My skin crawled, a horrible fluttering sensation in the pit of my stomach.

"Harry," I said, my voice scratchy. "Harry, do you—"

He looked up, his eyes twin pinpricks of flame. I shoved him again—but he was unyielding, solid like he was made of stone, and I couldn't get him to answer. When I looked back, my breath catching, the dark figure was gone.

There was no one there at all.

The distance through the floes was impossible to calculate, and soon the maze and snow vanished the *Fortitude* altogether, as if we'd left the real world behind. Our boat grew lower and lower in the water, and my arms ached like dying meat. The wind was wet and chill; our clothes chafed and scratched. Seeing Nicholls surreptitiously loosening his jacket, Clarke—leaning across the water—said firmly, "No, you know better," and, raising his voice, "Watch your gear! You'll need it."

I tried to tell myself I was in good hands. Capable hands. Randall knew the Weddell Sea: it had ruined his face, nearly killed him, but he had survived it.

In the distance, a loud muffled *boom* echoed and rebounded off the bergs. We stopped. We waited. It might have been the ice. It might have been the ship. *Coal dust, it'll blow*—no one said anything.

Then Clarke started rowing again, feverishly, and the rest of the men followed suit.

After many hours, it was obvious we couldn't make it to shore. The pack shuddered and creaked and contracted as the temperature dropped. If one of the "little" floaters—as we'd called them, so cavalier on the *Fortitude*—came up against us, we'd be done for. They bobbed and showed us their deceptive face: but jagged ice waited, unseen, beneath the surface.

Clarke scanned the horizon. The clinging snowfall was relentless and heavy, and he was knee-deep in slush. I realized my waterproofs were soaked through. I couldn't feel my feet. The dogs were drowned up to their haunches, and shivering all over.

Randall's voice came over the wind: "This one's big enough—haul up—there's no landing up ahead—but we must rest, and by God's good will—" and the gusts snatched away the rest.

Ropes were gathered, and we made ourselves fast to a floe the size of a football pitch, dragging the boats out of the water. The sea spun around us, black as tar. It was nautical twilight rather than true night: the cliffs visible above, bearing down on us, miles and miles of unforgiving ice. I watched Harry wiping his eyes, staring numbly back towards our lost ship.

I took a deep shuddering breath, curled my hands into tight balls, and allowed myself to remember Smith and Benham. Their happy faces in the mess hall. Smith, pronouncing everything "A-one." That horrible moment when it must have dawned on them that they were falling—falling down into the burning belowdecks—and no one would be able to get them out. I wished to God I could go back. I could have got to them. If only I'd been a little quicker.

Wild, our sailing master, who'd always been kind to me. And his smiling young boys. They were all gone.

It seemed monstrously unfair: they had died, and the *spare* was carrying on. But perhaps not for long. Perhaps to a slow death, the death Harry had talked about in South Georgia, when I'd refused our last chance to turn back.

X

I do not remember sleeping.

Morning came with Harry's weight pressing on me, head heavy against my shoulder. There were smudges of soot on his face, but he was warm, and breathing solidly. The sound of water lapping made me drowsy.

Then I remembered: the water was dangerous. Dark. Drowning. Killer whales. I struggled to sit, looked around. Ice had blown in overnight—our little channel had frozen solid—and the snow had stopped. It must have been close to three degrees Fahrenheit, and I thought about that *thirty degrees of frost* I'd once thought so impressive. The sun was a round ball hanging in a gray sky. Pale faces, as men stirred from sleep and cursed the day.

"Morning. You'd better wake him—another dog's gone." Nicholls was brushing ice from his clothing. I squeezed my eyes shut for a moment. They felt gritty and heavy, and all the joints in my fingers had a faraway ache.

I grasped Harry's arm, and his eyes flew open too quickly for him to have been asleep. He didn't breathe. A look of horror sped across his face at something in the middle distance. But it was only Tarlington, crouched bareheaded by the boat, hair shockingly red. His greatcoat trailed in the slush, bulking out his unimpressive frame, making him seem much taller, much less defined. Harry shivered as if the cold had crept its way into his marrow. He didn't say anything.

We bent to work.

Randall looked terrible—reddened eyes, face harder than ever. When we dragged ourselves off the floe, his boat was lowest in the water. Standing and surveying us, he started to say "Damn, *damn*," then caught Clarke's eye.

"Well," he called. "We must make land—we can't risk another night in the pack. We must find lower ground—or try our chances on those cliffs. We'll make it."

No one responded. I shook my head, trying to calm myself. Randall seemed to look right at me with searching eyes, and we were under way.

Hours passed. My hands were no longer part of me, and I dropped my oar with a thud, the dogs whining unhappily. The ice had started to fasten itself around us again, those invisible fingers clenching tight, and I watched it with raw eyes. I couldn't fend it off any longer. "It's nothing," I insisted, although my chest throbbed from holding in great wrenching shivers. My feet were leaden. I refused to think about the freezing water in the bottom of the boat.

"Nonsense," Nicholls said shortly. He clambered over and grasped me by the shoulders, pulling me close, and felt for my temperature with bare fingers in my throat. "Jesus, you're like ice."

I rebelled, but he hugged me tighter, rubbing briskly at my arms. I was too weak to fight back. "You shouldn't have stopped me," I said, my voice small. "You shouldn't have stopped me. On the ship. We left them. It's not right."

A clatter as Harry, too, dropped his oar. "Keep rowing, Cooper."

Nicholls uncurled my fingers, exclaiming at their color. "You *idiot*, Morgan. Why didn't you say?" He went straight past what I'd said about the lost sailors.

I laughed, and choked on it: my shivers were starting to unleash themselves, as if given permission. I was wearing a shirt—woolen jumper—Burberry windproof tunic—Burberry snow helmet—but it wasn't enough. It was like the cold was rapping on my heart.

Someone pushed at my arm. "Here," Tarlington said, holding out a pair of gloves. "They'll be better than nothing. If you get frostbite—lose the use of your hands—you'll hold us all up, you idiot."

Nicholls—raising his eyebrows—agreed. Once he let go, the cold smacked back, and Harry piled Sanchez onto me: a large docile heap of wet fur. The dogs made an unpleasant smell under the canvas—on the water we had to relieve ourselves over the side of the boats, which I'd loudly refused, thankful there wasn't enough to drink, until the sensation dimmed to a constant dull ache. I'd been trying my hardest not to think about the ice; about tents; no doors at all, where we were headed. No privacy. It seemed so unfair, so monstrously unfair, that I should have to worry about this, after everything.

I burrowed my face into Sanchez, clenching my fists. They might discover who I once was—that was all. I was on the ice, here and now, and every part of my body was freezing.

I felt I was watching the scene through a telescope. The shadows lengthened into nautical twilight, the horizon mocking, and the pressure gathered. We heaved to where the cliffs dipped towards the sea, and a narrow lane of open water swelled and seethed with newborn floes. I used my own family home to gauge height: the ice above us loomed four or five stories high, a dwelling built to no human proportions.

"The seams won't hold," Rees called. Randall waded through his boat to confer with Holmes, who was holding our mountaineering gear out of the water, teeth chattering.

"We won't make it," Harry mumbled, eyes dazed.

"Stop it," I said. I didn't have the strength to shove him. "Just—stop it."

"We have to go up," Randall growled. "We can't risk another night—" and he turned, expectantly, to his two mountaineers. They'd been intended for the interior: for beautiful clear snow slopes, not these jagged and unfriendly barriers to the continent. The pair of them looked up, lantern-light flashing off Ollivar's glasses as the boat wallowed.

Ollivar insisted we wait for morning, with more than an officer's confidence—when it came to mountains, he was clearly used to people listening. But Randall simply said, with an air of terrible restraint: "No, I don't think that will be possible. We'll be on the bloody seabed by then. Holmes?"

Holmes was shivering hard, trying to avoid Randall's gaze. But all eyes were on him. "Come on!" Randall barked. "Three ascents by twenty-two—you know why I brought you here, eh? I have complete faith in you both. We all do."

"We'll—we'll try, sir," Holmes stuttered. They'd have to pull themselves up that sheer façade inch by inch, carrying their own safety ropes. My stomach lurched.

Randall landed his mountaineers on the fast ice at the base of the cliffs, where the swell broke and the tide eddied, cracking the perimeter into brash ice and spray; the rest of the boats hung back. Then a floe rose up out of the water right on top of Randall's boat—kept rising and rising, screeching like chalk on a board, as the men tried to fend it off. The crunch of timber made everyone hold their breath.

The first warning came from Duncan. He'd been given morphine for the pain, to keep him still, and I'd heard Staunton despairing of the unclean conditions. Duncan murmured: "What—" as water gently sloshed over his face.

"Oh, *hell*," Randall said with feeling. "Clarke! We've sprung!"

The second boat came swinging around, started taking on men, the dogs leaping and howling, tents and sleeping bags being thrown across the gap. Staunton yelled, "My case!" and Randall searched in the cold slushy water at the bottom of the boat until Staunton's red leather medical case surfaced, throwing it into Clarke's waiting arms. It contained the morphine and chloroform: infinitely precious.

Randall's boat pitched lower. The tide rolled it back towards the cliffs. Distance opened up between us.

Someone bellowed, "Duncan!"

Randall dived into the blackness of the Weddell Sea. I took a shaky breath, gripped the side of my boat, feeling my pulse pounding in my temples.

"Come on," Nicholls whispered beside me. "Come *on*."

Above us, on the cliffs, a light swung. They'd found a narrow gulley in the ice, dark and invisible from the water. "All well, sir?" a disembodied voice yelled.

No one answered. All eyes were on the inky water. Ripples. I knew if I breathed it would come out as a sob.

Randall appeared again.

Clarke dived straight towards him, showing no signs of the terrible shock of such cold water.

"Keep him up!" Staunton shouted as Randall struggled to get Duncan's face out of the water. Clarke reached them—but grabbed straightaway for Randall, arms closing around his chest. Randall shouted something, almost hit Clarke in the face. It took both of them, pushing and heaving, to get Duncan to the other boat.

The water streaming off him like a sea leopard, Randall shouted, "How dare you!" to Clarke, who calmly ignored him. Then: "Good work, lads!" to Holmes and Ollivar, two pinpricks of light nearly halfway aloft.

Randall's boat paused for a moment. Then the sea swallowed it up with emphasis.

A whip-round for dry—or drier—clothing. I covered my eyes when Duncan was stripped, the raw flesh on his limbs exposed. Wet and pink like something from the bottom of the ocean. He was bundled back into the warmest things we had, men and dogs and provisions pressed in around him on all sides. "Keep him moving," Staunton cried, pumping his arms and legs.

"How dare you," Randall hissed at Clarke. "You know the drill! To put me above the men—"

Clarke shrugged. Low: "They'll need you now."

My head swam. I stared up at the cliffs, my heart in my throat as I looked for our mountaineers. I'd been so proud of my skills in the rigging. But my brothers' tree house—the ship herself—had been one thing. This was quite another, and it dwarfed me.

Harry had been right: some of this *had* been a game. I'd played at storming the citadel, and it was as if Rufus had abruptly pulled up the treehouse ladder and shut the hatch in my face. I'd been childish. My fingernails dug into my numb hands through the damp, scratchy gloves.

This wasn't a game.

Two boats, twenty men, and an uncertain number of dogs. When Ollivar—laboriously—gained the top of the cliffs, we lost more provisions to the abuse of the winds as we winched them up with tackle and boom. We huddled in a small sheltered spot on that immense ice sheet, seamed by crevasses, slowly sloping down to the sea before dropping like a stone. Even with its whiteness, the ground looked gaunt and unfinished; Nicholls thought he saw some signs of a penguin rookery on the shore ice below, long abandoned by its occupants. I could finally see, in the distance, the suggestion of a mountain range like a chick tapping through an eggshell.

I tried to sleep, but I could only think of my brothers, my bright shining brothers, and how they'd said, so cheerfully: *Antarctica, or die trying.*

I'd thought I'd find them here. I didn't know what I'd found instead.

XI

"So, are we going to talk about it?" Boyd said abruptly. He looked into his mug, but his voice carried clearly across camp. "Why we lost the bloody ship?"

No one answered him. The winds had briefly abated. The pull and hiss of the sea at the cliffs was like an animal pawing at a locked door. Our "Shore Camp" was a small dark blot tucked into a fantastic landscape, snow hummocks and sastrugi making the long line of the horizon knobbly and uncertain. We had made flags out of bright scraps of material—hung them everywhere we could, like a garden party. But they were tiny, and we were utterly alone, hundreds of miles south of the whaling channels. No one would be seeing our signals.

Clarke had called a halt to our work, and Macready served cocoa, loaded with sugar and condensed milk, tasting like the galley. Like home. It raised no spirits. Laurence and the stokers talked in hushed voices over a crumpled sketch of the *Fortitude*'s belowdecks. Mortimer stood a little way off, facing the horizon, silently sucking on his pipe, as if he refused to acknowledge we were on land—or what passed for it. A captain without a ship.

They'd held hope for the fireproofing: Wild had thought he could flood the lower decks, contain it at the bulkheads. If she'd burned out without breaching the hull, she might still have offered some shelter as the winter closed in. But my heart plummeted at Boyd's stark acknowledgment. Boyd, practical Boyd, thought the *Fortitude* lost. I believed him.

I could see Harry looking over. He was exhausted, and we couldn't keep the dogs muzzled forever. They howled for their master: a sound that put my teeth on edge, made me want to shut them up however possible. In a tent with a hissing kerosene stove, Staunton was trying to dress the dreadful burns running all down Duncan's left leg and arm. Save for a few muffled whimpers, Duncan wouldn't be answering.

"The engine was low," Boyd said. "An open flame in the coal bunkers— no one's that stupid. It traveled up the shaft—should've been locked at both ends." He paused. "*Somebody* left it open. Otherwise we'd have stood a chance."

"Mistakes happen. People get careless. There's little use dwelling on it, not now." Nicholls took off his cap and ruffled up his graying hair, giving Boyd a meaningful look. "Gone is gone. We're lucky to be alive."

Boyd shook his head. "Something went wrong," he said deliberately, rubbing a hand up and down his scarred arm. "Seems to me—worse than wrong. The ship didn't burn, it damn well blew up—like a Jack Johnson went off under it."

I glanced around, saw nodding and agreement.

"The dust caught." Nicholls let his breath out in a big gust of steamy air, and I thought—my chest clenching—of the booming noise we'd heard on the water. "Doors were left open. It was an accident. Things happen down South." He sounded very calm. I tried to tell myself these were old hands, old Antarctic hands.

But I'd never heard of an expedition losing its ship and surviving.

"Clarke didn't blame that Spanish fellow," Macready added. "When the bearings were wrong, and he lost his fingers."

Nicholls smiled a smile that didn't reach his gray eyes. It seemed that would be the end of it. But Boyd glanced over to Randall and Clarke, perched at the lookout point. He said quickly, "There's someone to blame, all right. We just wish there wasn't. Someone left those doors open. And as for the bunker, Christ. Someone *started* that fire."

Nicholls coughed, mug halfway to his lips. "Now, hang on—"

"He's right," Ellis said.

"Sometimes coal just bloody blows," Laurence muttered. The cheap bituminous coal that had made Laurence swear, and complain about the foolishness of supplying the *Fortitude* so cheaply. It was liable to spontaneous combustion—explosion. And that had crippled her.

A hubbub of voices. Harry put his hand, very wearily, over his face. A familiar expression: someone who'd been on their feet for days, was living on their nerves. A *Jack Johnson*. I bit my lip hard enough to hurt. Harry had been an artillery officer; I didn't need to ask what he thought. If he thought the fire deliberate, if he and Boyd agreed the ship had blown up—

I pulled off my hat, beat the ice from it, put it back on. Keeping my hands moving as they shook. "But it'd be *suicide*."

We couldn't expect a rescue party—Randall had made no plans for our relief. We might survive for months on the ice, on whatever provisions we'd salvaged. We might even sit out the long dark winter, if the blizzards spared us, if our camp could be dug in and fortified. But no one would be coming for us. It was all down to Randall, now: Randall and his officers. Whether we lived; whether we escaped.

Or how fast we died.

"Worse than suicide," one of the stokers spat. "Fucking murder." We'd lost their ship: they'd never expected to end up on the shore. "This place'll be the end of us."

"Not what we need right now, lads," Macready said, a scowl passing over his tanned face.

"Whoever did it killed Smith and Benham—Wild and Perry—might as well have killed Duncan, too." Boyd gestured to that ominously silent tent, from which Staunton still hadn't emerged. "As good as killed us all."

Sideways glances around the circle. My throat locked at the sound of those names. That moment when I'd felt the deck hot under my feet. My conviction that I could save them.

"Randall's not blaming anyone," Macready said.

"Well, he wouldn't, would he? But someone here had no business—no bloody business at all—being in those bunkers. He's been sneaking about like a spy." Boyd spat on the dead white ground. "Look at his sleeves."

Silence.

Tarlington put down his mug, hands trembling slightly. Long, pale hands in biscuit-colored, red-trimmed fingerless mitts. He'd tried to shove his shirt cuffs up under his jacket, but they peeped out like naughty children refusing to go to bed. Smudged and sooty with coal dust, they looked as though he'd wiped his hands on them after touching something very dirty.

I thought of that clean handkerchief—"JWT"—he'd offered me, the little twist of disdain on his face. My chest clenched tight.

"Boyd," Nicholls said dangerously.

"He's got some fucking explaining to do." Boyd shot a quick sideways glance at me—and at Harry, who was staring across at us as though something large and fast was bearing down on him.

Tarlington stood up, jamming his hands into his pockets. "Gentlemen—" He strode off towards our tent, looking very small. All eyes followed him. Mortimer knocked out his pipe on the ground.

"Well?" There was an ugly tone to Boyd's voice. "Wonder what tricks he was learning in those camps. Which of his chums put him up to this. Getting his own back on Randall—"

"Boyd," Nicholls said. "We're all tired. But to suggest *he* of all people—"

"Careful," Macready said quickly.

Boyd stared at them, jaw set. Around the circle, men were getting to their feet. Some fast, some slow. With their Burberry snow helmets cinched tight, hoods concealing heads and necks, they were faceless ruffians. Our tent flaps billowed in the slight wind, and Nicholls blocked Boyd's path. I hugged my knees, stayed on the ground. *Murder*. I turned it over and over in my mind. I tried to fit it to Tarlington, green with seasickness, scowling his thanks for a mug of tea. His tentative attempts at conversation. But he was right. The prediction he'd made had come true: this would surely be Randall's last expedition.

"Stand aside," Boyd said. "I'm not going to hurt him—I won't. But who knows what that sort's capable of?"

Saboteurs. Randall. Boyd pacing in the *Fortitude*'s chart room, forehead deeply furrowed. I'd felt even then that we'd gone too far; Harry's talk could have *consequences*. These were men who'd fought and been wounded; seen friends die and be buried; naturally mistrusted those who made common cause with their common enemy. And now the ship had gone, it seemed very plain what those consequences might be. I found myself standing up, teeth so clenched I felt they would shatter out of my skull. I didn't know what I was going to do.

A sudden noise. Clarke blocked out the wan sunlight. Randall had come upon us unnoticed, his hood revealing only the sanded-off side of his face. Boyd stood very, very still, like an animal before a snake.

"A word, *Richard*," Randall said—like a curse—and took him by the arm, dragging him over to the lookout point, where they cast long shadows together. No one said anything. Our camp's small flags stirred limply in the breeze, as if signaling surrender.

"I will not have it!" Randall suddenly roared. "By God, speak like that again and I'll have you—"

He broke off, and strode towards us, breathing fast and hard. "That goes for the rest of you. If I hear rumors again—about traitors on my ship—about *him*—amongst my crew—any of you, telling tales about your shipmates—well, I'll—I'll throw you off the cliffs and you can *swim* home."

The stokers set their jaws. Clarke made a small tense movement.

"Don't think I won't do it. To any one of you. Officers. Men. No one could have intended *this*. I'll lead you out of here. But I won't bloody well lead a bunch of quarreling schoolboys." Randall seemed to crouch as he stood, clothing more ragged than ever.

"It was an accident," Nicholls said, clearly and quietly. "You all know it. You're looking for something to make it easier." He looked towards the cliffs, the dark sucking water that had surely swallowed the ship. "Nothing will make it easier."

Boyd nodded, once, his face unreadable. "My apologies." An uneasy silence. I saw Nicholls puff out his cheeks and loosen his shoulders. He'd been at Ypres, leading more than a hundred men. With all his jokes, it was so easy to forget about Nicholls and his cool command.

Clarke broke the silence. He'd lost his fancy custom-made gloves, and his reindeer-skin mittens steamed as he held them over the stove. "You can all do the maths," he said. "There are too many of us. We can't just sit here and *hope* for penguins returning to that rookery. We can last three weeks on what we've salvaged. Four—if we stop moving."

The earlier cocoa had been a lie, to keep our spirits up. Bile burned the back of my throat. Harry looked ready to shoot someone. No one said a word. Four more weeks until we started to starve, and shiver, and lie down to die.

"So we need to *get* moving," Randall said. "With all of us—and the dogs—we're only a week or so, God willing, from assistance."

It was as if he'd announced we would walk to Timbuktu and fill our pockets with sapphires. Boyd, refilling his mug, finally looked up. "What?"

"The German expedition," Randall said. "Karlmann and his men. They were carrying huts and provisions, intended to land and make base camp not far from here. I have the coordinates. As you all know, they didn't—return on schedule. That's no reason to believe they failed." He paused, looking around at our drawn faces. "We might not be welcomed with open arms! But they could hardly turn us away. Let's get working. Rees, Laurence—let's have sledges built. We leave tomorrow."

XII

Mortimer turned on Randall on the fourth day. "The ship's still there, damn you. We could have saved her—saved all of us."

Jones and Archer stood with him. The argument had started in their tent overnight, Laurence's voice rising and falling like a cantata, cursing and angry words until he'd decamped with his sleeping bag and crammed himself in with the other officers. The wind had continued its unearthly whistling sounds until we rose. Stepping outside the tents, it had simply stopped. As if the curtain had risen, the audience had fallen silent, and we were the stage production.

At breakfast, Archer had openly blamed Tarlington for the fire. His voice muffled by his balaclava, held back by Bedloe, he shouted—almost petulantly—"Come on, you coward!" Tarlington's refusal to rise to the challenge made me deeply uneasy. It had ended when Randall grabbed Archer and punched him in the face. In the stunned silence, I'd have sworn I could hear his nose break.

Before Archer could retaliate, Clarke had set himself squarely in front of Randall, more forbidding than I'd ever imagined a man could seem. Archer thought better of it. He pressed his wet gloves to his face, winced. The chilly air must have been like breathing knives.

We'd struggled silently through the indifferent sunlight; light glimmered from the eastern mountains to the westerly coast, and our southward course through the middle was lit up in muted and fantastic shades of blue, green, and gray. The beauty couldn't impress. Our dogs were hard to control; on each sledge, a grim-faced man with wide shoulders—Clarke, Boyd—hauled beside them in man-harness, and the rest of us did what we could to keep it on track. Breaking for cocoa, we huddled for protection from the biting winds. My legs were so sore, I felt every bone in them was fractured; my feet were numb stumps. We wore every item of winter clothing, from knee-length windproof tunics to heavy blue fleece-lined trousers. I was indistinguishable from the rest, but for once it brought me no joy. We were a crew of shapeless, baggy, exhausted ghosts.

Finally, Mortimer had poured out his dregs on the snow, and stepped up to Randall. "We need to get back to the *ship*," he said, scowling as though we were conspiring against him.

Randall grasped his shoulder, turning him away from us like umpires politely discussing a cricket match. The air was crisp and white. We could hear every word.

"We must stay together. Find the Germans. Not take to the water so late in the season. Good God, you saw how it was out there."

I shivered, thinking of the crushing pack. The mad lurching of the boats. The threat of killer whales in the dark water. We'd cached one boat at Shore Camp—Clarke had buried it single-handed—and cannibalized both to build our heavy makeshift sledges. I was glad to see the back of the sea, and the malevolent glistening of the bergs.

"No," Mortimer said coolly. Men were getting to their feet, abandoning tools and mugs. "The ship's still there—Wild knew what he was about. We shall take our chances, with or without you."

Movement beside the sledges—Jones and Archer, struggling under laden packs. I scrambled to my hands and knees.

"You wouldn't dare—" Clarke said.

"We're in enough trouble, Christian," Randall said, his hands out, palms up, as if trying to tame a beast. "Don't risk their lives. We'll have more of a chance—for survival or rescue—if we stay together."

"The Germans disappeared two years ago," Mortimer said. "During a one-season trip. No one's heard from them since. Their wives sent you telegrams; implored you to search for their bodies—begged *you* to be their relief expedition, when their government wouldn't act."

Silence.

"Karlmann is a—a veteran of the ice. I'll be damned before I'll give up on him. This from you—eh? A Navy man on his first time South!"

Mortimer gave a bitter smile. "You've become a fool, Randall. An old fool. Obsessed with glory."

"By God, *you're* the bloody fools. I'll not split the party, nor risk our lives in the pack. Supposing she's still there—how do you propose to sail her out, eh? There won't be a scrap of coal left." He snorted. "Are you going to wait for the wind to—*blow* you five hundred miles to South Georgia?"

Jones stumped up alongside Mortimer, his jaw set. "We know where the ship is. I won't go marching towards God knows what." He kept a picture of his wife and three little girls in his front pocket. He hadn't meant to come this far: in Argentina, when the *Fortitude*'s engines were serviced, Randall had persuaded him to stay.

"This is my expedition, damn you. A gentleman would honor his contract."

Mortimer laughed—an unfriendly sound. "A gentleman? *You*, Randall—you'd speak to me of being a gentleman?"

"Think about it," Nicholls said hastily. "Even if she's still there—making the attempt would be risky enough. If the weather turned—"

He stopped—looked up at the dark storm clouds to the east, dogging our steps since the cliffs—then stepped in front of our ramshackle sledges. I scrambled to my feet, realizing what he feared. We might carry our own packs—but there was a limit, a painful limit, to what each of us could bear. For fuel and food and shelter and a hundred other things, everything we needed to survive, we needed those sledges, and the dogs. Needed them desperately.

I looked around. The circle had got smaller.

A brief twitch of Archer's right hand, hidden behind his back. Clarke tracked the movement like a big blunt-headed shark. "Archer," he said, very low. "*Don't.*"

Behind him, Laurence shook his head. "I swear, I didn't know—"

"You're not going to stop us," Archer said, sullenly wiping his nose. It had started bleeding again, dark as crude oil. In his other hand, the gun.

Randall put his hands up.

The air crackled. Clarke carried his revolver everywhere; others, too, were always armed. If Randall had given the nod, they'd have shot the treacherous bastards. I might have tackled Mortimer myself, ground him into the snow. An *old fool.* It made me tremble with impotent fury.

But Randall backed away, giving Clarke a small shake of the head.

The deserters took the one decent sledge. Most of its contents. The remaining sledges were heavy as anything, and every day dragging them over the plateau would be horribly exposed. If a blizzard stopped us in our tracks, or we met bad surface conditions, couldn't haul fast enough—we'd have to start eating the dogs. Then travel slower still. I knew enough about true man-hauling—backbreaking and awful—to know I never wanted to try it. God only knew what we'd do with Duncan, who was dead weight. Strapped down onto a stretcher, bundled up with tarpaulin, he was confused or sleeping, not even waking when his handlers managed to drop him face-first onto the snow.

I thought, horribly, of what we might eat when all other food ran out.

But Archer held the gun, so they took what they wanted. "We're not robbing you," Jones kept saying. "We're not thieves—this is just the ship's share. We'll leave what's left at Shore Camp."

Boyd spat on the ground. "Fucking cowards."

Jones took up the harness. They could possibly have convinced Clarke to release some of the weaker dogs—useless mouths—with a little time. But from the jumpy, white-faced way they kept looking around, they obviously knew they didn't have it.

Archer waved his gun at Tarlington. "We'll take him off your hands, too, if you like," he said nastily.

Silence. Tarlington stood like a scarecrow, all sharp edges and elbows. A pinched expression on his face that looked like resignation. I found myself walking over to him, keeping my eyes fixed on the mutineers. I didn't think—whoever he was, whatever had happened—that he deserved to be dragged off to die on the ice like an animal. He raised his eyebrows at me.

"By God, begone," Randall hissed. It was more frightening than his most violent rages.

When they left, we froze in place. Waiting for the danger to pass—although no one said it aloud—we were quite deliberate in turning to our chores, performing small tasks of maintenance. Macready served hoosh, the Antarctic sledging stew of boiled preserved meat—*pemmican*, that was the word—and crumbled ship's biscuit, hot enough to burn the roof of my mouth. We made a huddled semicircle facing south around the stove. Three blurry figures struggled over the terrain to the north. Getting smaller and smaller, until they vanished entirely.

The wind came at sundown, screaming across the icy plateau from those distant mountains, and its ferocity caught us by surprise—made the dogs scream too. We couldn't travel any farther into that seething hell.

The tents went up in haste. Tarlington scrubbed at his sooty sleeves in the thin light, wearing a look of disgust. Harry curled into a ball. His silence was unnerving—as immense as the cliff face, and just as hard to scale.

"It's like it's—testing us. The wind." He only gave me a hard stare in response. "Look—I know how it sounds."

Tarlington glanced across, perhaps the beginning of a sneer on his wide lips, and I fell silent too. The sound outside was raw and lonely. When I struggled away from the tents to hastily relieve myself behind a ridge, at the farthest end of a shaking rope line, I saw no horizon and no sky; no ground and no stars. The wind had brought the snow down from the secret interior. It was white all over. A great white darkness, so complete in its *absence*.

"A terrible mistake," Nicholls said, making the rounds. His growing beard was flecked with snow—opinions were divided as to whether a beard made one more or less susceptible to frostbite—and it made his face look older, more noble. I thought of Randall, saying Nicholls *knew the white spaces*: I hoped to God he was right. "If she's still there, if they make it, and we return—well. There'll be a reckoning. He's not a forgiving man."

The wind tore at the tent, secured to the ice by mounding drift over its skirts. There was little purchase to this land. My hands were weeping blisters, and I hissed as I peeled off my Shetland mitts to inspect the damage.

"And you—you need to give more care to what people think," Nicholls snapped at Tarlington. "If you'd only denied it, instead of being so damn stubborn—"

Tarlington said nothing. I couldn't quite believe I'd been ready to stick up for him. I let out a long, shaky breath as I pressed a handkerchief against my blisters. "We'll get through this, Morgan," Nicholls said. He put his hand on my shoulder—a capable, veteran hand. "Now, who's up for a game of cards?"

I didn't need to ask what had happened outside, in the first gusts of wind, as we bent to our tasks. The story told itself: Randall's nod to Clarke. Clarke's disappearance into the gray mist beyond camp. And much later, when we were under canvas—making Harry jump and clench his fists—the sound of gunshots, so far away and indistinct they might have been on the moon.

XIII

The storm ended and the winds died. In the strange white light, we could finally see the eastern mountain range, curiously closer than expected. Jagged rock disappeared into the misty sky, a single black peak sitting squatly in the center. Mountains to the east, where the land sloped upwards, the shore out of sight to our west. We were caught between the deep water and the unforgiving rock. I caught Harry staring at the mountains as we struck camp, frozen in the act of rolling up his sleeping bag. His brown eyes were wide and dark.

I shoved him, rather harder than I intended. "Stop it." I wasn't sure what, exactly, but his silence was starting to grate on me. "Harry—"

"You can see them, then?"

"What?"

"Nothing," he said.

"Did you see . . ." I found my voice trailing off. "Harry, did you see—something on the ship? When Duncan said . . ."

I wished I could believe I'd seen Smith limping across the ruined fo'c'sle, or Benham making his way through the flames to a lifeboat. But it had been a tall dark shape, unwavering, unmoving. Smoke swirling around it; a hollow in the world. Even now—in the open air, surrounded by men—the thought of it made me glance over my shoulder, into the white wavering horizon, feeling sure I'd see it waiting there.

"There was someone on deck. Harry, did you see—"

"Nothing," Harry said again, his voice clipped, and turned to work with more purpose. I let him get on with it. And if I noticed a strange twitch about him throughout that morning—cocking his head to the side, as if listening for something—I decided it would have to wait.

I rubbed my sore eyes. My face was dirty and wind-bitten; the icy plateau was horribly exposed. Tarlington's freckles turned rust-brown under the glare of pale reflected light. A harsh, uncompromising place. The sun splintered into sun dogs, two hovering spheres that seemed to move every time I took my eyes off them. I had a powerful sense they were watching me. Bearing down on me—*pressing* down on me—and the dark mountains were what I'd felt waiting below the horizon.

I set my jaw and tried to ignore it.

We made good progress until the wind came sneaking back. "What the hell?" Nicholls looked up at the clear sky. Clarke turned and stopped, shielding his eyes.

Harry was doing all he could with our dogs, but their hauling instinct was weak, these were hardly proper sledges, and they just wanted to fight and run. Jamieson had taken such a chunk from Samson's leg that Staunton had suggested butchering him—it would be a mercy, and we could use the meat to stave off scurvy. I tried to stamp down my rolling disgust.

The dogs howled when the mountain winds returned; sat down in their traces and howled, and Harry was utterly unable to budge them. Just like they had howled at the winds on the ship. The hairs on the back of my neck stood up. I turned around, squinting.

"Cooper!" Randall shouted. "We've only a few hours of daylight!"

"I'm trying!" Harry sank to his knees. "Come on, come on," he muttered. "Don't do this—"

I grabbed another dog by its collar. It barely seemed to notice, and I set my teeth—dragged it by its neck.

Clarke called, "Randall, it's starting to—"

"Yes, thank you, I'm aware!" Randall strode over. "Can you get them to haul, or not?"

"I don't *know*," Harry said. "Just let me—"

"You have fifteen minutes!"

Clarke looked at the sky. "We can't spare fifteen minutes." Dark clouds were massing, shadows scudding towards us.

"We must get under way," Randall said. "A little farther at least. I know you can do it, Cooper!"

"Australis—"

It was as if twilight had come early; the wind was so fierce I had to jam my hat down to stop it being snatched off. Again, the horrible sense that something was watching me.

"Then stop mucking about—get them under cover," Randall snapped, and strode off to shout orders elsewhere.

I flinched at the deep indentations from the sledge harnesses; the dogs weren't used to any of this. Some of them bled sluggishly in the cold, tried to bite my numb and prickly fingers as I untangled them. They were *resources*—not pets. Leashes whipping in the wind, the dogs howled louder.

"Can't you shut them up?" someone said nearby, and I noticed Tarlington was there, unclipping the harnesses as if he'd been doing it his whole life.

"Oh—you try, if you like!" Harry said.

A burst of wildness: the first real strength of the storm.

"Take cover!" Clarke yelled. We scrambled back towards the sledges, our only shelter on the barren plain. I stumbled, and the screaming wind lifted me up whole, like the Rapture, pulling at my arms and legs. The drift whipped up into the air, clouding my vision with pure dead whiteness, until everything—even the horizon—disappeared. I couldn't see.

The wind roared like distant guns. I was weightless. I crashed to earth, rolled, and grabbed the leashes again.

Harry fell to his knees and wrapped himself around the dogs. They seethed and growled at the air, a gray-white frenzy of movement, jaws snapping so wide I thought they'd bite his arm clean off. Tarpaulin crackled and boiled like thunder. "Harry!" I yelled. "What's wrong with them—"

"Jonathan!" He was only a few feet away—might as well have been miles. I fell again, a sharp thud knocking the breath out of me. I had two leashes in my hands, two dogs.

Then none.

Instinct took over. The dogs pulled away smoothly—never achieved when hauling, the beasts—harnesses bouncing along behind. I ran, my boots kicking up powder snow, panting plumes of steam into the cold air. A frenzy of howling, joining with the wind, rising and falling, like they were *singing* together. I tried to snatch a look back. The sledges were already gone, the wind directly behind me—the mountains behind me—and the dogs racing away.

"Jonathan!"

The muffled sound of someone else running nearby. More dogs, in a confusion of fur and teeth. Samson and Sanchez, followed by Harry. Despite his injury, Samson was running as if hell itself were on his heels. Sanchez was barking at the air, and I saw—for a moment—the terrified mad light in his blue eyes. I'd never seen dogs bolt like this, and it made me run harder myself. As though they knew something I didn't.

Shouting in the distance. The dogs ahead were blurry, scudding shadows, like the suggestion of fish beneath the surface of a pond. Whiteness all around. I'd never catch up. I came skidding to a halt, my heart pounding. Took one breath, coughed, then another. Wrapped my arms around myself. My chest ached. I couldn't see the sledges. I couldn't see *anything*.

I was alone.

"Harry!" I yelled, whipping my head around. "Harry!"

The wind screamed back at me, mocking. I shouted again, cupping my hands to my mouth, throat burning and tearing, voice high and desperate. There wasn't the slightest chance anyone would hear me.

Out of the snow rushed a shape in a long coat, making me freeze in place. A hat with earflaps. A furious expression. "Stay there!"

Tarlington. I let out a sobbing breath. "Thank you—" But he vanished into the roiling snow. I'd been abandoned again.

I took a faltering step, but it was no use: I'd completely lost my bearings. I could be walking towards the sledges—or away, forever, into all that white. I made myself stop, wheezing, and looked down at my feet as though they were no longer part of my body. Somewhere, a dog howled on the wind.

I told myself Randall wouldn't leave me—that wasn't his way. He'd send men out into the storm. But I'd been stupid—impossibly stupid—to run off. If they died looking for me, it'd be my fault. I started breathing hard, unable to control it. Perhaps I deserved to be left.

I found myself thinking of Clarke—the ice cave—his lost fingers. "Sometimes the South takes a piece of you," he'd said at Grytviken, flexing his stumps in the glow of the fire, appearing neither bitter nor resentful. "And will come for the rest of you soon enough."

I crouched into a ball, panted into my own cupped hands. I'd have some time before the cold got to me. Perhaps it would lull me, show me home on the horizon, like a mirage. My feet and hands would go white, then black, and lose all feeling. I wouldn't care. It would be like falling asleep.

I tried to think of my brothers—hide-and-seek—when we were all so much younger, so much closer. They laughed at me from behind the heavy damask curtains. My mother would be annoyed; I wasn't meant to be playing with them. I could hear her small sigh of exasperation. She'd tried so hard. I must have driven her to distraction. She told me stories, tried to interest me in my piano lessons. But I always escaped and ran off after my brothers. I was small, good at hiding. Terrible at finding them. I closed my eyes.

I was ready to find them again.

"Get off me!" Harry shouted, somewhere close. "You bloody—"

The sound of dogs, over the wind. Tarlington shouted: "Listen!"

I scrambled to my feet, blindly following the voices. Indistinct black shapes loomed in the haze; the wind picked me up and threw me down again, scraped me across the ground. My ears rang. I tasted blood, drying chill and sticky on my lips. I wasn't strong enough for this place.

They took form: Harry was struggling with a leash, dogs invisible at the other end. He was being hauled along, in painful fits and starts, Tarlington trying to pull him back.

"You have to let go!" Tarlington yelled.

"I'm not leaving them!" Harry shoved at him. "Get off me—*leave* me!"

They were evenly matched, but Harry elbowed Tarlington viciously in the stomach. A sudden snapping motion—the leash pulled whipcord tight—and Tarlington put his arm around Harry's neck. Harry struggled and swore, calling Tarlington a coward and a monster. Screaming in language I never thought I'd hear him use.

"Stop it!" I stumbled towards them, legs weak and uncoordinated.

"Let go," Tarlington snarled. "You think you're being so bloody brave—"

"Stop it!" I yelled at Harry, high-pitched. Every moment, the dogs pulled him farther from any chance of rescue. "Let *go*!"

"Oh, you—" Tarlington said viciously, and hit him hard in the face.

Harry staggered and dropped the leash, reaching desperately as it snapped through his legs. The dogs were free; they seized their moment. With a final mournful *awoo*, they disappeared into nothingness.

"Look at me!" Tarlington shook Harry. "We need to get back to the sledges! We can't be out here!"

Harry shielded his eyes from the beating snow with his arm. He wouldn't move. For a moment, I thought he would just lie down. Give up.

"Oh, you—" Tarlington pulled him up before I could. "On your feet, *soldier*." He looked around. Up at the boiling sky, the wind battering his sharp face. Dark blue eyes. He seemed to scent the air. He pointed. "That way! Come *on*!"

I grabbed at my throat and followed, dragging Harry by the hand behind me.

"You lost us the dogs," Harry said when we were back at camp, shaking and punching the life back into our feet. His eyes were wide; he was breathless. He wouldn't stay still, even after Staunton had bandaged his ripped hands. "The dogs, you bloody—"

Beside us, the remaining dogs—the teams that Tarlington had lashed to the sledge—continued to bark at thin air, shaking their tails. The winds mocked them in return.

"Shut up," I said, my own voice sounding low and raspy. "He saved your life."

"I saved *both* your lives," Tarlington hissed with as much dignity as he could muster, his teeth chattering. "You idiots."

XIV

We had lost so much.

Duncan swam in and out of consciousness on the sledge, Staunton walking beside him. Bedloe, who'd been so cheerful at sea, proved to be dreadfully sick on land. And only a handful of dogs left. There were whispers—aggressively suppressed by Clarke—that we were going nowhere. Marching to our deaths, as Karlmann had before us. That there were no huts, or none we'd be able to find.

We had only two weeks of food, then we'd shoot the dogs.

We waited out a viciously uncomfortable night, the silence inside our tent oppressive. I tried to force myself to sleep, but the ground prodded at me, and my fingers and toes were numb. I screwed my eyes shut and willed myself back into my bed in Portsmouth. A proper mattress underneath me. My mother's bedtime stories—the ones she'd told me when I was very little. Snow White. Rapunzel. The sound of my brothers talking quietly in the next room. Rufus's pealing laughter. I tried to hear their voices in the whistling, sobbing wind. I was not rewarded; there was nothing human about that sound.

Man-hauling over the morning's soft, uneven snow was like trying to drag a dead horse through mud. I was harnessed alongside the remaining dogs and the other smallest crew members, having to set my shoulders square to prevent the makeshift harness slipping. We'd barely left camp before my back started shouting at me to straighten up. Ellis and Parker, too, were bent almost double. "Not as bad as the mines,"

Ellis said, grudgingly, trying to help. "It's all right for you, pipsqueak." But my shoulders were raw, and I knew how the dogs felt.

I kept my head down. It was all I could do.

Randall hauled on the other sledge. "It'll be a long march, and a hard one. But we'll shake their hands and tell them the War is over, and share and share alike until we can get out of here. We're all men, down South."

I wanted so badly to believe him; couldn't believe he'd be lying to us, not about this. Curling my hands into fists—agonizingly—one of my blisters popped. No one smiled. No one made eye contact. There was a certain cool determination. When Tarlington slipped on the uncertain ground, Randall helped him up without a word.

It was so still I could hear my boots breaking through the surface of the snow. The scrape and slide of the sledge, the dogs panting. Silence had taken possession of the world, and the sky was a sinister gray. The men complained of headaches, worsening as the days passed. Daylight shortened; shadows lengthened. The winter was waiting to pounce.

And the constant threat of those winds returning: the winds that had driven the dogs mad. It sounded ridiculous when I thought of saying it aloud. *Terrible winds*—as if they had a personality of their own. Antarctica was full of dangerous weather and harsh conditions, but that easterly breeze felt somehow aggressive. Territorial.

Harry had taken the loss of those dogs very hard. Whenever we stopped, on that long and painful march, he made a fuss over the ones that remained, scratching behind their ears, burying his face in their wet fur. I wondered what he would do now. He'd hardly been a dog handler in the first place, and we were hardly an expedition. We were a retreat. A rout.

"They might live," I said, trying to cheer him up. "If they make it down to the sea ice, they could hunt. Penguins and seals. They're meant to survive these places."

"Oh, honestly, Jonathan," he said, with a heavy sigh. "Believe what you like."

I opened my mouth, then closed it. I realized that perhaps the lost dogs would outlive us all.

XV

On the seventh day Clarke returned from scouting with an uncharacter-istic air of excitement, skidding ungracefully over the snow. "Look," he called to Randall, pointing. The sledges stuttered to a halt. I collapsed in harness, my breath coming as long plumes of steam, eyes fixed on the ground in front of me. It took me a few moments to raise my head, a series of pops and unfriendly cracks all down my spine.

I untangled myself, shielding my eyes from the glare. Harry shoved his binoculars at me. I could see—like a mirage—a small valley made of dark rock, as if the mountains were sneaking up on us. "It's there," Clarke said, his face splitting in a rare smile. "We've found them!"

A ragged cheer. "The huts?" I blurted out, hearing my voice shake. "They're real?"

"And the flag?" Boyd called. "Are they flying the German flag?"

"No flag at all," Clarke said, slowly. "But they're there."

Weak with relief, I dropped my harness into the snow, looking up at the sky for the first time in hours. Macready clapped me on the back, wheezing a little, and I grabbed his arm, trying to pass some of my strength into him. Randall shook hands with his officers. He looked cool; his blue eyes burned. "Well, then," he kept saying, smoothing down his sealskin cape and looking around, as if wanting to take in this moment from all angles. He'd led us to safety.

The sledges grew no lighter now that our destination was in sight, and I thought back longingly to all that idle time on the *Fortitude*, when I'd read in my hammock, played cards in the mess hall: I could have been lifting irons, doing calisthenics, preparing for this. My legs felt like dull, uncompromising lumps. Each step a torment.

The valley ahead of us took shape. The dark speck at its center became a low hut crouched amongst rocks. It was perhaps thirty feet long and twenty across, roof slanted, surrounded on all sides by an overhanging veranda and railings. The pale weather-beaten timbers gave it the air of an Alpine chalet. Smaller shacks, barely bigger than cupboards, made a little village on the side away from the easterlies; kennels tucked away against the rocks in its shadow, although—as our dogs pulled and champed their leashes, making Harry snap at them—no sound of barking, not at all.

It reminded me of somewhere, and after a while I realized it was South Georgia: the way the station had seemed frozen in time. The huts were still. No birds, not even clouds scudding across the sky. A feeling of oppressive quiet. Karlmann and his men were the only other expedition that had tried to land on this coast. A mystery—the subject of rumor amongst the whalers, bets amongst our crew. These were their huts; they'd got this far.

And what had happened after?

I strained to overhear as the scouting party returned. They pointed at the huts, speaking in subdued voices. Worried glances. Randall shook his head.

Nicholls wore a frown as he surveyed the area. "Look at that," he said thoughtfully, showing me: the horizon behind the huts was a shimmer of dazzling blue. "A glacier—that means pressure. This whole ice sheet might be veined with crevasses, like the Great Barrier on the other side of the continent. The wind always following us, coming from nowhere—this weather doesn't make sense. *None* of it makes sense. Randall encourages me to be grateful, instead of wondering why."

I shivered, rubbed my arms. To fall down a crevasse would be a slow, lingering death. "Perhaps we're just lucky."

He flashed me the slightest of smiles, not reaching his eyes. "I don't know. Do you feel particularly lucky, Morgan?"

I turned in my harness and looked at the mountains. The wind hit me in the face, teasingly, almost flirtatiously. But hard enough to hurt.

We gained steadily on those silent huts. I'd never seen anything so sterile that should have been welcoming. The empty flagpole twitched in the breeze. The windows were black glassy holes, reflecting the dying light as nautical twilight bloomed around us. It was the dark of the moon, and the sky was speckled with stars, distant and alien.

"Shouldn't there be a lookout? A—nightwatchman?"

Nicholls nodded.

"Something's not right," Boyd called.

"Well," Randall said sharply. "Let's wait and see."

I could almost forget the harness flaying my shoulders. I stared at the windows, half-expecting to see a figure appear. A face. Anyone.

Randall finally called a halt. A dog whined, then stopped instantly.

The huts were motionless. Small signs of inhabitation: a storeroom with a tarpaulin awning sagging under the weight of snow, large storm lanterns on each side of the front door. The porch was covered over with decking, to ward off the deep chill of the rocks, and old packing crates waited for people to sit on them. Someone had made this place a home, but the snow had drifted right up to the door, an inexorable and slow-moving wave. On the rocks behind, the anemometer made a creaking revolution in the wind. There were no lights inside.

Randall puffed out his cheeks and strode up to the front door, a lantern in one grubby mitten.

"Hello?" he called. "This is the 1920 British Coats Land Expedition. James Randall commanding. Is there anyone here? The War's over, we've come a long way."

He rapped on the door and called out again. No reply. Clarke and Boyd flanked him, their boots sounding unnaturally loud on the creaky porch.

Randall tried the coiled rope handle, and the door swung straight open, ricocheting against the frame, loud as a gunshot. "Careful—" Boyd pushed him aside, his service revolver drawn. "It could be a trap."

A small yelping whimper from the dogs; made by one then taken up by the others. I tore my gaze away from the open door. Harry was kneeling in the snow, holding them by their collars, and shook his head when I looked his way. They looked uneasy. In fact, they looked frightened.

"There's no one here," Randall said, coming out and pulling off his gloves. "Absolutely no one here."

THREE

THE HUTS

THE GERMAN HUTS, AUSTRAL AUTUMN 1920

I

Karlmann's expedition had gone.

Inside the front door, flecked windowpanes looked out over the porch; galley shelves strained with supplies; and a long wooden table, handsomely crafted from abandoned timber, served as mess for officers and men alike. But the patent stove sat with its steel chimney piping all buckled and warped from heat, its doors filmy with soot, as if it had been left burning for some time. I didn't know who would leave with the fires still burning.

A tin of cheese remained half-open and half-nibbled on the galley dresser. A chess set on the mess table had been left midway through a game. It was as if the occupants had simply stepped outside and would be back any minute. We traipsed through with wide eyes, frozen boots loud on the timber.

"Hello?" Nicholls said, pulling open the canvas curtain of each little sleeping compartment in turn. "Anyone here?" Boyd clamped his hand down abruptly on Nicholls's shoulder, and he stopped. Glass crunched underfoot: the interior walls had been built of packing cases, and the bottled goods inside had frozen and shattered once the stove had gone out. Pieces of glittering shrapnel had buried themselves into the timbers. From the wall above the mess table stared down an unsmiling portrait of the Kaiser.

Macready knelt in front of the stove and coaxed it back into life with his box of lucifers and kindling. The faint wind outside made a moaning sound down the pipes, and Ellis jumped—then laughed. Our lanterns sent shadows dancing over the blackened timber of the hut walls. I

sighed, feeling my body release a weight I'd been dragging along since
the ship. I might have at least a few nights sleeping indoors, and some
small measure of privacy. No more trips into the snow. No more awkward
cramped tents. I'd been lucky, immeasurably lucky, that no one had seen
or noticed anything; it was a blessing beyond measure that our glowering
tentmate had always been so *absent*.

I looked around, still feeling there was something missing.

Clarke ducked through the back door and beckoned at me with his
large gloved hand. "Come and help us with the dogs," he said, keeping
his voice low. He glanced around at the activity inside. "Quick—quiet."
Beside him, in a small, dark boot room, rows of abandoned clothing—
gray and khaki—swayed in the breeze.

Outside, the darkness baffled me, and I blinked—hadn't known it was
so easy to become accustomed to light. There was only a sliver of moon,
and the lights from the huts extended barely a few feet. "Astronomical
twilight," Clarke said briefly, striding down the steps. "In a day or so."

I could see the horizon, and nothing else. Another step towards *true*
dark. I shivered, my boots crunching on the scree.

The German kennels had been built against the lower rocky slopes.
("Probably the same rock as the mountains," Nicholls had said, thoughtfully,
giving it a kick). A long building, waist-height on Clarke, the space inside
was divided into a series of yawning mouths with wire-mesh doors, each
large enough for a single animal. Harry held up a guttering lantern, and
the light danced. He was letting our dogs tug at their leashes, yapping and
hissing—a sound that made my skin crawl; I'd never heard anything like
it. He just stared at the kennels, pressing his other hand to his pale face.
Covering his nose, although nothing in this frozen world smelled very much.

"Harry?"

"I can't bear it," he muttered. "I can't bear it."

The first kennel door was unlatched, moving limply in the faint breeze.
I knelt, and Clarke held the light up above my head.

For a moment it wasn't obvious what I was seeing. The roof had
partly collapsed, snow drifted in. A huddled shape lay at the back of the
little compartment. I took a deep cold breath and crawled in, my shadow
looming huge on the back wall.

It was a dead dog. A big one—perhaps from the Russian stock Randall hadn't been able to afford. It had frozen solid, curled up into a ball, its ribs nearly poking through the leathery gray membrane of its skin. I pressed my lips together, determined not to make a sound, but realized—gradually, as my eyes adjusted—that I felt only pity, as if my body had lost the ability to conjure horror. It had been a long way from the dog deck.

I wouldn't falter—not like Harry.

A growl outside startled me, made me come to my senses. I held my breath as I crawled back out. "It's dead," I said stupidly, and Clarke nodded.

"All of them—there's more," he said. "We need to get them out."

"They won't—" Harry hissed, and his voice was thick, choked. He indicated our own dogs—backing away from the kennels, their hackles raised.

"They'll have to," Clarke said. He looked around the still camp, narrowing his eyes. "We can find somewhere else in the morning."

The morning. I tried to imagine this black-and-white scene under the unforgiving Antarctic sun. Turning to the huts, I saw faces in the windows, distorted by the double panes. It seemed unbelievable that someone had troubled themselves to bring plate glass to the South; the Germans were as unknowable as they were absent. I saw gestures, as the men noticed the fuss our dogs were making—Harry, standing stock still—and the yawning kennel mouths.

"Now," Clarke said, giving Harry a shove. "Let's get on with it."

I crawled into the hole again—reached out—got the body by its collar, and heaved it free with a crackling and splintering of ice. I'd never touched anything dead. Never killed. Perhaps I was the only member of the expedition who hadn't. I coughed, then covered my mouth with my scarf, in case something was lingering in the pin-sharp air. Harry said, quietly, "At least they're not—"

I stared at him; couldn't work out what he meant. But a phrase came to me from one of his letters—*a pale waxy green*—and I remembered all the things Harry had seen. My brothers had been pulled off the battlefield by the stretcher-bearers, taken behind the lines, not left out in the open. Not left to rot slowly into the mud; to slither down bonelessly into the shell craters, faces turning blackened and shapeless with time.

They'd been the lucky ones.

We set to—Clarke and I—with a makeshift tarpaulin graveyard. The German dogs were still leashed, each one tied to a metal bolt, but the leather was brittle, crumbling away. I found myself looking for teeth marks on the leashes, scratches on the walls. Any evidence there'd been a struggle. Any evidence the dogs had fought to get away from their fate. A crawling feeling made its way down my spine.

"Come on, Cooper," Clarke was saying, and by the time I'd reached the end of the kennels, Harry had started to coax and chivvy the reluctant dogs inside. They moaned. Jamieson looked at me with wide ice-blue eyes, and I wanted to pick him up and take him inside the huts with me, just for one night. Just until the Germans returned from whatever mysterious errand had taken them out onto the plateau.

I looked up. Those faces were still in the hut windows. I could see Ellis and Rees, noses pressed against the glass, making them look like trolls. A tall figure that had to be Tarlington at the far end, his pinched face distorted. I couldn't think which was worse: to be out here with the limp pile of frozen dogs—not dogs any sensible expedition would leave behind, even if they had to leave in a hurry—or to be inside, watching our small human shapes in the snow, the endless dark behind.

II

A blast of cold air swept straight through the front door and all the way to the boot room at the rear, making the windows rattle and the stove howl.

"Hey!" Macready shouted, and Ollivar—wiping steam from his glasses and stamping snow from his boots—apologized. The hut smelled like the evening's stew: the last of the ship's pemmican bulked out with lentils and flavored with curry powder. The brown smell had saturated every inch of the common room, as well as the laundry—British and German alike—hanging on washing lines from the beams above. Clarke had spent the last two days making an inventory of what the Germans had left behind: a great deal of candles, clothing, and sundries like ink and photographic plates; a good supply of anthracite coal, but not enough kerosene for the lamps; and no weapons or ammunition at all. But the storeroom on the rocks outside appeared plentiful to me, crammed full of packaged food with cheerful yellow brand names I didn't recognize. "Six months' worth," Macready had said to me with a nudge. "We might as well start eating it."

More men were appearing from every inch of the small building: behind the canvas wall of Staunton's "sick bay" and Randall's room beyond; the warren of pallet-board and crate partitions that housed the rest of us, crammed in like a bird's nest, all the way back to the hut's drafty southeasterly walls. In the boot room the Germans had even left their flag, lying on the floor, covered in tracked dirt. One or two of the men spat, discreetly, but Randall insisted it should be washed, and carefully pressed, so the Germans might see—on their return—we meant no offense.

"Eat up," Clarke said, barging me aside. Maybe casual to him, it was hard enough to make me bite my lip. "You'll take the next watch." I lost my appetite immediately.

He picked up a rifle and passed it to me. "Ever handled one of these?"

I shook my head. It felt unwieldy, far too large for my hands. Looking up, I could see some of the men taking an interest, and I nearly put the wretched thing down immediately.

"You'd only have to point it," Clarke said. "Nothing more." Daily we expected the return of the Germans—the sound of their boots on the porch, harsh voices in foreign tones, the door banging open on its hinges. They'd left civilization in 1917, when the guns still rolled on—when the South Atlantic whaling trade rendered sad-eyed mammals into oil and glycerin and a hundred other things necessary to those guns—to establish the smallest toehold on this bleak coast. To claim this place for the Kaiser. If they still believed us at war—believed us a threat, or an occupying force—we were prepared. Two men on watch around the clock, from the twelve hours of bright white daylight to the varying grays and blues of the twilights. First civil; then nautical; and finally astronomical, nearly as dark as true night itself.

I forced myself to straighten up. Once, I'd have been proud as anything to hold a gun, would have strutted up and down. But my mouth was dry, and I felt like an impostor.

"We'll need every man—or boy—on watch," Clarke said to me. "You're up to it."

Macready picked up my snow helmet from the bench, pulling it ungently over my head and cinching the toggles tight around my neck. He surveyed my dirty hands; bitten fingernails; tanned face. "Now you look the part," he said, punching me in the shoulder. I scowled at him, then grinned.

"Get on with it, Morgan." Clarke turned away.

A babble of voices as the table filled up elbow to elbow. Nicholls was wearing a ridiculous hat with earflaps, rubbing his hands together to get the blood flowing: the Germans had left skis, and he'd been trying to sketch in the barren landscape around us. There was a caved-in glacier tongue that might have made a fine ramp—surely where the *Drygalski* had once landed.

"Cooper," Clarke called. "Watch, if you please."

"No need," Randall said, coming through from the sick bay, tugging his braces up. "Tarlington's out there already."

Clarke looked as if he were about to say something.

"He can shoot," Randall said. "Captain of his school's rifle club."

Clarke shrugged. "All right."

The other men didn't seem to like it. Parker didn't think Tarlington could bring himself to hurt the Hun, and Ellis mimed a fluttery swoon. Randall drew up a chair at the head of the table, shutting them both up with a deep bushy-eyebrowed glare.

None of this gave me confidence, although at least Nicholls showed me how to load the rifle, hold it properly, as I struggled to pull on a damp pair of windproof trousers and my Burberry. He clapped a hand on my back, making me jump. "That jacket is bigger than you, by far."

I opened the door onto a still night. The new moon had not yet appeared. It seemed darker than it should, and I felt very small under that wide, pitiless sky. My sunburn from the plateau had flaked and peeled, leaving raw skin; the cold made my cheeks smart as if they'd been slapped.

The wooden porch ran around the hut like a belt, enclosed by railings, steps down onto the rocks at each door. Faint light spilled through the windows. I paused, blinking, as my eyes adjusted, and thought I could smell the salty frozen sea.

I slung the rifle awkwardly over my shoulder, walking until a dark shape leaning against the front railings became Tarlington. His distinctive hair was hidden by his hood, but the way he held himself, stiff across the shoulders, was instantly recognizable. I opened my mouth. Without turning around, he hissed: "Tread a little softer. How on earth did you find every creaky board on the whole porch?"

I stopped dead, suddenly self-conscious again—I didn't know anything about being on watch.

I reminded myself that neither did he. "Does it matter?"

He turned. It appeared he'd been expecting someone else. He exhaled, softly. "Morgan. You must weigh the least of all of us. How you're making that much noise—"

I scowled at him. "If they don't already know we're here, I hardly think that'll be what does it." I waved my hand at the sledges, under tarpaulin for the night; our dogs, sheltered in a hastily constructed lean-to far from the old German kennels; the sound of voices from the common room, as the chimney exhaled smoke into the clear sky.

"Still, we've set watches," he said. "Randall's orders."

"As if *you* care what Randall thinks."

I made sure to tread particularly loudly as I returned to my post.

Time passed excruciatingly. There was little to see from the back door to the cliffs. The biscuit-case room, grandly called "the bathhouse," consisting of a nail to hang a towel and a tin pan for melted snow. The latrines—one for the men, a larger one for the officers, with a door that locked; I was grateful to be considered *a bit posh*, and given this extra privilege. An abandoned meteorological screen crouched on the slope some distance away. Then rock and boulders, dark hummocks blanketed by drifting snow. The blue-black sky crammed full of stars. Inside, men would be keeping the stove going; playing cards at the common-room table; curling up in their sleeping bags, unaware of the dark bearing down on them outside.

A sense of crushing loneliness came over me, and I shook my head, remembering my duties.

It shouldn't come to that, I told myself—the idea of shooting some-one, down here where there were so few of us, seemed like blasphemy. My gloved hands were suddenly sweaty. I didn't think I'd imagined those gunshots I'd heard on the plateau. I could well believe that grim-faced Liam Clarke—sitting in our common room, eating with his boots off—had shot three of our shipmates. But he was a pragmatic man. He'd made himself a shovel from a food tin; had crawled into the ice to survive; had volunteered on the convoys, when they wouldn't send a fingerless man to the Front. He wouldn't have willingly left their sledge—just like the Germans wouldn't have willingly left those dogs. It didn't make sense.

Tarlington materialized like a tall, slender ghost.

"You—" My heart hammered. "Why on earth did you do that?"

"To prove it could be done. Lord, Morgan, I could practically hear you breathing." He joined me by the railings for a while, scribbling in his notebook. Nicholls had been very excited to see the meteorological screen and the anemometer, which measured wind speed and direction, and I wondered whether we might finally be able to steal a march on the weather. But most of the German equipment was missing or smashed, including a wireless receiver, now well past salvaging.

I tried to play Tarlington at his own game. Once he'd returned to his post and a long, weary hour concluded, I crept delicately around the porch as if playing Grandmother's Footsteps, pausing at every creak of the boards.

No one was there.

At the front of the huts, the plateau stretched off to the mountains, dark knuckles punching up into the stars. I turned around several times, my neck cracking. The storm lantern was still. There was no noise from the dogs.

For a moment I pressed my hand to my mouth, eyes still darting back and forth. Then I shouldered my rifle, hardly daring to breathe. I hadn't heard anything. But I'd been concentrating on sneaking up on Tarlington. All the men inside, all depending on me—

"Tarlington?" I whispered. No reply.

Light danced across the boards as the lantern creaked from side to side. "Tarlington—"

He tapped me on the shoulder from behind.

I swore, a shaky feeling released in all my limbs, and punched him hard in the chest. "That's not funny!"

"Yes it was," he said, smirking. "You, creeping around, loud enough to wake the dead."

"I could have shot you!"

"It seemed unlikely. Your finger's nowhere near the trigger, for a start."

My rifle was still raised. I lowered it sheepishly. Realizing how absurd I must look, I started to laugh.

He looked surprised, and a little hesitant, then gave a low chuckle that didn't quite reach true laughter. "Your face. As if you thought the Germans had arrived to murder us in our beds."

"I was worried about you—"

"I'm touched by your concern, Morgan."

The denial was on the tip of my tongue, but instead I said, "Well, if they'd taken you, they were a short step from taking all of us."

Tarlington nodded, a slow smile on his face.

"Thank you," I said in a rush. "For going after Harry, out there. On the way here. You know."

He looked at me from under his hood. "I'm surprised he's lasted this long, running off into a blizzard like that. None of us have any idea what's out there. A crevasse field. Sudden losses of visibility. Perhaps a whole expedition of dead Germans, buried under the snow."

"That's stupid."

"Is it? We don't have the slightest idea what happened to them—why they would abandon the only shelter in thousands of miles."

Randall expected them back before winter; said it would be a matter of days before we'd be slapping one another on the back, sharing our stories. We'd relate the doom of the *Fortitude*; the Germans would reassure us that their own ship, the *Drygalski*, was waiting in the pack or a snug little inlet just out of sight. A second route off this continent. Randall said it with unshakable conviction: a few days more.

But I pictured the huts when we'd first reached them, and shivered.

"A whole company of live Germans, perhaps, waiting out there in the snow." Tarlington was almost talking to himself. "The Hun. Ready to fight us tooth and nail for this place, outrage the bodies of the dead, all that nonsense you heard in the War. Maybe this is a *trap*."

He picked up his rifle, very deliberately, searching my face. "Maybe I'm in league with them—that's the sort of thing you lot think, isn't it?"

The blood thundered in my ears. He wouldn't shoot. Wouldn't dare. Clarke had trusted him with a gun. And Randall didn't believe him a threat—despite everything.

I hardly think he'll be brought low by bloody no-fight Tarlington.

Tarlington's teeth flashed white and wolfish in the moonlight as he smiled, bitterly. A whine came from the dogs in their makeshift kennels— tentative and thin, as if uncertain whether anyone was listening. "Come on," he said. "You'd scare penguins at least, soldier boy."

It didn't make me feel any better.

III

"Well," Randall said. "Well, it's time to count these our winter quarters. They're out there somewhere—mark my words, they're still out there! But they don't show any sign of returning before the dark. Lucky for us, eh?"

The sun had a halo, three brilliant rings like a target, and the daylight was so bright it hurt my eyes. I slipped off my hat, rubbed my short greasy hair. Although winter seemed far away, I knew it was waiting to fall like a hammer. We'd had an untroubled week, save a squally gust of wind that blew down our lanterns, whipped up tarpaulins, danced around camp then departed again. From the confusion that followed—men spilling out into the cold night—the Germans might as well have been launching ordnance at us.

Randall had joined us on watch after that. Those nights were a great treat, despite his terrible singing. "Lads," he'd say in his growly voice, "lads, let's have a song—"

"Maybe not," Clarke said quietly. He leaned against the porch railings with his bare arms folded; had already debriefed each of us individually. I'd felt that the lack of incident disappointed him.

His interruption made Randall pause. I held my breath, could see others raising their eyebrows. "Winter quarters, yes," Randall continued, as if he and Clarke had been in conversation. "We're well-stocked. And they can't have gone far"—a tiny moment where it hung in the air, and I could feel the German kennels looming at my back—"so the *Drygalski* might not be far, either." He gave a nod to Nicholls. "We'll see them sooner or later, and I know Karlmann well—a cautious man. We'll be getting out of here together. We just have to sit tight until then!"

Some of the men muttered at the idea of joining up with the Hun, despite Randall's claim of friendship; he turned his scowl on them, cracked his knuckles—appallingly menacing, coming from Randall—and silence fell.

"We'll keep up the watches," Clarke said. "And make this place safe for winter. There's plenty of work to be done." He looked as if he were going to say something else. I'd overheard him speaking to Rees about the wraparound design of the porch, with its windows on all sides; features that would make the huts shockingly cold in the depths of winter.

Randall shot him a look. "Yes, I suppose there is. But we've ended up somewhere decent, and got it to ourselves to boot. I bet some of you thought we'd never make it!" He smiled his animal smile, half up and half down.

A laugh. "Three cheers for Australis!" A ragged cheer went up, for the immediate danger that seemed to have passed us by, and I joined in. But the light flashed off the hut windows, pitiless and fresh, and something about the after-image—burned into my eyes, shimmering like a ghost—made my smile falter.

"And the ship?" Staunton said, unrolling Duncan's damp and stiffening bedsheets over the railings. They were changed daily: Duncan sometimes shivered, teeth chattering, as though he were caught in a blizzard. The next moment he'd be sweaty, glassy-eyed. "Just keep him quiet," I'd heard Clarke growl to Staunton. "If nothing else—" It was apparent the Germans had their own surgeon, who'd left behind his anatomy books, pincers, needles, and saws. But nothing of use; the burns on Duncan's limbs had, slowly and inexorably, turned bad.

There was an embarrassed silence. No one had talked about the ship for quite some time.

"Forget the ship," Boyd said. "She's gone. And we barely made it here. The dogs are played out, the sledges—"

Unbidden, our gazes turned to Laurence, his mustache grimy with engine oil. A motor sledge had been found in one of the outbuildings, tightly wrapped, like a Christmas gift from our hosts—ours, of course, had gone down with the ship. Hundreds of pounds of expedition money; probably Harry's money.

Boyd folded his arms, shaking his head. "Winter's on our doorstep. You saw the conditions out there."

Randall held up his hand. "I *won't* split the party," he growled, although no one had suggested it. "D'you hear me? I won't do it. We'll stay together, and wait for the Germans. We'll be safe here."

"Not yet," Clarke said. "We need to reinforce the camp. Put up windbreaks, shutter the windows. Dig in. We don't know how long we'll be staying."

"Perhaps we should install window boxes too, eh? A nice surprise, when they get back!" There was a laugh. "All right, all right. Let's preserve some of this fine Hanover glazing. Clear up the mess they left—"

Glancing behind me as I set to work, I saw Laurence and Clarke speaking quietly and confidentially. Neither seemed entirely convinced that sledges wouldn't be needed: "It never pays to get comfortable," I'd heard Clarke say, darkly. And Harry, too, was harnessing up our dogs—had been running them in teams around the huts, day after day, exercising and encouraging them for a journey that might never come. He'd seemed very restless since the night we arrived. A watchfulness. A nervous energy that made me uneasy.

"Do you really think they'll be back?" I asked Boyd, struggling to lift the wireless frame, which had been dumped outside to become rimed with ice.

"I would. Wouldn't you?"

I looked around. We were a small anthill of activity on a frozen wasteland. The sun flashed as a skua flew out to sea. Frost glittered on the timbers, and we were fast approaching the last days of autumn. The

Germans couldn't have meant to be gone this long. They'd even left their boots, lined up neatly under their coats. I scuffed mine against the rocks, wondered what would make me abandon them.

"They'll be back," Boyd said shortly, shifting the weight towards him. "It's nice to suppose we're *safe* here. But we don't know where they went, or when they'll be back, and these supplies won't last two expeditions for the winter. Then it'll be us or them, and I know I won't be starved out. We need to be pretty bloody wary of throwing our lot in with the Boche, that's all I'll say."

Nicholls came past with his skis; Boyd broke off, and we carried on working in silence. Inside, muffled exclamations as men claimed their bunks; the high-pitched scraping sound of glass-studded crates being dragged across the floor. "Laurence!" Staunton called. "Randall says put that down, if you please, and come and have a look at the gasworks—"

I shaded my eyes. There was a small, narrow darkroom beside the front door, with the copper pipes and drums of an acetylene-gas plant, to light the huts through winter with a blazing cool light. At the other extreme, hammer blows made the huts shudder as Rees started to reattach the discarded shutters; we'd found them some distance away, as if they'd been whisked through the air. I'd thought I'd feel glad to keep the winds out, and with them my half-theories about the dogs and their *madness of storms*. It would be dark outside, but inside there would be light and conversation, whiling away the hours until the Germans returned—or winter passed.

I'd thought I'd feel glad. Instead, I had the strange sense we were shutting ourselves in.

IV

I was woken before dawn.

A movement of air, and the sound of a door opening. My shoulders and arms were suddenly cold: I slept in my Jaeger combination underwear with a jumper over the top, and my sweat had dried stiff overnight. I exhaled, trying to see my own breath.

The Germans had divided the huts into smaller sleeping compartments, some barely large enough to turn around in, and Harry and I had been kept with Tarlington: no one else had wanted him. Our new "Nursery," right next to the boot room door, was dark as the grave when the daylight went down and the shutters were closed; our tarpaulin curtain blocked some of the smoke but very few sounds. I could hear men snoring, creating a faint vibration in our connecting wall of wooden Venesta cases. Harry stirred in the bunk beneath me, fighting invisible battles in his sleep.

A thud. Someone was outside. It didn't sound like one of the night-watchmen—rather, like someone blundering around in the dark.

I pulled up the blankets and tried to go back to sleep, but it was no use: I was wide awake, my heart racing. Footsteps on the porch outside—two sets of them—hurrying. Someone called out, and a muffled curse came from our neighbors in the "Coal Hole" compartment. The laborious sound of one of the stokers turning over in his heavy sleeping bag. I held my breath, but no one went to the door.

I shook my head, steeled myself to pull back the covers. It seemed a long way to the floor before I could jam my legs into trousers, my feet into boots, pull on my shapeless Burberry tunic, and rub my hands sharply against my arms to retain a few degrees of warmth. I tried to persuade myself that I was going outside; my chilly limbs rebelled. I knocked the fuel-can lantern hooked up beside Tarlington's box bed. He didn't stir.

"Jonathan?" Harry said drowsily.

"Go back to sleep," I whispered, and ducked out into the common room, where a faint light was burning in the galley. The open door of the boot room looked like a large black mouth filled with jagged teeth. Rubbing my eyes, the teeth turned into our jackets, swaying in the breeze, empty and slack, like the shells of dead men. The external door should have been bolted at night—Clarke had insisted on fitting bolts—but chill air blew through from the outside world.

Someone appeared in that second doorway.

I sucked in a breath. It took me a moment to recognize Ollivar, the light gleaming off his little round glasses: he was so wrapped up they looked like a beetle's eyes.

"Morgan," he said. "Out to use the facilities?"

I craned my neck to see around him. He wasn't carrying his rifle, and I could hear distant voices in the snow. "Who's out there?"

"Stay inside," he said. Then shook his head. "Well—I suppose you might take a look."

The porch had turned orange, as if dawn were not far off, and I assumed civil twilight was on its way. But as I paused, it shifted like a kaleidoscope, bright light and smeared patches of darkness. I gasped.

The South had taken off its mask at last: the eastern sky was on fire. The mountains wore crowns of red flames, shimmering and flickering like beacons in the night. A corona radiating out from the distant peaks, like a child's drawing of sunbeams. The aurora australis.

The back of my neck prickled. I felt very insignificant, and very vulnerable. It was bitterly cold, the orange cast of the aurora glimmering on the frost and icicles of the porch, like icy fingers reaching across the distance to us, setting the huts ablaze.

"It's all right," Ollivar said hurriedly. "I'll fetch Staunton. Go straight back to bed—promise me?"

I remembered the sounds I'd heard: someone blundering around in the snow. Dragging my gaze from the mountains and their unearthly fire, I could see two figures on the rocky slope that marked the limits of camp. Dark stick figures. One walking, the other scrambling to catch up. I followed instantly, cinching my tunic tight.

When I walked out past the porch—crossing its barrier of lantern-light—the wind had stopped, and all was silent. I found myself holding my breath as my boots crunched through the rocks and snow, as if the figures would dissolve away at any moment. In the darkness it was hard to gauge distance: I thought I might walk for miles without catching them, but in an instant Clarke was looming over me, casting a very long shadow. Blocking my way with an outstretched arm. "Don't wake him!"

A stray gust of wind plucked at my hood, whispering in my numb ears. The shape in front of us had stopped walking, was standing frozen like a statue. I shook my head at Clarke—"I won't"—and tiptoed forwards. It didn't notice my approach.

Randall. He was barefoot and undressed: he slept in just his combinations, saying our reindeer-hide sleeping bags were *the best in the business*;

that was the slogan he'd agreed on with our sponsors. His dark blue eyes were open, distant. The aurora glimmered orange over his face, making a distant hissing noise in the frozen air, as if it were filling him up.

Australis Randall. Named for the Southern Lights—now I was seeing him under them. A homecoming of sorts. My chest swelled painfully, and it was hard to breathe.

"What's wrong with him?"

"Go back inside," Clarke said roughly, shouldering past me. "You won't be any use carrying him."

I opened my mouth, winced, feeling the cold to my bones. Randall's naked feet. His burning eyes. I stumbled back to the huts and used the latrine in bitter cold, my teeth chattering. I tried to crawl back into bed, but my heart thumped as if I'd run a race.

Macready was clattering around by the stove. I made some excuse about nightmares, restless sleep, and he accepted my offer of early-morning help.

Randall had looked so terribly *absent*. I felt I'd intruded on something private, and wished I'd turned over and stayed in bed: the aurora would come back soon, might be our constant companion over winter. I kept stealing glances at the easterly windows, looking for those tormenting lights, until I deliberately put them at my back.

"No one's been resting easy." Macready took a moment to cough into a grimy handkerchief. "I get an hour or two here and there, but—it's like something in the air. I grew up in the Highlands, lad. Miles from bloody anywhere, and in the winter all the roads would be shut. Pure deadly ice. There was no way to get a doctor out, unless they wanted to go riding through the snow—nor a priest nor coroner. My aunt died when I was about ten years old, and it took a week before anyone could come and pronounce it. We shut her in the front parlor, and tried to go about our business."

The boot room door creaked open, and I turned to see Randall being brought in. He was covered with Clarke's coat, limp as a drowned man. He opened his mouth, formed a word. With chills down my spine, I recognized it instantly.

Charlie.

I fumbled with the knife. Put it down before I cut myself.

Macready nudged me in the back. "Come on," he said. "Anyway. We tried our best, you see, but there was something about the house, while she was lying there. It felt wrong. No one could sleep."

I thought of Harry: how he fought with his nightmares, sheets drenched in sweat. "Are you talking about a—ghost?"

I knew how childish it sounded.

Macready laughed. "Hardly. I'm not that type, Morgan. No such thing. But something makes men uneasy, particularly when they're cut off like this."

His words hung in the still morning air. *Something makes men uneasy.*

Randall's bunk in "The Clubhouse" was accessible only through the canvas curtain of the sick bay—he'd insisted he should be the one to take it. Duncan sometimes made muffled sounds, although he now struggled to open his mouth. He'd never be handsome again; the fire had seen to that. Every day Randall would have to pass his bed. Every day Randall would be reminded the expedition had failed, horribly, and we were at the mercy of strangers.

"Do you think Duncan will die?" My voice sounded small.

Macready nodded, light glimmering off the pink scars on his scalp. I'd never asked him about them: a man was entitled to his secrets. "It'll be a mercy when he does, all things considered."

I found myself agreeing with him.

V

Clarke came to find me after breakfast. The front door was open to let out smoke, and work continued outside. Everything had iced up overnight. The mountains seemed to have advanced across the plateau towards us: a mirage in the frost-crammed air, a Fata Morgana. It was impossible to tell how far away they were.

"Morgan." I followed Clarke wordlessly around the porch. The boards creaked and popped under the weight of his boots. There were dark circles under his eyes, and he rubbed his hand over his face, staring off towards the construction of his windbreaks.

"Is Randall—"

"He's sleeping," he said flatly. "There's nothing wrong with him. Just frost-nip."

"I didn't mean—"

"No," Clarke said, turning with some effort to look at me. "I don't suppose you did. You haven't told anyone, have you?"

I shook my head. "He was just sleepwalking." It felt wholly inadequate.

Clarke leaned against the railings and sighed. "Just sleepwalking. Exhaustion from getting us here. Nothing more."

I looked at him sharply, thinking about the words he'd almost used. I'd heard, of course, of *nervous exhaustion*. The euphemism they used for shell shock. But that seemed impossible—unthinkable—of Randall. We were counting on him to know what to do, how to get us out of here.

"No one needs to know. All right? We're all tired, and worried."

"I won't tell anyone."

"Good," he said, and looked straight at me. "We're on our own, Morgan."

On our own. It sounded like a door closing. I thought of the kennel doors frozen shut, the German dogs left inside, abandoned to their fate. We'd pulled down those weathered planks, broken them up with saw and crowbar, and all that was left was a shadow on rock, gradually being erased by the drift.

"Something—happened here, didn't it?"

He didn't answer. Just rubbed his rough beard with the palm of his gloves, making a rasping noise.

"We need to stay together as an expedition. If we lose morale—terrible things can happen. Men turning on each other. Fighting their best friends for the last scrap of biscuit. Arguments can go bad, very bad, if there isn't a proper—order—to things. The moment they think Randall—"

"I wouldn't!"

Clarke raised his eyebrows. "You went to Boyd, didn't you?" he said. "You and Cooper. About Tarlington. Look how that nearly turned out. We can't afford to have any more rumors."

I looked down, not trusting myself to say anything. My ears stung as if I'd been smacked.

Clarke softened his tone. "We just can't afford it. Not now, not here.

We need to get on with it—the business of survival. It's a good thing those mutineers left when they did, or we'd have to deal with them too."

I thought of the tent out on the plateau. The claustrophobic half-light. The wind whipping around us. Those gunshots in the distance. It was what they'd have done in France, after all. Deserters. Traitors. Dreadful or not, it was necessary. And I might have to shoot someone myself, one day, if the Germans returned, and Randall was wrong about their intentions. It felt wild and terrible to fight a man for his food, even a perfect stranger. But if it came down to it—I knew I might have to.

Clarke loomed over me, blocking out the sunlight.

I matched his tone. "I understand."

Clarke smiled, the grooves around his eyes narrowing into the tributaries of tiny rivers. "Good," he said. "I knew you would. Randall has only one thing on his mind, and that's the welfare of us all."

Clarke was lying: what was on Randall's mind was his son. *Charlie*. Left for dead on some faraway battlefield. His memory had followed Randall here.

"There's talk going around." Clarke rubbed the side of his neck. "The Germans. That this is some sort of—trap. Some of the men are spoiling for a fight, can't be trusted not to do something stupid. If you hear it getting out of hand—"

"I'd tell you."

"Good," he said. "I'll be counting on you, Morgan."

Clarke clamped his hand on my shoulder as I turned to leave. For such an icy day, I felt quite warm. It was the longest conversation we'd ever had.

VI

The huts became hemmed in by an obsessive maze of windbreaks, closing off our line of sight to the plateau, creating shadows and cramped corners, not a single one a right angle. The wind whistled around them with small shrieks and moans. And the doors and shutters were bolted every night.

"Where do you think they've gone?" I whispered to Harry as we bundled ourselves into our windproofs, covering every inch of skin. "There's just—nothing out there."

And nowhere else to go.

He gave me a sideways glance that I couldn't quite read. Tarlington interrupted in his scratchy voice: "You'd better hope there's *something* out there."

I clenched my teeth. He was poring over an anatomy book and a dog-eared German dictionary in the thin shaft of light coming through the Nursery shutters, legs hanging over the side of his bed. It was breakfast time: as usual, no one would tell him.

"If you're such a keen shot, you should come."

He shook his head. "I don't think I'm welcome—I'm a scientist, re-member, not one of you dashing young things."

I took in a long, even breath, and he gave me a half-smile—I fought the urge to snatch the book from his hands. We worked from dawn until dusk, which seemed to come half an hour earlier each day. There were dogs to be exercised, windbreaks to be maintained, snow to be shoveled, stoves to be cleaned. Tarlington contributed nothing to our survival. He'd set himself up in the small cold locker outside, where the frozen gray spoils of German hunting parties hung from the ceiling on rusty hooks. Although offered the disused darkroom next to the galley, he'd refused.

He didn't seem to have grasped that science was useless.

"Shouldn't you be out in your cell?" Harry muttered.

"It's actually a good deal warmer here than it was—there," he said faintly, turning back to his book.

"Oh, look—Jonathan." Harry pulled me aside as we ducked into the common room, seeing the look I was giving him. "Whoever he is. You just can't forget he was one of *them*. Even if Randall doesn't mind—or Nicholls—plenty of us do. You used to, as well."

I jammed my hat down over my ears and strode towards the door, where Boyd was waiting. I'd once thought Antarctica a barren desert, white and empty, but that wasn't entirely true. Birds populated the empty shoreline to our west. Skuas, petrels of all sizes. We needed to hunt while we still could.

The table was filling up for breakfast. Nicholls said, "We'll save some for you!" and Ellis grumbled, "Every man for himself." Laughter broke out; they'd be following in our footsteps, heading to the cliffs to build a lookout tower. From the sea ice, it was impossible to see the huts, or any signs of our occupation. If the Germans' ship was still in the pack, she might pass us—leave us here—unknowing. We'd be out of sight and out of mind.

Randall stumped to the head of the table, a little unsteady on his frost-nipped feet. He'd have to watch them carefully if he wanted them healed by spring—and being frostbitten once, I knew, made you more and more susceptible. The killing cold worked its way into your bones.

"Look out for seals," Clarke called.

Boyd raised his eyebrows. "Chance would have it."

While I didn't relish the thought of stinking of seal blubber, it would at least be another source of fuel; Clarke was already such a miser with kerosene and candles, I wondered what the middle of June would be like. The darkness all-consuming. The huts lit by stove-light, men huddling in the common room against the night outside. Feeling my way out to the latrines by running my mittens along a rope line, as blind and defenseless as something that crawled underground.

Randall was certain there'd be a ship, I told myself.

Climbing out of the valley towards the coast was a long, exhausting trudge; Nicholls and the mountaineers were adept on skis, but we'd never learned. The sun wavered uncertainly on the horizon, like a plain girl at a dance. I kept looking around, trying to get my bearings in the spare blue-and-gray landscape. But ice and snow covered everything, making it impossible to see what lay beneath. Harry spoke little, and Boyd not at all.

When we stopped, the salt-fresh sea breeze made me suck in a deep breath, trying to clear my lungs of all the smoke and sweat and cooking smells. The horizon fell away as a straight black line, and the air was a beautiful white, no birds in sight. Harry unfastened his jacket and pulled off his overgloves to retrieve the binoculars, wrapped in leather to stop his skin blistering on the cold metal. I hadn't seen him using them since the ship. I peeled my scarf off my chin, my neck muscles straining as I stared up at the great cathedral dome of the sky.

"There," Harry said, passing the binoculars—still around his neck—to Boyd, who had to stand a little on tiptoes.

"Are you sure?"

Harry nodded. "Behind that hummock."

Boyd looked again. "Well, if you say so." His tone made it quite clear he could see nothing. Harry crouched down, flattening himself against the ground. Unnecessary, as the birds didn't seem to have much fear of humans. With his binoculars and rifle, though, it was as if I could see another Harry superimposed on this one: crawling out of the gun pits for reconnaissance, everything sepia and gray under thick cloud, too dark for planes to fly.

"Here." I jumped as Boyd thrust the other rifle into my hands. "Have a go after Cooper: if Clarke's going to insist on putting you on watch, I'd rather you learn to shoot."

"It'll be a waste—"

"Scared?" His tone was so scathing I bit the inside of my cheek to stop myself answering.

"It *is* a waste," Harry murmured apologetically, not taking his eyes off the birds, and I felt the blood rush to my face. He knew very well I'd never fired a gun in my life. I wished he were better at bluffing—just for once.

"You can talk," I hissed, shouldering the rifle as Nicholls had shown me. Since my conversation with Clarke, I'd been out on watch more often. I wanted to pull my weight; earn my place, as I'd always intended. And to be taunted by Harry, of all people, about my reluctance to shoot—

"What?"

"You flinch," I whispered. "Harry, you know you do."

"I do not!"

"I've seen you."

"You have *no idea*—"

"Oh, shut up, both of you," Boyd said softly. "Here we go."

A turn in the wind. Harry took the first shot, and my criticism proved just: he did flinch, as if scared of the noise—the *crack* that echoed around the hummocks and made the birds erupt into flight. Suddenly I could see the display of their black underdown: three snow petrels, invisible on the ground.

"Go!" Boyd shouted. I squeezed the trigger, and the butt of the rifle came hammering back.

A bird fell to earth, struggling, moving crablike in agonies. I rubbed my collarbone, wincing, pulled back the bolt—and looked around, trying to stifle the grin that threatened to write itself large across my face.

"Winged it!" Harry didn't sound at all pleased. "Really, Jonathan—that was something."

"I'll say." Boyd squinted at me. "But it's too big for you, isn't it? The recoil. A small lad like you."

Harry said, "Oh, for God's—" and stood up, putting his rifle down on the snow. I ignored him.

"Stay there, Cooper," Boyd ordered. "Morgan, see if you can finish it off. Try this."

He reached under his jacket and pulled out his Webley service revolver. I'd seen them enough, although never handled one. They were on mantelpieces all over England, tucked into bedside tables: the remnants of the War, brought into our homes as souvenirs or talismans. My father had put Rufus's on display; Harry had left his behind. Boyd handled the revolver reverently, wrapping my fingers around it, dwarfing them with his roughed-up greasy gloves.

I swallowed, lowering the pitch of my voice. "I don't think I can—"

"Nonsense," he said. "It was the size working against you. Try it now." He steadied me from behind, shockingly intimate; no grown man had ever held me so closely. Like everyone on the expedition, he smelled of sweat. Like everyone, I'd stopped caring.

The gun was already loaded, but I didn't remark on it. I reached out under his control, cocked the hammer, took aim. A few shots—staccato against the rocks—before Harry, looking sullenly through his binoculars, called: "That's it."

"See?" Boyd patted my shoulder. "You'll do a damn sight better with that."

I stood up awkwardly, nodded my thanks, again squashing down that light-headed grin. The clean air was expanding my chest, making me feel bigger—but my arms and legs were all pins and needles, horribly cold, and I grimaced as the blood rushed back.

Harry retrieved the bird, held it up to me like a relic; I examined the carcass, its jet-black eyes beginning to dull as the light left them. The image of the German dogs—stiff, balled, as if sleeping—crowded into my mind, and I nearly dropped the revolver. Clumsily, I offered it back to Boyd. My five bullets were a waste, and my trousers and coat were heavy with crackling ice. Come winter, there'd be no place for shooting lessons.

"Keep it." Boyd waved me away. "I want to try you on a moving target. Some of our best snipers were your age, you know—steady lads, good in a spot. You could grow into that gun."

In the wardroom, months ago, he'd said those boys *barely made a mouthful for the Boche*. His views had changed—maybe I had changed too. For a moment I thought of my own father: pipe smoke; arms folded; that stiff, square set of his shoulders. Determined to bear the loss of his children, just to show how well it could be done. I'd hated him for that—it had always seemed as if some part of him was eager to experience the worst. "This is War," he'd say, and I could hear the capital letter.

He'd lost another child now. I looked up at Boyd. "Let's hope you'll never need it for anything larger," he said. Harry's mouth twisted, and it looked like he was going to say something. But he just gave me a small, tight smile that obviously required effort.

On our return journey, a dark, skinny finger that looked—from a distance—as tall as Nelson's Column turned out to be the backbone of Nicholls's lookout tower. The timber frame had been sunk into sheeny refrozen ice, pointing at the sky, standing stark against the sheared-off glacier tongue like a warning. There were scrapes and drag marks in the snow, but no sign of its invisible architects.

I turned and looked out to sea, shielding my eyes. Tiny cracks marbled the farthest ice, thin and dark as the veins on an old woman's hand. Everything else was glittering, sharp—dead white. In the distance the bergs made a low, untroubled *boom* as the current crowded them in around the continent, settling them into place. The faint pinpricks of movement didn't make the scene any less desolate, or make me feel any less insignificant against its wild expanse.

I could see why the lookout post had been abandoned. The vast Weddell Sea had frozen shut for winter, and there was no ship in sight.

No *Drygalski*. If the Germans were still on the continent, they were as trapped as we were.

Turning back to the huts, the top of the anemometer was just visible on its pole, spinning around with its cups gleaming copper in the dying sun, surrounded by miles and miles of nothingness. It would be dark before we returned, and our boots on the frozen porch would sound exactly like gunshots in the night.

VII

I polished the service revolver with mineral oil, working it carefully into all its secret places. After days of practice, I could take down a skua; I still begrudged the ammunition, but Boyd had saved three full boxes from the chaos of the *Fortitude*. "Enough," he'd said roughly. "You take it. And keep it on you."

I was on second watch, and it wasn't worth trying for a few hours' sleep. The huts were quiet after our sing-song, but there were usually some night owls in the "lounge" beside the stove, under the hanging laundry: Macready mended socks in return for cigarettes, and Staunton wrote bad poetry about the English countryside. Sundown came in the afternoons now, the air so dry and cold that fur trimmings on hats and gloves crackled with static, like the aurora coming to earth.

Nicholls stuck his head through the door and asked for a cup of tea. He'd swapped places with Harry, who seemed increasingly reluctant to be on watch after dark. Perhaps my comment about his shooting had hit home, and I was sorry; he couldn't help it.

"You should get some sleep," I'd told him, looking at his pale drawn face.

"Don't you think I'm trying?" he'd snapped.

I rarely saw Nicholls inside, although he'd found nothing in the snow, not a single harness or boot, that pointed to the Germans. They were . . . gone. Vanished, leaving nothing but a nagging uncertain hope behind. *A ship will come*, we were told. Whether the lost *Drygalski*—which might already be at the bottom of the Weddell Sea—or a German relief ship.

The possibility of that relief ship had made Randall frown hard at Captain Hvalfangeri, I remembered. It hadn't seemed anything like certain.

Get through the winter, we were told. Our windbreaks made the wind scream unpredictably, and Laurence had looked gloomily at the acetylene-gas plant, seemed pessimistic about his chances of lighting the place up.

Nicholls, though: his good humor never seemed to waver. "A good outdoors life," he'd say; deep grooves appeared around his eyes when he took off his snow goggles.

Handing him his tea, I glanced towards the Nursery. The wind raced inside at the least opportunity, and our curtain did nothing to stop the icy blasts whenever the doors were opened. A laugh from the corner: Ollivar and Holmes were playing a game of consequences with paper torn from one of the unreadable German books lining the shelves.

I walked quietly through. Harry was a small dark ball in bed, our shutters open to the night outside. They were meant to be bolted after twilight fell, but I'd noticed—on more than one occasion—the Nursery's pair left open, exposing the glass to the chill black air. "Very funny," I muttered: the stokers must have been playing tricks on us again.

It was the first night of *true* night, and the sheer depth of the darkness made me dizzy. The aurora was just over the horizon, colors shifting across Harry's blankets. The movement was erratic, organic—like watching the waves on a beach, sucking and eddying and erasing the sand.

"Jonathan?" Harry murmured drowsily. "Outside?"

Harry used to talk in his sleep. I knew because Rufus would make fun of him in the mornings, pretending that he'd given away all his secrets—such as they were. Cigarettes nabbed from the warehouse fore-man's office. Girls from the Catholic school on the quay. All as innocent as Harry himself. This Harry, though, had curls stuck to the pillow with sweat; he'd refused to hack his hair short with me. His hand lolled over the side of the bed, as if trying to reach out to something.

I bent down to pick it up and place it back under the covers, stopped myself with a grimace. Such a little thing. But the easy physical familiarity we'd once had was gone.

The Nursery seemed very empty, and I realized Tarlington hadn't been in the common room either. I'd heard scraping chairs and boots, squeaking bunks, soft murmurs, and now there was no one left at the long table; just that lonely chess set, still a few moves away from check. I was sure I'd seen him after dinner, hauling a pail of hot water from the stove towards the door. The first of several: he'd been yelled at for letting the heat out, and Boyd had pushed past him to get to the sick bay, a long, hostile look passing between them.

I checked the boot room pegs. His fancy greatcoat was gone. It was easily thirty degrees below. I couldn't think why Tarlington would choose to be outside.

I thought—just for a second—about waking Harry. Quashed it down.

Sitting at the table, I forced myself to take a deep breath. I wished the shutters didn't make the room so dark: it was somehow worse to have the auroral colors half-glimpsed, green giving way to red, like a child coloring in the sky. I heard Clarke shift on the decking, and exhaled quietly. It was a powerfully comforting sound.

Then I heard him get up. A short conversation between two muffled voices. The front door opened, the aurora making a crown of fire out of Tarlington's hair.

"Where have you been?"

"It doesn't matter," he said quietly. "Help me with this, please."

His coat was unbuttoned. When I finally made myself move, he'd already shrugged it off. The arms of his jumper underneath were wet and dark, part-frozen, and it took me a few moments to see that they weren't covered in tar—or soot. The spatters looked bloody. My stomach lurched, but I couldn't look away.

"I need more warm water," he said. "I don't want to take my skin off."

A sound outside made me jump, and he gave me a despairing look. "Hell, Morgan—" He glanced at the other curtains and partitions leading off the common room. Soon Boyd would leave the officers' quarters—the drafty "Whitechapel Tenements"—and join me on watch. The thought of him folding his scarred arms, furrowing his brow, undid my paralysis.

Tarlington's jumper was stuck to the long fingerless mittens underneath, and needed to be peeled off. He stood very still, watching me through half-open eyes, like a cat. His damp clothes steamed. Although Macready had managed to fashion a smoky coal burner out of an old fuel can—

saying unassumingly that it was a typical Antarctic trick—Tarlington's makeshift laboratory would be very dark and very cold.

I chewed at my lip until it became too much: once again it was night, and Tarlington was prowling the edges of the lantern-light.

"Where on earth have you been?"

"Trying to find some answers. Finding none, as ever."

He pulled the jumper over his head. Underneath, his shirtsleeves were brownish against his freckled skin, and a shallow cut ran from his wrist to the crook of his elbow, parting the fabric like a fin in water.

"Not all of it's mine," he said, seeing me stare. "And not all of it's blood!" A fastidious twist to his mouth. "The knife slipped, that's all."

I looked at him in horror. Our dogs—our remaining dogs—were vital and excitable, perfectly healthy. My stomach clenched. I strained to hear them, but no sounds came.

"Not, not them," he said hastily. "Of course not." He took a damp cloth off me and dabbed at the ragged cut, hissing a little, then wrang it out. Blood bloomed in the water, like mud disturbed on the bottom of a pond. "I'm meant to be a scientist. I thought I could work out—what happened to the German dogs."

He sat down ungracefully. "I hid one of the bodies—thawed it out this evening." A small flicker of his lips told me it had been a long and unpleasant task. I lowered myself onto the bench opposite, trying not to look at what had washed out of his sleeves, trying not to ask how long those dogs had been dead. "I thought we should know how it died. If something spreads to our own dogs—"

I remembered Tarlington protesting when we reused the wood from the kennels to make windbreaks, saying it should be burned, in case of disease, and someone hissing at him to *shut his fucking mouth*: he was the last person to talk about burning things.

"What happened?" I whispered. We were pressed close together, knee to knee. His wrists were very white and very slender.

"I don't know," he said. "But—well. I don't think it was sick. At least, not in the sense of having any discernable illness. I think it starved to death." The stove flickered. The movement caught my eye, making me take a small sharp breath. "They just stayed in the kennels and starved."

Tarlington rubbed his hands through his hair. "You saw them, Morgan. Do you think they fought, or just . . . gave up?"

I'd looked for signs of a struggle: signs that the dogs had tried to chew through their leashes, break open their kennel doors, escape their darkening prison. But there were none. Like a command to *sit*—and *stay*—had been taken to its logical conclusion.

I shook my head, and he seemed to guess. "I don't know of any dog acting against its instincts like that."

A shudder unfolded itself languidly down my spine. I found myself listening, desperately, for the sound of Clarke outside—needing to be reassured there was someone watching over us. Clarke had made windbreaks; seemed to mistrust this place. Randall, on the other hand, thought us safe for winter, though the winds—

"What are you thinking, Morgan?"

I hesitated. I didn't think I could bear to have Tarlington scoff at me. I remembered how Randall had snapped at him: *You're meant to be a scientist.*

"Nothing. Does Randall know?"

Tarlington gave a small, surprised laugh, looked down at his hands. "As if he'd be interested, when they're dead and no use to him. I'm not to tell anyone else, but—well, you were here. Cooper, though—he would have gone snooping, trying to find me with arsenic in hand, or goodness knows what."

"He wouldn't—" I started, then stopped myself. Drummed my fingers, very softly, on the table.

Tarlington's mouth twisted. "Precisely."

I stood up, pushing the table away. The bench made a long scraping noise against the floorboards, and he hushed me furiously. I looked at Tarlington's bloody sleeves. "You'll need another shirt."

"You don't have to," he said faintly.

The Nursery was darker than before, and smelled of body heat and damp. I felt my way to Harry's kit bag. His clothes were dirty; all of us were dirty. But at the very least we could have Tarlington in someone else's dirty clothes, rather than his own bloodstained ones. Clarke had put his trust in me. I could keep a secret.

I hugged the shirt to my chest, quashing down the image of Tarlington out there in the dark, bent over another dead dog. We were stuck with him now—whatever he was.

Harry turned over, made a deep groaning noise. I did put my hand on his shoulder then, telling myself he wouldn't know it was me. And I was completely right. "Rufus," Harry whispered. "They're here . . . out . . ."

The hairs on the back of my neck stood up. I thought of what Harry had said to his parents, refusing to be taken out of the lines, refusing to be carried to safety: "The Morgans are here, and will look out for me." An impossible promise—clearly something said by someone who'd say anything—but the way he groaned made me remember it now. I could hear the blood pounding in my ears, feel the darkness of the Nursery and the Antarctic night bearing down on me.

"Harry," I said. My mouth was so dry. "Wake up."

"I'm so sorry," Harry mumbled. "God, Rufus! I'm so sorry for everything."

"Harry!" I shook him—I couldn't bear it. But he was impossible to wake. In the distance, deep red lights flickered.

"It's coming closer," a voice said behind me, and I sucked in air as a figure appeared in the doorway.

Tarlington. "The aurora," he said. "It's coming closer. Something to do with the magnetism, or the prevailing temperatures. I should think it'll reach us soon."

VIII

Sprays of diamond dust fell like glittering rain across the plateau at sundown. I told myself I was lucky to be alive, and to see such wonders. Macready had cracked open a crate of "Morgen" tinned fruits, and we'd had peaches for our pudding, shockingly sweet: "Good Morgan" was the predictable joke. I would put out of mind those poor dogs, the aurora, and my growing sense of unease. *Get on with it*, as Clarke had said.

My eyes were gritty. The previous night's watch—after Tarlington had shrugged on Harry's shirt and turned in—had me jumping at shadows. I'd found myself wide awake at six in the morning, my heart thudding, refusing to slow down. Seeing blood, blood everywhere, so powerfully that I had to check, more than once, that I wasn't bleeding myself—*no, no, please no* going around my head in its rat-tat-tat refrain. The relentless cold made me wish to stay in bed, draw the curtains, and bar the shutters.

I placed my empty mug on the porch railing. I wasn't foolish enough to touch it with bare hands; knew from experience I'd leave ghostly fingerprints as the top layer of skin was ripped off. The winter was starting to steal our flesh.

Even Laurence had stopped whistling while he worked. The acetylene-gas plan had been abandoned: we'd have to rely on candles and lanterns to hold back the crushing dark. Turning to the motor sledge, he made it periodically roar to life—stutter—then die again. But it would see no use: Randall's wishes were known. The last man to suggest finding what had become of the *Fortitude*—splitting the party—had been hauled up from the table by his collar. We were stuck here for the winter, and had to make the best of it. Skuas were hauled in by the brace, to dangle in the cold locker over Tarlington's head; large cables had been passed over the roof of the hut and frozen in on each side. Joints hammered down, seams checked. Discussions around the fire were full of forced jollity; men in twos and threes, in their bunk rooms, might talk of other things.

Diamond dust, falling to earth as the moisture in the air froze solid. It was beautiful, I told myself. Stark and alien. The last rays of sunlight lit up the mountains, ice crystals in the air creating a double image, upside down, suspended: mountains on mountains on mountains, like a hall of mirrors. An illusion, nothing more. But I thought of Harry, watching them incessantly from the ship—of that figure on the flaming deck, the bite of darkness taken out of the burning air, the tall shape that had seemed to be watching us in turn—and shivered.

I was surprised to see Harry appear for the next watch. I'd been preparing to catch someone (probably Ellis) latching the Nursery shutters open, and make him *stop* it; the time for games was over.

"I thought you'd swapped—" I broke off awkwardly.

"He's got the best eyesight." Clarke gave Harry a push to his shoulder, as if chivvying a reluctant child. "Seems a waste."

I gave Harry a quick smile and handed over the rifle, frowned when he put it down immediately. Some nightwatchman.

"Look," he said. "Do you think you could—stay out a little while longer? Keep me company?"

"Harry, it's freezing—"

"I know. Just for a short while."

I rolled my eyes. The light slipped away, and the shadows cast by the windbreaks lengthened. I didn't make any move to go inside, although I hadn't said I'd stay. There was a strange expectancy in the air as civil twilight ate the day.

A crunch in the snow. Boots squeaking in the silent air. A tall shape—too tall—appeared at the far side of one of the windbreaks. Appeared to pause, surveying the scene before it. Didn't come any closer.

"Harry—" I hissed, my heart pounding.

"Evening, lads."

A chuckle; the shape in the twilight turned into Nicholls, wearing his big ridiculous hat. I straightened up, gave him a smile as he disappeared inside. Cutting a glance towards Harry, I saw he hadn't moved. He was frozen. Transfixed. Staring towards the windbreak.

I punched him in the shoulder, my heart still racing. "What was that?"

He let out a long breath, shaking his head. "Nothing. Just—jumpy, I suppose. Just—stay awhile, please. I'd like you to be here." He looked embarrassed. "It won't happen again." His eyes were very earnest, the circles under them very dark. He leaned against the side of the hut, hands jammed into pockets, the rifle still untouched. "What happened on the ship, I mean. I know you—don't. I won't lay a finger on you, I promise."

I felt sick. I felt like I wanted to claw my way out of my own skin. Tear off whatever it was he saw in me. Make him see me—really see me. Not as he wished I might be, but as I really was. I coughed again, grateful for the distance between us.

"I just can't stand it," he said, his eyes downcast. "The dark. Those winds. That . . . bloody . . . aurora." He rarely swore. He didn't say what else he couldn't stand. I could guess, because I'd heard him using their names in the polar night. He dreamed of mud: was buried in it; woke choking on it; and they were there. Blown to pieces. His memories were stalking him, and he couldn't lay them to rest.

My hands were shaky as I steadied myself on the railings. It was colder than I'd ever thought possible, and I tried to believe it explained the prickling of my skin.

"I know it's hard," I said, and swallowed past the knot in my throat. I thought of their empty beds. Listening at the door as they climbed out the windows. Always in the next room, up in the tree house—always out of reach. And only the two of us here to remember. At least I could remember them at the railway station, hugging me amidst the smoke and steam, the sound of people calling to one another, the sound of engines.

Handsome. Whole.

I knew how Harry remembered them. Those ruined tunics, that bloody fabric—smelling of earth and sweat—had only been the half of it.

I shuddered. "God, Harry, I know it's hard. But we're still alive. We've made it this far. And we have worse things to worry about. The winter—"

"I know!" he hissed. "Honestly, I *know*. They expect us to believe that if we just sit it out—get through the winter, I'm sick of hearing *get through the winter*—somehow everything will right itself. You're not stupid—you know how bloody unlikely it is—and the Germans are all—"

The air tasted like static. I could very easily complete his sentence, and found my hand back on the service revolver, had to consciously ease it off. "Randall says—" I started, then swallowed again, thinking of him sleepwalking under the aurora. How *empty* he'd looked.

Prickles ran up and down my spine.

"It doesn't matter what happened to the Germans," I said. "We're here now. And we've got to—things are bad enough without you—"

"Seeing ghosts?" Harry's pale face was almost hidden by his scarf. "Don't you? Didn't you wish—more than anything—that you could see them again? We might as well wish for them now. Don't you ever think you've heard them speaking to you—like they're just around the corner?"

I opened my mouth. It was so easy to say that sort of thing, wasn't it? I'd heard it from family, even from members of the clergy. It was meant to be a comfort: the idea that the dead weren't truly gone. As if imagining them was the same. But I hadn't thought Harry was the sort to engage in such fancy—no, he was always so earnest, so unvarnished.

My traitorous heart pounded off-rhythm at the thought of seeing my brothers again. At the huts, waiting for me. I'd thought I'd heard them calling me to Antarctica. I'd thought I'd followed them here.

"Harry—"

"How can you *not*?" he snapped.

I looked up and didn't answer. The full moon hung low, hiding the aurora from sight. I could feel it, though—as if the face of the sky were rippling, quivering, moving invisibly above me. Tarlington was right. It was coming closer, creeping up on us. That storm of lights. Harry's eyes were wild, the moonlight sketching him in gaunt black and white. He'd become much thinner since the ship. Again, that slow, horrible crawling sensation.

"They're not here." I was barely able to get the words out. "Harry. You're tired. It's just your nightmares." The hut was a single dot of light and warmth, the snow crowding in all around us. The night approaching. "You're—imagining things."

He looked about to shake me. Footsteps, and the silhouette of Clarke loomed around the corner of the hut. "All right, you two?" His tone was kind.

"Just passing time," I said, flashing a half-smile, and he resumed his post. The ice cracked and spat with every step on the timber, the night air magnifying the sounds. Out here you could hear a ski blade scraping through snow several miles off: he might well have overheard us discussing night terrors; hallucinations; madness. The thought of confinement—in the sick bay, or worse—swam to mind. I couldn't let it happen, not to Harry. Not to me.

"It's just the light," I said. "Just—magnetism, or the temperatures."

Harry said nothing.

"You've got your duties." I nodded at the binoculars around his neck. "Clarke's counting on us. It'll help, I promise."

Damp curls escaped Harry's helmet. Despite his mustache, he looked much younger—as if we were the same age. But he'd gone to war, and

I hadn't, and now he was scared of the dark. I pitied him. And rather meanly wished he would *get on with it*. Do his job, as I'd been doing mine.

"Of course I—wish I could see them again," I said. "They were my *brothers*. But this—these morbid thoughts you've had—you've got to stop. We've got a long winter ahead of us." I didn't like to acknowledge the rest, although Harry had conjured it up effortlessly: it hovered unspoken, waiting for me to dwell on it in my bunk, alone, as the dark pressed down and the winds tried our defenses. What would happen if Randall was wrong, and the Germans—or the *Drygalski*—never returned?

"Then they won't abandon Karlmann," he'd growled when finally baited into a response, rubbing his eyes with the back of his hand. "Mark my words. One year late—of course they wouldn't waste a relief ship! But two years late—no, they'll send someone in the spring."

"You need to stay calm," I said. "We all need to stay calm."

Harry let out a small, wild laugh. He pressed his hand to his face. "I should just be brave, that's what you're saying. Be a *man* about it, Jonathan?"

"Harry—"

I took a step forward—watched my fist come up, my body acting of its own accord. I think we were both equally surprised; Harry's mouth twisted into an odd shape, and he looked away, waiting to be punched, as if he knew it to be inevitable. I flexed my fingers in my gloves—exhaled, long and slow, my heart racing, watching my breath plume out in front of me. Lowered my fist.

He should have left us at South Georgia. As soon as I thought it, I knew it to be utterly, damningly true.

"I'll stay with you," I said. "But let's walk around. Keep moving. And talk about something else. Anything but them."

IX

Several nights passed without incident, until I took the midnight watch.

With a mug of cocoa, it was possible to stay warm for a few precious minutes at a time. The air was still, save for the creak of boards as Nicholls paced up and down at the front door—sometimes the rhythmic thump-thump-thump of him running on the spot. It was desperately cold, the cocoa soon chilling, and I abandoned it.

I looked around. The scene should have been beautiful. Instead, there was something watchful about it: the relentlessness of the night, the rolling unbroken sky. The moon was on the wane, and the aurora hung in a shivering, rippling pathway between the mountains and the huts.

Listening intently, I could hear occasional bumps and groans inside. Harry moving restlessly in his sleep. A creak of floorboards—Tarlington hissing, "Oh, do be quiet!"—then silence. Yawning, I pressed my back against the hut.

"All well?" Nicholls called from around the porch.

"All well," I said, quickly standing. The cold air hit me like a slap, through combinations and trousers, Shetland wool and windproofs, all cinched tight. It was impossible to imagine it getting any colder, but this was just the beginning. Soon our teeth would freeze.

I glanced at the waning moon, then away. I was trying not to think about the days and nights to come, but Harry's words had hit hard. The Germans were gone, the *Drygalski* vanished; we were surely the only humans left on the continent. The sun would soon disappear over the mountains for the last time, leaving a darkness as profound as any tomb. We'd been buried alive. Trapped in the loneliest and most desolate place on earth. Randall had said a relief ship would come with spring, but that was October—six long months away.

There was a lot that could happen between now and then.

"Shut up," I said, very quietly, and watched my breath freeze. "Shut up."

Leaning on the railings, I allowed my eyes to close for a moment. Harry kept us awake in the Nursery, and others were having the same problem: restless sleep, filled with voices and unsettling images. Some had asked Staunton if there was anything he could give us. But those supplies were finite. All our supplies were finite.

I do not know how long my eyes were closed.

I woke to find a chill breeze playing over my face. A sound; someone moving inside. I heard Harry say, quite distinctly, "Francis? Is that you?"

The aurora made a clapping noise overhead, and a slow convulsive shiver of dread moved down my spine. Those lights had shifted through scarlet to brilliant green. "Red sky at night," Nicholls had laughed at the start of our watch. "No sailors to delight—not for thousands of miles."

The wind increased steadily, until the sound became a low note—almost a hum—which made me feel a strange sense that *something was happening*. I couldn't say what made me decide to unbar the Nursery shutters; they often stuck fast, needed hot water to be eased apart, and I was surprised they opened. I told myself it was curiosity at hearing my brother's name. But it was like walking in a dream; time moving slowly, my steps seeming to hold no weight at all, as if walking underwater. That continual low note sounded in the sky.

It was too dark inside to see much. I could make out Harry, curled in on himself, blankets drawn tight around him like a winding-cloth. The strap of his binoculars spooled out from under his jumper. The faint moonlight illuminated Tarlington's ginger hair, picked out a slice of freckled skin. Condensation on the windowpane made the room seem hazy and indistinct, a long way from the endless night outside.

I meant to close the shutters, of course. Clarke was adamant: every night they were closed and barred against the winds. I told myself I'd only leave them open for a moment. Ours were often left open. There'd be no harm.

I scrunched up my fingers inside my gloves and took a few steps around the porch. My hands seemed to act without my intervention. The shutters to Whitechapel Tenements were firmly frozen shut, and I needed all my strength to pry them open; strength I was surprised to find. Inside, a blackout curtain prevented me from seeing the occupants as they slept.

The next window was Randall's. He was sitting on his bunk, head in his hands. He didn't look up at the sound of the shutters opening—perhaps he thought it was the wind. The candle burning beside him cast a soft orange glow: I could see the veins on the backs of his hands, the white hairs in his beard. The crevices on the ruined side of his face blown red-raw by the weather. He looked like an old man.

He looked like he'd given up.

He moved. My heart thumping, I hid myself along the side of the hut, coming face-to-face with the darkness of the night sky, the source of that deep ceaseless hum.

On the other side of the dividing wall, the sick bay was well lit, and Staunton was in his shirtsleeves. One of the huddled shapes in bed, moving restlessly, must have been Duncan. I sucked in a breath of cold clear air, had to press my hand to my mouth to stifle a cough. His wrists were strapped to the bed, in case he tried to break free in one of his intermittent bursts of confusion. He was leashed like one of his dogs.

My chest felt suddenly very tight. Something in the fire, or in the boats, or in the cold unforgiving ground of Antarctica had got into his burns— had turned them bad. Duncan would never recover from the burning of the *Fortitude*; if Macready was correct, he would never leave these huts.

But no one had ever talked about it. Not even Randall.

And I hadn't visited him, in all the time we'd been here. I'd meant to—of course I'd meant to. But I'd been needed on the hunt, or on watch; I'd worked in the galley, or helped Harry with the dogs. I hadn't quite been able to bring myself to cross that line. Seeing him on the stretcher had been bad enough: reduced to cargo, his sightless staring eyes, his weeping bandages. He'd been so young and sarcastic and brash.

Sepsis. Stretcher-bearers. *Rot.* It made my skin crawl.

I steeled myself to look again, but Staunton was pacing about, repeating something to himself. I couldn't tell what it was.

The aurora sizzled and seethed.

I unbarred more shutters, one after the other, and paused at the corner. I listened. I couldn't hear Nicholls anymore; hadn't heard him for quite some time. The wind was now loud enough to drown all human sounds. As I looked at the shutters, all down the eastern side, I didn't know how I'd opened them—or why. There was a buzzing in my head. Something lay behind the wind, as if instruments were being played some way off.

The storm lanterns creaked and swung in the growing breeze. Where the aurora touched the ground, it was green as summer grass, and flickered like gas lamps going out. The sky was a gently rippling veil, lights carried upwards on a vast invisible wind. The hairs lifted on the back of my neck. A pathway. Something was nearly here.

I had to get away. I scrambled down the steps and onto the rocks. I left the blankets behind, the rifle propped by the back door. I would have left my own jacket if I hadn't been wearing it.

The wind was gaining in volume: a crash as it upended something behind me, but I didn't look back. I was aware—distantly—that I was shivering, my muscles sore with the effort. My breathing sounded terribly loud. The first windbreak towards the cliffs loomed in front of me. The light ended there.

And a voice called from the darkness on the other side.

I'd been in the common room when the men turned in. I'd seen the others—Randall, Staunton and his charges—through the windows. Nicholls was on watch. We were all accounted for, even Tarlington. It was a ridiculous thought, an awful thought. There could be no one out there.

No one at all.

I fumbled at my jacket, forcing my hand under the stiffened material, and grasped the service revolver. It stuck in its leather holster at an awkward angle, and—holding my breath—I worked it from side to side until I felt it heavy in my hand. Anyone beyond the windbreak would be an enemy. An enemy, or in dire need of assistance.

Back at the huts, things were moving. I could see the wind tugging at the lanterns, the latrine doors slamming open and shut, open and shut. A figure had reappeared on the porch: Nicholls. I could call out to him. I could go and get help. Reinforcements.

I hesitated. But whatever was happening—I knew it was for me alone.

On the other side of the windbreak, darkness dealt a hammer blow. The flickering of the aurora made the landscape dance about. I closed my eyes briefly; when I opened them, the movement was more languid, almost tidal. A faint sinister popping overhead told me the aurora had reached us.

The wind nearly blew me backwards. It was stronger out there, and with a curious twist to my heart—a feeling of *longing*—I realized I'd never hear the voice over that gale. I drew down my hood with shaking hands, pulled off my cap, exposed my ears. Biting pain. I stayed very, very still, and tried to quiet my breathing. In, out. In. Stop.

I thought I heard it again. Someone just around the corner, speaking very low.

"Who are you?" My voice caught in my throat. I sucked in a breath, freezing and sharp, then said, louder, "What do you want?"

The wind whistled.

Backing up against the windbreak, I scanned the snow. No one there. Nothing. I brought up the revolver, fumbling to load it with gloved hands, and found my breath coming faster and faster. I couldn't see anything. Indistinct shapes seemed to loom about me. "Come on," I muttered. "Come on."

Green lights everywhere. Green lights, dark sky, snow and ice. I sobbed a little, not quite trusting myself, and peeled the glove off one hand to get better purchase on the weapon. I felt my fingers clenching, curling, as chill air reached them—winter, eating my flesh. My glove fell into the snow, along with my cap. It was strikingly cold.

The voice returned.

It was a man's voice, just at the edge of hearing. Somehow familiar—coming from a long way off. I took several more steps into the darkness; my movements were starting to slow. I didn't know how long I'd been outside.

Someone was shouting in the distance. It didn't sound important; not like that other voice, the quiet voice from the snow. I craned my neck, trying to make it out. There was something almost unbearably sweet about it.

A rushing sound. Like a flock of starlings, stirring and trembling the air. The wind from the mountains swooped into the valley, hitting the huts dead on. The slam of doors; shutters; the screaming of dogs. Loud and keen, the high mournful howl they'd had on the plateau. "Jonathan!" someone was shouting. "*Jonathan!*"

My name broke the spell—whatever it had been. I was myself again. It made me stagger, realize my fingers were burning hot fire, my teeth were chattering, and I was in terrible danger. I returned the Webley to my belt. Scooped up my gloves from the snow, although I didn't remember dropping them. My legs barely cooperating, I started to run.

The snow was whipping up and over the windbreaks like sea spray. It stung my face, and I put my hand up to shield my eyes. The shutters slammed back and forth, like the huts themselves were trying to outrun it. Randall was roaring, "Everyone outside! To the stores, damn you!" and there were shapes in the snow. A piece of tarpaulin crackled past, making me duck, and struck the windbreak with the force of incoming mortars. Stones and pieces of shrapnel strafed the huts; I heard the crash of breaking glass as windows gave way.

The moon went dark. The lanterns had gone out. Everything was green. The aurora made that horrible distant crackle, and I begged it, "Please—"

Men fought their way through camp. The canvas storeroom roof was wrestling its way into the air. A windbreak danced past. Randall stood in the doorway, still as a statue, the door trying to tear itself off the frame. I expected him to move—shout at us, help with the shutters, lash things down; know I was missing; call my name.

But he didn't. He was staring at the sky.

I ran towards him, and the wind slammed me into the side of the latrines. For a few moments, everything went black. I raised my numb fingers to my head. They came away sticky.

"Jonathan!" I could finally recognize Harry's voice.

I sat with my back against the wood; I could no more walk than I could fly. I curled up, trying to make myself a small target for the barrage. We were under attack. My head buzzed and swarmed. Men were running through the snow, fighting to save what they could. Another crash in the distance as more glass shattered.

"Get inside!" Clarke bellowed. "Leave it—just get inside!"

Someone shouted, high-pitched and mad-sounding: "Who goes there?"

I knew where to look. The windbreak was nearly drifted over, but—in the choppy green light—it was much wider than it should have been. The dark wood giving way to something else. A shadow.

A tall dark figure standing in the snow.

I shut my eyes, willed it to go away. But when I opened them, I let out a sudden gasping sob—put my hands to my mouth to hold it in. I couldn't breathe.

Francis was standing by the windbreak. Tall, red-haired, wearing his deployment uniform. Even at a distance, I could see the freckles sprayed across his face, the upwards tilt to his lips. His hands in his pockets, he was standing up straight, as if the wind couldn't touch him.

My brother.

I crawled upright and took two faltering steps towards him. My heart was beating straight out of my chest, my mouth so dry. Painful *love* in my veins. He'd returned. I reached out—then pulled my hand back. Because it couldn't be him. The winds screamed and beat me in the face. The aurora sizzled.

Something wasn't right.

"Morgan!" someone shouted. The figure blurred, turning to face me. Then—as if it had heard my doubts—it was gone.

Nicholls was pulling me along. "Morgan, come on, come on." He was pressing my hand—my bare hand—inside his coat, and I leaned into him, barely able to stand. The huts seemed miles away. Greenish light rippled over the decking: I had the crazy impression the aurora was finding its way inside. The windows were full of darkness, and I struggled.

"No, no, I can't—"

"Easy. Come on, Morgan!"

My boots dragging along the porch, Nicholls half-carried me through the dark doorway, and men rushed to bar it behind us. The common room was alive with light and movement, loud voices, concerned faces. Rees was hammering at the walls, nailing boards over the broken panes, swearing as he hit his fingers and thumb. I staggered into the table and fell to my knees, Nicholls saying, "He's in shock—"

"Get off!" Harry pushed him away.

My hand had started to jump and spasm, as though no longer connected to me. Macready took it in his. "This will hurt, but you'll have it back."

I looked around. Counted. I could see fourteen men. There might be a chance that the voice I'd heard was from the expedition, someone missing, a real and *living* person—

"He's gone," Staunton said.

"What the *hell* do you mean?" Randall shouted. The room fell silent. The winds shrieked outside.

"He got loose." Staunton took off his glasses with a wavering hand. "I don't know how. He was sedated. And Bedloe. They're both gone. They've both—vanished."

My hand burned and crackled in agony as Macready rubbed it. He held my wrist fast, tightening whenever I tried to pull away. The pain rang around my head. I was still bleeding. Not much.

And the figure I'd seen—who'd looked so much like my brother, in the confusion, but it couldn't be—

By the time the storm blew out, I was shaking all over. A fine tremor, like the vibration on a gramophone needle. Certain I was going mad. Restraints; institutions; straitjackets. White-coated orderlies. *Hysterical*.

Duncan had disappeared. Bedloe, too, although no one had seen either of them leave. Their footprints were erased by the snow and the wind, but a single boot—unlaced and discarded—was found at the windbreak leading to the mountains.

X

"Sunset and evening star." The growl in Randall's voice had transformed to something somber. "And one clear call for me."

There was no point holding the service outside: there was no grave. As soon as nautical twilight had revealed the horizon, search parties were sent out, but no bodies had been found. Staunton said Duncan couldn't possibly still be alive. "He shouldn't have been able to get out of bed," he kept saying, restlessly smoothing down his whiskers. "He was too weak—"

Bedloe had been cheerful on the ship, quieter and quieter with its loss, with the death of his bunkmates Smith and Benham, with the news that the Germans had disappeared, with the sea freezing over, until he barely spoke at all. He'd been no Richard Boyd: he wouldn't have been able to carry Duncan, even in his reduced state. They might have crawled, on hands and knees, into the night.

With all of us gathered—the broken windows boarded up—the common room was stuffy, oppressive. I clenched my fists, fingernails biting into my sweaty palms. Something had summoned Duncan from the huts. Something so inexorable—so impossible to refuse—that he'd disappeared despite the pain, his injuries, the restraints. The dark. I drew an unsteady breath.

"Twilight and evening bell, and after that the dark."

Randall didn't care much for the Bible, was reading from a small scuffed poetry book. Men stood side by side, hands clasped, heads down. The chess set on the long table had taken on a horrible gravity: in all the chaos of the storm and that long confused night, shouting, hammering, crates dragged inside, a search party for the fuel cans—it hadn't been moved. It sat smugly, undisturbed. I wanted to upend it, scatter the pieces. But I knew I wouldn't.

After that the dark. Two more weeks before the austral winter set in, and we would live in perpetual night. No one would dare suggest we leave—not now. There was no other place to go. The stokers had accosted me, demanding to know why the shutters were open. "They're always closed after dark," Ellis had kept repeating. "Always. You never know what's out there." He'd been desperate for an answer. I had none, and it terrified me beyond reason.

Nicholls had led search parties all day. They'd gone as far as the cliffs, to see if clothing, the signs of a fall, told a story we could—God willing—one day take to Duncan's relatives. But the stokers were right: even Nicholls didn't know what was out there. Unbidden, horrible, the image of Francis by the windbreak—turned away, looking down, clearly expecting me to *follow*—jostled its way into my head. I pressed my fists tighter, begged it to go away. To leave me in peace.

Randall finished the poem, said a few words about Duncan's reliability, his sharp sense of humor, their first meeting in a Sydney dockyard. Macready told an anecdote from the lower decks, met with laughter. "And as for Bedloe—"

"Thank you, Robert," Randall said.

Randall refused to believe Bedloe was past rescuing; the fruitless search parties would continue. But I'd seen the conditions beyond our little circle of humanity—the shrieking winds, the billowing snow. It was still blowing now.

Macready closed his mouth with a snap, folded his arms. For a moment they were face-to-face. Macready had carried on shaving his head and chin, and his bare brown skin looked shiny—almost slippery—next to Randall, who was all beard and rough angles. I wondered if some of the scars on Macready's head had been gained in Randall's service. Randall clapped his hand on the cover of the book, and Macready tightened his jaw. Something swept around the room, over the faces of the men, then was gone.

I counted. It had become a habit. Fourteen of us inside, and no one on watch; all present, apart from Nicholls. My mind skipped back—a gramophone needle slipping into its groove—to count and recount for the night of the storm. I still couldn't come up with a name for the person I'd heard beyond the windbreak.

No *living* name, at least. But I had to be wrong. I'd heard Harry calling to Francis—the idea had been put into my head. Then the winds had come. The winds that—awfully, inevitably—seemed to drive dogs mad.

Perhaps Harry had been right. It could affect humans.

"Jonathan." Harry nodded at my hand. I looked down, saw that my fingernails were drawing blood. I shrugged, and wiped the sweat off my face.

"It's all right," he said. "You're not alone." The storm had seemed to come as a relief to him; almost as if he'd expected it. I couldn't tell him what I thought I'd seen.

I would confess, and face my punishment. The windows shattering— the shutters open, banging, tearing themselves off—that was my fault. I still didn't know why I'd done it—not entirely. I told myself I'd been checking our defenses. I told myself I'd been worried about Harry.

I knew that wasn't it.

Those damnable winds.

"I can help—"

I elbowed him, furiously, in the ribs.

The service finished with the boot room door opening. Staunton flinched, then looked around, pretending he'd been moving his feet to keep the blood flowing. But it was just Nicholls, pulling down his snow goggles and balaclava. He made eye contact with Randall, shook his head. *Nothing.* Someone cleared their throat.

"Well, back to it," Randall said. He pressed the book into Clarke's chest.

I dawdled as the gathering broke up. At the common-room table, Ellis, Parker, and Holmes buttoned their Burberries and checked the nails hammered into the undersides of their boots. Rees stood watching, his mouth twisting, as if he both wanted and didn't want to join them. Nicholls looked at me with concern. "Morgan, are you feeling—yourself, again?"

I could smell the cold on him, somehow: a clean white smell like salt water, the sea just out of reach. People looked over at us. I hated him, for a moment, more powerfully than I'd hated anyone in a long time. For his long legs; his black-and-white beard coming in strongly; his broad, capable hands, explorer's hands; his utter self-assuredness. I wouldn't have him making digs at me. Pain flared in my jaw. For all I knew—I'd hit my head badly—he'd told me to open the shutters. He'd told me, and I'd somehow scrubbed it from my memory. Someone had to have told me.

"Morgan," he said, softly.

I clutched at it. I couldn't remember when I'd heard his restless footsteps stopping. He'd left his post, I was sure of it. But there was something I couldn't quite grasp, like tiny fish in a tide pool; the memories twisted away from me.

"You'll feel better in a while." He squeezed my shoulder. I shrugged his hand off and ducked away, reflexively rubbing the back of my head. The wound wasn't deep, but had bled copiously, and my hair had been shaved right off; I was as bareheaded as Macready. The bruising was coming up strongly. I'd stared at myself in the mirror, trying very hard to see the back of my skull. I liked the angles it put on my face, and the obvious disapproval on Harry's. The person in the mirror was unmistakably Jonathan Morgan, myself as I was meant to be.

I took a step towards the sick bay. Randall's room beyond would be a dark little box. The *fine Hanover glazing* was all gone.

Someone came up behind me. I stiffened, expecting more from the stokers. But it was Clarke. "Here," he said, marching me towards the boot room.

"Randall—"

"No. Come with me."

XI

With the door closed, the boot room felt barely bigger than a wardrobe, dim light shining through the cracks. It was already ten degrees colder than the common room, despite the sacking nailed to the walls, and I tugged at my clothing as Clarke leaned over me. "You tell me what happened," he said, low. "People are starting to talk. Those shutters should have been closed. Explain yourself."

I swallowed. I'd been ready for Randall: his terrible roiling anger and sudden explosions. Clarke was steady, the leash to Randall's rage. This was worse.

"I opened them," I said, fighting down my shame.

"Why?"

"I don't know."

"Did someone tell you to do it?"

I let out a small, unexpected laugh. "Nicholls was the only other person out there. You'd have to ask him." I'd never talked back to Clarke. My face prickled and burned.

"Did they?" he asked again.

"I don't know."

A horrible silence. I thought of Duncan, strapped to the bed. All that might happen to someone who admitted to . . . hearing things. I squeezed my fists. "There was something strange." Just saying it made my skin crawl; brought to mind that quiet, persistent voice on the edge of hearing. "I heard—someone, beyond the windbreaks. Before the storm. A voice."

Clarke was a silent figure in the darkness.

Recklessly, in a rush, my voice catching: "I think the wind here—sometimes—gives the impression it's *calling*—"

"Stop." Slowly: "Do you think you heard the Germans?"

The idea was so utterly divorced from what had happened that my mouth fell open. I hiccupped a little, and slapped my hand over it, said "No" through my fingers. "I don't think the Germans are out there. They're all dead. Aren't they?"

My eyes must have adjusted to the dark, because I could see, stamped over Clarke's left shoulder, the black stenciled letters on the hut's exterior wall. The whole building had been brought here as a kit, like a doll's house; I realized Clarke's constant grumbling about its construction had been born of bafflement. In a place where winds reached forty below, it was preposterous to construct something that offered a clear line of sight on all sides, rather than tucking it away against the rocks. We'd found a lockbox under the bunks, its lock pried off with a crowbar, but no guns. A slow crawling feeling. I knew about the *overwinter*: how men could be driven mad by the dark. By the winds. By the sheer crushing claustrophobia of six months in a small space. Maybe they'd turned on one another.

Our invisible hosts were dead and gone, leaving no clues behind them.

Clarke shifted, exhaled loudly. "Did you—" He stopped. Seemed to steel himself. "Did you recognize it?"

I'd told myself I didn't. But there had been something hollow about the voice: an echo, as if it came down a corridor. It reminded me of nighttimes in Portsmouth; the adults talking downstairs, my brothers in their room. I'd tried not to think about it, because it was a short step to believing that Francis had been talking to me. Had been trying to make himself understood, across all the miles of ocean and time and— everything that now separated us.

My mouth was very dry. I didn't know what to say. Again, that horrible fear bubbled inside me: I might be dragged out in restraints. I might be tied down. *Hysterical.* I might be examined. Restrained. A danger. A liability to the expedition. I tugged shakily at my scarf.

"Don't mention this to Randall," Clarke said suddenly. "I mean it, Morgan."

Caught as I turned, I stumbled back against the wall: splintery wood and sackcloth, just thick enough to make this conversation a private one. I could see the set of Clarke's shoulders, the tension in his jaw. I remembered him dragging Randall in from the snow. The night I wasn't allowed to talk about. The night Randall had said the name of his dead son.

Charlie.

"He heard someone, too." I felt my stomach turn over. "Didn't he? When he was sleepwalking."

Clarke rubbed his knuckles. "He doesn't need to know."

I looked at him sideways. This was Randall's expedition. Randall's ship had burned; Randall had led us to safety. But since we'd reached the huts, Clarke had taken over, so capably and seamlessly that we'd hardly had occasion to notice.

"But if there's something out there—watching us—"

"At least it wasn't the Germans." He exhaled. "We can't do anything about it, whatever it is." He looked tired, but the set to his jaw told me he wasn't to be trifled with. Six dark months until the relief ship: someone would need to lead us to that point. "You're not to take watch again, do you hear? Stay *inside*."

When Clarke opened the interior door, the light made me screw up my eyes. I heard the search party at the table stop talking. Randall was looming over them, his jumper so ragged it looked ready to fall off him. He hadn't shaved in weeks. I thought about how he'd looked in that glimmering light before the storm: a man who'd given up. Maybe these huts—*get through the winter*—was Australis Randall giving up. No vainglorious last hope; no dashing escape.

"Well, Morgan," he said.

"I've dealt with him," Clarke said firmly.

Randall opened his mouth. Then seemed to change his mind. "Well, then. Go on, and you've got off lightly, Morgan—very lightly indeed."

Clarke took Nicholls aside, said something in a quiet voice, nodded towards me.

Nicholls shrugged. "I think I can weather it," he said, a smile on his face. The story went around that Nicholls had got me to help him clean ice from the windows—some of the men didn't like it too much. But I knew the truth. He hadn't told me to open the shutters, or given me any orders at all.

Someone—or something—else had, and I'd obeyed.

The night hadn't yet fallen, but already it was preying on me—perhaps preying on all of us. Making us weak; susceptible. Encouraging us to make mistakes. It was a long time until the thin pale light of dawn might find us at that cliff-top tower, waving to the ship, pointing back to the huts. Maybe—I let myself think it, just for a moment—there would be no ship. No huts. No people to wave.

And there was something outside, walking with the weather, peering around Clarke's windbreaks. Not the Germans. Maybe not anything *real*—not as we knew it. Francis was here, somehow; down here in the white spaces. They'd buried him in France. But he was here. Harry had called my brother's name into the night, into the winds and the aurora. Summoned his ghost.

XII

I awoke with a start. Francis had been standing in the doorway of my room again, watching me sleep. Although I was on the top bunk, he loomed over me, far too tall, fox-bright hair and shadowy face. He'd been speaking, but I couldn't quite make out the words; his was the voice I'd heard in the snow. It should have been wonderful. It should have comforted me.

I pressed my eyes shut, willing him to go away.

I opened them again. The Nursery was pitch-black, as if someone had abruptly blown out a candle, as if Rufus had come in to say: "You shouldn't have a light." He'd always sided with our father: if lights were permitted only in the back rooms, then nobody in the house would have one. It was all or nothing. The two of them were cut from the same cloth, and sometimes I'd snuffed the candle out myself, knowing that Rufus would pause at my doorway and—smiling quietly—move on.

It could have been day or night. The wind was howling and sobbing outside. The walls were squeezing in on me, my blankets itchy. I was alone.

I crept my way to the floor; the curtained doorway; and came out into the common room. It seemed to be night. Ollivar sat in the lounge, reading a book, and looked up at my approach.

"What time is it?" My voice sounded very loud.

"Four in the morning, or thereabouts," he said. "The aurora's here."

I shivered, and felt the kettle with the back of my hand, then poured myself a mug of warm water. "Who's on watch?"

"Rees out back." Ollivar paused. "Cooper at the front."

I no longer liked the idea of Harry being our nightwatchman. *We might as well wish for them now.*

The wind tried the doors like an insistent but unwanted guest. Outside, other doors were banging, slamming open and shut repeatedly, muffled and far away. Footsteps creaked on the porch, and I swallowed, listening hard. Ollivar took off his glasses and polished them with a nonchalant air. I noticed his hands were shaking.

"Rees?" Harry called. The wind roared. "Rees?"

Ollivar straightened up. "Stay here," he said, seeing me put down my mug. "No—you stay here, Morgan." He opened the front door carefully. The auroral lights flooded in across the threshold, bright as sunrise, a deep and unsettling crimson. The wind made the stove flicker, the laundry billow, the boot room door rattle on its hinges—then shut the door obligingly behind him.

I waited, staring, fingers tracing my mug's chipped enamel.

Noises outside made me jump. Then someone shouting: Tarlington. I went to the door. It opened—the aurora flashing, urgently, above us— and Ollivar returned in a hurry, nearly falling over me. A strange sharp smell blew in with him. "You shouldn't wake a sleepwalker," he called to the unseen watchers outside.

I'd thought so when it was Randall. But I couldn't bear the thought that this time it was Harry walking out under the aurora. His feet bare, his eyes sightless. "Let me go—" I said, trying to push past Ollivar. He grabbed me roughly, saying, "Stay *here*," and his face was white, his eyes wide behind their glasses.

A crash came from the kennels. The wind whipped the door wide, and I saw that it was dark outside, so very dark, dry static electricity thrumming in the air. My skin prickled. The aurora was low in the sky, sitting on top of us, giving off a thin hissing sound. Green waves crashed over invisible shores. The drift was blowing around camp, making everything hazy. My heart stuttered with relief to see Harry on the steps, holding onto the railings like a drowning man. The air was thick—it was alive.

"Help me—" Tarlington shouted from the vast swimming darkness. "Damn you, Cooper, they're your bloody dogs—"

Boyd ran past, his thudding footsteps loud enough to wake the dead. "Stay inside!" he shouted, door slamming shut behind him. A scream of wind; sobbing; howling; growing to an almost unbearable high pitch. I wanted to cover my ears. The door juddered back open to the night and Harry appeared, the aurora in the whites of his eyes.

"Get Staunton!"

I obeyed instinctively; I returned to the common room along with a hubbub of voices, curses, as men roused themselves from their bunks. Ollivar and Boyd were nowhere to be seen. Harry stood with his hands planted firmly on the table. I watched as he squeezed his eyes shut—as if banishing a bad dream—then opened them again.

"Harry?"

"Rees's smashed up the sledges," he said. "Everything Laurence—then took his hammer to—the kennels. He was stopped, before—"

I bit down on my knuckle, tasted blood. *It never pays to get comfortable.* I suddenly recognized that sharp smell—blown in on the wind, so foreign to Antarctica—as our fuel. I thought of the sledges under canvas, the roaring thunder of the motor, the cans of oil, the dogs being trained to harness, day by day: Clarke and Laurence had been so careful to make sure we had a way out of here. In case something happened; in case we had to get ourselves out. But even if we'd wanted to leave before winter—now we couldn't. There were too many of us. We were trapped, like animals gone willingly into a snare.

Trapped with whatever was outside.

I sat down hard. The smell of kerosene was now overwhelming, and I found my gaze drawn to the flickering lantern on the table. The corridor to the sleeping quarters, yawning dark as an open mouth, and how the men's shadows rose up the walls and onto the ceiling.

I took an unsteady breath. I wanted to shake Harry, scream at him: "Where were you?" But he wasn't a coward—not exactly. I knew why he hadn't been able to stop Rees. I knew why Rees had betrayed our expedition, because I'd felt that same spell myself, with the low hum of the aurora bearing down on me. It was like morphine—like being whispered to without words. I breathed through my mouth, big shuddering breaths, and tried to compose myself.

Staunton and Ollivar dragged Rees in like a carcass. He was missing his jacket and hat, and his slicked-back raven-wing hair stuck up in wild peaks. He made a constant pained noise, but couldn't speak; fixed and glassy, his eyes appeared to bulge from their sockets. His nose was clearly broken. Tarlington followed, holding a rag to his face. He caught my eye, shook his head brusquely. His mittens, once trimmed with red, were now dull brown. Harry turned to me, and I avoided eye contact.

Boyd strode back in, rifle slung across his shoulder. "We need someone on watch," he said, grabbing me. "Hell—you go. You two."

"Not them," Clarke said roughly. "I'll see to it." He turned to the men who were huddled in the doorways and partitions, blinking in the light.

Boyd leaned against the supporting beam, and I could see the blood matting his woolen cap to his skull. "The fucker got me," he said, throwing Rees's hammer down on the table. "And the fuel's all over the snow. Someone put him up to this. When he wakes up I'll bloody well—"

"Enough of that," Clarke said. "Get yourself seen to."

"He's lucky I didn't *shoot* him," Boyd said, very darkly, then ducked through into the sick bay. From behind the curtain I heard Rees start to stammer. Boyd said something in response, and there was a thin moan.

Randall appearing in the doorway silenced us all. He'd been sleeping in his boots and coat. His eyes looked as if he'd been staring into the sun.

"Well, now," he said brusquely, then seemed to lose his train of thought. He swayed slightly. "Laurence—go and take a look. Rees—we'll have him sedated. The rest of you—the rest of you—"

"The rest of you, try to get some sleep," Clarke said.

"Attacked in our beds," someone said. "There's something out there, mark my—"

"It doesn't matter." Clarke's face twitched. "High winds tonight. Macready, brew up some cocoa? Let's just—batten down the hatches. Get through the night."

XIII

"No need to be afraid," Staunton said. "There's a perfectly reasonable explanation. It's dark nearly twenty hours a day. The effect of the southern night on a man; even the most sane, well-adjusted mind. And we're all tired. Cold. Worried about the Germans. Our fates. Whether we will—"

He broke off, not looking at me.

"Rees lost everyone. Heaven knows he's not the only one. Every single family back home missing husbands, fathers, sons; an empty place at every table. Some mothers had aches, terrible pains, where their sons were shot—like red-hot pokers, they said. Others couldn't sleep, for fear they'd miss the sound of them coming home, ringing the doorbell, and finding no one to let them in."

I thought about the first few nights here—waiting for the Germans' boots on the porch. Staunton sipped at the cocoa, steam curling in his whiskers. "Some of the young men who didn't go became melancholic, anxious. Wishing *they* had died instead; traumatic events can take us quite strangely. What I'm saying, Morgan, is that it would be perfectly natural if Rees—particularly with his history—if anyone thought they'd heard—"

"I know," I said abruptly, grabbing the bucket. Staunton had barely been outside since we'd arrived; he couldn't lecture me about the *over-winter*. "I should get on."

The sick bay gave me the creeps. On the night of the storm, Staunton had wanted me on a bed to examine my head wound; I'd struggled and sworn, Harry staring him down with every inch of his officer's bearing. Staunton was a decent sort, I supposed. But in my imagination he cast a long dreadful shadow: Duncan strapped to the bed. The little leather case. Knives and scalpels. I wouldn't let him touch me. I wouldn't let them hold me down—examine me—declare me insane.

A cough and a muffled curse from the bed stopped me in my tracks. Rees was blinking his way awake. "I don't want to sleep anymore," he said, slightly slurred. Raising his voice: "Why am I—what—"

Dog leashes, stiffened with salt and age, held his wrists to the frame. "For your own good," Staunton said apologetically, and knelt to shine a light into his eyes.

Where Duncan had been quiet, drifting in and out of consciousness, Rees was loud, struggling against the restraints as he swam back into our waking company. The bed shuddered, and I found myself backing towards the far corner, bucket forgotten.

Clarke appeared in the doorway; I let out a small huff of relief. "Staunton, you have to keep him quiet—"

"No." Boyd appeared behind him. "Too much is being kept quiet—by you, Liam. Why the fuck d'you think you're in charge here?" He pushed Clarke aside, muscling his way in. I saw people massing in the common room. Voices, angry voices.

Staunton stood between Boyd and the bed, looking like a dandy by comparison, with his waxed mustache and neatly knotted scarf. "Listen—we need to keep him calm. He's in shock."

Boyd laughed. "*He's* in shock?" He gestured at his head. "When he whacked me with a hammer?"

"What?" Rees said urgently. "What did I do?"

Boyd turned to Clarke. "But it's not just him, is it? I know you've been covering something up. Keeping us all nice and quiet, while we wait for God knows what to come over that horizon. It started at the ship, didn't it? Started at the bloody ship."

There was a sour taste in my mouth.

"No," Rees said. "No, you have to believe me, I'd never, I was asleep—"

"Who set that fire? Why haven't we put fucking Tarlington outside, or—in chains? He's still out there—doing God knows what. Signaling to them, perhaps, with that bloody weathervane of his. What's Nicholls doing on all those day-trips?" Boyd gestured at me, and I shrank back. "Getting poor Morgan to open those shutters? Next they'll leave the bloody doors wide open, so he and that slinky-eyed coward can welcome them in."

His voice was loud enough to carry around the entire hut. My stomach plummeted. This was the disaster Clarke had feared.

Rees was twisting his shoulders, trying to pull himself upright. He looked dazed, eyes too big for his face. I thought of the newspaper photographs I'd seen of the *shell-shocked* soldier—my earlier conviction, on the ship, that my brothers would have beaten the secrets out of a man. Rees looked utterly incapable; didn't look the slightest bit like a conspirator. He mouthed my name, nodded at his straps.

I shook my head, the movement jerky. "No, Boyd—"

I knew it hadn't been Nicholls. He'd been somewhere else, although the memory remained stubbornly elusive. The creak of a door shutting: the cold locker. Had I heard Tarlington, perhaps? He was red-haired. Tall. Although I'd made the comparison more than once, he was as different from Francis as a man could be. I bit the inside of my cheek hard enough to taste blood.

I wished to God it were some sort of plot. I wished to God it were that simple.

"If you've got something to say to me"—Nicholls appeared in the doorway, quiet and determined—"you can say it to my face."

"I've got nothing to say to *you*."

Nicholls laughed. "Same old Boyd. Always looking for someone to blame."

"He's right," Ellis called from the common room, and more voices agreed. "As if there'll be enough to go round when the bloody Krauts come back—"

"We should get it out of him," Boyd said. "Find out what's really going on here." He grabbed one of Rees's wrists.

Staunton said: "Have you gone *mad*, take your hands off him—"

"Let him go," Clarke growled, suddenly seeming to take up all the space in the room.

"Where's Randall?" Boyd twisted Rees's hand further. "Randall!"

"This business isn't for you," Clarke said. "And not like this." And he grabbed Boyd from behind. I released a sudden breath, and a moment later—as if that had been the signal—someone shoved Clarke. The first punch was thrown.

XIV

"Boyd!" I shouted. "It was me!"

I'd acted alone. I'd let it in—whatever it was. A half-heard voice, an impulse or instruction coming with the wind and aurora, as wild and unknowable as the patterns guiding a flock of starlings. Boyd could turn his anger on me. He'd believe in hidden German encampments, trenches in the snow, caves and dugouts hiding our enemy in the landscape—not ghosts, or cursed winds. I'd be declared mad, or a traitor—strapped up like a prisoner on a rack. Perhaps he was right; perhaps I *was* a danger to the expedition. But no one would be punished in my place.

I took a deep breath—my chest expanding, my fists squeezing—and shouted: "Boyd!" Then caught an elbow in the face and staggered back.

"You'd betray us—" someone yelled. "For the sake of a—"

I choked, found myself pushed about by the scuffle, drowned out by

Randall bellowing, snow on his coat, "Why is no one on watch, you lot of—"

A sudden shocked lull. Rees's wrist was broken, and he was making a whining sound, still trying to pull away from his restraints. His eyes still popping from their sockets. My heart thudded in my chest so painfully that I clutched at it.

It was over as fast as it began. I'd come out unscathed, though I didn't deserve it. Boyd nursed a split lip. Clarke dragged Ellis through the common room by his neck. And Randall's head was wet, where he'd been struck—unthinkably—from behind. "Cowards," he growled, feeling at his hair with dirty stubby fingers. "I should like to see the man who'd fight me face-to-face."

A sullen silence in the huts. Outside, the dogs had barked themselves out; slipping their leashes, they'd run around in chaos, quarreling and attacking one another while we'd been distracted. "It's not their fault," Harry said. "This place is bad for them."

"It's not good for us, either," Macready replied. "At each other's throats." The furrows on his forehead seemed very deep. "It's never been like this before. Not when we were on the Barrier—or the western Weddell, up Mount Haddington way." Both expeditions had been far from this coast. "We just need to be sensible. Stay inside. Wait it out."

"Easy for you to say," Parker said meanly. "You lot've come out of it all right." He hovered by the Coal Hole, grimacing for the fate of his bunkmates, glancing towards the door. Clarke and Ellis had been outside for half an hour; it felt like much longer. The faint sounds of shouting echoed in the distance.

"Ellis should've known better," Macready snapped.

"Well, then," Randall's voice said from the sick bay. "I'll help you out, eh?"

An ominous silence.

"Don't use it," Staunton said hurriedly. "Rest it entirely, for as long as possible. You should really stay—"

Randall half-dragged Rees through the common room. His wrist was splinted, dark hair plastered to his face with sweat. His feet were uncoordinated. He seemed incapable of speech.

Harry hissed, and I turned back to him. He was very pale in the lantern-light as Macready tended to his bite wounds. Blood swirled in the water, and I dipped in a finger, watched a droplet run down my hands. I flexed them; saw the muscles working under the skin. Stronger than I expected. I was queasy, but it wasn't the sight of blood. "We should never have told him, should we?" I whispered. "Boyd. He's a fanatic. He could kill someone."

Harry made a face and looked away.

The front door opened. Behind Clarke, the sky was the dark blue of fathomless water. He gripped the doorframe on both sides, seemed to feel himself pulled back into it. The warmth started to be sucked out of the hut. The lanterns flickered. Someone shouted, a small hint of panic in it: "Close that bloody door!"

"Morgan," he said, and I jumped. "Take Ellis tea, and a sleeping bag. We won't have him freezing."

"He's outside?" Macready said.

"The fuel store. One night, that'll be his punishment. For this." Clarke gestured to his black eye.

"Randall—" Macready said carefully.

"Randall knows," Clarke snapped. "And he'd have done worse." He looked at me, bushy eyebrows sending a clear warning. "Well? Tea. Don't make me tell you twice."

I braced myself for the night outside. The route to the fuel store was well trodden, a new padlock on chains looped through the corrugated-iron door, making it into a cell. A great deal of our fuel had been spilled, and the interior stank of kerosene, lamps that wouldn't be lit. Ellis said nothing to me, although his scarf hardly concealed the bruises starting to come up, livid in the freezing air, around his sinewy neck. The outline of Clarke's big hands.

Locking the door behind me, I paused. Shadows dominated all the corners of camp. The dark of the moon. That strange sensation the sky was a void, a hole or an absence, waiting to whisk me up. Being outside felt hazardous. I pressed my hands to my temples, feeling horribly sure I was being watched.

I looked over at the windbreak.

But there was no one there: when I picked my way through the darkness, the windbreak was accusingly ordinary. Solid wood against my hands; a faint lean towards the south; snow drifted up on the other side. My stomach roiled. Francis had been real, I was sure; as real as the aurora, at least. The word *ghost* felt far too small for my dead brother. If I called out—if I said his name, like Harry—perhaps he would answer. I hesitated, chewing my lip, tasting blood.

He'd surely come if I called.

The creak of the cold locker door was like a gunshot. I spun around, breath shuddering out.

"Morgan?" It was almost a relief to see Tarlington standing there.

"Go back inside," I snapped. Beyond the windbreak the hummocks stretched out like sand dunes on a sunless beach. I ran my hand over the wood again, where Francis had been, and heard the door close.

"Damn it," I whispered. What Clarke had predicted was coming true: we were barely an expedition anymore, just a group of desperate men hoping to last out the winter. But Tarlington still carried on as if science meant something here. An image slunk into my head: that shallow cut down his forearm. *The knife slipped.* The German dogs.

The aurora was starting to eddy across the sky like seaweed in a rock pool, and I could feel an answering tide in my spine. Macready was right: there was something about this place. These huts, crouched on the rocks—facing the mountains—in a part of Antarctica not yet firmly on any map.

It was barely above freezing in the cold locker, despite the coal burner flickering away. A small table was wedged against the wall, and the broken wireless set served as a chair. Splayed out on the table—my heart hammered for a second—a big fat snow petrel, partly decomposed, black around the eyes.

Tarlington turned to me in surprise. "You could close the door, you know." His breath steamed in the cold air. He was at least wearing proper gloves, not his dainty fingerless mitts, although he still stubbornly preferred his double-breasted greatcoat.

"What are you hoping to find?" I asked, nodding at the dead bird.

He shrugged. "What were *you* hoping to find? By the windbreak?"

I felt myself grinding my teeth. "It's cold out here."

He flashed me a sudden but confused smile. "Thank you for noticing the *extremely* obvious." He turned back to pulling out feathers by the fistful. The smell made me cover my mouth. "Oh, I know," he said. "It's unpleasant. That's also obvious. But if something got to the dogs—did it also affect the birds? Sadly my studies had nothing on the topic—whatever topic that might be."

"You should come inside," I said. "It's not good to be out here alone."

He ignored me. "I am staying busy," he said distantly. "I'm doing my *job*. I'm meant to be a bloody scientist—didn't you hear? I heard all the shouting. And I seem to have a cellmate, just like the old days."

A lump in my throat, which I choked down: telling myself I would warn him, no more. "There was a fight. You should know, they're still talking about—someone setting the fire. On the ship. Plotting with the Germans. Betraying Randall."

Tarlington pressed a glove to his face. Screwed up his eyes. "Don't tell me. It always comes back to this in the end. Because I didn't . . . bloody . . . fight. It's like having the mark of Cain." He gave a short laugh. "The scarlet letter."

It struck me that he was the same age as Rufus and Francis—the same age as they'd have been, had they lived. Dark blue eyes. The barest suggestion of ginger stubble, no mustache, in stark contrast to my brothers, and Harry's own neat facial hair. Without it, Tarlington had a wide sarcastic mouth. *That slinky-eyed coward.*

"I'm sorry," I said. "Sorry, Boyd was—I thought you should know."

"You don't think so—do you? That I had anything to do with the fire—because I didn't, Morgan. There's no reason I should try to murder us all. You; that sanctimonious idiot; Randall. If I'd wanted to kill myself, there'd be less elaborate—and warmer—ways to go about it."

"I believe you," I said quickly, and met his eyes. "I do. But there's something strange happening here. Something about this place. You shouldn't be outside."

He stared at me. "Then why are *you* outside? What are you looking for?"

"Nothing." I fixed my eyes on the dead bird. It seemed impossible it had ever flown, called out, walked the ice.

"Morgan," he said quietly. "You've seen it, haven't you?"

"Seen what?"

He narrowed his eyes at the falseness in my voice. "People talk, around me. I don't suppose they think it matters if I hear them. The men are seeing things. Hearing things. People they lost."

"Ghosts?"

He smiled slightly. "I don't believe in ghosts, or devils. And you, Morgan?"

I shook my head, tongued the blister inside my cheek. "I've seen nothing."

"Heard anything?"

"Just the wind," I said quickly.

He laughed. "You're a terrible liar, you know?"

I took a step away, looking down, trying not to snap at him. Being called a liar by Tarlington— who was hiding so much—felt like a slap in the face.

"All right," he said. "*Don't* tell me. Clarke knows, though—he's been keeping a lid on it all since we got here. And you look like you've seen a ghost." Offhand: "Lord knows Cooper has."

I felt my fingers tingling, the confession on the very tip of my tongue. Bit it down again. "What about you?"

He shrugged. "There's no one I—it doesn't matter. It's nothing; Staunton thinks it's cabin fever. Hallucinations, or some sort of group delusion—men getting paranoid. I've wondered whether there's something contagious; but there's no signs in the dogs, or the birds."

I couldn't help myself snorting.

"Oh, be like that," he said. "You can't imagine how I feel the . . . want of someone with qualifications." He kicked the broken wireless set. "Even a physicist, anything! But I need to try."

I found myself staring at that radio equipment; the Germans had smashed anything that might transmit or receive. They'd come here to stake a claim, but the Prussian eagle had been torn back down. Ripped along the side, covered in bootprints, as if it had played some key part in whatever had happened here—perhaps in a hasty and panicked decision to leave. We carried no flag of our own. We were meant to be many miles from this place. But this was where we'd ended up.

The men had started to call it Expedition Point, as if it was so very important to give it a name.

"You don't still believe they're alive, do you—don't be stupid." I shook my head. "Or that they're coming back. Or that there's really a relief ship coming."

I sucked my teeth.

"Exactly," he said. "Get through the winter. Then what, exactly? You look at them—go back in there and *really* look at them, Morgan—they have no idea."

"Randall—"

He just looked at me. "There's a reason," he said very quietly. "He believes the Germans are still alive."

"Clarke, then—"

"Clarke doesn't trust—or believe in—anything he can't put his hands on. When spring comes without a relief ship, he knows what we'll have to do." A pause. "Our chances aren't much better than Karlmann's—worse, even."

The name made my spine prickle. He raised his eyebrows at me, waiting for a response.

"Then we—batten down the hatches." I tried to keep my voice measured. "All we can do is wait it out, whatever it is. And no one will think less of you—if you just come inside. Wait by the fire with the rest of us."

Out of the wind; out of the dark.

Tarlington gave me a sideways look. I was reminded, powerfully, of Harry on the ship. Sitting on the dog deck, alone, waiting for something, although perhaps even he didn't know what he was waiting for. "I don't suppose I should be welcome," Tarlington said. "I'm not stupid, Morgan. The masses will want a scapegoat. When winter arrives, and we turn on each other in earnest—well. They'll come for me. I might as well give them what they want."

XV

A week of storms confined us. The sun slunk off behind the clouds, the aurora hid away, and the snow screamed down over the windbreaks. The huts started to smell, and Randall apparently developed a passion for housekeeping: we scrubbed the walls, washed the sacking, turned over all the mattresses. At least it kept us busy. Under the dripping laundry Clarke ran a hotly contested bridge tournament, keeping score in cramped left-handed writing, the dogs trying to steal scraps from the table. We'd allowed no animals inside when we arrived. But this had become less important, and the stokers suggested—with a nonchalant air, a small request—they be allowed to keep a dog in the Coal Hole overnight.

What they really wanted was a guard dog. No one would say out loud that they were scared—nervous, jumpy. But Ellis was certain that Tarlington had knocked on his cell door, gently and persistently, when the night was darkest. "A fucking stupid trick," he said.

When asked what he'd heard, Ellis looked defensive. "All I'm saying is—it wasn't the wind." A waver in his voice. "It was someone knocking. Saying something I couldn't quite hear. Just outside but—far away."

I wanted to like Ellis, who was fiercely keen on the dogs; when confronted about the story, Tarlington had just smiled his wry smile and shrugged.

As I opened the boot room door, the mongrel on the blankets by the stove growled at me, bared its teeth. The men in the common room stiffened. "Wind's getting lighter," I said, stamping my feet. I'd been shoveling out the latrines; an unpopular task, but I'd taken it uncomplainingly, using the duty to draw attention from how frequently I used them. The wind outside had seemed to find its way into the smallest knot holes, every crack in my clothing. Cold, greedy, insistent fingers. But the worst of it had ceased.

No one moved. I swallowed. I was instantly too hot in my outdoor gear, and the thought of peeling it off wasn't appealing; the group by the fire no longer seemed so welcoming. Harry caught my eye—chewed his lip, deliberating—and stood.

The boot room was cramped, and Harry smelled powerfully of wet fur. He pulled on his jacket. "Don't start at me about the dogs—I know they're not pets."

"I wasn't going to say anything."

"It's just—they make the men feel better, that's all."

I opened the door to the dark, the sun a pale glow far below the horizon. We were losing light at an abominable rate, caught between two advancing fronts of night like a specimen in Tarlington's pincers. The aurora retreated across the sky. Harry exhaled, the magnetism making the hairs stand on the back of my neck. I couldn't stop myself looking towards the windbreak.

Harry met my gaze, held it. It was suddenly very hard to catch my breath, and I gulped air like someone finishing a race. I couldn't hide it from him any longer.

"Harry—"

"You've seen them, haven't you? Tell me the truth."

I nodded. Wished, instantly, that I could take it back. The mixture of awe and love on his face was worse than I could ever have imagined. It made his cheeks look even more gaunt; it gave him a faraway stare, like a man looking towards a distant explosion.

"You've seen them? Here?"

I looked down, rubbing my temples with my thumbs. It felt as though saying it would somehow *call* him—his long officer's coat, his red hair shining with the aurora. "I saw—I saw Francis. Outside."

Harry nodded, once. Then put his arms around me. His skin smelled of smoke, a faint impression of body heat. I leaned into him, my heart hammering. My face was hot, and I buried it against his collar. I felt my eyes prickle. I'd never cried in front of Harry before; I didn't know how he'd take it.

I didn't care what he thought of me anymore.

"Then they're here," he said. "They're really here. Walking at night—under the aurora. Out in the snow. We came here to find them, Jo, and—they've found us."

I nearly corrected him. *Jonathan*. But the way he said it stopped me: the devotion and fervor in his voice made the breath stutter in my throat, and I couldn't get the words out.

"More than anything, I longed to see them again. Didn't you?" He made a small choked sound that might have been a laugh. "I got what I wanted."

I wasn't sure that I had.

"Harry." I peeled myself away. Swallowed, realizing I wasn't going to cry if I breathed very carefully. He stood swaying, the last glimmers of green light catching in his eyes, making them burn cold. "Harry. *Why* are they here? Why aren't they—in France? Back home?"

I'd had days and nights to wonder why their ghosts were haunting a hut in the Antarctic wasteland. I thought about it while the men muttered about Germans and saboteurs, and Boyd sat with his scarred arms folded, watching Nicholls coming and going. While we played cards and discussed our favorite meals, and Macready finally, carefully, moved that chess set—and was cursed out of the room for disrespecting the dead. I'd kept glancing at the cracks in our boarded-up windows, knowing my brothers were still out there. Wondering if they felt the cold—if they were able to feel anything.

And what they wanted with me. I shuddered all over. In the depths of winter, when the air was like slate, and the winds ruled the continent—

I might finally find out.

Harry opened his mouth, and I heard the faint *ah* . . . as he drew breath. Clutched me by the hands, his grip tight.

The door opened behind us, Clarke bellowing something. There was a general moaning and reluctance to leave the huts. We let go of each other immediately, shuffled an awkward inch apart.

Work outside recommenced, with men wielding shovels and axes against the drifting snow. The crates in the storeroom had iced up, needed to be pried free with crowbars. As with the dogs, we'd held off on bringing food inside; better to keep it in the lower temperatures, and it was only a short few feet to the store—capable of being walked in the worst blizzing possible. But now we'd cleared out the abandoned darkroom, and Clarke said we'd bring in as many crates as we could.

Things had changed. I shivered again.

Civil twilight had fallen already, and a figure trudged through the snow to the anemometer. "What's the bloody use—" someone said, then was hushed; talking back to an officer was still an offense. Climbing the ladder, lantern held high, the long coat and hood was unmistakably Tarlington. The wind exposed his face, and I could see—or imagine—his pinched expression.

There'd been mutters about allowing him outside—although no one wanted him in. That platform was the highest point in our little kingdom, the wind tugging at it, bouncing the anemometer's pole from side to side like an invisible hand playing badminton. Soon we would lack a dawn, and all true light was man-made: "Signaling," they'd said, about Tarlington's trips to read it. "I suppose you'd rather the weather surprised us," Nicholls snapped, and someone had jeered, "Doesn't it always—"

Tarlington had been right: they wanted a scapegoat. Clarke hadn't said anything more about the German expedition, or the possibility of a relief ship. He'd gone to great lengths to avoid discussing it, keeping us busy throughout the hours of dwindling light and beyond. *Getting through the winter* had started to seem like an obsession. A talisman. Something to hold up against the night, as we stayed away from the door and the vast dark spaces that waited outside.

I recalled what Tarlington had said: *go back in there and* really *look at them.*

And if there wasn't a relief ship—then what?

"Harry," I said. "You know we were wrong, don't you? Tarlington doesn't mean us—or Randall—any harm. He didn't start the fire. If anyone did, it wasn't him."

I heard a hitch of breath. I balled up my fists, thinking Harry was about to needle me again for talking to a *conchie*; to remind me of Tarlington's cowardice, my brothers' sacrifice.

"You're right," Harry said. "It wasn't him." His mouth twisted as he looked back at me. But my gaze followed Tarlington to the darkness beyond, the men grouped in the snow, drawing their hoods back.

"Come away from there," Boyd shouted, sharp.

"I just need to—" Tarlington called back, the lantern swinging crazily as he examined the instrument.

A horrible expectant air below.

"Come down. Or I'll come up and make you—"

Clarke pushed his way to the base of the ladder. "You'd better do as he says."

Theatrically, looking around at the gathered men, Tarlington put the light out. Someone spat on the snow. I exhaled, then trudged off towards the kennels, trying not to look back. One of the dogs snuffled at my approach, poked its nose through the bars to lick me. Absurdly, my heart ached for Sanchez, and his almost human *awoo*.

But they exploded into howls, abruptly, when Nicholls came blundering into camp, skis under his arm, his face flushed under his helmet. "Where's Randall?" he panted. The dogs keened, and Harry tried to quiet them.

Clarke looked up: he was fitting reinforcing bolts on the kennel doors, his screwdriver held daintily by two fingers and thumb. "What's the news," he said without enthusiasm.

Nicholls skidded to a halt. His eyes were wide, and the dogs were all barking. It echoed around camp in that way only Antarctic air could achieve, hollow and stark, making everyone look up from their tasks. I followed his tracks with my gaze. It looked like he'd come from the mountains—or that direction, at any rate, where the last glimmers of light had faded. It would remain dark for a very long time.

"Nicholls?"

He shook his head. "It could be—nothing."

Clarke stood up, and I heard something pop under his weight. "Let's hope so." He gave those of us nearby a suspicious look, then glanced towards Randall's window—or where that window should be. Boarded up, with sacking nailed over the joints, it looked like a wounded man wearing an eyepatch. "Come on."

He put his hand on Nicholls's arm; they disappeared towards the door.

I caught a snatch of excited conversation from the stokers. "*That's* where they've gone," Ellis was saying. "Dug in and watching us. This whole thing—it's a bloody trap." He glanced towards the cold locker, his mouth twisting. "No wonder it doesn't feel right—"

"They're still at war," Parker interrupted, to nods of agreement. "They're going to take the place back from us—"

"Waiting to catch us off guard—"

Nicholls had seen something. I clambered, on legs that seemed suddenly unsteady, up the rocky slope. Looking out towards the mountains, I watched my breath plume in fits and starts against the aurora. A sense of foreboding seized me. We were battening down the hatches against the oncoming night; soon that aurora would be the only light we had.

Whatever had happened the previous winter—whatever had happened to the Germans—was starting to happen again. Disappearances. Madness. Violence. All the things I'd feared from the mythical *overwinter*. I stared at the mountains, at the way they seemed to undulate and curve. Subtle and maddening, always seen from the corner of one's eye. Maybe the light, so far below the horizon, was picking them out at an unusual angle. But standing there on the edge of camp, I was able to put my finger—horribly—on the feeling: it was as if something out there was trying to get our attention.

I shuddered. Harry was shading his eyes and looking over: I'd be nothing more than a little dark silhouette against the white plain beyond. He was turning his binoculars around and around in his hands, but I was grateful he hadn't put them to his face. I had the sense that we were being lured out. Someone was putting a helmet on a stick and poking it over the edge of the trench, to see if it drew fire. No Man's Land.

FOUR

THE DARK

EXPEDITION POINT, AUSTRAL WINTER 1920

I

Winter was upon us: the sun would soon set for the last time, no daylight for months. The mountains would be indistinct shapes on the horizon, visible only in civil twilight, or by the aurora. The next morning dawned with Nicholls and Clarke both absent; the half-light had revealed Tarlington's cold locker flying that German flag, and I was sure I detected Ellis's hand in the poorly spelled message daubed on the door. But it was unfinished, stuttered to an end, as if the author had been interrupted halfway through.

As if he'd looked up and—seen something.

A bark made me jump. The stokers had got their guard dog: a big boy called Jesus slept in the Coal Hole on Bedloe's abandoned sleeping bag. All our ammunition had been taken out of the salvaged lockbox overnight, poured onto the common-room table, sorted and counted: the smell of powder made my nose prickle, and I couldn't help picturing Smith struggling past me in the smoke of the burning *Fortitude*. I'd slept poorly, awoken to find everyone in the hut looking around themselves with uneasy choppy glances.

In the Nursery, Harry was throwing a ball against the wall, a regular thud-thud-thud that jostled the bottles in their crates; it set my teeth on edge, made me want to grab and shake him. On the other side, Jesus barked again, then growled and fell silent. Our room was in near darkness, dull fingers of firelight reaching through the curtained doorway. Blankets were bunched up in Tarlington's bed, and for a moment I mistook them for the man himself.

"Where did he go?" I said, fingers twisting at my scarf. After the incident with the German flag, Randall had refused breakfast to all of us, saying that if we were so concerned about our finite supplies—were worried one of our number would sell us out for a place at the Germans' table—*well then*—we could get used to scarcity. His jaw set, he'd shot a baleful glance at the empty place at the end of the table, the oilcan where Clarke normally perched. Hunger and cold made us short-tempered. If Tarlington was outside, I didn't know whether I could stop someone hurting him.

Harry shrugged. As my eyes adjusted to the dim light, I could see his binoculars were still under the bed. We'd talked—frantically—about what Nicholls might have found. Whispers were spreading through the huts. I'd heard someone say a depot, another—a grave. Harry had latched on to that, and shoved those binoculars under the bed as far as they could go.

"Does it matter?" he said now. "There's nowhere he could have gone, is there? Nowhere else for any of us." He laughed, shortly. "We've ended up in the last place on earth. The end of the line. It's no wonder they're so close."

I felt a chill pass over me. I hadn't seen Francis for some time. I kept thinking about him, though, out there in the snow—the way I'd wanted to go to him. But my blood had frozen. Something had stopped me.

"Now we're trapped," Harry said. "Like Karlmann was. Maybe *our* dogs will die soon. Lie down and die. No one's coming for us, Jonathan. And we're all going to—" He gulped in a breath. "It all started with the ship, didn't it? With that *bloody* fire."

I glared at him. "It wasn't—"

"I know," he hissed, so violently I took a step back. "I *know* it wasn't Tarlington—or whatever his name is." And he swore again, in a choked voice I'd never heard him use. The ball reverberated against the wood. Jesus growled. "Whoever did it deserves to be shot," Harry said, his mouth twisting. "They've damned us all—haven't they?"

I sat heavily beside him, the bunk creaking under my weight. I wanted to put my hand on his shoulder, but stopped myself; I knew this was no longer possible. I thought of us reading books together in my hammock on the *Fortitude*. Miles away and lifetimes ago.

He stood abruptly. "I'll go and find him, if you want."

I lay back on his bunk and stared at the ceiling, a horrible cold foreboding in the pit of my stomach. The voices in the common room rose and fell; Ellis and the other men spoke with lowered voices now, looking across at the officers, their accents becoming more and more exaggerated each day. Making themselves impossible to understand.

On the other side of the wall, in the Coal Hole, someone was whispering. The break to Rees's wrist was healing poorly, despite Staunton's best efforts, and he kept himself to his bunk. Sometimes he sobbed, the sound carrying uncomfortably. "I'm no bloody use anymore." He buried his face in the pillow. "A carpenter with one bloody hand. Leave me alone. Put out the light." Clarke had raised his eyebrows, and shut the curtain carefully, saying nothing.

And now Clarke had gone to see whatever Nicholls had found. A depot. A grave. I thought how sure I'd been that we could get through the winter, if we just stayed inside.

No one's coming for us.

I'd once felt so very glad of that.

My parents might have put an end to all of this with a single letter to Australis Randall, care of the magistrate's office, Grytviken. When none had come, I'd thought myself lucky—I'd been so sure they could guess where we had gone. Randall's exploits always made the papers, and Rufus would snatch them out of my father's hand at breakfast to flatten them on his plate, toast and jam forgotten. "Listen to this!" he'd hiss, all wild excitement, he and Francis bending in together. "Australis has returned to New Zealand with *no losses!*"

A look, an indulgent look, passed between my mother and my father—a look that then slid, curdled, to me: paused with my toast halfway to my mouth, as spellbound as my brothers. The awful thought had never occurred to me—that my parents hadn't known me well enough to guess where I'd be headed.

But now the wind was trying the boarded-up windows, rapping on the boot room door, sounding like a whisper—then an anguished scream. I held my breath until it stopped. I'd made my choices. I wasn't a child, to be afraid of ghosts. I wasn't a coward, to be afraid of my brothers, in whatever form they had found me.

II

A door slammed. "This is *my* expedition," Randall shouted. "You have no right, damn you!"

I scrambled to my feet, heart pounding. The Nursery was in pitch darkness. The rest of the hut felt horribly still—expectant. My boots were loud on the floorboards, and I held my breath as I pushed the curtain back, trying not to draw attention. I needn't have bothered: the common room was full of men. Some were in shirtsleeves, others wrapped head to toe in their Burberries, obviously called in from watch. Randall was wearing his large sealskin cape, so heavily and badly patched it looked like someone had performed botched surgery on it. The wound on the back of his head had healed red and crusted beneath his hair.

Harry was right: there was nowhere left to go. The hut seemed impossibly small.

"Australis—" Clarke said. "Not in front of the men."

He stood by the galley, holding a rifle, snow still clinging to his beard. Macready was slowly polishing a large copper pan, skis were propped against the common-room table, and Nicholls was struggling to take off his windproof tunic. The light shimmered off the pan, off Macready's bald head. The three of them looked, abruptly, like conspirators.

"I won't have anything else behind closed doors," Randall snarled. "There's been too much of that, by God—you've presumed too much." He took a few steps forward, grasping the beam above him, leaning down like a large predator scenting for weakness. "Signs of life in the mountains. And you'd go off without telling me—"

"It's nothing," Nicholls said quickly, pulling off his snow-covered hat. His tight curls were whiter than ever. "On my word, Randall," he said. "It's just a cross. Revealed by the storms, in the foothills, and nothing to suggest there's anything more to it than a grave. I'd stake my life on the Germans being dead and gone." He glanced at Clarke. "And those mountains are a death trap. Unknown terrain. Winter on our heels."

So it was true, then. Just something left by some dead men. I found I could picture it easily, with Clarke and Nicholls in their snow gear, the wind whistling down the chimney: those strangers overcome by the mountains, lying down in the snow. Someone surviving just long enough to bury them.

My skin crawled. The wind had scoured those slopes over the last week, while we were all safe inside: clawing away at the snow inch by inch until that cross became visible. I thought of the malevolence I'd felt in the wind. The watchfulness of those mountains.

I told myself not to be paranoid. The *overwinter* was getting to me, too.

"We don't need this," Clarke said. "Not now. Let's talk this over sensibly. Something clearly happened to them. And we need to consider our options." A small crack as he rubbed his knuckles. "We need to think about how we're getting out of here."

"What we need!" Randall snapped. "That's for me to decide, damn you. We have proof positive there are men out there. A few days away! As many as twenty-nine fellow men, here at the bottom of the world. The only men in a thousand miles—and you'd have kept me in the dark? By God, this is—this is bloody well close to—"

Boyd snorted, his arms folded. "It's more than *close to*. I'd say it's plain insubordination. Plotting." There was a most unpleasant look on his face: the look of someone who'd been proved right.

Randall cut him short with a glare, the fallen slope of his face twitching a little. He seemed to gather himself as he turned back to Clarke. "I know you've been working—despite me. And I've been willing to overlook it. But the Weddell Sea—"

The Weddell Sea. The left side of Randall's face hadn't survived that accident: he'd bear the mark of that sea for the rest of his life. I couldn't think why he'd mention it now. But then I looked around and saw the darkroom table, disassembled by the door, broken down into a neat assortment of planks. Clarke's solicitude towards Rees, which had struck me as uncharacteristic. Lots of things had been broken down for timber recently, awaiting a carpenter.

It hit me in the chest: Clarke, sensible Liam Clarke, was planning to build *boats*.

"It's likely a grave," Clarke said, shaking his head. "Just some dead men. They won't tell you what you want to hear. And as for that ship—"

"Convenient, eh?" Randall growled. "Isn't it? To stay inside, stay quiet, when there are men out there that might need our help—might be starving, injured, stranded by weather or accident!" He turned, slowly, looking around the room. "How do any of you propose to live with yourselves, eh? Knowing you left them to die?"

No one met his eye. My hands were curled into tight, painful little balls. Randall would never leave anyone behind. Not after Charlie. He simply didn't have it in him.

"Germans," said one of the stokers.

"I don't give a damn whether they're German or not!" Randall roared, pulling his cape off so violently the buttons clattered to the floor. "Whether they're German or English or—damn you—I don't care whether they're fucking American or African! Petty cowards—the lot of you! That you'd dare to—have the cheek to—sit indoors and make yourselves comfortable amongst their funeral goods. You're a bloody disgrace to me—to your country!"

Think of the press. Randall had built an industry of exploration around himself and his reputation; lionized in the papers, by people like my brothers. *Fortitude—or devastation.*

He had no choice but to send a rescue party.

He jabbed at Ellis with his broad finger. "If that isn't enough for you, think of this—who knows where the *Drygalski* is, eh? The Germans. Who knows what arrangements might have been made for a relief ship? The bloody Germans. We need to know when it's coming, so we don't have to—so we can avoid—"

"Randall," Nicholls said quietly. "It's just a grave." He paused, and the next few words seemed to be dragged out of him. "A depot, maybe."

A look passed between Randall and Macready; Macready inclined his shoulders the smallest fraction of a degree. I couldn't stop myself looking towards the galley shelves. The growing empty spaces. The storeroom was chained and padlocked. No more tinned peaches. No more "Good Morgan." "We won't eat you, *yet*," Rees had once said, and winked.

Randall swallowed, his mouth curling inwards on the frostbitten side. Then, looking up: "Stores, and—and men! For when we leave this place, together."

Someone snorted; it was Clarke. "I won't be part of this," he said. "We could have got on with it, over winter—come up with a way out, not gone haring off after rumors of some relief ship. You told me—"

Randall turned on him. "And you—*you*! You have no right—no right at all. To keep this from me—try to turn my own men against me—"

Boyd shouldered his way forward to stand beside him, saying to Clarke, "We're done taking orders from you."

"I know *some* of you have been loyal," Randall said to the men. "Some of you. But when cowards and upstarts—"

Two steps, and Clarke was on Randall, grabbing him by the collar. Randall was large, but Clarke towered over him. "You'll take that back, James!"

Silence. Randall's harsh breathing. The sound of the wind outside, rattling at the door, trying its luck on all our cracks and crevices and weak points. My heart hammered. I'd never heard Clarke use Randall's first name.

"Let go of me," Randall said. "I'll have my expedition back."

"There's no one out there," Clarke said. "There's—damn it—there's no one!"

Ellis laughed like a goblin, a small twitch showing in the corner of his mouth. All eyes turned to him. "Someone's out there, all right. We've heard them."

Macready scoffed. A dark look came over Clarke's face. He loosened his hands, let Randall go. Took a step back.

"*You* know what we mean." Ellis gave Rees a hard nudge to the ribs. "Tell 'em."

But Rees froze, opening and closing his mouth, a puppet.

"Calling to us," Ellis muttered. "Those as are dead."

Silence.

Randall rubbed his hand over the scar on the back of his head. "Someone outside," he growled. "Someone—dead—outside." He seemed to forget where he was, looking around the hut as if he'd never seen it before.

"Morgan knows." Ellis pointed at me. "They want you to go with them, don't they? And make you—"

My skin crawled. My head felt suddenly full of ants. Everyone was looking at me. I took a step back, straight into Laurence. He steadied me, but did not smile.

Randall's terrible gaze seemed to take an age to turn to me. "Morgan, eh? Our *spare*. You wouldn't leave someone out in the snow, would you? You once told me so. Wouldn't leave a fellow on the battlefield—wouldn't leave—" He rubbed distractedly at that scab until it reopened, and something wet ran down his neck. He didn't seem to notice.

I opened my mouth, taking an unsteady breath. But it seemed plain to me that Clarke was right. Pinning all our hopes on the Germans, on a relief ship—going into the mountains to hunt for them—was a huge gamble, one wagered with our lives. For a moment I hated myself. This was Australis Randall, hero of the South, and this was who I'd become: this Jonathan with his shaved head, face tanned the color of weak tea.

"We need to settle this, once and for all," Boyd said, cracking his knuckles. "Where they've gone. Who's *outside*."

"There's no one," Macready said. "No need to jump at shadows—"

"We need to survive," Clarke said, stepping in front of Randall. It felt like a shutter had been closed, a pitiless searchlight extinguished. Laurence loosened his grip on my arms, gave them a pat. "Even if the Germans *are* still alive—we can't all go. And it's too close to winter—you won't split the party, you know it's madness. We need to stay together."

"It's madness, eh?" Randall said. "You've always thought yourself capable of reading my bloody mind. Boyd—you and Laurence start preparations for a search party. Pick the men to accompany you—four should do it—Staunton, in case there are casualties. We won't leave Karlmann and his men to die out there. We'll put an end to this."

"I reckon we will," Boyd muttered.

Randall turned back to Clarke. "Whatever you may have thought, Liam, you're my man no longer. You've got no authority here. No rank. We'll get you home, but by God—you'll not make something of yourself at my expense. Get out. Get out!"

In silence, Clarke walked to the front door. Opened it. And stepped outside, exhaling a long hard breath into the wind.

III

The creaks and groans of pressure outside, as the wind battered the eastern side of the huts.

Drifting in and out of half-sleep, my thoughts—sleeping and waking—arced, always, back to my brothers. Francis, standing in the snow. He'd been so proud of his uniform as a newly gazetted lieutenant, the cap still peaked and wired, the boots polished to a mirror shine. After purchasing their commissions, they'd spent the autumn and winter in training, showing off their eagerness and appetite: doing everything they could to shove themselves to the front of the queue for France. Their big adventure before they turned south. They'd wanted it all so passionately, in a way I had never been allowed to want anything. I was to be packed off to boarding school. Made *appropriate*. Forced to be someone else.

They'd worn those crisp khaki uniforms with their battalion at the railway station. Deployment. My mother, crying. Rufus's cruel smile, as he spoke of the battlefield ahead. Glory, and death. His eyes were gleaming—as though her discomfort gave him strength—but at the end he'd folded her up in an embrace, told her not to worry.

I'd felt desperately sorry for her, the feeling tugging at my heart from a hundred different directions. She'd always . . . tried. She looked so tiny and fragile in his arms: Rufus was larger than Francis, taller, his face carved from stone; capable of setting into disapproval at a moment's notice. He'd towered above Harry when they were younger, resented every inch of Harry's sudden leggy growth. A stray shouldn't outgrow those who took it in. Should be grateful. Should know its place.

Harry turned over in the bunk beneath me, his breathing ragged. The sound of him saying "Whoever did it deserves to be *shot*" came back into my head, familiar as the refrain of a song. I imagined Rufus saying to me—with those cruel eyes—"He's damned us all." Rufus wouldn't hesitate: he'd have dragged the culprit outside in a second. Put a gun to the back of his head. Pulled the trigger. He'd always been so sure, so certain, in everything he did. He'd have been Boyd's right hand.

And I was—what?

I sat up. My heart was fluttering in my chest like a captive thing. It was so dark. I couldn't bear it a moment longer. I felt my way into the common room, blindly seeking out the light.

I'd expected to find people there. But the room was frozen, absolutely still, save the flickering reflections of the stove. Tongues of flame, licking at dry timber.

Whoever did it deserves to be shot.

Shot at dawn, like the deserters: Clarke had taken care of Mortimer, Jones, and Archer. This was my world, now. I rubbed my hands reflexively over my forearms, noting with distant satisfaction the muscles firm under the skin.

A growl. I jumped. Jamieson was curled possessively around the stove, tail twitching. His pale unblinking eyes fixed me with a warning. Then I noticed Laurence lying on the long bench of the common-room table, one hand dangling over the side. His rifle rested across his knees. He wasn't outside. He was asleep on watch.

I let out a *tsss* of disapproval between pinched lips.

At our sullen teatime—when Randall had sent someone to eat outside for doubting the very existence of the relief ship—Nicholls had swapped onto the night watch. Casually, darning the earflaps of his ridiculous hat: "I'd like to take some observations, as it doesn't look like an auroral night."

Laurence had yawned. "You'll have to keep me awake, then."

Now he was so fast asleep, he was drooling. Nicholls was on watch—*outside*—alone.

Jamieson stared at me, hackles slowly rising. "Good dog," I whispered, and backed away, my boots sure and certain on the uneven flooring. On the dog deck I'd learned to keep eye contact, and the dogs were much less skittish around me than Harry.

I glanced at Laurence, but he didn't stir. I resisted the urge to shake him roughly awake: he'd left us defenseless. Again, I thought of Rufus. He'd have made Laurence regret it bitterly. But I wanted to go outside myself—I wanted to *see*. Because Nicholls had let me unbar the shutters. Nicholls had let me walk out into the storm—

Maybe Boyd was right. Maybe it was all a delusion, and I was seeing what I wanted to see. Maybe there were no ghosts at all.

I clung to the idea. It was almost easier.

Whoever did it deserves to be shot.

I slept wearing the service revolver, at Boyd's insistence, although it was uncomfortable. I found myself feeling for it now. Boyd had been so sure, on the ship: Nicholls was above suspicion. The navigator who'd stayed loyal. Likable, easy Nicholls. But Boyd's certainties had evaporated; and Nicholls seemed the exception to the unspoken rule that we were staying indoors for the winter. He'd been the one to see that cross. *Signs of life.*

I could imagine him coming across a German camp. Hands up, a smile on his face. Making a deal. Trading his place with Randall—sleepwalking, erratic, *haunted* Randall—for a place with Karlmann, when the time came.

I swallowed, tasting the metallic taint of blood, and found the boot room door at my back. It was stiff; the huts were starting to warp as winter approached, settling themselves into the landscape. Jamieson looked at me steadily, but made no sound. A poor guard dog.

I didn't waste time finding my own gear, but dragged a random jacket over my head, shoving the sleeves up and rolling them into place, tightening the belt like a tourniquet. I didn't bother to wish myself taller or bigger; found myself muttering in the dark, "Come on, come on—"

I steeled myself against the outside world; took a good deep breath; checked the Webley.

The night was warmer than I expected. No wind and no color. I felt incredibly relieved, then told myself this was stupid: there was nothing brought by the aurora. No need to jump at shadows. I gripped the gun tightly. *Nicholls.* I turned it over and over in my mind. Gray-haired Nicholls, lines etched around his eyes.

Meet me on the dog deck, later.

It made my stomach churn. I should have watched him more closely, back on the ship, when I'd had the chance. I didn't know how I'd been so trusting. I'd wanted to believe in the safety of this new world of men; my own unquestioned place in it. But if the Germans came back—my heart beat hard in my chest under all those layers of clothing. Harry had said, once, that the whalers were to be feared. Strange men, uncivilized, perhaps less likely to take me at face value; who knew what German bootsteps on the porch would bring?

There was no one at the front steps. No lantern, no rifle. No sign of Nicholls at all.

"Damn," I whispered, and crept down into the snow.

It was incredibly dark. As my eyes adjusted, I could see the new moon filtering through the clouds, the pinprick dusting of a hundred stars. The huts crouched under the endless sky. I turned around, slowly, searching for signs of life.

A sudden noise. My hand clenched on the gun. But it was only the dogs, growling softly at one another. They stuck their noses out of the kennels and whined as I tiptoed past. They looked alert—bright-eyed and healthy—and I thought of Tarlington. He hadn't been in the Nursery. I'd seen the stokers jostling him at dinner, barely pretending it was a game.

If Tarlington was outside, he'd be in the cold locker, its squat little door just outside the circle of lantern-light. I turned around, again, looking for Nicholls. Nothing.

But I was increasingly sure: I'd heard that door on the night of the storm, when Nicholls had left his post. And that foggy night on the ship—there had been a second person in the foredeck locker. A second tall shape, walking quickly away. It might mean nothing. But Harry had had his suspicions about Nicholls, too, from the very start.

Plenty of those officers came to regret it, over there.

What if we'd got it the wrong way around? It made my fingertips tingle. Everything would be easier for a veteran—someone who knew the ship and the expedition inside out. Maybe he'd been trying to make common cause with the one person he knew would share his . . . disillusionment. Drawing him in. Using him.

I suppose you'll show him.

Tarlington—whoever he was—might be in terrible danger.

I drew the service revolver, looking at it dumbly. My hands shook. I couldn't imagine I'd have the courage to point it at someone and pull the trigger. I wasn't like Rufus. But this was my world now, and I had to fight for it.

My footsteps muffled by the drift as I approached, I could see a light burning in the cold locker. I edged around the side of the ramshackle building, my heart dancing in my chest, hearing low voices. And a sound that made my mouth fall open—I wasn't sure I'd heard it before—Tarlington laughing.

I found a crack in the wood.

Macready's fuel-can stove was hissing away. A lantern hung above Tarlington's examination table, and I could see the coppery flash of his hair. A swaying tern carcass blocked my view of the two figures inside, its stomach distended, feathers turned a dull stiff gray.

I looked away—then looked back immediately, pressing my face to the timber. Tarlington was partly undressed, his shirt unbuttoned to the waist and shrugged off his pale freckled shoulders. The light picked out sweat glistening, gemlike, on his bare neck. Nicholls sat on the examination table, hand tangled in Tarlington's hair.

"James—" Nicholls said. Then tightened his grip, pulling Tarlington closer. There was a look on his face I'd never seen before. Some sort of hunger.

Tarlington said something very quietly, a smile taking up his entire face. And he must have reached up to push Nicholls away—I couldn't quite see around the carcass—because there was suddenly not an inch between their bodies.

I turned away, stumbling on the snow, staring at the revolver in my shaking hands. My breath came in wild and uncontrollable bursts. I had to help Tarlington, although I wasn't sure what the danger was. Something was—wrong. I went towards the door as if my legs weighed a hundred tons each. As if they were completely out of my control.

A noise inside. Nicholls said "Shh!" and the door creaked open.

Tarlington appeared, silhouetted against the warm glow, and I came crashing to a halt. He scowled at me. I sucked in a breath, staring at him. "For God's sake, Morgan!"

His eyes widened as he looked down at the Webley. Up again, to search my face.

"Come here." Nicholls shouldered roughly past him to grab me. If he was afraid—if he even noticed the gun—he didn't show it. He pulled me into the close damp air of that little room with enough force to make me tumble onto the floor. I scrambled to my feet, shoving the gun back into my belt.

Nicholls's curls were wild and messy. He refastened his trousers with a dogged air of bravado. Tarlington—with what looked like a bite mark on the side of his long pale neck—stared at me, then pressed his fists into his eyes, as if trying to dispel a bad dream. He didn't appear to be hurt. They were waiting, I realized, for me to speak.

"I thought you were—plotting against us—"

Tarlington let out a high helpless laugh. Nicholls towered over me, using my jacket to push me up against the wall. The dead birds swung wildly from side to side. All laughter lines were gone from his face. "How long were you there?"

"I was only—I saw—" I cleared my throat, and stopped. I was no longer sure what I'd seen. My ears were hot and prickly.

"You idiot," Nicholls said. "You little *idiot*, sneaking around like that with a loaded weapon. In camp. God knows what could've happened— this is no place for war games." He released my collar, but didn't back away. My Burberry was far too warm, and the sweat beaded on my face.

"Are you going to tell—anyone?" Tarlington said, a catch in his voice. My expression must have given away my horror, because he went on, urgently: "Are you going to tell Randall?"

I stared at him, then looked away, my cheeks burning. I knew what I'd seen: the way he'd gone willingly to Nicholls; his warm easy laughter. I thought of the flash of—something—when he'd seen me and Harry sharing a hammock on the ship. How he'd shaken his head and turned away. My face grew so hot I thought it might be on fire, at the idea he'd thought, even for a moment—

But there hadn't been any danger—not to us, to the rest of the expedition, at least. Assignations in strange places around the ship; Tarlington had found me in the storage locker; Tarlington had soot on his cuffs, and hadn't dared explain, even when it put him in terrible jeopardy.

They must have been—*together* for some time.

But it was strange, so utterly unlike anything I'd ever confronted, and my mind whirled. Nicholls looked ready to strike me down where I stood. I opened my mouth, and he shook me roughly. "Well. Are you? You should know, Morgan, there's nothing about me which Randall doesn't know, and—and tolerate. I've been at his side since the beginning. Tell him, for all I care. He wouldn't think less of me."

I bit the inside of my cheek, thinking of all the other people I could tell. Harry, with his downcast eyes—his clumsy pass, that night in the rigging. He would think this very different; would insist on that differ-ence, cling to it. And the crew were on a knife-edge, ready to name a *scapegoat*—anyone would do. Anything could tip them over. It would be a disaster. A witch hunt.

We'll settle this, once and for all. Who's outside.

My mortified silence seemed to satisfy Nicholls, and he stepped away. I exhaled slowly.

But Tarlington caught my hand and squeezed it. I looked down in surprise. It was the first time he'd really touched me since finding me a stowaway. His hands were bare, and quite warm. "Please, don't tell Randall. Just—don't."

My words didn't want to come out. Tarlington was *touching* me.

"We're no threat to the expedition," he said in his low hoarse voice. "Morgan, *please.*"

I shrugged him off. He snatched his hand back, like a boy caught doing something for which he'd receive a whipping. I backed towards the door, not wanting to look at either of them. "I know you're no threat," I said slowly. "But—"

Tarlington's high uncertain breathing. A look passed between them, Nicholls's gray eyes hard as granite. Tarlington passed me my scarf, sodden with snow. "Do as you like," he said, then swallowed. "We can be separated. I'll move out of your room, and sleep—and sleep wherever. But please, Morgan, don't tell him."

IV

Tarlington kept his end of the bargain.

His absence made the Nursery seem dangerously lopsided, like a lifeboat that would shortly be taking on water. "Good riddance," Harry said, commandeering his bed and all the extra blankets immediately. The condensation now froze on the walls overnight, and we tacked up sacking for insulation. Soon April would end, and during the long, long night, the temperature outside would drop to forty below.

I felt restless when I thought about Tarlington, out in the cold locker. I had no wish for him to freeze to death—none at all—no matter what was said. He took catnaps by the stove, head placed on his folded-up arms, greatcoat drawn around him, tucked into a small nook where he could not easily be poked or shoved. Macready shrugged, but let him get on with it. At mealtimes, his eyes followed me eagerly down the table. He looked away when I wouldn't return his gaze.

I'd told him, once, to return to the Nursery. Stop going outside. Stop making himself such a target. But now I found myself unable to do so. I wished I'd never seen what I'd seen. My cheeks flushed at how I'd almost been ready to use the gun, fancying myself—alone—able to protect the expedition. I was grateful beyond measure that I hadn't woken Harry.

My world revolved uneasily. Preparations continued for what Randall called the "rescue party," Boyd simply the "mountain party": Laurence had worked miracles, holding the German motor sledge together with a wing and a prayer. A smaller dog sledge team would scout ahead—try to make contact. But whatever Randall said, I could tell Boyd didn't intend to bring anyone back with him.

I weighed the service revolver in my hands. Nine in the morning: sunrise still some way off. A breakfast of porridge, prunes, and tea was served in the common room, but my stomach felt hard, and I couldn't face eating. Clarke gathered himself onto one of the benches, no longer at the head of the table.

Staunton emerged from the sick bay bundled up to his eyeballs. "I've left what I can," he said to Clarke. "Dressings. Some morphine—for emergencies only. Be sparing."

Parker nudged Holmes, and chuckled. Staunton had been little use at hauling—had never been on watch—and now he looked like an Antarctic explorer straight out of the papers. He said peevishly, "Perhaps you'd like to try to set a broken bone, or treat gangrene. Oh—shut up."

The front door opened. "All right, boys." Boyd leaned in. The stove flickered, the curtains swayed. "Let's get on with it."

I felt lighter as I made up my mind, unclipping the holster from my belt and walking outside. The cold morning air was like a physical blow, and I saw Staunton flinch, although he didn't have an inch of skin on display. I licked my dry lips, regretting it instantly. Tingling, prickling. The air *hurt*.

"Well." Randall cleared his throat. "Boyd, you have your objectives. Find the cross. Find the Germans. Offer them assistance as required—bring them back, if you can, with all supplies. We shan't be the expedition that abandoned men to their deaths. I won't have it said we were that."

He was about to say more, but there was a shuffling through the ranks of the mountain party—Boyd, Staunton, Laurence, Ollivar, and Parker—and a sixth figure appeared. Wrapped up like the rest of them, toes to eyes, snow goggles clamped over his face. My hand fell limply to my side: a thick black cap covered his head, but his hood was down, and I could see the nape of his neck. Pale from living too long in darkness, and the signs of someone taking a razor, clumsily, to red hair. He would feel the loss very keenly in the cold.

"Sir," Tarlington said formally.

Randall turned, his eyes narrowing.

"I wish to join the rescue party," Tarlington said in a rush. "I haven't been as much use to the expedition as I intended. I'm a quick learner—I could help Laurence. If I have your permission?"

I watched the expression moving slowly across Randall's ruined face. A fierce look came into his eyes, and for a moment he was so very like the Randall I'd met on the *Fortitude*. A believer in the wonder and allure of the South; a man we could trust to get us out of anything.

Boyd nodded. "We could use another hand on the motor," he said roughly. "And I'd be happy to have him where I can keep an eye on him."

Randall took his hands from his pockets and clasped them together; turned his signet ring, under his gloves, the movements muted and dreamlike. "Of course," he said. "By God, I will not turn down volunteers."

I glanced around the assembled faces: wearing balaclavas, they looked strange and skeletal. Nicholls wasn't there to see Tarlington leave for the mountains. He'd gone out to where the glacier plummeted into the sea; the sound of him thumping around with his skis had woken me, and I'd lain in my bunk, staring at the ceiling. I'd started looking at the faces of Randall's veterans, as Tarlington had once suggested, and had come to read—clearly—what I saw. Nicholls wasn't scouting for the sake of a relief ship; he was making plans for the absence of one. Clarke knew that one day we would have to leave the huts; find our way to the thrashing open water; try to row ourselves to safety. *Desperate men.*

And a long, long winter to survive first.

"Good man," Randall said, clapping Tarlington heavily on the back. "That's what we need, eh? Good men. When the journey will be difficult, and the ending uncertain. Men you can count on."

I couldn't smile. I could only stare, noticing that people were talking over him in a way that would have been unthinkable on the *Fortitude*. He continued to speak—telling us we were showing the true spirit of exploration, the best of our country, risking our lives for others—while Ollivar adjusted the weight of the dog sledge under Rees's rather nervy supervision. While Macready said consoling things to Holmes, who hadn't been chosen to go, and was looking longingly at the horizon: no doubt thinking about the glories that might once have awaited him. His disappointment was naked on his face, and Ollivar avoided his eyes. Even Boyd himself rubbed his jaw, glanced at Clarke, then said, before Randall was done: "Come on, then, let's get this over with."

Tarlington—the shrouded figure that was Tarlington—took a last look at the huts. Slowly, his gaze found me in the crowd. It was like being looked at by a plague doctor, or a creature from a fairy tale. Barely human. I rubbed my gloved hand against the back of my neck. I wanted to speak to him. I didn't have the faintest idea what I would say.

When Randall finished—perhaps noticing how we were stamping our feet, burrowing hands into pockets, resenting every second of this protracted good-bye—I slipped over to Boyd. "Here." I held out his service revolver. "It's yours."

I'd been so proud.

I thought about what Nicholls had called my *war games*. Unmasking a plot. German agents. Saboteurs. I'd been wrong about everything, and having the Webley—Boyd's gun from the trenches—disgusted me. You couldn't shoot a ghost, after all. It was worse than useless. My stomach lurched and pitched. In the distance, Tarlington conferred with Laurence in his scratchy voice. For a moment, I thought of begging him not to leave.

Boyd looked at me through goggles and balaclava. "Keep it," he said, and reached out a big hand, closing it over mine. "Keep it, Morgan. I gave it to you for a reason. You'll know when the time comes." He turned away, shouting instructions. I exhaled at length, feeling the cold stab at me.

Whirring; smoke; fumes. The dogs howled as the motor reverberated around camp, loud enough to wake the dead. It would haul steadily over flat ground, barely faster than walking—far slower than dogs—and Laurence and Tarlington would bring up the rear, struggling with the beast alone. Sentiment made me wish to watch them pass out of sight. To see the back of Tarlington, bent double.

"Two weeks should do it. Three at the very most," Boyd said to Randall. "If we're not back by then—well. Don't expect us."

Nearly half the expedition had been . . . drawn out. Out onto that windswept plateau, winter dogging their heels. They turned away. My teeth chattered. The skin froze on my lips; cracked and bled. My fingers stiffened and lost feeling. Blinking hurt my dry eyes.

It was too cold to be sentimental. I had to go inside.

V

"We should never have left the ship," Ellis said.

The galley was quiet. The stove was banked to conserve coal, and the pot water was cold enough to numb my fingers. Ellis was a poor companion at chores: he kept leaning against the stove, trying to engage me in conversation. His demeanor casual, so it might be mistaken for a friendly chat, but there was nothing very friendly about his flinty eyes.

Over at the table, Holmes raised his eyebrows. "You saw the state of her. Think she's still there?"

"Doesn't matter. If she's a wreck, if she's drifted, or frozen in. We were safer on the water. Anywhere's better than being stuck *here*."

The winds banged on the door, peremptory, demanding admittance, and he shuddered. They'd started when the mountain party left, with a ferocity that surprised us all. Hammering at the boarded-up windows, pulling off roofing, bringing down lanterns and weather equipment. Nicholls had ventured out in the screaming blizzard, and come across nothing of our comrades but a discarded tobacco tin. Their tracks had long since blown away.

We had no way of knowing where they were.

I hoped they'd simply ground to a halt; taken cover, dug in, waited for the storm to pass. No senseless heroics. Holmes had a grisly theory that they'd encountered Mortimer and the mutineers—making their own desperate attempt to reach the safety of the huts—and it had come to murder. Shots ringing out in the whiteness. Blood in the snow.

"Clarke shot them, though," I'd blurted out.

"Are you sure?"

"I heard it."

Holmes had given me a skeptical look—and I'd fallen silent. I shivered. The idea of *hearing things* had become dangerous.

"Are you going to play, or gossip like a pair of lasses?" Macready said. "Ellis. Stop swinging the lead over there."

The chess set had reappeared. Holmes and Macready were passing the time by trying to teach Rees, take his mind off things. I could see from the horrible tremor in his good hand—the other held awkward and crabbed—it wasn't having the desired effect. He was reluctant to even touch the pieces. I couldn't blame him. Karlmann had brought with him that beautifully polished chess set, china dinner plates, all the trappings of civilization. But the South—or something else—had refused him.

Ellis shook his head. "Back off, Macready."

"If you're heard talking like that—"

"What?" Ellis laughed. "If I'm heard talking like that, *what*? You should've seen the fireproofing. She'll be there now, frozen in like a cork in a bottle. Maybe even her boats. *Proper* boats."

He put a lot of emphasis on that last point, and I braced myself against the table. It would all come down to boats. We'd have to retrieve the one left at Shore Camp, tear down the huts for timber to make more, then scramble back down into a shifting maze of ice, four hundred miles from the whaling routes. Live off whatever we could shoot. Get ourselves out. Or die trying.

I stared down at the cold greasy water. I still had nightmares about the sea, about killer whales rising up out of the water to look at us with their yellow piggish eyes. Their snub noses and glistening teeth, welcoming prey to their territory. "You're here!" they seemed to say, with wide and malevolent smiles. "We've been waiting!" And they hammered on the ice beneath us with cunning and efficiency, tipping the floes, trying to split us up. Backing away—redoubling. Taking their time, because they had time to spare.

We'll take a piece of you—then come back for the rest.

Our short journey in the *Fortitude*'s well-maintained lifeboats had been bad enough. I looked over at Rees, at the way he was holding his hand, thumb splayed towards the wrist. A nervous tapping of his knee against the underside of the table. I tried to imagine him wielding a hammer, building those makeshift boats. Exposing them to the stern face of the Weddell Sea.

We'd all drown within the hour.

"If Randall hadn't dragged us here—" Ellis continued.

"We all went along with him," I snapped, my voice louder than I intended. "What's done is done." I attacked the pots with renewed vigor, as if I could drown out the voices clamoring in my head.

Get through the winter—

"Morgan. You're still a young lad. It's worse for you, hey? To die down here—"

We're all going to die down here—

"Just because our crippled old leaders—"

"What's that?"

Randall: standing in the sick-bay doorway, his shirtsleeves rolled up. There was a slight side-to-side sway in his stance, as if he were back aboard ship. "Who said that?"

"It was nothing," Macready said.

Randall looked directly at me, his dark blue eyes piercing. "Morgan?"

I shook my head. I didn't dare glance at Ellis, whose Northern drawl was unmistakable.

"An old man, am I?" Randall growled. "Or a cripple? I've commanded three expeditions, show some respect—"

"Oh, shut up," someone else said.

My heart stuttered.

Randall spun around. "Who said *that*?"

Jaw set hard, he tried the weight of his stare on each of us in turn. Rees pushed the chess set out of reach with a shivery fingertip. Holmes met Randall's gaze, looking bitter. Harry—over by a chink in the boarded-up windows—closed his journal with a deliberate thump.

Ellis smirked, as if delighted to have provoked this. Any one of us might have said it: Clarke would have identified the culprit instantly. Clarke could recognize us all by the backs of our heads; by the way we coughed; by our bootprints.

"Outside," Randall snapped, shaking his head. "If none of you will own up—"

"I don't see why," Harry muttered behind him.

There was an audible intake of breath.

Clarke, appearing under the dangling laundry, had just finished tying off the fingers on another pair of gloves, making his disability plain. He was so large his ice axe looked like a toy. "We should do something about the drift," he said, with the air of someone thinking aloud. "Before it splits the timber."

Randall's mouth pressed into a tight, hard line. For a moment, it looked like he would strike him. "All of you! If no one wants to own to it. If you're going to sit indoors and gossip like a bunch of hens—questioning and second-guessing—we'll have no more talk. Outside, until the snow is cleared—until I tell you to stop. I'll give you something to do, damn it."

When I dragged myself outside, the aurora was a dull green glow in the sky, the snow set hard as iron. It was so cold I let out a tiny sob, fearing for my toes. Nicholls was a tall blurry shape at the anemometer: an unmoving sentinel against the emerald light, the smattering of stars. Then, as if realizing he was being watched, he clambered down and trudged past us, ice caked around his boots like elephant feet.

"I've been watching the weather, Morgan," he said sideways. "Not signaling to the enemy, or plotting against the expedition." He slammed the door with a flourish, and I heard Randall's growling voice rising to greet him.

I swallowed, feeling strangely dirty.

Clarke had included himself in Randall's punishment, swinging the axe as though he could chop his way through the globe and come out back in Ireland. He didn't complain, even when Harry slipped down the porch steps, upending our pail of slushy water—warm only minutes before. It hissed as it froze on the decking like a field of cut glass.

It had been Harry who'd told Randall to *shut up*; absolutely unthinkable, for a boy who'd had to be so carefully coached to lie to the recruiting sergeant: my brothers had told him how to hold himself, what to say. I'd once thought him utterly transparent. But now we were all being punished on his account.

"Watch what you're doing—" I grabbed his jacket. He felt like a puppet whose strings had been cut.

"Easy," Clarke said.

I paused, realizing I had the jacket bunched around Harry's neck, and his throat was working against the taut fabric. His officer's mustache—he hadn't shaved it off or grown a beard like the others. He'd always looked exactly like the Harry Cooper who'd come home from the War. Neat and disciplined. Dutiful. But now—

We're all going to die down here.

"What do you think has happened," I said desperately to Clarke. "To—to the mountain party?"

He didn't look at me.

"The mutineers?"

"They're no threat to us, not anymore." Clarke clamped his hand down on my shoulder. "Courage, Morgan."

Courage, Morgan. I tried to keep it in mind as I swung my axe. But the memory of Clarke shooting them gave me no courage at all. The dead were not staying dead. If my brothers could find us here—all the way from France, dragging themselves through mud and ocean and ice, when they bore no possible grudge—then the ghosts of Mortimer and his men were to be dreaded.

The front door opened, startling me. Randall appeared on the threshold, half-dragging Rees under one arm. The wind grabbed the door and slammed it closed again.

Clarke stood up.

"You bloody coward!" Randall was shouting.

"I don't *want* to," Rees sobbed. His eyes were popping, staring sightlessly ahead. The whites appeared to protrude too far beyond the sockets, like a poorly executed marble carving. It made him look utterly inhuman. "I can't bear it, please—"

"He's lost his nerve," Macready shouted. "We shouldn't—"

"Everyone works! I made myself quite clear."

"There's something outside." Rees was crying. "It's made me do terrible things. And we need to stay inside, shut the doors; it won't stop, it's coming back—"

"Leave him, Randall," Macready said. He kept his voice steady, his hands up. As if speaking to a wild animal. "You know what this is. You've seen it before."

No one took a single step towards Rees, half-crouched on the porch in front of Randall, holding the railings like he'd been put in the dock. A man on trial for his life. The lanterns creaked. The aurora shimmered, turning the snow a delicate green, and Rees cringed from it.

It's made me do terrible things. My skin crawled. He looked like the shell of a man. And Randall looked like a beast.

"I'll do his shift!" I shouted. Randall turned, and appeared not to recognize me. But we were all the same to him now. We were soldiers— pawns. Infinitely expendable.

"By God, you'll—" He snarled, and pried Rees off the railing. Pulled him up, a few steps along the porch, then onto his knees in front of Clarke, who took a step back. I held my breath. Rees was limp and shivering, his mouth open, like he was already suffocating.

Randall grabbed him by the scruff of his neck and plunged him headfirst into the slush bucket, as if to drown him. Rees flailed and struck out. Clarke made a single abortive motion with his own good hand, and I stared at him, willing him, begging him to intervene. The sound of Rees in the bucket was the sound of ice around the boats, the sound of the sucking dark water, the sound of Harry flailing in his nightmares of mud, the devouring mud.

I couldn't bear it. "I'll do it!" I shouted again, scrabbling one-two along the frozen decking. I *hated* Randall. Would have punched him if I'd dared.

Harry made a low noise of wonder. A dim crackling in the sky. And then, horribly, Randall turned; the aurora caught in his eyes. He appeared to recognize someone—just for a moment—standing in the void space behind the kennels, where the ice marched away for unbroken miles.

VI

True winter arrived with the mountain party two weeks gone.

I was back on watch—Randall's orders. The aurora was a storm of lights, capping the mountains to the east with fiery crowns, giving the weird impression of a burning city somewhere beyond. Ice in the air became embers floating to earth. Nicholls, as always, took the front of the huts. I paced up and down outside the Nursery, feeling as if I would wear the boards thin.

Clarke was in and out to bring us hot drinks. Once, I'd have found it patronizing. But now there was nothing I could dislike about his large shape looming at the back door; warm tea; the creak of the railings as he leaned next to me.

"Anything?" he said quietly.

I knew he wasn't asking about Germans. "Nothing."

He looked past me, towards the aurora. "Nicholls?"

"He's all right. Harry?"

"Asleep." In Tarlington's bed, binoculars stuffed into his pack. He'd traded or given away most of his small comforts from home: his shaving kit—we "shared" the same one now—and his writing instruments. The room looked emptier and bleaker every day.

I followed Clarke around the porch, ice shattering under our feet. Nicholls, too, was pacing, never taking his eyes off the mountains, the point where dark horizon was menaced by burning sky. I looked up—then had to avert my gaze.

"A few hours of civil twilight," he said briefly. "That'll go soon, as well."

Clarke checked his watch and nodded. "Right on schedule. Then that'll be it till mid-August."

I shivered; wrapped my arms around myself; bounced up and down. Almost four months without a sunrise. We would be utterly at the mercy of—

What, exactly, I didn't know.

Clarke pulled out a tin of tobacco, gestured. "Disgusting stuff," Nicholls said, taking it anyway. His fingers trembled slightly.

"Anything?" Clarke nodded towards the mountains. Nicholls swore under his breath, shook his head.

"I'm sorry." Clarke placed his hand on Nicholls's back. My heart thumped in my chest, heat rising to my face. I stepped cautiously out of the light of the storm lanterns. Nicholls hadn't been bluffing when he'd said I might tell Randall. It was obvious that Clarke, too—Clarke with his large weather-beaten hands, wide shoulders—knew about his liaison with Tarlington.

Randall opened the front door, narrowing his eyes at us. He gave Clarke a small nod as he let him inside. The faintest of acknowledgments. Then the warm glow of the common room disappeared again.

"Look," Nicholls said, pointing towards the back of the huts. A blur of light in the sky, like fireworks, as a shooting star fell to earth and extinguished itself in the Weddell Sea.

I cleared my throat. I didn't know what to say; the art of asking another man if he was all right. Talking about something so—intimate.

"Nicholls."

"You know I lost most of my men?" he said, absently. "In France. *Wastage*, that's what they called it. We were supposed to pretend it didn't much matter, that it was all inevitable. Couldn't show it, even to the other officers. But it did." He looked at me, gray eyes clear like pale running water. "It did matter, Morgan, every single one."

My pulse hammered. I wasn't sure what I wanted to apologize for. Everything.

"They might not come back," he said. "That'll be another six men. I can't keep pretending." Silence. The wind delicately tried the lanterns. "I suppose he thought—oh, hell. At least I'm grateful you didn't tell anyone. For his sake." He walked off along the porch, footsteps measured on the timbers. Squared his shoulders against the railings, looked towards the anemometer, and let out a sigh. I thought about Tarlington walking around like a cat in the dark, light and quiet, being the villain he was sure we needed.

He must have learned a lot, in the camps, about the nature of man.

I balled up my fists, looking at Nicholls's back, and resumed my post. Harry called out inside the Nursery, and no one answered him. It made me cringe with misery. I knew why Tarlington had volunteered. Shame might have sent him to his death: I'd been the occasion for that shame. I tried not to think about how scared he'd looked, as he'd buttoned up his shirt and begged me not to tell Randall.

His laugh—that warm laugh—rang in my ears. I'd been so *childish*.

The aurora moved restlessly over the clear sky, creeping closer. I worried at the dry skin on my lips and tried not to watch it; was infinitely grateful when Clarke reappeared. He looked up, eyebrows furrowed, the anemometer starting to squeak-squeak-squeak, and I realized his appearance at that moment was no accident. Something was coming.

"Randall?" I asked.

He hesitated. "Asleep. His room is dark. No light gets in."

I took a deep long breath. "Good."

"Winds!" Nicholls called out of the darkness. "From the mountains!"

The air trembled. My heart sank.

Clarke swore, looking angrily at the back door. He'd asked Rees to fit bolts to the outside as well as inside. But he couldn't give orders anymore, and Rees was hardly fit to work. More so, after his ducking: the cold had set into his lungs, and he breathed in ragged, straining gulps.

"Stay here—don't let anyone outside. I don't care how you do it. I'll say it was me. Just keep them out of it."

When Clarke left, I put my back to the wall and looked towards the cliffs, where the windbreak had been—where Francis had appeared— then away, a tightness clutching at my chest. The first gusts of wind were freezing blasts that made me screw up my eyes and cough. I put my hand in front of my face, tried to keep my eyes fixed on the back door. The massed black clouds blotted out the stars with a speed that startled me. The huts were plunged into gloom.

A few minutes later, the winds were screaming against us. Snow whirled into my face, biting like a punishment, making it impossible to see clearly. I flattened myself against the hut, found my hand going—unconsciously—to my revolver. It almost made me laugh. I had no idea what I'd shoot. The weather?

The faint sound of the front door opening, Clarke yelling—"Get back inside!"

"The dogs!" someone shouted. It almost didn't sound like Harry: hoarse, angry. I kicked the boards in frustration. He couldn't be outside. Shouldn't be outside, not in this. The storm was a howling, whistling thing that whipped the drifted snow around us like leaves caught in floodwater. A sudden crack overhead made me look straight up—then blink hard, my eyes smarting.

The lantern guttered. Went out.

I fumbled with the little box of lucifers, but it was useless with gloves on. The air was so cold that it felt malevolent. The darkness surged towards me across the snow, as if given permission, and all the hairs on my arms and neck lifted up. A faint suggestion of buzzing, like an engine running at a distance. The smell of thunderstorms, in a place where thunder was vanishingly rare. The effect was uncanny.

I knew I was being watched.

"Clarke?" I shouted. "Nicholls!"

There was no chance they'd hear me. In the hissing nightmare I could barely make out the sound of kennel doors slamming, dogs howling. I turned around, stared at the back door as if it were the most beautiful thing on earth. I could go inside. For a moment the urge struck me very powerfully. I could leave my post, crawl into bed. Shut out the night. Shut out the winter. Wait for it to all be over, one way or another.

That wasn't me.

Sinking to a crouch, I checked my revolver. I had the impression someone had just said my name. I pressed the heels of my hands into my eyes, taking in a deep breath and holding it.

Again. Someone calling my name. Just a little above me. I had to look.

I stood slowly, keeping my eyes squeezed shut until the last possible moment. Where the lantern-light ended, a bite had been taken out of our world. Shadows, flickering moonlight. And a figure in the drift, watching me.

Francis.

He was closer than before, and the lash of the snow didn't seem to bother him. His fox-red hair was neatly combed back under his hat. He wore no windproofs, his trench coat exposing a triangle of brown-green tunic, the flash of a gold button. He should have been desperately cold. He uncrossed his arms, stretched his shoulders back, as if he'd just finished a long piece of work. His mouth folded into a smile.

Then, appearing to see me watching, he ducked his head. Paused for a moment—looked up at me. His eyes were warm and sincere. I'd been so determined to think of him as a ghost. A delusion. To look away. But he was utterly, unmistakably, my brother.

And he saw me now.

"Francis!" My voice cracked. He reached out his hand, fingers curling towards me in silent invitation. Then turned away.

"Wait!"

I used the railings to pull myself down the porch steps. The snow whipped and sizzled. The drift came past my knees, swallowing me up. I didn't care. It was Francis, it was really my brother. He wanted me to follow him. He needed me. I couldn't let him down.

I caught the impression of his coat—swishing against the flickering snow—then vanishing. "Francis!" I howled. I sounded like a desperate animal. I stumbled on into the darkness.

Away from the huts, the winds strafed me pitilessly. My clothing scraped. My breath froze and was whipped away. Going to my knees, there was nothing. No windbreaks—everything was gone. No huts, no meteorological screen, no lantern-light, nothing. A gray and dark land-scape. My limbs rebelled, and I couldn't climb to my feet.

I called out to Francis. I strained my eyes. Nothing. The crackling in the sky was like a war in heaven. It filled me up. It seemed impossible to think of anything else.

I turned in the snow. Faintly, the sound of dogs came on the wind.

"Harry!"

He shouldn't be outside. I had been the least of the Morgan siblings. Now—*here*—I was stronger than him.

Expedition Point wavered, a murky hunched shape through the

blanketing snow. Then it was snatched away. I clapped my hand over my mouth, tried to silence the sound that wanted to come out. I was alone. I hadn't paid attention to where I was going. There were no landmarks. And if the blizzard grew any stronger, I might never find my way back.

I stood up, shaking. Francis was nowhere to be seen. But I knew he hadn't left me—I knew he was still close by. Watching silently. He was *waiting*, half-real and half-made. I took another step forward, ready to follow him into that howling darkness.

"Francis?"

The dogs.

I turned towards the sound. If Harry were outside—if he'd seen Francis—he would surely go to him. I knew, powerfully, it would be his death.

I swore, throwing up my hands, and made one last attempt to find Francis in the barrage. My movements were becoming more and more erratic. My breath no longer steamed and froze. But there was no one there. The moon glimmered. The huts appeared and disappeared, vanished by the seething wall of snow.

I fought my reluctant way back towards the sound of the dogs, stopping every few moments to look for my missing brother. "Harry!" I called, pulling myself along the windbreaks, doubled over like a drunkard.

I was grabbed from behind, all the breath whooshing out of my lungs. "Thank *God*," Clarke said in my ear. "Where's Nicholls?"

I stared at him. "What?"

"He saw—something. Went off after it."

"What?"

"Are you hurt? Morgan, are you hurt?" I shook my head numbly, looking around me with dread.

Clarke trained his rifle on the point where visibility ended, backing us into camp, into the maze of buildings. He must have known what I'd done: left my post, left the huts, abandoned them. I couldn't meet his eyes. But he simply added, "Cooper's safe—the dogs are safe—"

I clenched my jaw. I'd been close to Francis—so close. Perhaps if I'd gone farther—if I'd looked harder. Harry had made me turn back, and I resented him for it.

The front door was open—damaged—men swarming around it. Clarke shouted a few instructions, then slipped back into the snow. "Stay there—" he shouted at me, and I shook my head, scrambling to catch up with him.

I took a deep, shuddering breath. For a horrible moment I feared what he would think of me. But I shouted into his ear to make myself heard. "The gun's no use. It's not a person. It's a—ghost."

Taking another breath, my throat sore: "This place has *ghosts*."

"I don't care what it is!" he snapped, pulling away. "We're under attack. I'll show it! That it won't take me without a fight."

I could feel every hair on my body thrumming, caught up in the vast pull of the invisible aurora. The dogs made a keening sound. I sat down, hard, against the porch. Nicholls. It had taken Nicholls.

I pulled the service revolver out and turned it over and over, trying to calm myself, trying to stop my teeth chattering. The snow hissed off my helmet, slowing. Muffled hammer blows. The wind moaned. Every time I raised my head, I was sure Francis was there, just beyond the light. Back here at the huts, back in the living world, I felt traitorously glad he was too far away to see. Then hollow with guilt.

I'd wanted so badly to see him. But not here. Not like this.

A door slammed. Shapes coming through the snow. I stood up, calves and thighs screaming, as Clarke pulled Nicholls out of the cold locker. The moonlight picked Nicholls out in black and white; he was shivering so hard that his teeth looked about to smash. He dropped something small and shiny on the ground.

The winds threw another blanket of drift over us. Then stopped abruptly. The lanterns ceased swinging. Stillness. I looked around. The eye of the storm was here.

"Why did you leave your post?" Clarke shook Nicholls roughly, battering snow and ice from his jacket.

"There was someone—" he said, full of horrible awed wonder.

"I know," I said wildly. "I saw it too."

Nicholls looked at me. A grief so intense I thought he might die from it. "You saw—him?"

"Who?"

A pause. "Tarlington." Nicholls's voice shook. "His *ghost*."

"Come on," Clarke said. "Both of you."

His tone of voice was eloquent: he didn't bother telling us that ghosts weren't real. I wondered whether Clarke—formidable Liam Clarke—would shoot a ghost, right between the eyes, just to show it he didn't believe in it.

Coming inside, the front door was bulging at its seams, as if someone—something—had thrown itself against the huts from outside. Snow had drifted in. The winds had upended the galley, thrown the chess set off the table, pinned Nicholls's charts to the beams. They were torn straight through the middle. I had the sudden impression that this place was laughing at us—toying with us. Resisting our attempts to know it.

Everyone was so quiet. Muttering. Looking at us strangely, looking behind us, as if waiting for someone else to walk back in.

Clarke was right: we *were* under attack, I was sure of it. The winds. The aurora. The ghosts. Drawing us out into the snow. For some reason I couldn't fathom—they meant us harm.

"Where is he?" Macready was breathing hard, staring wildly at Clarke.

I realized no one was threatening me with a whipping for leaving my post. No one was shouting or ranting. Something was wrong.

Outside, the winds had vanished. All was darkness, perfectly still.

Macready grabbed each side of the frame. Leaned out. Yelled: "Randall!"

He had left us. And the sun was no longer rising.

VII

"How on *earth* did he get outside?" Clarke bellowed.

I'd always thought of him as utterly controlled: master of the moment. Master of his own emotions. Now his rage was as fearsome as Randall's, and his voice rang in my numb ears.

"Oh, like *you* could've stopped him," Ellis snapped. "He insisted. Said there was someone out there, and he'd go if no one else would."

Clarke looked wildly at Macready.

"He heard something," Macready said, his voice hard. "I thought it was one of you calling for him."

"You let him outside—" Clarke pinned Macready up against the wall. The cold air made jets of steam come from his nostrils. "You knew damn well he wasn't in his right mind—"

"No, I didn't—because you didn't tell anyone!" Macready shouted. "You knew how bad he'd got, damn you, and you kept it from us!"

"Just because he demoted *you*," Ellis said nastily. "Doesn't mean he was mad." I clenched my fists. A wheezing cough came from the Coal Hole as Rees fought for air.

"Liam." Macready pushed Clarke away. "Liam. You think any of us could have stopped him, if he thought he'd heard—"

Clarke stared at him, jaw working. He nodded. Then swore—punched the table with an almighty crack. There was a horrible wetness about the sound. He didn't appear to feel it. I thought, queasily, about our lack of a surgeon.

Macready looked around, clearing his throat. "No time to waste, before the storm returns. Come on—we need to get moving!"

Grumbling, the men obeyed, pulling on coats. I tried—and failed—to hide the tremor in my limbs, the shaky one-two shiver that made my breath catch and hiss. "Morgan—you're staying here," Clarke said, rubbing the life back into Nicholls's hands with rather more force than was necessary.

In the distance, something like thunder rumbled. The wind was back, pulling at the door: I watched as they disappeared one by one into the night. Though the hut was cold, I'd become sweaty, and constantly wiped my hands on my trousers. I could feel the pulse in my wrists, throat, temples.

The door banged open again. I jumped, bracing myself against the table, the rumpled mess of Nicholls's charts. The darkness was absolute around Harry, his hair a halo of shadows. "The dogs—they're safe, I've dug them out." No one had asked; I had no idea where he'd been during the storm.

"Jonathan." I met his eyes. "Did you see them? Are you—" He grabbed my hands, clung to them. He was icy cold. "You *came back*."

"Stop it," I whispered. "Harry, stop it." Nicholls was trying, numbly, to piece his charts back together. The white paper was grimy. But there were no features, and vast portions of the pages remained blank, entirely obscure. Our little cluster of rectangles was surrounded by miles and miles of howling emptiness.

"What did they tell you?"

I shuddered. "Nothing. He didn't—speak."

"Why you?" A curl to his lips that was almost petulant. "Why would they come for *you*?"

I pushed him away, wanting to put as much distance as possible between us. "Harry, it's not what you think. Not what you—wanted. They're trying to hurt us."

He looked at me as if I were very stupid; pressed his mouth tight, collecting himself. Then picked up a light and left.

A sudden stab of grief hit me. I bit my lip, busied myself with boiling water and making a pot of tea. Tried to stop shaking. Tried to stop seeing Francis, standing tall against the wind, his eyes urging me to follow. The quiet sent cold fingers down my spine.

Another rumble of what sounded to me like thunder, thick and ominous. The wind outside was tugging at the flagpole, and the sound of it squealing and clicking set my teeth on edge. Clarke spoke to Nicholls, too low for me to hear. Something seemed to be decided. He strode to the door—clenched his fists for a moment—opened it, and leaned out.

"Everyone back in!"

Footsteps on the porch. Macready appeared in the pool of light at the doorway. He scowled at Clarke, the rising wind plucking at his clothing. Behind him, I could hear the muffled sounds of men calling Randall's name.

"Where are his tracks?" someone shouted. My stomach turned over. *Vanished without a trace.*

The wind shrieked, and everything rattled. I glanced behind me at the boot room door—was relieved to find it shut. "We don't have much time," Macready snapped. "We need to go farther. Nicholls—"

The plateau was vast, all-consuming darkness. Nicholls was the only one who knew the terrain beyond the lantern-light. He'd warned us already that it might be full of hidden dangers, crevasses, the currents and moods of the ice invisible beneath the snow—would only send men out in daylight, with ropes and ice axes. Not this mad dash into a blizzard with handheld lanterns. He stared into the middle distance and shook his head slowly. "No," he said. "Clarke's right."

"Right about what?"

"Everyone inside!" Clarke yelled again. To Macready: "You'll never find his tracks in this. The storm's returning. I won't send men out onto the plateau."

"What?"

"You heard him," Nicholls said. He looked very sick. I caught his eye, then had to look away. We were abandoning Randall to his fate. My thoughts stuttered: I couldn't quite grasp it. The huts looked the same as always: dark timber, cast-iron stove, billowing laundry. I swallowed.

Clarke held the door, freezing blasts of wind coming in waves. The rest of the search party gathered on the porch, and a sudden gust extinguished Ellis's light. He looked around, eyes wide. The static was lifting up the fur trim on his hat, making him look like a mangy, starving lion. Once again, there was a loud deep bellowing sound in the distance.

Harry turned around in a slow circle, staring at the darkness. His expression was searching—a dreadful *yearning*, like a sick dog waiting to be put out of its misery. I realized that I, too, was staring into the yawning blue-black, trying to see Francis again. Just for a moment. Just a glimpse.

I squeezed my eyes shut and gripped the table, trying to stop myself; whoever was out there had taken Randall. They meant us harm.

"Everyone back inside!"

"To hell with you!" Macready shouted. "It's not your decision to make. He'll freeze to death."

A muttering amongst the men.

"I don't care," Clarke said. "I'm making it anyway. I've been with him for years. Since before the War—before *Charlie*. The real Randall—the one I knew—would never have asked men to risk their lives for him. Not like this."

"You're not in charge," Ellis snapped. A dog made a screaming noise, and he cringed.

"I'm the most experienced," Clarke said. "And next in command, with Boyd gone—"

Nicholls. He looked up, and said, very clearly, "Clarke's right. You don't know what's out there."

I could see nothing beyond the porch. Macready swore, throwing his lantern to the ground, where it bounced down the steps, flickering out. He looked around, seeking support. When his gaze fell on me, I ducked my head and shook it. Clarke was right. There was an ominous buzzing as the barrage resumed, the huts shaking and rattling with it. The door was slammed shut.

Pacing up and down, Macready paused beside me. I could smell the cold on him. "I'd have thought *you*, Morgan—you'd be better than this."

"You don't know what's out there," I muttered. I found my gaze drawn to the sick-bay curtain, swaying in the breeze we couldn't keep out.

"Bloody superstition," Macready hissed, then raised his voice. "All of you! Tired—paranoid. There's no such thing as ghosts! You're afraid of your own shadows."

"Did the Germans come, then?" Clarke said abruptly. "Steal Randall out from under our noses?"

"Jesus Christ. He was tired. Exhausted. He'd have been bloody well invalided out of the lines—you know that. His nerves were shot. It wasn't some *ghost* that burned our ship. Nor a *ghost* that smashed up our stores." Macready dragged a hand over his face, looking around at us. A group of desperate men, the storm howling outside. "Am I the only one in my right mind?"

"I've seen something," Holmes said quietly.

Ellis shook his head, thin-lipped.

"Me too." My voice wavered. I sounded small, and scared. "I've seen it—twice. It wants me to follow."

Clarke set his jaw. His cheeks were white, showing the first signs of frost-nip. "I won't have men getting lured away. Wandering off and getting lost. Not now."

Macready snorted. "The only thing outside is a storm. And for *that* and the bogeyman, you're willing to let him die." He looked around. "Some loyal men."

It stung like a whip. He threw down the metal matchbox—it clattered off the table—and stalked off towards his bunk. I let out a long breath, and nearly slumped over with exhaustion.

Clarke sat down and pulled off his glove, rubbed his thumb over the dark bloody patches on his stumpy knuckles. He flexed his hand, checking for bone damage. The stokers called their dog, firmly tacked shut their curtain. I could hear Rees's voice, hoarse and plaintive, asking them to put out the light.

The drift hissed off our roof.

"Well," Clarke said to me. I couldn't look at him.

I knew he was right. I *hated* him for being right. Because when the search party had gathered on the porch—swinging lantern-light, moon stalked by clouds, the storm rolling in—I'd known what waited behind them.

We'd all lost people. We all had our ghosts. I knew, sure enough to make bile rise in my throat—my hair stand on end—they were coming ever closer. Waiting for us to call their names into the indifferent night, follow them into darkness. They didn't mean for us to last the winter.

They meant us harm.

VIII

"We need to stop them," I said, shivering. "Fight them."

Harry shook his head, hugged his knees to his chest. "We can't."

We were side by side in Tarlington's bed: having the doors open for so long had dropped the internal temperature below freezing, and condensation had frozen into sheets of ice on the walls. The Nursery shimmered in the candlelight, a scene from fairy tales. I'd protested, backing away with hands in front of me, when Harry had suggested we share a bed. But it wasn't like that. We were wearing all the clothes we owned, and it was *still* cold. Other men were sleeping two to a bunk. The dogs weren't all tame enough to be brought inside, or we'd have done that too.

"We need to—to stop them," I insisted. "We can't just wait it out, not now." I was on the edge of the bed, but my feet were resting on Harry's side, and the warmth was glorious, made the rest of my skin prickle.

I could see pink ears under his hat: Harry had always blushed easily. "They're *taking* people."

Our candle guttered, throwing the room into shadow. Harry said, quietly: "Maybe some people deserve to be taken."

"No," I snapped. "Not Randall. Not anyone." He hushed me furiously. On the other side of the compartment wall, the sound of someone muttering to himself.

I paused, listening to Harry's breathing, staring at that faint and wavering flame. The glimmering light. I pictured it illuminating Nicholls's map. The glacier, the crevasse fields—hidden by the snow and the dark. We'd somehow avoided blundering into them on our way here, although we'd been traveling blind. It had seemed miraculous at the time. Lucky. The wind outside howled, and the hairs rose on the back of my neck. *We've ended up in the last place on earth*, Harry had said. Maybe by chance.

Maybe not.

"They—the ghosts—wanted us here, didn't they?" I whispered. "Harry—why?"

He looked around at the cramped room. The frost, come inside. The miles of night surrounding us. "They always loved Antarctica. I don't know if this is what they wanted—to pass a winter here, with us."

They always loved Antarctica. The blank spaces on the map, the adventure novels, Randall and the heroes of the South—this was the natural end point of all that. I thought of Rufus and Francis going out to toboggan on the boating pond, their cheeks flushed with excitement; I wondered how they'd like these leaden skies, those howling winds, this desolation.

A small hiccup of breath. "But—Randall gone. The ship gone. No hope of rescue." Then, in a rush, "You're right. They wanted me *here*." He paused. "They're here for me, not you."

I stared at him, my pulse hammering. The ashen cast of his face had nothing to do with the candlelight.

"Why—" I stuttered, and balled my hands into fists under the blankets, trying to resist the urge to shake him; trying to swallow down the unexpected sob that had clawed its way up my throat. They were my *brothers*, however much I'd fallen short. However much I'd been left behind. I'd always longed to be like them.

Or so I'd thought.

"Oh. Oh, Jonathan." Harry reached out to put his hand on my side. His face twisted, as if struggling with something huge. "It's not like that. I'm just trying to keep you safe—that's all I've ever done. I thought if I did what they wanted—"

He put his hand over his mouth. Silence.

My chest squeezed. The wind flung pebbles at our walls in small explosions. The roof creaked. I looked around, wildly, in the darkness. The walls of the Nursery were closing in on us. Just as they must have closed in on Karlmann and his men, in their own longest winter: this place clearly had its seasons. The Germans hadn't just vanished. They'd *been* vanished.

Maybe they'd been called outside one by one; maybe they'd all left—or been taken—together. I didn't know which would be worse.

"Harry," I whispered. "Please. It's too much—we need to stop them."

He turned. His shirt was warm and damp, and I could feel the look of disgust crossing my face. "Maybe I don't *want* to stop them," he said indistinctly. "They're your brothers. We have them back."

I thought of Francis. His slight, sincere smile. He could have asked anything of me, anything at all, and I was terrified of it. "Harry, please—"

He twisted suddenly, coming up on all fours to stare into my face. I recoiled. He looked like a starving wild animal. "You don't know them!" he hissed. "You don't know *anything*."

I opened my mouth. He clamped a hand over it. His palms were callused and split. "You didn't even *want* them back—not like I wanted! Telling me to just get on with things—God, Jonathan, if you only knew. You never heard them. You were too busy—following Randall. Being part of the crew. Doing all the things they'll never be able to do. It was so easy for you to leave them behind. You wanted to—forget them. I *loved* them."

The candle flickered. The winds outside sounded low and threatening like thunder: I'd have been grateful for lightning. But it was just the dark. The pitiless dark.

Harry dragged his hand off my face. "I thought I could make up for what I did." Something about his expression made my stomach drop away, as if I were falling from the mainmast, the *Fortitude* swooping beneath me.

All those nights on deck. The fog. The dogs. The ship, bathed in the solemn white light of the ice, winds whipping around her. The tall figure I'd seen on the dog deck—on Harry's dog deck—as the ship burned. Untouched by heat or cold. From the maze of the pack to this tiny room in the snow; with the winds and the fire, they'd herded us, like animals driven before the slaughterman.

Silence.

"Harry," I pleaded, choking on the cold. A horrible idea was filling my mind, drowning out everything else. "Harry. What did you *do*?"

I thought I'd push him away. But as I reached out, my treacherous fingers wound around his collar instead, pulling him close. I looked at them in amazement—then at the dark pools of his eyes. He put his arms around me stiffly. "They've been waiting for us," he said into my shoulder. I could feel his breath hitching. "And I'm glad, I—I really am. That they're not really gone."

An uncontrollable shudder swept through me. The storm seethed outside. We were down to our last inch of candle. Tomorrow, we would wake as an expedition without Randall. Harry smelled of wet dog and soot. My breath was starting to come in short, hard spurts.

I thought if I did what they wanted.

I turned it over and over in my mind, trying it from all angles, as Harry's breathing slowed. As his fingers clenched and unclenched against my back. His heart-rate evened out. For once, incredibly, he was sleeping.

He wouldn't answer me. It didn't seem possible. Not from Harry.

I *had* my answer, though: he'd done something awful.

I pushed myself away and stumbled out of the bed like a newborn animal, all arms and legs. Pressing my hand to my mouth, I stood over him, a roaring in my ears. I could have punched him—kicked him—kept on going, through skin and blood and bone, until he was smeared on the bed. I felt sure I could do it; in the candlelight he looked like a boy. Just a boy. I raised my fist.

Then I brought it down. The others would hear me. I couldn't. I couldn't give him away, see him dragged out by his neck. I thought of Tarlington, somewhere out there on the ice; the things Harry and I had set in motion.

Maybe some people deserve to be taken.

I came out into the common room, where the wind was howling down the chimney, the cracking of timber outside sounding like distant cannon. I wanted to go to the door, stride out into the snow. Take a few deep breaths of air. The hut was damp and cold despite double boarding on all the windows.

But we were trapped inside. By weather. By ghosts. Stretching out their cold dead hands on the wind, across the miles of snow, they'd reached across the pack ice to Harry, in those nights alone on the dog deck. He'd wished for them with every inch of his being. So desperate. So keen to follow orders. To make amends for living, while they died.

IX

The storm blew out on the second day. No search party had been sent into that hissing darkness. Although Macready had called him a coward and an upstart and every other name possible, Clarke had said, very calmly, "I don't care if you disagree. We're not going." And that was the end of it.

We'd dug the huts free of drift, surveyed the plateau in all directions: nothing except fresh unbroken snow. When I went to my watch at noon, I looked for pale lemon light beneath the horizon, to remind myself of sun; but the civil twilight dropped away fast, and no matter where I turned, the light had faded.

"Hey!" Ellis shouted from the other side of the porch. The click of his rifle was like an explosion in the still air. I fumbled to get out the service revolver, skidding around the decking towards him.

"Stay back!" Ellis yelled again. He turned to me. "You see it?" He sounded panicked. "You can see it, can't you?"

Clarke shook his head, snuffed out the storm lantern, leaving us in the gloom. I scanned the horizon. Again. Again. Heart thumping, I expected to see Rufus or Francis, walking inexorably towards camp. They were coming closer, closer. The thought made me shiver.

"Easy, Morgan." Clarke lowered my gun with one push of his large gloved hand.

"There." Ellis pointed. "It keeps—moving."

I saw an irregular black blot on the snow. Too big to be a dog, too early in the season to be a penguin. "It's not moving," I said, stupidly.

Then it did. An arm reached out, then another. Bit by bit, pulling itself along. My skin crawled at the way it moved: like something clawing itself back to life.

"Don't come any closer!" Clarke's shout echoed. The door opened, worried faces looked out.

"Harry," I said, grabbing him roughly. "Get your binoculars." He shook his head. I shoved him, hard. "*Go.*"

He was pushed to the front when he returned. Clarke raised his rifle. "Go on." His voice was steady, but I could see his fingertips flickering, a small intake of breath as he steeled himself.

"I think—" Harry said. Then he lowered the binoculars, took a step back. "What do you see?"

"I think—" He turned to Clarke, blinking. "It's Randall."

Clarke shook his head, mouth pressed into a thin hard line. His finger hovered near the safety. "He's not coming back." A murmur of voices: angry, dissenting. He hushed them with a motion of his arm. "After two nights? In the storm? There's no chance he's coming back."

I grabbed the binoculars off Harry, pressed them to my face. The figure in the twilight was inching its way forwards using the ridged snow for leverage. It was painful to watch, like a butterfly in the killing jar. I thought about Rufus and Francis: how the cold and the weather had passed right through them. This figure was real in a way they hadn't been. Left tracks on the snow where they'd left none.

"Clarke," I said slowly. "Clarke, it's Randall."

He shook his head again.

I put my hand on the barrel of his rifle. He looked at me, startled. "It's too—broken—to be his ghost."

I was right.

When we reached him he'd crawled another few feet, and was trying to use a snowbank to shelter from the dark. His eyes were closed, but he was clearly awake, and in great pain.

"Get him inside!" Clarke roared. "Ellis—Macready—Morgan, *keep watch.*"

Randall couldn't walk. When they lifted him, his legs were dead weight, two pieces of rotting timber. The left side of his face—already ruined by frostbite—was blue-black and swollen, closing up his eye, tilting his lips into a rictus grin. But he was talking, constantly talking, a slurred mumble that made the hairs stand up on the back of my neck.

"My feet are burning . . ."

"Morgan, damn it!" Clarke shouted. I tore my eyes away, kept my gun on the horizon. Nothing approached. Not a flicker of movement. I stepped carefully back through our footprints, watching the mountains; the snow was frozen hard. Randall's body left a dragging, stumbling track stretching a little way into the distance. He'd clawed his way back to us, although I couldn't see where from.

My skin crawled. Something had—let him go.

Back at the huts, I was sent to fetch fresh snow. It seemed a ridiculous suggestion in thirty below, but I didn't ask why. On the lee side of the kennels, the drift was still powder; the dogs were uneasy, whining and pulling at their leashes. One growled at me with mistrustful eyes. Harry couldn't calm them, and wouldn't speak. He'd gone to his hands and knees at the sight of Randall returned—ruined.

Beyond the sick-bay curtain, Randall thrashed in Duncan's bed. They'd managed to remove his outer layers—he hadn't been dressed for the cold—and the clothes steamed in the relative warmth, sending wet fingers of melted ice reaching across the floor. He appeared not to know where he was, or how long he'd been gone. He talked about the aurora, a great glowing city beyond the mountains. Voices on the wind. His lost son. *Charlie*.

"We need to rub his legs," Holmes said. "I've seen it done—"

Clarke nodded, taking the bowl from me. "Hold him."

Stripping his trousers off was a horrible business: they were stiff as a board, stuck fast. But when we reached the frozen skin below, Randall screamed. I dropped his legs as if scalded. It was clear from the way his joints worked—alien, cramped—that there was something very wrong with his limbs. "He'll lose his feet," Holmes whispered. "Maybe the rest."

When the clothing was finally cut away, I could see what they meant. Randall was cold as frozen metal; his skin just as hard, refusing to yield to the touch, a deep and unearthly shade of mottled gray. His fingers were black and swollen, the area around his signet ring leaking pale fluid. White patches ran up his thighs and chest. It was apparent he had lain facedown in the snow for some time.

I couldn't see how he was still alive. But this was obviously Randall, not his ghost. He moaned: his feet were on fire, and we should take away the heat.

"Hold him," Clarke said again.

"We could use the straps—" Ellis said.

Clarke turned with a coiled ferocity that sucked the breath from my lungs. "Not on him!"

I was at Randall's feet. We couldn't find his boots. We'd looked. "Where would they *be*?" I said helplessly. He was in his fur linings, so deeply encrusted with ice that we needed a saw. Underneath, both feet were unrecognizable.

"Sometimes people take them off," Nicholls said. "They undress, when the cold gets to them. But Randall, Randall knows better, he wouldn't—"

"He'll need more morphine," Holmes said. "If we can get it in him . . ." There was a tourniquet around Randall's upper arm, weeping blisters, the evidence of desperate attempts to find his sluggish veins.

Randall screamed again. Clarke was rubbing the snow on his hands, massaging the white flesh. It steamed in the dim light. I put my hand to my mouth, tasting bile, then clamped Randall's feet to the bed. Tried to look away, but couldn't. The skin was sloughing off his fingers. From the grim look on Clarke's face, I could tell something was terribly wrong.

And still Randall fought. Called for Charlie. Wished, at the top of his voice, that he were dead.

When we moved on to Randall's feet, I had to leave the room to be sick. I staggered back through the doorway, seeing the figures crouched around the bed in the lantern-light, the ceaseless roll of Randall's neck as he strained. His movements were getting slower.

"His pulse is dropping," Nicholls said. "The shock . . ."

It was the worst pain I'd ever seen; pain that made me fist my hands until they cramped, looking wildly around the huts, wishing I could do something, anything, to make it stop.

Again, Randall begged to die, and I could *taste* our despair.

"We need to splint his legs," Clarke shouted—there was a commotion as we found long pieces of wood and strapped Randall onto them. His muscles twitched hard under the bindings.

"He needs more morphine," Holmes insisted. I flailed around the small shadowy room, turning over shelves, benches. Staunton had left books, bandages, and sticking plasters; the knives and saws of the German surgeon. Not enough of anything that mattered.

"There'll be none left," Clarke said. "Not for the mountain party—any survivors. Not for us."

He didn't have to say that Randall would likely die. His face said it plainly enough. "But we should give it to him," he said, and took in a heaving breath. He looked at Macready, who nodded. Across the circle to Ellis, who gulped, then said, "All right." Then to Holmes, who was already preparing the syringe.

Nicholls pressed his hand to his face. Turning away from the bed, he looked at me pleadingly. "You saw Tarlington, didn't you? Outside? In the—the storm?"

"I didn't see him," I said in a rush, thinking of the roiling darkness of the blizzard; the confusion; a trench coat swishing on the snow. "It was—someone else. Someone who looked similar." I knew I'd seen Francis, or his ghost: as clear and vital as the day I'd seen him last. "He could still be alive."

Nicholls shook his head. "It was him." He shuddered. "Hell, you think I wouldn't know him? It was James Tarlington, just beyond the light. Every lanky redheaded inch of him. His ghost. He's *gone*."

An awful heat behind my eyes. Nicholls turned back to Clarke, who didn't believe in ghosts. "Give him the morphine," he said briskly. "Do it."

Randall tried to fight off Holmes, but his movements were erratic, like a clock starting to stutter and wind down. "Charlie," he kept saying, "Charlie." Then, pulling his ruined mouth into a startled O of surprise: "I should never have brought him. He should never have been here. He didn't want to come."

"James." Clarke's voice was soft. "James, you're safe. Everyone is safe. We're trying to help you."

Drugged, Randall's thrashing subsided. We worked quickly to splint his ruined limbs, rub what life was possible into his pale gray legs. "He'll lose them," Holmes said.

Macready scowled. "We don't know that."

"The *color*." Clarke flexed his hands. "They're already gone."

Something had let him go—to die in front of us. Like some terrible animal dropping a kill half-eaten at the mouth of its lair.

I ducked back out of the sick bay, stumbled to the front door, and sank to my knees on the porch, heaving. The fresh air didn't help. It was so cold and dry, my nose started to bleed, and I wiped the blood away as it froze on my face. Someone shut the door—pragmatic—and I was left alone, shivering.

I looked into the darkness. I looked for Tarlington's ghost.

Nicholls had given him up for dead: and he should know. I'd done this. Trusting Harry's stories—his *war* stories—of saboteurs and soldiers. Valuing my place in the expedition too highly; being too proud, and too stubborn. My failures were crimes against Tarlington. They must have led to his lonely death in the mountains, among people who despised him.

I doubled over again, fought the sobbing as long as I could. My knees felt like ice. My breathing came in fits and starts. The aurora pressed down on me, green and malevolent.

When I looked up, a dark figure was watching me. I thought—for a moment—it was him, and reached out. But it didn't speak. Standing at the edge of camp, it lifted a hand towards its face. I was struck with the horrible certainty that it had pressed a finger against Cupid's bow lips. *Shhh.*

And then, as if satisfied, it walked off into the snow with long, silent strides.

X

"You know what to do," Clarke said. "Get Staunton. Get the morphine. Leave everything—everyone—else. They'll follow later. Come back as quick as you can." He clapped Nicholls on the back. "Quicker, if possible." The dogs were straining at their leashes, scuffling in the snow, eager to be out of camp. Harry quietly disentangled them.

"Shoot anything out of the ordinary," Clarke said to me, and pulled his balaclava back up, his next sentence muffled. "I mean it, Morgan. Shoot first—I don't care what you see."

I nodded, jumping from foot to foot. "And no time to be—sentimental," he added, raising his voice, carefully not looking at Nicholls. "D'you understand?"

The mountain party had been gone too long, had nearly reached Boyd's grim calculations. *Three at the most—don't expect us.*

Clarke's briefing—chillingly explicit—had encompassed the worst: finding a tent in the middle of nowhere, flapping in the wind, full of dead bodies. An abandoned sledge, to be looted for medical supplies. We'd have to leave the corpses, pause a moment to lace their sleeping bags over their faces—building a cairn would take too long. There was no time for sentiment. Everything was to be sacrificed to the impossible: saving Randall.

My breath had already frozen my scarf and balaclava onto my face, and it would be a long time before I'd be able to pry them loose. We had few hours of civil twilight, and Nicholls wouldn't want to waste any of it.

"Send up the flares," Clarke said, finally, as Macready kicked the sledge from its furrow of snow. The dogs quivered with anticipation. "Twice a day. We'll do the same."

The Webley & Scott flare pistols had been distributed, although we might well be the only living beings left on this unspooling featureless ribbon of land. "At least the Hun'd be real—if I'm going to cop a packet, I'd rather a *man* did it," Ellis had said bitterly. He'd be remaining at the huts, along with Rees—we didn't need a surgeon to tell us our cheerful carpenter was dying of pneumonia.

I'd watched Harry as the guns were handed around. He took one with trembling hands. His lip was split. He'd been the first to volunteer for the search party, even though he'd obviously be needed to drive our remaining dogs. But he'd wanted me to stay behind—it had come to blows. "You'll be safe at the huts!" he'd shouted. "Jonathan, *please!*"

But Randall needed a surgeon, and medicine. As he grew steadily weaker and more distressed—pulse visible in his neck; shivering despite blankets; trying to claw his way from the bed with ruined hands—he called out for the darkness. His cries seemed to summon the aurora. The men were uneasy. No one slept. Rees coughed up his lungs every night. It felt like my blankets were becoming heavier and heavier, suffocating me.

He'd been returned to torment us.

Mutiny bubbled and seethed beneath the surface. Macready was set against Clarke. Both were Randall men through and through: lower class, picked out of the shipyards and the merchant navy, worked to their limits, instilled with unshakable loyalty. But one was just a cook. The other was—once—Randall's second-in-command.

Clarke sat alone at the common-room table. He wouldn't presume to take Randall's desk. He'd been right to leave him; he'd been wrong. It didn't matter either way. The choice had been made. The aurora sat above the huts like hellfire, and still no one slept.

He was finally forced to give in. Nicholls knew the mountain party's route. The weather might have slowed them down. Running extremely light, pushing ourselves mercilessly, we might catch up. Macready insisted on coming with us—eyeing Nicholls with a most unfamiliar distrust. And Holmes might finally get the chance to use his ice axe.

I had to do what I could. Even if we were only prolonging the inevitable, even if we were only *saving* Randall for months or weeks or even days. I couldn't wait anymore. And someone had to keep an eye on Harry, who didn't sleep, just stared at the sky.

Nicholls looked up, sighted his compass against the stars, and we left our little world behind.

XI

We made good progress out of camp towards the mountains. The dogs keened, wagging their tails at the joy of being out, finally pulling like a proper team.

I hated all of it.

After so long in the huts, the plateau felt horribly exposed. I found myself turning to walk backwards, staring into the darkness behind us; imagining tall, dark, faceless figures watching me from the shadows cast by our lanterns. The echoing silence made it sound as though another sledge were following, always invisible when I turned. I pulled my scarf tight as armor around my neck, checked my belt for the Webley, the flare gun beside it.

I disliked the thought of announcing our presence to that alien sky. The twilight was going down in measured fashion, civil to nautical to astronomical, the aurora meandering lazily across the heavens. A steady, pulsing glow. Like a heartbeat. But my brothers could surely find me without a flare, wherever I was. I stared into the distance. They could surely find Harry, if he was right: if they were there for him, bearing some unfathomable grudge.

And if so, I wondered—what did that make the rest of us? *Wastage?*

No one was inclined to talk. Perhaps we were all thinking the same thing: it seemed impossible that anyone could have survived a blizzard out here. The sweat on our backs froze, rubbing us raw. The dogs had learned to haul, but our boots sank through the top crust of snow with each step, like wading in mud. My knees swelled and popped, but I wouldn't be the first to complain.

The huts vanished behind us. The mountains seemed only a few miles away; I felt I could reach out and touch them. Harry stopped in his tracks, and the dogs did too. He shook his head.

Nicholls scowled at the aurora. "Let's press on," he said. "A little farther."

Macready and Holmes challenged him, shoulders set square in their frost-caked windproofs. We'd made good progress, nearly thirteen nautical miles. We needed to get warm—tend our feet—give our bones some rest.

"We need to get on," Nicholls snapped, pacing with nervous energy. "You know what's at stake."

Macready swore, said he knew very well. Randall needed us, and he'd be damned if he'd let him down—just look at the mess Clarke had made of things. His tone was bitter; he hadn't tried to jolly us along for a very long time. Nicholls didn't look at him. Just bounced on his heels, surveyed the mountains.

"You really think we can catch them?" I asked Nicholls.

He stared at me. With his hat and balaclava, only his eyes were exposed. He blinked several times. "Perhaps," he said finally. "The motor will be moving slowly—if they haven't abandoned it already. But I have to know. If there's the slightest chance—"

Nicholls's pale eyes slid off me, towards the aurora, in a way that made me deeply uneasy. He'd seen Tarlington, at the huts—seen his ghost.

But I'd done this. I would make it right if I could.

"I'm sorry." I ducked my head, too cowardly to face him. "About—about Tarlington."

He sighed. "You set it in motion. That's all. He'd cared far too much for far too long about what Randall thought of him. At least this way, if he . . ." He seemed unable to say more.

"We should send up the flares, if we're not stopping," Holmes came over with an aggressive air. "Let them know where we are."

"There's no chance they'll be seen," Harry said. "Not over *that*."

Nicholls paused. "Very well. Just in case. But we keep moving—another hour at least."

When the flares went up, they were brilliant spots of light, burning and beautiful. Then the aurora swallowed them entirely. The dogs howled. Macready pulled me aside. "He's lost his head—he'll get us all killed. You know, don't you? How dangerous a winter journey can be. We need to stop him."

I drew myself up to my full height. We were leashing ourselves to the sledge, in case something happened—so we wouldn't lose one another in the vast darkness. There was something to be said for going forwards. *Onwards.* I clipped on, my movements precise and efficient. "I'm not stopping," I said. "If Nicholls says it's safe. He should know."

XII

When the aurora died, the darkness was complete. No horizon, no mountains, just an endless sea of blacks and grays, and our little lanterns bobbing around in it.

Harry had a terrible nightmare. It was the worst one in weeks: he didn't cry out, but his mouth worked itself open and shut, jaw lengthening and distending, as if he were trying to say something but all the words were gone. He thrashed, though, and in his sleeping bag kicked out at the rest of us. "Morgan," Macready said threateningly, so I shook Harry awake, pressing my hand against his mouth so he wouldn't scream.

He clutched at me, eyes glassy, curls frozen to his forehead. "The flares."

"What?" I whispered, my heart suddenly lifting. "What did you see?"

"No—no. We used them over there—in France." He gulped for air. "Flares and whistles. Red means—it's time to go. I was dreaming of—I think I was dreaming of the final advance."

He retched, shockingly loud in the cramped tent. "Morgan!" Macready said again, this time with a note of concern. I put my hand on Harry's back and rubbed it. The final advance—my brothers' last engagement. I'd never asked him to describe it further. I knew it had been patchy cloud, a thin drizzle: they'd gone over the top in choppy sunlight. Everything visible. They might have seen their deaths coming towards them. I imagined the rolling guns, thunder loud enough to split the sky; Harry directing it from his position in the rear. An unstoppable machine.

There was nothing I could say that would comfort him.

The dark morning wasn't a morning. I woke with my ribs aching, and the weight of Nicholls on top of me. One tent for five of us: we were crammed in head to foot, piled upon one another like bodies in a mass grave. The tent flaps froze as we untied them. The air was so still an open flame didn't flicker but burned unwaveringly. A thick wet blanket of freezing fog had descended, and there was no way to tell up from down, north from south. The gray atmosphere made my head throb, and I looked around, trying to find the aurora.

Nicholls finished his tea in a hurry. His lips were cracked and bleeding, as if he'd been gnawing on them. "I know where I'm going," he said when Macready suggested we wait for visibility to return. It was very obvious he hadn't slept.

"We can't even see the ground in front of us—"

Nicholls stared at him. "Are you tired—Cooper—Morgan? Do you want to wait?"

I shook my head, met Macready's gaze full on. Nicholls gave me a nod of approval.

"Hell," Macready snapped, "just because you and he were—"

"I know he's dead!" Nicholls hissed, fists clenched. "I *know* it."

My heart thumped painfully. Harry looked at them both, not understanding—then flinched as the flares went up. We looked to the west, for answering flares at the huts: nothing. To the east, for lights in the mountains: nothing. The fog blotted out the sky, muffled our voices.

We carried on into that dead white wall. The dogs went faster and faster, straining harder and harder, propelled by an unseen force. Holmes held up a storm lantern, and it did nothing to penetrate the gloom. A compass glinted as Nicholls searched the gray, his eyes desperate. No mountains. No moon. No stars.

When the sledge hit something, I felt the juddering blow deep in my bones. Macready looked at me with mute appeal; I swallowed and nodded. Unclipped my harness to walk around the back to Nicholls. The void swirled thickly around us. I worked my mouth free of the scraping ice on my balaclava, put my hand on Nicholls's shoulder. "Shouldn't we stop—at least scout ahead?" I thought of what he'd said on the way to the huts: *this whole ice sheet might be veined with crevasses.*

"You, too?" Nicholls screwed up his eyes.

The dogs started to howl. The howling echoed and reverberated around us, returned by the fog, until we were at the center of a swarm of devils. Nicholls stared over my shoulder, transfixed. Something gripped at my chest until my ribs felt ready to crack. He wasn't looking where we were going; hadn't been looking for quite some time. I knew he'd seen Tarlington: might be seeing him still. Standing behind me. *Blaming* us.

If my brothers walked, so must he.

"What are you following?" I grabbed Nicholls's windproofs. He was a dead weight. "Who do you see?"

They meant us harm.

"Everyone—stop!" I yelled. It came out too high, and the cold air hurt my throat. Harry looked at me, eyes wide with surprise.

Nicholls said, "No—" in a broken voice that hurt to hear.

Holmes exhaled loudly, putting his storm lantern down in the snow. The dogs were still pulling hard, howling and yapping. "Cooper!" Macready shouted. "We're stopping."

"I can't!" he called back. I grabbed the dog harness and put all my strength against it. After days and weeks and months of hard labor, I could hold my own. But still there was a jerking, erratic forwards motion as the dogs danced on their leashes, growling, dragging the sledge with them. A breeze caressed my face.

The fog was eddying around us. A pinprick of light to the east. I followed it instinctively: all my life, that had meant sunrise. But the mountains were—in the wrong place. The aurora glowing behind their fog-covered peaks. "We're going the wrong way!" I shouted. "Hell—*stop!*"

A crunching sound. Holmes, furious, tried to wrestle the compass off Nicholls, and they slid on their backs together in the snow.

A sudden high-pitched whimper as one of the dogs stumbled. Then a crack. Loud enough to stop everything. Loud enough to make my entire world narrow down to that one sound: the certain cracking of the snow bridge underneath us.

"Everyone stay still!" Nicholls yelled.

The fog had hidden it: we'd finally found the crevasse field.

Harry grabbed the harness and fumbled with the carabiner, eyes wide. The sledge stuttered to a standstill. The lock was iced shut like a vise, and I flinched as Harry discarded his outer mittens. Then his gloves. He hissed, sucked in air, as he worked at the cold metal. Finally it clicked. The lead dog flattened its ears, started to back away from the sledge, harness trailing. We might be on solid ground; might be safe without their weight.

I breathed out.

Then the front end of the sledge tilted down.

I screamed. The sudden movement made me grab at Harry. The sledge runners were sinking into an invisible hole. A rushing feeling—like a strong wind—and I saw Holmes vanish beneath the surface.

Another cracking sound, slow and ominous. The dogs skidded on their hind legs away from the widening gap. "It's going—" Harry shouted.

The glassy roof caved in. We fell, shouting and kicking.

I was falling forever.

A convulsive jerk. Lights flashed behind my eyes. Great white spots of nothing. My harness had stopped me facedown over the edge of a sheer cliff, and I frantically tried to get purchase on the glassy ice. The leash holding me was frozen and brittle—could snap at any moment.

A deep black pit yawned beneath me. The growing aurora showed a crevasse going straight into the depths of the earth, all jagged edges, flickering ice, corkscrew turns, and the large dark shape of the sledge beneath. Mad green lights danced and pulsed. It was like looking into the mouth of Hell.

I could no longer hear the dogs. I hoped they'd escaped. Dimly, I realized Harry had the other end of my harness—had managed to wedge himself into an ice crack at the crevasse mouth. We were both on a small ledge, barely eight feet down. "Jo," he said harshly. "Are you hurt?"

"I'm here." My heartbeat thrashed. "I'm here, you can let go."

Down below, the sledge was suspended on its side, dangling off into nothing. Gouges in the crevasse walls where it had slid, smashing away at the ice as it fell. The cave was too deep for me to see anyone else. I could hear Macready, though—somewhere very distant, his voice horribly distorted. He was shouting for Holmes. A moment later, Nicholls joined in.

"Holmes?" I shouted. It rang around me, booming, mocking. "Holmes!"

No reply.

"It's too deep," Nicholls shouted from somewhere beneath us. "I can't see him—"

"Can you pull him up?"

A scuffle. The sledge shifted and creaked. A crate teetered on its straps, and I shouted, "Watch out!" It fell into the green-tinged darkness— crashed off more of those corkscrew turns—then disappeared. No sound of it landing. None at all.

"We've lost Holmes," Nicholls called. "His leash is snapped. He's gone. What's happening up there—are you—" He broke off. A fit of wet-sounding coughing made my stomach flip.

"Nicholls?"

"I'm here," he said. "Macready—"

"I'm *under* it, God damn." I could hear something moving a long way below. A scraping sound. A small grunt of pain. I tasted bile, thick in my throat. I recalled the dizzying moments of free fall. The sledge stopping beneath us with a muffled thud.

The sound of it hitting Macready.

"Jo," Harry said. "Jo, we need to climb."

I could see the sky, the aurora, the mouth of the crevasse. Behind

Harry, the ice led straight up like a ladder. I poked my head back over the edge of our little ledge, as far as I dared, and tried to make out their figures in the darkness. My harness pulled tight around my heart.

"Macready?"

"I'm here—Jesus Christ—" A horrible, desperate sound. "I can't move." A pause. "I think my legs are broken."

"Hold on," Nicholls said. "Hold on, Robert."

"Nicholls?"

"I don't think there's anything—" But he didn't complete that sentence. "I'm just—caught on something—" The sound of Nicholls struggling against his harness. The crevasse was a yawning green void, and I stared at it.

The sledge shuddered. Harry jerked me back from the edge, shouting down: "It's moving!"

I let out a sob. Scrabbled back to flatten myself against the wall of the ledge, trying to find a handhold. The ice was unforgiving.

"I've got you," Harry said. "I've got you."

"We have to get down to them—"

The wind blew stinging snow down the wall into my face. I swallowed, breathing through my mouth, trying not to think about it drifting over the entrance. All light blotted out. The crevasse collapsing, burying us alive. It was the most terrible death imaginable.

Everything suddenly seemed very fragile.

"Morgan—Cooper—stay where you are!" Nicholls shouted. Then: "Robert, I'm coming down for you."

The sledge was dead weight; there was no way he'd be able to lift it. With every small movement, I could sense it shifting. It was getting ready to crash through the cave like a wrecking ball.

"We can make it," Harry said to me. "I won't let you fall."

I shook my head. It was a long way over to Harry—the ledge very narrow—and moving from the wall felt impossible. A sudden burst of nausea hit me as I looked down. I shook my head again.

"I've got you." Quiet. Authoritative. More sure of himself than he'd been in months. "You need to come over here. I can lift you."

I kept shaking my head, hearing myself making a whimpering noise. There was an echoing sound below. Someone in great pain, trying to stifle his cries. I felt certain I was going to fall—was going to be trapped there too. But if I stayed on that ledge, I'd never get out.

Light-headed, breathing small, jerky breaths, I inched away from the wall; teetered, sickeningly, towards that dark chasm. If I fell, the force of it would almost certainly dislodge Harry. We would fall together. Hit the sledge, knocking ourselves out; then fall past it, down into the depths of the earth. Becoming part of the ice.

I exhaled, letting Harry take my weight for the last moment. He hauled me up against him, chest to chest. He opened his mouth to say something, and I shook my head, wild-eyed. Tried to calm my breathing, stop my heart hammering.

An insistent trickling sound, like rain.

"Nicholls!" I shouted.

The ice cracked again. The sledge shifted.

"You two get yourselves *out*," Nicholls said. "That's an order. I'm going down for Macready. Take this."

From my new position at the crevasse mouth, I could see straight down to Nicholls. He was holding up an ice axe with the very tips of his fingers. The aurora glimmered green across his face; his hat and balaclava had come off, and he was bleeding blackly from his head. I thought about those wet coughs. His eyes were steady, determined. He was not so far beneath us. With the axe, he might still be able to climb out.

"The sledge—"

"I know," he said. "I know. But I'm going down. He hasn't got long."

Harry wriggled down to retrieve the axe with the toes of his boots. Nicholls exhaled, and nodded to us. I closed my eyes, briefly, gulping in air. The tears froze on my cheeks.

Another crack as the ice field contracted, trying to swallow us up. More provisions lost their battle with gravity, more straps gave way. Our human bodies were warming the cave, making the ice yawn around us. "It's going to go," Harry said, indicating Nicholls, crouching and looking into the darkness below. "When he does. We need to be ready."

It took several attempts to cram the ice axe into a fissure, Harry holding me tightly. We started to climb.

Crack. The crevasse vibrated as the sledge started to move.

"No, please, no—"

Macready cried out—once—far below us. The sledge disappeared into the lower darkness, dragging Nicholls with it. He scrambled. He fought to arrest his fall. He grabbed on to something. Said, awfully, "I'm not—"

He disappeared into the black.

The walls were sheer and dangerous, and I could hear dripping. Soon it would be impossible to climb out.

"Jo!" Harry shook me—it was like a bomb going off in my chest, splintering through my ribs, cracking me open from the inside. I shoved him away. I didn't trust him.

"Put your weight on me," he insisted.

"No," I said, gritting my teeth. "Let *go* of me." And I swung around, held myself up on my own arms, started to pull steadily. I was strong enough to get myself out.

XIII

I screamed for Nicholls until I choked on it. Then for Macready. Made Harry hold my legs as I crawled to the edge of the crevasse, stared down into the narrow black mouth. The sledge had wiped away all the ledges and corkscrew turns. Now it was just a void. A pit. No one returned my screams.

I rolled over onto the snow, retching with effort, and looked up at the sky. The fog had receded, and the aurora was sneaking off into the distance. Pale, watery civil twilight. I could see Harry's worried face as he dragged me back; shook me; tried to speak to me. I couldn't make my arms and legs work. Everything seemed a long way off.

I thought I would die.

Dogs barking above me. I opened my eyes. Two of the mongrels were worrying at our packs, tails wagging, leashes trailing. I stared at them. It seemed blackly comic that they were here, when Nicholls and Macready and Holmes were gone.

"Jo," Harry was saying in the distance. "Listen to me. You have to *get up*."

I started to shiver as I came back to myself. The snow had got into my windproofs, and my skin was on fire. Every touch of raw flesh was an agony. I could see Harry rubbing mechanically at his hands, which were jammed inside the front of his jacket.

"Here—" I crawled over to him. He'd taken off his gloves to release the dogs. The carabiner and ice axe must have been like grasping molten metal, and his palms hadn't survived, were battered raw meat. He hissed with pain as he shoved his mittens back on.

Our tent, our stove, everything we needed to live: gone with the sledge. I found myself drawn, blinking, back to the hole. It looked like it went on forever.

"They're already dead," Harry said bluntly. With two claws he put his binoculars to his face, scanned the horizon. Pragmatic. I could see the soldier my brothers had known.

I tore myself away and looked at the mountains, trying to recall Nicholls's charts. The huts were somewhere behind me in the swimming whiteness. The dogs were starting to yap and pull at their leashes. After all that time on the dog deck, I didn't even know their names.

Harry waved his arm. "We're not where we expected," he said. "The glacier's over there. We're southeast of the huts—started making a circle."

Neither of us had a compass. But I could see our tracks in the snow, the drag path of the sledge. Five men walking alongside. Then the horrible rolling scuffle at its end.

"Here." Harry kicked the ice axe across the snow to me. I took it, seeing Nicholls holding it up, his eyes clear and steady. Looking at the sky for the last time. Making his peace.

I shook my head, drew a shuddering breath. "They might still be—we have to get help."

"They're gone." Harry fumbled with Holmes's storm lantern; looked through his precious binoculars, hiding his eyes. "I shouldn't have come," he said, very low.

The blood pounded in my veins. My head throbbed. It felt like ice was burning and sizzling under my skin. I launched myself at him, grabbing the front of his coat, pulling him down to the ground with me. His wide eyes stared as I took a hand off and swung at him.

I thought if I did what they wanted—

A crack. Blood gushed out of his nose, then froze. I flexed my fist, hearing the bones pop. "You shouldn't have come!" I screamed in his face. "You shouldn't have left Portsmouth! This is all your fault—all of it!"

Harry shook his head mutely. He made no move to defend himself.

"We should have left you in South Georgia!" I shouted. "*You* were the one we should have left! And now they're all dead—Nicholls—Randall—Tarlington!"

"I'm sorry."

The dogs keened.

"It was you, wasn't it?" I could feel the ice in my fingers, throat, lips. I hadn't wanted to believe it. I hadn't wanted to think it was possible—not Harry. Not honest, dutiful Harry Cooper. "You set the fire. You burned the ship."

He opened his mouth. I shook him, and his head slammed down on the ground like a dying thing. "It was you—wasn't it?"

He cringed, looking very small against the ice, then nodded. Hair bobbed over his forehead, escaping from his cap. I stared at him.

I thought if I did what they wanted—

He'd seen them all along—had wanted to see them. He'd called the ghosts, and they had come. Creeping from the mountains, reaching over the ice, in the faintest breath of wind. Harry must have been like a beacon in the darkness.

He'd burned the *Fortitude*, to deliver us here at their command.

"Why?"

"To keep you safe."

"You didn't need to!" My voice was a howl. I thought of the ship; the clear uncomplicated pleasure of the rigging; nights in the mess hall. Being called *Morgan*. Accepted, unquestioned, for who I was.

"I didn't need you—God, Harry! I didn't—"

I punched him again, barely feeling the blow. There was no satisfaction in it. A sick feeling in the pit of my stomach. Everything seemed to be watching, listening: Harry and I on the ice, utterly alone.

"Please—please understand. I thought Randall was—I thought we were all going to die down here." A hollow laugh. "I thought the expedition was doomed. I was so sure there was—sabotage. Or something would go wrong, like it always does. I *knew* we were in danger, I just didn't know how—and I thought if something happened—before we got stuck—he'd turn back." He gulped. "I meant to waste some of the coal. Scare them. I didn't mean to leave the hatches open. I didn't realize it would be so *big*."

The dogs howled at the scent of thunderstorms. For a moment, I thought I could smell burning. Harry's sooty clothes, discarded on the Nursery floor. I should have seen it earlier.

"You bloody idiot," I whispered, fist unclenching. I wiped my mouth with the back of my hand.

"I didn't know! When they came, it was—it was like something whispering, at first. Little voices in my head—telling me things I already thought. It was easy to believe it was just—me speaking to myself. And then in my dreams, I started to hear them—see them. The voices got bigger and bigger. It was like a whistling—a hissing—like radio static." He swallowed. "Like someone was speaking to me on the wind, if I listened close enough. They were your brothers—*keep Jo safe*, they told me. They told me you were in danger—the ship—the men—I thought we'd go back to South Georgia, and I could get you home. I thought that was what they wanted."

He had the decency to look ashamed.

It made my skin crawl. My brothers had told him precisely what he wanted to hear: that he was the only one who could protect me. That I needed his protection. That I was *Jo*, still, and all that came with it.

They'd both been wrong.

I knelt over him in a daze; fumbled with the revolver. It was frozen into its holster. The ship—the fire—all the deaths that followed. Someone should be punished. Someone should be *shot*. That was how this world worked. Harry's eyes tracked my movements. He nodded. "Do it."

But my fingers clenched, and wouldn't touch the trigger.

"You need to go," Harry said, distantly. "You can make it back to the huts. Follow our tracks—take the dogs. It can't be more than a day away."

I stared at him. Then shook him, hard. He was limp and unresponsive as a rag doll. "Get up!"

"No," he said. "No. Don't you understand? I'm staying here. With them. With . . . the sledge. Nicholls. The others. This is all my fault."

"Like hell you are." I pulled him savagely up. "You'll freeze to death.

I'm not leaving you here. I won't—I won't tell anyone. I'll keep it a secret. They won't kill you."

"But it's my fault," he said again.

"Yes *it bloody well is*!" I yelled. It echoed around the plateau. The dogs barked. That burning wind blew in my face, making me stumble away from him. "But I'm not leaving you—they'll come for you if you stay."

"I'm sure they will." He unlooped the binoculars from his neck, motions jerky, the leather straps coated with sweat and rime. He weighed them in his hands. "Then the rest of you might have a chance—if I can draw them off. They're here for *me*, after all. This is my—punishment, for what happened over there. They want me to face up to the things I've done."

We were standing on a precipice. He looked as if he would continue his awful confession, and I couldn't bear it. I raised the ice axe, trembling, to ward him off. "Stop," I rasped. "Stop talking."

He walked up to me. Very calmly, he pushed the axe aside. Took my face between his ruined hands, icy mittens on my raw cheeks. Blood and tears. His brown eyes were dark, the stars starting to come out. I'd thought him handsome, once. My lips parted.

"I'm very sorry," he said. "Please believe me, Jonathan. I never meant it to turn out like this."

He kissed me, briefly, and this time I didn't pull away. Faint eclipsing warmth; I kept my eyes open, felt the scrape of his skin, the ice starting to cling to him. I knew this was good-bye.

He stood back. Pressed his binoculars into my hands, curled my fingers around them. They felt unbelievably heavy. I'd been thirteen when Harry had enlisted: always underfoot, always left behind, always shouted at for playing with my brothers' things. They'd gone away to war and we'd been just children—left behind again—until Harry had followed suit, running off into the ranks to play with toys of his own. He'd grown up so fast. It had truly, as my father had once said, been *the making of him*.

I looped the strap around my neck, watching him for a few moments. The invisible tether between us wouldn't let me walk away. My childhood. The War. All the miles between us and England. Then I turned my back, wound the leashes around my aching hands, and started my journey.

Zero hour.

XIV

The dogs were tamer once I'd left Harry behind.

They pulled me along when I was weeping too hard to walk. Tails straight up, breath pluming in the twilight, paws sure and steady through our tracks. Once or twice they stopped, looked around abruptly, and scented the wind. But though I watched for the aurora, it never came.

I had to keep moving.

My boots became blocks of ice. My balaclava welded hard to my face. Francis's scarf, blood-red in the gloom, formed a frozen noose around my neck. I found myself repeating snatches of poetry, songs, my voice cracking. Anything to stop the vast silence consuming me whole.

"Sunset and evening star. And after that the dark."

The words seemed to follow me. I pressed my gloves against my eyes, wiped away tears; I was in danger of being blinded if they froze. "Shut up," I told myself fiercely. "Shut up. Don't cry."

I might make it to the huts if I just kept walking. One foot in front of the other. The dogs lurched as they found dents and depressions where the snow had settled unevenly. But this route, at least, was safe: it had taken the weight of all five of us, and the sledge, and the dogs. Nicholls, following a figure only he could see.

I wiped my nose on my sleeve. I could cut corners: leave our tracks, squaring the circle across the uncharted places. It would be quicker. But the thought made me sick: the snow could hide anything. Again, I saw the sledge disappearing, heard Macready screaming. Saw Nicholls, handing up the ice axe, climbing down to his death. He was a hero. Not the sort of hero my brothers would have recognized. But that didn't matter so much anymore.

I hoped he'd died quickly. That would be a mercy. For any of us that would be a mercy. But I had to carry on, stumping through the snow on my own funeral march.

The dogs skidded to a halt. I looked up. The waning moon was like a silver coin. The stars had come out, dusting the sky with brilliance, and I wished—desperately—I knew what they said. How to find Jupiter, how to guide myself home. But this was exactly the sort of thing I'd overlooked: I'd dreamed over the romantic map of Antarctica instead of studying navigation, and the heavens were indifferent to my suffering.

One of the dogs yelped. "Let's go, then." A screaming gust of wind made us huddle around one another. It was cold, so cold, and for a moment there seemed to be an urgent whispering, everywhere and nowhere all at once.

"Stop it," I said. "Just stop it!"

The dogs growled at the air.

I had the impression that something had just stepped out of the sky— had come to Earth. The wind ceased, as if it had never been there at all. My skin crawled. Someone was approaching. Just a little out of sight.

And after that, the dark.

The cold caught in my throat. I froze, clutching at the leash, resisting the urge to turn around. I forced myself to stumble onward.

"Don't look," I whispered.

Night came. I managed to light the lantern. My path was unbroken and unending. The aurora started behind me—I could tell from the green reflections on the snow, in the dogs' eyes. I didn't turn around. I knew that if I did, it would show me a city over the mountains, steepled summits flashing in and out of existence. It was a mirage, nothing more. I wouldn't play its game.

The darkness pressed in on me, making me feel small and insignificant. We'd been nothing to this landscape. I crouched in the snow; I gave the dogs names, made a fuss of them, wanting to hear my own voice out loud. I called them Coats and Weddell, for the landmarks on the map in my brothers' room, its white center reflecting the bright Portsmouth sunlight. When they'd still been at home, I'd sneaked inside whenever Chloe left their door open after cleaning: if Rufus caught me, I was in for a disapproving look. "You're not allowed in here," he'd say. "Run *along*."

The dogs whined, eyes wide and watchful. Whatever followed me—I knew it was coming closer.

"Come on," I whispered. I found myself humming, under my breath, a thin, ragged tune. It took me a while to recognize it as a popular marching song. I wondered if my brothers had sung it, over there: Rufus had a fine baritone voice. But that was something I'd never asked Harry—like everything else—and now never could.

I couldn't keep up with the dogs, and found myself falling farther and farther behind, until the leashes were fully extended and they were just bobbing impressions ahead. I dug my heels in to make them stop.

I crouched in the snow over the lantern, breathing hard, and flexed my numb fingers. A sense of shifting. Movement in the darkness.

I wasn't alone.

"Francis?" I said quietly. The dogs growled, flattening themselves at the ends of their leashes. "Rufus? Is that you?"

"But of course," came a voice from the darkness. It *echoed*, seemed to come from miles away, and a great height. "Who else would it be?"

He'd come right up to the edge of my pool of light. Red hair, neatly pressed uniform, broad shoulders, tiger smile. The eldest Morgan brother had finally arrived: twenty-two forever, sketched in night.

It turned my heart to lead.

"What are you doing out here?" Rufus said. "You idiot. You'll catch your death."

His voice was sharp, but concerned. "Rufus," I croaked. I was cold, exhausted. Felt I could just lie down in the snow, let the darkness wash over me. I'd stop shivering, eventually, as my muscles forgot how. My heartbeat would slow. I'd fall asleep. It would be easy.

And Rufus would watch over me.

"This isn't for you," he said, looking around at the aurora playing over the snow. At the mountains. The moonlight. The dogs, now pulling as hard as they could, yelping and whining and trying to get away. "I don't know why you came. You're so—small. So defenseless. Everyone you loved—everyone you cared about—all dead."

I swallowed. "I came for you." It sounded inadequate—as I always did, with Rufus. I hugged my chest; remembered, at the last moment, to keep hold of the leashes. He was right, though. I was utterly alone. I'd neither killed Harry nor saved him. I was wasting my strength on the long march. There was nothing left for me back at the huts. Just a dying leader, and months of night.

Better to end it.

Rufus looked down, smiling his secret smile. "You'll catch your death," he repeated. "Here. Come with me."

There was a swarming sensation in the air, as if we were surrounded by a flock of flying creatures, and I saw black spots in the corners of my vision. When I looked back, Rufus was closer, holding out his hand, his face in shadow. Just a hand, held out of the Antarctic night, waiting for me to take it.

I gulped back a sob. "Where's Francis?"

"Oh, he's here too," Rufus said. "Just a little farther away. I can take you to him."

I knew why people followed their ghosts. His bare hands looked warm, although his breath didn't steam in the night air. He was sure and confident. He knew I was going to reach out to him. It would be like falling down a crevasse: the sudden drop into nothingness. To whatever was on the other side of the aurora. It would be quick.

"And—Harry?" I choked slightly on his name.

"Soon enough," he said quietly. "It's getting darker. You'll lose the tracks. You'll lose the dogs. And we both know you're just—drawing things out. It's inevitable."

I pressed my gloves to my face, took in a long, shuddering breath. He looked more solid every moment, *wished* into being: first by Harry, then by me.

We'd longed to see him.

"Jonathan," Rufus said. "I'm your brother. I've come to take you with me."

The aurora flashed like a knife.

Slowly, very slowly, I stood up. "What did you call me?" My voice shook. There was a vise around my heart.

Rufus didn't reply. He remained on the other side of the lantern-light, like a bird of prey using the sun to hide. I wanted—more than anything— to take his hand.

But I knew that I wouldn't. My brothers weren't in Antarctica. They weren't to be found in the white spaces. This wasn't my brother—or even his ghost.

"You're not him," I said. My voice came clearer, my spine grew straighter.

Rufus looked at me and smiled. "Of course I am."

I'd waited so long. All my life, perhaps. But Jonathan was my *real* name. The name I'd chosen for myself, for the person I knew I really was. I'd never wrestled with my brothers; never played football with them; never run barefoot on the beach. I'd never been allowed on their adventures. Always underfoot; always left behind. Wherever they went, it was no place for a *girl*. No place for their little sister. Whenever I'd tried to follow them, Rufus had called me by my full name—a name painted with flourishes, garlanded with lilies, on the door of my childhood bedroom. And smiled, knowing how much I hated it.

This thing wore his face. Spoke with his voice. Called me *Jonathan*, and saw me at last.

It was just showing me what I wanted.

I had to get moving. My legs were numb. I remembered Randall, raving, his feet two solid lumps of blackened flesh. Perhaps it was already too late for me. Perhaps that was how I'd die: screaming in agony, Clarke wielding the saw. But I preferred it to giving up. The quiet death in the snow. This thing—whatever it was—that *lied* to me.

I'd continue onwards, for as long as I could.

I took the first step, snow crunching under my feet. Then stopped. I realized what it meant: they were really, truly gone. I'd never see them again, never be caught up in Francis's embrace. I'd never hear Rufus laughing. My brothers were dead, and the world had changed.

I sobbed, suddenly, choking on the cold air. Pressed my gloves to my eyes, feeling the ice setting hard like diamonds. Remembered the risk of blinding myself. My chest ached as if it were turning itself inside out; I could feel screaming, an eternity of screaming, waiting to be released. I swallowed it down. Swallowed it all down.

Rufus—the thing that pretended to be Rufus—looked interested in my pain, like it gave him strength. He came further into focus, until I could make out his burning green eyes, the sharp precise lines of his face. He was coming closer. A predator. Something that belonged to this awful place, using our weaknesses against us.

I'd talked to it for long enough. Allowed it close for long enough. "You're not him," I said, my voice loud in the echoing darkness. "Get out of my way."

The lantern wavered. The aurora spun sickeningly overheard. I took one step forwards, then another. The dogs started to pull. And in an instant, Rufus was gone.

FIVE

THE DEVASTATION

EXPEDITION POINT, AUSTRAL WINTER 1920

I

I'd die if I stopped walking.

Even so, I found myself turning around, feet like lead. I shouted, "Come and get me!" towards the mountains. The aurora. Rufus.

I received no answer.

Coats and Weddell flattened their ears, gave me low warning whines, and we continued. In the silence I could hear their paws breaking through the crust on fresh snow. Occasionally they spoke to each other in yelps and snaps.

"Good dogs," I said shakily. "Good dogs."

I'd been walking for an eternity: it was painfully obvious I was running out of strength. I'd already run out of fuel for the lantern, and had trembled as I looked around in the intermittent moonlight, trying to relight it anyway. The presence had come closer, closer, and the darkness had *laughed* at me as I'd cried.

My legs were very numb. I might have lost my feet already. But it was impossible to pry off the snow-encrusted boots, see if my flesh was white or black. I tried not to think of Randall's agonies. I just had to keep going. One foot in front of the other.

Stopping was death, and I didn't intend to die yet.

I looked around wildly when nautical twilight arrived. It was possible I was walking in the wrong direction, out into the heart of the continent. I'd left our tracks behind—struck out to what I thought was the west— hoping the dogs could somehow find a way back to their kennels. They were dumb beasts. I was asking a lot from them. But they'd always hated the winds; had always been able to sense the presence of something awful.

They'd hated Harry, too, at times.

I trudged hours into the false dawn. The air tore at my nose. My jaw felt as if it would snap. The horizon remained stubbornly blurry.

When the light in the sky lifted a fraction, I could see the jagged outline of the peaks, and nearly choked with relief. I was no closer to the mountains. Coats and Weddell gave wolfish growls of excitement; pulled harder.

After only an hour the sky started to turn deep navy again. I couldn't believe there'd ever been a time of pale blue skies, white clouds, birds flying, daybreak. A different world.

But as velvet darkness gathered me up, the moon scudded out from behind a cloud, showing me a shape in the distance. Several miles off, over the flat unbroken plateau. The camp's anemometer, whirling at the top of its pole. No one to take its measurements. Not anymore.

I took a great gulp of cold air, nostrils stinging like they'd been sliced open. I turned, deliberately, to look behind me.

Rufus wasn't there.

"I didn't think so!" I shouted, relief bubbling up in my chest. "I didn't think so!"

II

The huts were blazing light.

Nestled in our snowy little valley, they looked like a Christmas gingerbread scene. Icicles glittered from the porch roof, nearly long enough to touch the railings. The kennels, latrines, stores: all had lanterns hanging outside, creating a clear perimeter. I couldn't believe the extravagance. A circle of pale orange light fought against the dark cupped hands of the sky.

Snow had drifted, and hadn't been cleared—soon it would be impossible to open the doors without a struggle. No one came to meet me, and the boarded-up windows were eyes that had been deliberately put out. I shivered.

I let Coats and Weddell into the kennels. Their eyes glimmered in the musty darkness, and I sank to my knees, burying my face in the warm fur of their necks. "Thank you," I said, my voice muffled.

A door slammed somewhere. I clung to Weddell's collar, unwilling to let go. He was something solid, something real. A rangy black-and-brown mutt that had stayed by my side all the way across the plateau. I could feel his ribs as he breathed in and out, and I crawled across the kennel floor to see whether Harry had left any food I could give him. I was suddenly starving.

Outside, the sound came again.

I went still. Something told me Rufus—the creature with Rufus's face—wouldn't come into the light. Not yet, at least. But I wouldn't call out. I crept slowly to the kennel door. Nothing moved, the lanterns shining steadily. From inside the huts—ten or fifteen feet away, it might as well have been miles—I could hear raised voices.

As I watched, the cold locker door swung open sharply. It completed a whole swing on its hinges, reached its limits, and slammed itself shut again.

Weddell growled, backing away.

"Stay here," I whispered. "Good dogs."

I carried the ice axe. It made me think of Nicholls, his steady eyes at the end. *Idiot. War games.* This time, the Webley stayed on my belt. The fresh snow crunched loudly under my feet. The cold locker door swung open for me, and I looked around, shivering, for Rufus. Francis. Harry.

Anyone.

It took a moment for my eyes to adjust to the darkness, and make out the shape of someone tied to the examination table. Long legs—just able to reach the door and kick it open.

"For God's sake, Morgan," he said. "Untie me."

I'd have recognized his raspy voice anywhere.

"You're not him." My mouth was numb. It felt like my head was full of insects. Swarming. Beating their wings.

"Don't be stupid. I'm tied up. I'm a *prisoner*."

I knelt beside him, pulling down his scarf with shaking fingers. It was clever, so clever. The imitation was perfect, right down to the red fuzz of his hair growing back, pale slashes of scalp where he'd cut it untidily. Macready's stove glowed in the corner, light glimmering on his angular face. But he didn't move. He didn't burst free of his restraints, tower over me, demand that I follow him. He just blinked his large blue eyes and looked at me. A pause.

"Are you going to kill me, then?" He sounded very weary.

A sudden gust of wind made all the lanterns swing. My stomach roiled as I heard the low crackle of the aurora approaching, the dogs beginning to howl. His mouth twisted. "Hell. Get on with it."

My fingers on the ice axe were tight enough to ache. He had a black eye. His chest moved erratically as he exhaled, breath steaming. He was shivering.

"Tarlington?"

"For the love of— Morgan, it's *me*." His voice cracked.

He was affected by the cold. And I knew, then—he was as alive, improbably, as I was.

I moved back. For a moment I wanted to run, head away from the huts and into the snow and just keep running. But I bent to fumble with Tarlington's restraints. He let out a shaky sigh. "It's not too tight. They did it quickly. No one wanted to be out here."

"Where—who—"

"The mountain party," he said, lip curling. "What's left of us. Boyd brought me back—Laurence insisted. The rest are gone."

I clapped my hand over my mouth. Staunton, our surgeon. Ollivar. Parker. I hadn't—really—expected to see them again. But even so—

We were so *few*.

"We returned yesterday. Barely got halfway. But when those infernal winds came, so did—something else. Your ghosts, perhaps—I don't know. The men were drawn away from camp, one by one." He pulled at his free hand and flexed it in his gloves. "Boyd wanted to leave me there. This"—he indicated his restraints, the cold locker's ghostly interior—"this was the compromise." A half-laugh. He scrambled away from the table, his movements uncharacteristically clumsy.

"They saw—"

"Boyd saw what he wanted to see. What he expected. The evil— degenerate—villain. I'd burnt the *Fortitude*, sold you all out to the Germans. Gone on a rampage. It was *me* outside."

My cheeks burned. He accepted my hand to pull himself upright. He was heavier than I expected, shockingly cold, and we stumbled back against his dissecting table. "But now you're back. I'm glad. I'm so glad, Morgan. Now we have a chance to stand up to him."

I opened my mouth. Tarlington stopped suddenly. He looked out the door, at the pools of lantern-light, the frozen stillness of our gingerbread world. No sledge returned. No dog team.

No one else.

He turned back to me, and I could see the hope dying on his face. "Nicholls?" He shook his head. "No. Don't answer. Don't you *dare* answer, Morgan." He rubbed his mouth jerkily. Took a deep breath. For a moment, he was very still. Then he steadied himself against the table. "Damn. Damn."

"I'm sorry." My voice was very small. I couldn't look him in the eye.

Tarlington sighed. "I suppose—the others, too?"

I nodded, squeezing my fists. "All of them. There's—just me."

"Then it's not safe for me inside," he said simply. A faint expression of horror flickered at the corner of his mouth. "Not with Boyd on the warpath. You don't know what he's capable of—" He glanced at me as though something had just occurred to him. "Cooper?"

I thought of Harry, standing in the snow as I walked away, and my knees went weak. He could have been here—alive. The instrument of our downfall, but *alive*. I'd have lied, shielded him from the others. I'd have done nearly anything to keep him safe.

"He could—could have made it. There was a crevasse, the others fell—but Harry escaped. We both did. But he wouldn't come back with me."

There was a curious look of understanding on Tarlington's long face. "I'm sorry, Morgan." He made an awkward gesture, as though he wanted to put a hand on my shoulder. "What a bloody stupid waste."

For once, I knew exactly what he meant.

III

The air inside the hut was rank: unwashed men in desperate circumstances, and the sweet sinister smell of something rotting.

"Morgan—what the hell?"

Clarke looked at me as though I were a ghost. I let out a small, painful laugh, sinking down with my back against the door, fumbling to free myself from the heavy windproofs. My hands didn't want to work. The questions washed over me.

My answers were short. The hut had once seemed friendly. Now I was powerfully aware of the squatness of the ceiling, crushed under the weight of all that darkness. The stove made shadows leap and crawl. The empty doorways and passages became people standing just out of sight, waiting for their turn to speak. Clarke had stopped tidying his beard, and his eyes were bloodshot. The long table, where I'd spent easy evenings; where we'd shared meals and laughter—

Randall lay on it. His eyes were shut, but once the bare essentials had come out, he'd growled, "That's enough," and the room had fallen silent again. I listened to the stove howling as the winds sucked our heat into the sky. Tarlington had taken the ice axe—Nicholls's ice axe—off me, hefted it in his hands, then sat down in the cold locker to wait. I felt very light-headed.

Laurence brought me a mug of soup, supported my arm so I could drink it. Despair was written all over his face. Ellis and Rees were nowhere to be seen, although a hacking, gulping cough came from the Coal Hole, making me start.

"Is he—" I whispered, my eyes fixed on the table.

"He's conscious," Clarke said heavily. "Sometimes. We had to take his leg off."

Looking around, I could see the saw in a steaming pot on the stovetop. Blood, spattered on the pale timber floor. I understood the rotten smell must be coming from Randall, who was shivering, and appeared to have fallen asleep. I pushed the soup away.

Boyd had his head in his hands. He was in shirtsleeves, although the hut was chilly enough that I could see my own breath. He'd glanced up when the door opened, then—seeing I was not Tarlington, or Nicholls—had sunk back down. I tried to see his face; tried to see written there the look of a man who'd dragged Tarlington back in chains.

"We need to take more off," Clarke said. "Can't wait any longer." He nodded at Laurence, moving slowly. "Let's get some air to it."

I stood up reluctantly, bracing myself. When they pulled the blankets back, the smell was deeper. Randall's right leg ended at the knee, wrapped in bloody bandages, the stump of bone clearly visible. His left leg was the unhealthy shade of rancid cream, the foot blackened and swollen beyond recognition. A solid lump of flesh—a hoof.

I covered my face and tried not to vomit.

"I've seen worse," Clarke said to me. I let out a sob and clawed at my throat, as if I could stuff it back in. My brothers had *died* of wounds like these.

Boyd snorted. "After all that," he said, as if carrying on a conversation. "After all we suffered—after I saw that bastard murder my men—you decided to go and look for us. Bloody stupid. Throwing good men after bad."

"I'm not having this out with you," Clarke said. "Not now."

"It's not up to you," Boyd said thickly. "I told Nicholls that fucking coward would be the end of him, one way or another. I told him."

"Boyd. I think you've had enough." He was drinking whisky straight from the bottle. The Germans must have brought it for a special occasion. But they were gone, and there would be no more Christmases for us.

Again, I felt the walls closing in.

"Why not? Hell, the stores will go a lot further now." Everyone found their gaze drawn, quite involuntarily, to Randall. He lay still. I was close enough to see his eyelids flickering.

"We should give him morphine," Laurence said.

"We don't have any more," Clarke replied.

"He's dying, isn't he?" I was embarrassed to hear my voice cracking. But my brothers had died somewhere like this: winter outside and strangers around them, rotting from the inside out. The look Clarke gave me was equal parts anger and despair. "We should—we should do something."

A sudden intake of breath, and I got the picture: I'd stumbled into an earlier discussion. There was something no one wanted to say.

The stove flickered. "Go ahead." Boyd wiped his mouth. "I'll do it. None of the rest of you have the balls. He shouldn't die in pieces." He picked up a rifle. "It'll be faster and kinder than what happened when the blizzard came. We'll deal with *him* next."

"No," I blurted out, my voice high and shaky. Boyd turned towards me, hands moving quick and sure to pull back the bolt, feed cartridges inside, return the rifle to readiness. I took a step back, pressing myself against the wall. "No. Boyd, you're wrong. We—were wrong. It wasn't Tarlington who set the fire. There's no German plot. It was—" I put my hands up. "It was Harry. He saw it, and—it drove him mad. There's something stalking us."

Silence. Clarke made a rumbling noise in his chest.

Boyd shook his head in short, choppy motions. "You weren't there. I saw him. I know what he is."

Clarke's hand clamped down on his shoulder, knuckles very swollen. "No more, Richard. No more. There are so few of us left. We'll need every man to get through the winter."

"Then what?"

"Leave here. Get moving—increase our chances of being found. If we wait here, we might as well have given up. And I won't do that."

"My *Fortitude* is gone," Randall said suddenly. He turned his head. I could see the muscles straining in his neck, sweat pooling on his forehead, his expressionless eye. "All that's left out there is—*you* know, don't you, eh?"

I was frozen in place. "Randall?" I said, weakly.

He nodded. "*Devastation.*" He closed his eyes again, the breath leaving his body like a hot-air balloon sinking to earth.

"I'll do it," Boyd said. "I'm not afraid."

"Yes, you are," Randall wheezed, his teeth chattering. "You're afraid of what walks outside."

"The only thing out there," Boyd hissed, "is that *bastard*—"

"Don't you dare—" An unsteady shout. Randall would never bellow again.

Boyd pointed the rifle in Randall's face. Then, slowly, he moved it down to press against the blankets. I could see something leaking onto the floor below, and shoved my sleeve against my mouth, too frightened to even retch. Ellis's pale face peered around the corner into the common room, framed by a sliver of darkness. Laurence gripped my arm.

"Damn you for a coward," Randall whispered. "I've led you this far—"

"You've led us *nowhere*," Boyd spat, and raised the rifle again.

Clarke grabbed him from behind. "Put it down!"

The door flew open, snow sweeping in. A furious blur of motion as Tarlington swung the ice axe at Boyd's head—Clarke was in the way, and Tarlington skidded to avoid him, caught off-balance, axe clattering to the floor. Boyd grabbed Tarlington by the throat, pulled off his cap, and pushed him up against the support beam. The muscles in his big arms bulged and flexed. Tarlington's feet scraped the floor: it looked like he weighed nothing. Blood flushed into his pale face.

There was no air in the room.

Boyd released Tarlington—to put the rifle to his skull. "I'll take care of—this."

"No!" I launched myself across the table without thinking, blood pounding in my veins. Laurence grabbed my collar. Randall was trying to drag himself upright, eyes popping. He roared in agony at my weight; gritted his teeth; was defeated.

"Don't, Richard," Clarke said, hands spread. "There's no going back from this."

Boyd shook his head, breathing hard. The barrel wavered and scraped along Tarlington's patchy red hair. I could see the spray of milk-and-biscuit freckles on his long neck as he strained to avoid it. "What do you think, Randall?" Boyd flicked his eyes to the table. "You brought your boy here. You brought this upon us. Seems you should watch."

"Don't," I begged, struggling to pull myself free from Laurence. "Please, Boyd, it wasn't him."

"I don't believe in ghosts!" Boyd bellowed, spit flying. He turned back to Tarlington.

"Give it to me," said a voice in my ear. Rumbling. Low.

I turned my head an inch, sucked in a breath. Randall. His ruined face pressed close to mine. His dark blue eyes fixed on me. His breath stank. He nodded to my belt.

I knew what he was asking. I couldn't.

I had to.

Slowly and quietly, I pressed the revolver—already loaded—into

Randall's cold, trembling hand. I rolled off the table, a heavy dull sound as I hit the floor.

Boyd glanced at me, eyes wide, mouth pulled into a tight line. His expression held such mute horror, I thought he would relent—release Tarlington, and it would all be over. We could trust one another once more.

The sound of a hammer being cocked.

"Boyd," Randall said. "Boyd!"

The gunshot was painfully loud. It sounded as though it would ring to the mountains; summon the aurora; travel all the way across the ice to the *Fortitude*. I saw Clarke lunging, Tarlington falling to the floor. There was shouting, somewhere very far away, and I lay with my ears ringing, face pressed to the bare wooden boards. Hundreds and hundreds of scuff marks from the furniture, from boots, from us and those who came before us. On the other side of the table, a pool of blood began to spread.

I heaved and pulled myself upright, still retching, clutching at my chest.

"James!" Randall coughed. "James! Are you—"

Clarke grabbed the revolver, dropped it with a loud clunk. Boyd lay motionless on the bloody floor. Rees was choking, hacking away in the Coal Hole, the sound of utter misery, more death to come. And the front door was opening and shutting, opening and shutting, hammering backwards and forwards on its hinges. Each time it opened, the rolling crashing colors of the aurora filled the sky, mad as Catherine wheels. All the lanterns had blown out. The sound of the wind was inhuman.

"Dear God, shut it—"

I reached for the handle blindly. There were voices in the snow. Hundreds and hundreds of voices, speaking horrors. *Death. Madness.* I thought I would feel, from the darkness, a hand reaching for mine.

I slammed it shut, pressed the bolt back into place.

Randall rolled on the table. I saw, horrible and stark, the moment he lost control of his limbs and started to fit. Clarke took a painful breath, hit him with the butt of Boyd's rifle. His eyes closed. He stilled.

"We'd better do it while he's out," Tarlington said, faintly. "I can hold him."

IV

Randall did not survive the loss of his legs.

We did everything humanly possible to save him. It was just too much. His right leg already gone, he was pale and sweaty, convulsing, shivering. The blackened hammer of his left foot was cold as ice and stank of meat going bad. We didn't have anything left to give him. There was nothing, nothing.

So he kept waking. Laurence wielded a mallet: large, blunt, meant for hammering pitons into rock. Laurence's mustache trembled, and he was often unable to perform his duties. Randall woke in terrible pain and panic. Trying to escape Clarke, and the saw.

I held Randall's leg. I heaved repeatedly, throwing up water; eventually we put a bucket down so I wouldn't need to leave the operating table. It was primitive. Barbaric. Randall's breathing slowed. He woke less and less.

The rotting flesh came away in pieces, at terrible cost: the knife stuck on the tough, stringy ligaments. The saw slipped and slid in the blood. The smell was unbearable, and I tied my scarf around my face, but still it crept in.

"We have to go higher. Get above it," Clarke said. He moved up another few inches, took a great shuddering breath, then tested the skin with the blade.

Tarlington tightened the tourniquet, his face paler than death. Randall called him *Charlie* and begged his forgiveness: "I shouldn't have sent you."

Clarke started to cut, and it was blood, decent red blood. We'd found the limits of the rot.

But it was just too much. Randall stopped breathing, and so did I, pressing my hand to my face. Clarke thumped on his chest and snarled, "Come on!" We rubbed his limbs, slapped his cheeks. Randall opened his eyes, fixed his clear one on Tarlington—appeared to recognize him, and called him *James*. Tarlington laid his hand on Randall's forehead and said, with great tenderness, "It won't be far now, old man."

Randall stopped moving.

Finally Clarke wept, shoulders shuddering as he turned away. The fingers of his good hand were clasped so hard around the knife that I had to pry them free one by one.

We covered Randall up. It was very quiet.

"We'll bury him in the morning." Clarke wiped his face. "Boyd, too. It'll take a while."

The body looked small—pitifully so. He'd been so *large*. The saw boiled away on the stove, death leaving a metallic tang in the air. I thought queasily of Macready's story, all those countless nights ago, about what happened when a body was left unburied. Ellis was shivering at the door, uncharacteristically silent. Not a sound from Rees, either, and I supposed that was a small mercy. "The lights," I said. "Someone should be on watch."

"I'll go." Tarlington stalked to the door, rubbing his hand over the stubble on the back of his head. He'd been silent since Clarke had put down the saw, said "He's already gone," then carried on, so Randall wouldn't be buried with a foot hanging off. Some dignity.

Clarke looked up. "Are you sure, Tarlington?"

He paused in the doorway, gave Clarke a piercing look. Nodded. He suddenly seemed very old. "You did what you had to do."

For God's sake. Get on with it.

I remembered my night alone on the plateau. I'd nearly taken its hand—nearly gone with it. Though Tarlington told us he was a scientist—though he seemed to want nothing, need nothing, as self-contained and fierce as a wild cat—he shouldn't be alone out there.

The night outside the porch was a hell of ice and darkness, wind whipping the powder snow into a thousand tiny knives. I shielded my eyes, edged along the railing to the tall angular shape of Tarlington in his coat. Most of the lanterns were out, but the kennels—at least—were still within our pool of light. Coats and Weddell barked desperately at the wind, and my heart went out to them.

"They kept me safe," I said, raising my voice. "I don't want to leave them—"

"No, of course not." Tarlington's scarf and hood covered his face, and his eyes were unreadable, fever-bright. He steadied me as I climbed down the icy steps, struggled against the wind to the kennels, the ceaseless beating of the air making me realize how bone-weary I was. I couldn't remember the last time I'd slept. The dogs threw themselves at me.

Tarlington's laugh sounded like a sob. They were trying to lick his face, pathetically grateful to be brought onto the porch and closer to home. I sat on the steps, winding their leashes around the railings.

I took a deep breath, trying to get the smell of decay out of my nose and mouth; winced at the thought that it was Randall clinging to me. I looked sideways at Tarlington, who'd been protected by Randall in so many ways. Who'd followed him to Antarctica, although clearly unwilling.

"I'm sorry."

He turned quickly, his gaze like a bucket of icy water. "For what?"

I exhaled. "For Randall."

He stared at me, eyes narrowing. Then nodded, slowly. "I'm glad we'll bury him properly," he said, in his smoker's voice. "He should have a grave. A monument. An entire fucking mausoleum. Here lies the people's hero."

I swallowed. The wind made it hard to speak, but I had to get it out. "You should know—it was Harry. The ship. He told me, before he—left. He was misled. The thing outside, it—persuaded him." Silence stretched out between us, and I started to regret telling him. "For my part, I'm—sorry. I should have watched him closer. I should have seen what was happening to him."

The lanterns guttered.

"What a waste," Tarlington said at length. "What a bloody waste." He paced back and forth on the boards, hands shoved into his pockets, Coats padding beside him. "Boyd, too. I told *him*, when he asked me to come: people would hate me, they'd find ways to make it—about the War. I told him it was a mistake to bring me. But he insisted."

I chewed my lip. I'd always assumed Tarlington was with us because he was cheap in some way. Young, barely qualified. Another of Randall's bad bargains. "So why come—"

"Because he asked me." Tarlington's voice was louder than I expected. "I didn't want to disappoint him."

"You didn't," I said immediately, thinking of the fierce, lion-like look on Randall's face when Tarlington had volunteered for the mountain party. It had made him seem quite young again. I could see, now, that it had been pride.

Tarlington shook his head, looking out into the night. "You know—they asked him where he'd been? He didn't know. They couldn't get any sense out of him. A man who knew Antarctica like the back of his hand, and—all he could say was that it was *Charlie* out there." A sigh. "He'd have preferred Charlie. I was the next best thing."

The lantern-light picked out the deep dark blue of his eyes. My heart seemed to stop, then pound like hammer blows. I thought of Randall calling him *James*, and the startled—almost scalded—expression on Tarlington's face.

Recognition, at last.

"I suppose you know he was my father?" Tarlington said, wrapping his long arms around himself. "Never acknowledged, of course. A youthful indiscretion. It broke my mother's heart. And then, when I wouldn't fight—I think it broke his."

"Tarlington—"

"My mother's name. I got that from her. That, and the hair. The rest of it—I was his secret. His shameful little secret. Can't ruin the legend, after all."

"James—"

He laughed, surprised. "It sounds wrong—I even tried out *Randall*, when I was younger, but—*Tarlington*, please."

I thought of those books Harry and I had found. A name written some time ago, then crossed out and recrossed, vehemently, in Tarlington's own sarcastic green ink. It must have hurt.

"He knew you," I said. I wanted more than anything to put my hand on his shoulder. "He knew you weren't a coward. I don't think he'd have preferred Charlie, in the end."

"In the end—maybe not." He kicked at the railings, stretched his shoulders. "I think that must count for something." The wind screamed, making Coats retreat on his haunches, growling at the dark. Another lantern had gone out; it was advancing on us.

"It counts for more than something," I said fiercely. "You've proved—whatever you were trying to prove."

He looked at me, eyes so unmistakably *Randall* I wondered how I hadn't seen it sooner. "So have you, though, haven't you—Morgan? Wasn't that the whole point of this adventure? Show us you were as good as your brothers? Good God, I'd like to have seen them do better."

"Not much use now," I said quickly—telling myself I would most likely die down here. I stood up, taking Weddell by the leash, but my hands shook. An uncontrollable feeling of lightness was blooming inside me, as if a weight had finally been lifted. *As good as your brothers.*

"Don't," he said sharply. "Don't be like that, Morgan, like it means nothing to you."

I exhaled, slowly allowing the lightness to take its place in my chest. I'd resisted Rufus on the ice. I'd left Harry behind. I'd thought I'd follow them anywhere: would answer their call, wherever I heard it. But now, standing at the huts in the middle of the polar dark, whatever happened, however it ended—I was finally and truly the last of the Morgan siblings.

And a brother to my brothers. A man to myself.

"Now come on, soldier boy," Tarlington said, putting his mouth close to my ear, his tone only half-mocking. "Let's fend off those—ghosts."

V

We wanted to bury Randall outside the back door—Clarke said it was tradition—but the rocks of Expedition Point resisted. We had to climb out onto the plateau and dig at the snow in a small ring of lanterns, just us and the dogs against the vast blue-and-black horizon. It was hard, depressing work, after a night of too little sleep.

Tarlington swung the axe like a man possessed, until sweat soaked all the way through his greatcoat and froze. But he carried on until there was a shallow depression in the rock-hard snow—just deep enough for us to say Randall had been buried. Not left.

"Are you all right?" I panted as we turned our attention to the second grave. Ellis had already started, saying sourly, "I suppose you lot won't give him a proper one."

Tarlington shrugged. "I got used to it." His small, tight smile didn't reach his eyes. "The camps, remember? I was at Princetown for over a year. Building useless roads, in the winter, leading nowhere. In the sleet and rain. No use resisting, or speaking up—I learnt that the hard way."

He rubbed his throat, turned to dig for Boyd with pinched lips. I couldn't blame him. But I made sure to dig with as much energy and diligence as I had for Randall. Boyd had been mistaken. He'd been misled. He deserved a grave.

The dogs started howling when we finished. It was four o'clock in the afternoon, and all the color had bled from the sky. A quarter moon cast short clear shadows.

Randall's body was heavy. His sleeping-bag shroud had frozen overnight, and it took five of us—Rees incapable of leaving his bed—to drag it from the huts. We covered him with rocks, although there were no earthly predators to disturb the body. Clarke planted a small wooden cross: *JAMES AUSTRALIS RANDALL*. The dogs glowered and yapped at the moonlight, as if they could sense the aurora waiting behind.

"We need to get back," Clarke said, cracking his knuckles.

I hesitated. "Someone should say—something."

"Poetry?" Tarlington said, with a twist of his wide mouth. "He liked a bit of the stirring stuff. Well. James Randall. I suppose he was a great man. He was—not himself, these last few weeks. But he led us as well as he could." Tarlington's voice dipped. "The world feels smaller without him."

"*We* are smaller without him," Clarke said softly.

"He's with—Charlie, now," Tarlington said, swallowing. "One who never turned his back, but marched breast forward—never doubted clouds would break—never dreamed, though right were worsted, wrong would triumph—"

"Get on with it," Ellis muttered, eyeing the darkness.

"Held we fall to rise. Are baffled to fight better. Sleep to wake."

We filled in Boyd's cairn faster. It was unbearably cold, and I could feel my eyelashes fluttering with electricity. The two of them lay side by side in the emptiness, differences forgotten.

Clarke held out a hand to Tarlington. "Here," he said, voice rough. "This is yours."

It was a small scrap of bedding, reddened and torn. Tarlington unwrapped it with care, the moon glimmering silver off Randall's signet ring: *Fortitude or Devastation.* It had quite obviously been cut from his swollen hand. Tarlington curled his long gloved fingers around it, looked at Clarke, and nodded.

"It's yours, now," Clarke said. "The expedition. You're—the ranking officer. He always said a Randall belonged on the ice."

Tarlington looked at the grave. Then laughed. "That's exactly the sort of thing that got us here, isn't it?"

The stars watched. For a moment, I thought he'd throw the ring down, leave it on Randall's resting place, refuse to be a part of this. But he slipped it in his pocket. "You're in charge," he said to Clarke. "Obviously! If you need a Randall to reinstate you—I'm doing it now."

A prickling behind my eyes.

Clarke put his hand on Tarlington's shoulder. "Two expeditions and no losses. He was a great man. I'm sorry."

"What now?" Laurence said abruptly.

"We need to leave. Organize transport. Overwinter back at Shore Camp." Clarke looked at each of us in turn. "This place was no good for Karlmann. It's no good for us."

I agreed. There were only six of us left: the tail end of Randall's expedition. Even if we marched to nowhere, marched to our deaths—it was better than sitting in those dreadful huts as winter hovered over us like a pitiless bird of prey. Waiting to snatch us up one by one.

I hung back as they collected the stretchers, taking one last look. Laurence hissed at Clarke, "The motor won't last, you have *no idea!*" Ellis kept oddly quiet, kicking his broad legs to prevent his feet from freezing, and I wondered what he was thinking; what voices he'd heard. The lanterns were gathered up, the circle of light collapsing, until there was just me, the dogs, the moonlight.

"Come on," Tarlington said impatiently.

I couldn't take my eyes off Randall's grave. *Old Australis*, my brothers had called him, as if they knew him personally. All those newspaper cuttings. All those stories. I couldn't believe I'd just helped to bury him in the heart of Antarctica, with only the mountains to watch over him. He'd made it through two expeditions—had survived the Western Front—only to be overcome, finally, by this No Man's Land.

And my brothers were lying in some vast graveyard in France. I stared at my empty hands. I'd screamed at my mother when she'd suggested visiting them, taking flowers: I hadn't been able to bear the thought of those headstones marching away in all directions, reducing them to numbers. I hadn't wanted to admit they were so completely *gone*.

If I ever left this place, I'd visit their graves. Francis had loved daffodils, fresh and bright and scented. I'd take him all the daffodils money could buy. The dead should be remembered; honored.

Then left.

I wiped my face. The aurora was trying to come through, and Coats and Weddell looked at the sky with frightened eyes. One last glance. Randall's grave looked like someone collapsed on the snow.

I tried not to think about Harry. Disappeared, without a marker. As if he'd never lived at all.

VI

"Don't be a hero," Clarke said. "We can't afford to lose anyone else."

Ellis raised his eyebrows, his expression unreadable. "Could be it's over, whatever it was." He glanced towards the Coal Hole. "And we might not have to carry—"

"Don't," Clarke said.

"Would it really be so bad—"

"*Don't.*"

Work had been delayed overnight as the winds raged. The door had stopped rattling at some point after six in the morning, and pulling it open—just a crack—revealed fresh snowfall, the moon bright and low in the sky. The stillness was impossibly eerie.

I'd tried to sleep, but couldn't bear Harry's empty bunk beneath me, blankets crumpled up, clothes kicked on the floor. For someone so dutiful, he'd never learned to pick up after himself. It bothered me so much that

I'd climbed down and wrapped myself in his blankets, the unimaginable ache clawing its way up inside my chest. Tarlington pretended to be asleep as I pressed my face into Harry's pillow. Tried to smell his hair; dogs; that faint damned taint of soot. He was gone, he was gone.

For all he'd been wrong, for all he'd refused to see—I still missed him.

"Make it run." Clarke clapped Laurence on the back. "We need to get out of here, and quick." Tarlington was fiddling with a screwdriver, sleeves shoved all the way up his arms; finally turned to something practical.

Laurence gave Clarke a glare. A cough echoed, hollow, around the huts. It sounded weirdly as if it came from outside—came down the stove vents, dark with smoke. Rees sounded worse than ever. I thought about what Ellis had said.

Would it really be so bad—

I picked up the lanterns and followed Laurence out to where the motor sat. Coats and Weddell jumped up from the railings, trying to put their noses under my scarf. The circle of light made me think of a Spiritualist ceremony: summoning the dead. Or holding something back. We were running through kerosene like water.

Laurence looked up at the sky. I followed his gaze. It was a deep, deep blue, the aurora coloring the edges emerald, the moon looking close enough to reach out and touch. I remembered how beautiful I'd once thought Antarctica. He met my eyes, gave me a watery smile, and bent to work.

The dogs curled up in the snow. These two, at least, had survived whatever stalked this place. All Harry's efforts had been in vain—all his lies, his invented experience, about dog handling and hunting and the family estate. As if the Coopers had a family estate, rather than a warehouse on the docks. Harry had once shown it to me—in our other lives. We'd been chaperoned at a sensible distance by one of his female relatives; people were starting to take notice of the time we spent together. Eventually we'd managed to lose her in the maze of crates, the faint scratching of rats in the shadows. Leaned close and whispered of packet ships and South America, of Randall. We'd thought ourselves very clever. We'd always thought ourselves *so* clever.

And Harry had been proud, I now understood, of that warehouse, of the haulers tipping their hats to the boss's son. Back then, I'd thought it silly: everything was a means to an end. I hadn't given any real thought to how Harry might have seen it. How he might have seen the two of us.

My heart ached. It had all narrowed down to this. The cold polar skies, months of darkness, six of us left. Whatever had been important up there—it meant nothing down here.

Coats whined softly, pricking up his ears. The aurora was coming closer, sending its faint sense of *presence* across the world.

"Laurence," I made myself say, "are you all right?"

Silence. He used to whistle while he worked. He hadn't whistled in some time.

I said it louder, resenting the way it echoed and bounced around camp, and heard him swear faintly. One of the lanterns had already gone out.

Weddell barked, making me jump and flatten myself against the steps. "It's all right." I wound his leash through my fingers. "It's all right." But he continued to bark at the sledge, its shape becoming a monster in the half-darkness. The air hummed faintly.

I took out the service revolver. It was just an object, but I found myself staring, holding it limply as if hypnotized. The glimmers and gleams of moonlight, the scarlet of the aurora, reflected on the deadly exposed metal. We'd brought it from the living world, and it was alien to the snow.

I lost track of time.

Once or twice I thought I heard Laurence talking quietly to himself in Welsh. But when I listened more closely, there was nothing. The silence had a particular quality—as if waiting for something. The aurora was almost as bright as the moon, and its lack of movement unnerved me. The flagpole cast a shadow like a long skinny finger. We needed to leave this place.

A door slammed inside the hut, and I started. Weddell nipped at Coats. I worked to untangle their leashes, then looked back. The sledge loomed.

I felt pins and needles all down my arms and legs.

"Laurence?"

No reply.

I stood up, pulling Weddell with me. Taking a deep breath, I called out again, stepped hesitantly into the snow. The darkness pressed in behind the sledge, amidst the maze of tools and crates in our work area. I crouched down. There was a shallow indentation in the snow, from the heat of Laurence's body, but he wasn't there.

My heart swooped. Weddell pulled away from the sledge, whining, growling.

"Laurence!"

I couldn't say how long it had been—ten minutes, twenty. That hum or low note. That sense of oppression—the same one I'd felt so many nights ago. Nothing had come and *taken* him. He'd gone willingly. He'd followed.

His footprints walked off towards the plateau.

Heat raced through me, and I clenched my fists. I knew I should run back inside, call the others. But he'd gone so quickly, and I might still catch him. Bring him back, not risking anyone else, anyone who might be—tempted. Anyone who didn't know its tricks. I tied Weddell to the sledge, where he continued to growl. My fingers tightened so hard around the revolver I thought they might snap.

Laurence's tracks were clear in the unbroken snow: he'd walked with some purpose onto the rocks leading out of the valley. The moon edged behind a cloud bank. The aurora was bright enough to light my way, and once I'd left the huts behind, Laurence's tracks seemed to jump out at me in the unearthly glow. A strange optical illusion, as if they were elevations—rather than depressions—in the snow. There was a sudden chaos in the drift, like someone had fallen and got up again.

I shouted: "What have you done with him?" into the empty air.

A few hundred yards, moving quickly, and I came across a discarded Burberry helmet and cap. He would be desperately cold.

"I'm here," I said out loud. "I know you're out there. Give him back!"

A sound behind me—from the direction of the huts—and I whirled around, aiming the gun with numb fingers. It had sounded like someone coughing. There was no one there.

I blew out a big plume of air, stared down. I should turn around—go back to the huts. Get help. There was only one set of tracks. If it had walked beside Laurence, it had left none. It wasn't—quite—capable of touching our world. I waited a few moments to still the shaking in my hands.

Then the whispering began.

It was faint at first, like someone talking in the next train carriage, or a conversation between servants when the house was still. I turned, stumbling. It seemed to come from just behind me. I turned again, and it was still behind me. I couldn't make out the words. I was in danger of losing the footprints. A dark bundle in the snow turned out to be Laurence's windproof jacket. He wouldn't survive without it.

I ground my teeth. It was enough.

"I'm not afraid of you!" I shouted. My voice cracked, wavered. "You can show yourself."

The next sound came from right behind me. A laugh—but a familiar laugh this time, making my skin crawl. Rufus's laugh. I pressed my hands to my ears. I wouldn't look.

The footprints became confusing, as if Laurence had turned. I hugged my chest, desperate to keep a few degrees of heat. Laurence wasn't there. I could still go back. No one could say I hadn't tried. The whispering seemed to pause, waiting to see what I would do.

I bent down, examined the tracks and the night around. I could just make out the huts crouching in their valley. It was a beautiful clear night, the aurora breathtakingly bright. I thought, distantly, how my brothers would have loved it.

"I know you're there. Rufus. Francis. I know you're there."

The whispering coalesced into snatches of speech—human speech. Talking about a disaster in the mines, somewhere far from here. *Hillsides falling down, dust flooding the shafts. Men smothered. Crushed. The groaning.*

I clamped my hands over my ears, turned around blindly.

It got louder; changed. *Forty dead already, and the rest of us on the way. Fall back, fall back, but no retreat. A forest of barbed wire. We couldn't see it. But it was there—it was there, all right.*

"It's not real," I whispered. "It's not real." But my brothers had been killed by barbed wire, all the same: the advance trapped, pinned down, short work for the guns.

A mercy killing, a mercy killing, that's all it would be—

I caught sight of something behind a hummock, and struggled to reach it. Laurence, lying facedown.

I turned him over, holding my breath. He'd been using a pocketknife to trim the motor's wires, and it was buried in the side of his neck, gummy with frozen blood. His gore-smeared gloves were stretched out, as if he'd been reaching for something. There were no other footprints.

"You did this." I knew it was standing behind me, although it cast no shadow. "You did this, you—bastard."

Red hair, red eyes: the crimson aurora. His hands were hidden in the pockets of his trench coat, his collar turned up against the wind. But it was only a disguise; he didn't feel the cold.

Huddled next to Laurence's body, I met its eyes. "You're not my brother. Don't come any closer."

Francis looked at me fondly. "Don't be silly, Jonathan. Of course I am."

"No you're—not." My teeth were chattering. "You've been—killing us. You're a *monster*. You're not real."

"I'm as real as you are." There was an air of gentle curiosity in his voice as he squinted at me. "What are you doing down there?" He reached out his hand to lift me up, as he'd done so many times before. "Come on, you'll catch your death. We've a long way to go. We'll take you with us."

"You're—not—him." My hands fumbled on the revolver.

"We both know you won't use that." Suddenly it was Rufus staring at me, exasperated. He was tall—nearly as tall as Harry—but the monster wearing his coat seemed taller still. Francis had vanished; as if I could be shown only one brother at a time. As if whatever was behind this operated a magic lantern, and didn't yet have enough slides: I had the feeling that would change. I wedged myself against Laurence's corpse. I thought I could feel some faint heat left in the body, and it turned my stomach.

"I will," I insisted. "You're not them. You're not—anyone."

Rufus breathed out heavily through his mouth, shook his head. "As if you'd try." It was a picture-perfect imitation of the way he'd used to look at me: annoyed; frustrated; a bit embarrassed. I laughed. It turned into a sob. It was so *perfectly* Rufus.

But it still needed me to go with it. No one had been taken—dragged off kicking and screaming into the night. That was why it begged, and cajoled, and lied: it required my willingness, couldn't steal me away without it.

And whatever the real Rufus had said—whatever laughing suggestions he'd once made—he'd never planned to take me with him. Not really. It was all a game to him.

"You're not Rufus." I aimed the gun.

"Then what am I?" it asked.

The air tasted of storm clouds, the smell of the sky after rain. Fresh and clean, like I was looking at something made out of the weather. It crouched opposite me, close enough to touch. A shimmer—like clouds lifting, like a thunderclap—and it was Francis again, more solid than before. Stronger, more assured, taking up more space in the world. He wore his red scarf tucked into his coat; a pair of ocher-colored leather gloves, a birthday present to keep him warm in the trenches. "Nothing works, though," he'd said with a shudder when he'd unwrapped them. "I've never been so cold—or so wet. It comes up over your boots." He'd be going back in two days.

"Honestly—must you fill our sister's head with—"

"No—go on," I'd begged, wanting to understand; this was very rare. Harry was all horrified candor, but my brothers always insisted on platitudes: *don't worry about me; last night was an absolute bust; I should like to die doing my duty.*

"Francis," Rufus had said in a warning tone. "Come along."

Francis had finally pressed his lips together and turned away. "You don't want to know. Just—don't envy me, dearest Jo."

I'd understood, then, that he would always side with Rufus, no matter what I did or said. There'd never be a place for me. The two of them, and the War—they would always be another country.

Dearest Jo.

But this thing called me *Jonathan* to my face. Might have called me *Jo*—or any other name—behind my back. Whatever suited its purpose.

We were almost face-to-face. The whispering was all around us. The last day in the trenches. Awaiting orders to fall back. The attack would be futile—the sound of guns over the river lied to them. Confusion, efforts to prevent desertion, cowardice in the face of the enemy. The barbed wire was there, *it was there.* The sticky, cloying mud, flesh sloughing off bones. The rats. Shells falling from the sky, tearing through bodies. Like a child, greedy on Christmas Day, unwrapping presents.

Francis reached for me. "Come on, Jonathan. He's waiting. Surely you must want to see *Harry*."

I squeezed my eyes shut, so hard that white flashes bloomed behind my eyelids. "No." It kept making the same mistake, and I could think of nothing worse than seeing Harry worn like a mask. Talking to it was a mistake; acknowledging it; allowing it a greater presence in our living world. The temptation to go with it evaporated, like a mist passing over the snow. It wasn't Francis. It wasn't Rufus. Its lures were desire and despair.

I lurched forward, letting out a wordless cry, using the barrel of the gun as a club. In the confusion that followed, something broke—

I could see it crouching. A dark figure. Taller by far than my brothers. The whispering got louder and louder until it was screaming in my ears. The trenches. The mines. Deaths in the snow. Murder. Men eating each other. Shore Camp. Crouching in a little shelter, freezing, shivering. Clarke and Tarlington and the bodies of the dead. Flags fluttering in the ceaseless wind. Indescribable suffering and fear. Lying down on the cold ground, under that indifferent sky. *You'll never leave, you'll never leave, you came here, you'll never leave—*

It spoke with a voice as immense as the South itself. Seductive; cruel; looking at my tiny human body, and laughing at how unequally we were matched.

You came here.

You'll never leave.

"Shut up!" I screamed, and ran.

I looked back, my neck straining, my heart pumping. The thing wavered. For one moment it was Randall standing there, proud and certain, giving me a look of utter confidence. His legs were back. His face was in shadow. The imitation was perfect.

I ran as fast as I could. Each footfall on the snow was like a bell tolling. I'd lost my coat—I didn't know where—and my gloves. I had to get inside. I had to warn the others.

The approving look—that sudden hitch of breath when Randall had called him *James*, recognizing his son at last. It could come as anyone, anyone at all; and if it came for Tarlington, it would surely be Randall, whole and healthy and—proud.

He was in terrible danger.

VII

"It's out there," I shouted to Tarlington—a blurry shape beside the sledge. "Get inside!"

He scoured the snow and ice behind me, shielding his sharp features from the wind. "Where's Laurence?"

"Gone."

I pulled him violently up the steps. Coats and Weddell jumped up—then recoiled, cringing away, as if they could smell something terrible.

I crashed through the door and Clarke grabbed me, red-eyed, hands raw and blistered. I gagged at the reek of carbolic. "Where the hell were you? The lights went out. You know better—"

He shoved me onto the bench. The table was clean and slippery, glistening like a flayed body. Ellis turned away from the stove, steam wreathing his hard face. "Yes—where did you go, Morgan?"

My throat constricted. "I went after Laurence."

I saw the understanding pass over Clarke's face. "No." He sat down heavily beside me. "No."

"He left," I said. "Just sleepwalked away. He was there one minute and—gone the next. I don't know what happened. But he walked out of camp by himself, and—he must have seen it. It must have spoken to him, made him—"

"You saw him?"

I nodded, pressing my fist to my mouth. The image of Laurence in the drift danced around my head. The yawning skin of his neck, layers of muscle, blood freezing to ice. Ellis folded his arms. "He's going to puke." The hut spun crazily around me, the sharp disinfectant smell burning the back of my throat.

"He didn't believe the sledge would—well. It doesn't matter now," Clarke said, very low. We'd lost our engineer. It might come down to man-hauling. And I knew all about man-hauling, how desperate it was: slow, backbreaking work, exhausting, starving by degrees. A few miles a day. A horrible, grinding one-way trip, with God knew what waiting for us on the other side.

"I'm sorry—I let him go." My voice wavered, my eyes stung. I realized, with a slow dreamlike horror, that I was crying—*really* crying, tears hot on my face. It was worse than it had ever been. Worse than when Rufus called me "just a girl," or when Francis had caught me trying on that Derby enlistment armband, pinning it proudly around my arm, and I'd seen—just for a moment—an expression of sheer *bafflement* in his eyes. Faint embarrassment. All the worse for coming from him. Worse than the night after they'd left for France, staring at the plump curves of my face in my gilded mirror, like a wicked queen in a fairy story; wishing I wasn't the fairest.

My chest was going to burst open. I took deep, wrenching sobs. I'd let Laurence go, and it had taken him. "I'm sorry."

Clarke put both hands on my shoulders. "Morgan, don't—"

I sneaked a glance at Tarlington, who watched from across the table, tension written in the long lines of his mouth, and hid my face again.

I felt as if I would never stop crying. Ellis exhaled violently, then stalked over to the Coal Hole, swishing the curtain shut behind him. There was something impossibly eerie about the silence in his wake.

No living sounds in the huts, not anymore.

"We need to leave," Tarlington said.

Clarke tensed. "Yes," he said fiercely. "Yes, we do."

I took an uncertain breath, then another, unwinding my scarf and using it to wipe my eyes. I stared at it. Francis had tucked it into my coat on deployment day; he'd taken a moment to make sure it was sitting straight, his hands lingering. "There," he'd said. "Very dapper."

Rufus: "Don't tease our sister."

"You can have it back, if you want," I'd said to Francis, secretly hoping he'd say no, and he shook his head.

"It wouldn't be regulation." He'd kept his tone light, but the red scarf was bright against his khaki and brown and olive green, so I understood: he couldn't wear bright colors where he was going.

The monster outside was wearing Francis's scarf, though—making it into camouflage.

"All well, Morgan?" Clarke said.

I nodded.

The ache was worse than anything. Like a mask had been torn off, or several layers of skin. I felt lighter, though. Somehow *cleaner*. I thought, absurdly, of the hack job Tarlington had done on his hair.

"Morgan?" Tarlington drummed his fingers. I felt my face flush scarlet.

"We should leave," I said. "Right now. I saw it—it spoke to me. It's getting stronger. Bolder. The more people go with it—speak to it—"

"The more time we spend here," Clarke growled. It was May, and we were into true winter. "We need to leave while we still can." They exchanged glances over the engine parts strewn on the table, and Tarlington stood, making the bench screech. He'd be a poor substitute for Laurence. But he'd put away his long fingerless mitts with their jaunty red trim, and was as black-and-beige, greasy, as the rest of us. Snow goggles perched on his head. I could tell he was wearing his father's ring.

That settled it. I hesitated in the doorway, then took a deep breath and followed him out onto the porch. "Tarlington—"

He stood like a statue at the bottom of the steps, not quite looking at me. I'd wept at the common-room table, like a—a child. *Hysterical.* My face burned.

"I've seen plenty of men cry," he said, offhand. "Just so you know."

I gulped, the cold air almost making me sob again. "Thank you." He turned away. "Wait—"

"Your ghosts—whatever they are—might follow us, mightn't they?" he said. His back was tight. To anyone else, he would have sounded uninterested. "We don't know whether leaving will save us."

"They might. But I think it's strongest here." The air stung my wet cheeks as I thought about Nicholls's map—the emptiness of No Man's Land—this place at its heart, like a spider sitting at the center of an invisible web. Feeling for vibrations, tugging on the silk. "This is where it wants us." A hundred voices, whispering and screaming and howling together. "You'll never leave. That's what it said. Like it didn't even want us to *try*—"

Tarlington braced himself on the railing. "I'm meant to be a scientist." He swallowed, some of that dispassionate tone leaching out of his voice. "And I still have no idea what's going on here. Erratic winds. Blizzards out of nowhere. Animals committing suicide. Men vanishing without a trace." As if he were speaking to himself. "I don't think this place is real. It's like the shadow of a place, on a cave wall. We've dropped down a . . . hole in the cloth of the world. Been sucked into one of the white spaces on the map."

"Expedition Point."

"Yes." He gave me a sideways look. "I wonder what Karlmann called it."

I thought of that flag, ripped down. As if the Germans had realized—too late—that they had entered enemy territory. That they were trespassing.

"Something was here before them."

He met my eyes with an unhappy, pinched smile. "You say that, Morgan. I'm prepared to believe—maybe, *possibly*, in ghosts. I'm aware of a school of thought that ghosts are real; a kind of natural phenomenon. Maybe we're experiencing the *weather* of this place in all its forms." He looked towards the site of the old meteorological screen. "Or maybe it's something like—unusual radio waves. The Germans destroyed their wireless, after all."

"It's not that," I said quickly. "Not radio waves."

He raised a sardonic eyebrow. "With all due respect—"

"Or the weather. It—wants something from us. It's not—"

It wasn't so impersonal. I thought about what the voices had said: *You came here. You'll never leave.* Something down here meant to keep us now we'd come. Karlmann's flag had been a mistake; naming the huts had been a mistake. We were being punished for daring to know this place. It was closing up around us like a rat trap.

I saw Harry, on the dog deck, the wind whipping at his curls, his eyes bruised. *We shouldn't be here. We shouldn't be so far south.*

"It's something else. Not ghosts."

"All it can do is frighten us, Morgan. Whatever *it* is."

"*No.* It's—something that pretends to be ghosts. It can pretend to be anything." My voice wavered. "It tricks you. Pretends to be what you want, whatever you—want to see or hear. It can get inside you. It's a monster."

I paused, thinking about that giant presence I'd felt from the mountains. "No, that's not quite right."

He took a step towards me, raised one of his greasy mittens—as if he were about to lay his hand on my arm. "Seeing your brothers," he said, softly. "I imagine it must have been very difficult. As I said, I can just about—*just*—believe in ghosts. Things we might see only under certain conditions. God knows there's enough of a blank space down here. But some terrible . . . primeval beast unknown to science? No."

There was a thick, painful lump in my throat. Tarlington had never wanted to be here; he'd never heard the call of the South. But he'd followed Randall—as I'd followed my brothers. If *this* part of the South spoke to him, it would be in that voice.

I couldn't leave him defenseless.

"You don't understand," I blurted out. "I saw them, but it wasn't them. Or their ghosts. It's something else, something real. I could tell, when it was pretending to be them, because it . . . got things wrong."

He looked at me sideways, blue eyes impossibly kind. I could hear the start of a sigh. "Morgan—"

"It says—what it thinks I want to hear. Things they didn't see. Things they never knew."

"I'm sorry?" A flash of foxlike interest.

"It—calls me something they never did." The sensation of bees in my throat, a wild animal trapped in my chest. "It's . . . just a small mistake. But it means it isn't them. It's not . . . what's left of them. It's something using their faces and voices to *trick* me."

The thought of it made me furious, made my heart pound. *It's not a game.* Tarlington looked at me carefully, as if he wanted to take out a notebook and instruments; record all this, treat me as a specimen.

I could see he wanted to understand me.

"What does it call you, then?"

"Jonathan." A pause. "My name . . . when they knew me, when they were alive, they never—never saw me like this."

My voice cracked, becoming high and awful. If I'd been ashamed earlier, now I thought I might die from it.

He understood what I was telling him. He gave a single sharp nod.

"Don't," he said suddenly, a touch too loud. "Don't. God. You don't have to tell me if you don't want to." He paused, then looked me straight in the eye. "Jonathan. If you say it's—then I believe you."

It was the first time he'd called me that.

My fingers found my scarf untucked. I'd been grateful when the Burberry snow gear had been issued, because it covered me so completely. My pale, smooth neck lacked stubble. I'd kept up the pretense that I shaved—and the men, in turn, had teased me, thinking it was an affectation. I had to pay constant attention to how I sounded—risked exposure every time I shouted, every time I couldn't make the conscious effort to keep my voice low. I could get bigger through hard work; I could become grimy, and wind-beaten, and scarred. My shaven hair was growing back gradually, prickly and coarse. I was nearly eighteen, and dreading all the changes that might still come. All the ways my body might betray me.

Tarlington was a scientist. He'd lived in the Nursery with me—and Harry, who'd been careless at times. He'd always held himself apart: observed; catalogued; been sensitive to secrets. He might have known all along. It was impossible to tell.

"Thank you," I said, feeling it down to my bones.

Jonathan.

A small smile crossed his face. "Come on. If it wants to keep us here— whatever it is!—then I have no interest in acquiescing." He looked, for a moment, much less severe: a patch of light on a gloomy winter's day, the colors reflecting off his hair.

VIII

There was so much we had to leave behind.

I hovered in the doorway of the gloomy Coal Hole, looking at Rees's knot of blankets. Since I'd returned from the crevasse, his hacking, wheezing coughs had descended into unearthly whistles, whistles that seemed to come from everywhere all at once—a horrible trick of the echoes—then fallen silent. I couldn't think when I'd last heard him speak. Ellis refused to let him leave the room, saying he might be *infectious*. Or, looking sideways at me—a danger to us all.

The boarded-up windows were oppressive. It was somehow darker inside than out.

"Leave him." Ellis barged me aside. "Leave him, do you hear? Get on with your own business." Clarke stopped packing for a moment; resumed without looking around, so quiet it was ominous. Nearly all our weapons had vanished overnight, and we were left with what small arms we carried. And still Ellis wouldn't let Clarke examine Rees—saying he was no better than a butcher; saying there was no medicine *we* could give him.

Another journey over the ice with a dying man. It felt like a terrible omen.

In the Nursery, I stared at Harry's empty bunk. I made myself go through his kit bag, rooting around blindly, trying to find something to take with me. I smoothed his rumpled bedding, my eyes prickling. He'd given away everything but the clothes on his back: he'd known, one way or another, that he was going to let it take him. But it wouldn't stop until we were all vanished; until we all belonged to the ice.

It'll come for the rest of you soon enough. He'd underestimated the South, and it had swallowed him whole.

His binoculars were safe under my jumper, the gift from his men. *Steady.* Harry had been sixteen and a half when he'd joined up, desperate to follow my brothers to France. There'd been no temporary commission for him, no new uniform, no notice in the *London Gazette*: we were his only real connections, and his parents would never have put up the funds or signed the form. He'd lied about his age to join the ranks—like so many other boys—and been a *good soldier*, rising doggedly and inexorably through his own good qualities. And that had been his death, thousands of miles away and years later.

My hands stumbled on something shoved under the pillow. His journal, small and leather-bound. I clutched it to my chest. I could leave it here. Or I could burn it, keep his secrets. But I knew I wouldn't. I was certain he'd left it there for me.

Tarlington helped me lift my pack, and I staggered under the weight; it seemed impossible I'd ever carry it. He said nothing as he watched me tuck the journal under my jacket.

Outside, it was another clear night, a sliver of moon pale and bright over the mountains, casting long shadows. No wind. Again, that *anticipation* about the silence.

"It's waiting," Tarlington said. "Your—Adversary."

"Have you—"

He shook his head. "No, nothing. Maybe it knows I'm ready for it." His wide mouth was pulled narrow at the idea of seeing Randall. But as we loaded the sledge, he was as brusque as always; there was no indication at all that he thought of me differently. He knew everything, though—knew me right down to the marrow. I felt I would fly apart into a hundred pieces, and clasped my arms around myself, feeling Harry's journal against my heart.

Our eyes met. The first crackle of the aurora over the mountains.

"Jonathan—"

"I saw it. We need to hurry."

He nodded at the holster at my waist—I'd started wearing it over my windproofs. "Don't go anywhere. Keep talking. Anything—so I can hear you."

When he crouched behind the sledge, I realized he was considerably taller than his father—perhaps his height, too, came from his mother. There was no question about the stubbornness. "Tarlington—" I stopped, wondering how I'd react if someone suddenly asked me about Rufus. The golden boy. Compared me; found me wanting in every way. I rubbed my hand over my face.

A snort. "I can practically *hear* you thinking, Jonathan. If you wish to ask—now's the time."

"Did you—did you ever meet Charlie Randall?"

There was a small chink of metal on rock, as if he'd dropped the screwdriver. "No," he said at length, voice very even. "We were never introduced. I've seen photographs, though. You'd hardly know we were related. He could have been on the recruiting posters. Broad shoulders, blond hair, chiseled jaw, all that. A proper soldier."

"And you—"

"Yes, and me," he said sarcastically, pulling at the straps with emphasis so the whole sledge shuddered. "Everyone seemed to think it would be *good* for me. Make a man of me. But I always knew. I wouldn't do my duty, if my duty meant going across the sea to murder people I'd never met. All that noise, all that—trumpeting and hurrays and pageants. Play on, play up, and play the game. Like a bunch of schoolboys. Like the whole country had turned into a bloody rugby match, and I was the only one who didn't like *sports*."

I thought of my brothers. A dull ache between my shoulder blades, my hand going again to Harry's journal. But my usual fizzing indignation was entirely absent.

"I wasn't afraid to die, it wasn't that!" He was nearly shouting. Then, quieter: "I don't know what I was afraid of."

I stamped my feet in the cold. "What did . . . Randall say?"

"He hated me, I suppose." Tarlington's tone was surprisingly light. "We'd never exactly been close. I was too—intellectual. He tried to visit, and write, but he just wanted someone who could shout a bit with the boys. Perhaps if I'd been—different. But then I was locked up, and he fell over himself to have nothing to do with me. Would have disowned me, if he'd ever *owned* me to start with, which would have meant acknowledging I existed, that he wasn't the man people thought he was. And I was left in the camps, and it was a bloody wet miserable—"

"Your voice." Heat rushed through me.

"It wasn't pneumonia, if that's what you're thinking, although God knows I could have died from it. I was badly beaten by some—proper soldiers. There was no use fighting back, it would have only made it worse. My windpipe was crushed—I couldn't speak for months. I suppose they thought they were teaching me a lesson, for—the War, and everything else I was. My—ah—*nervous condition*. All that."

I stayed silent, my fists clenched hard enough to hurt. I'd heard that particular euphemism before. Whispers. Rumors and unkind things. People had been trying to tell me what was proper—or manly—my whole life. But out here, at the end, I couldn't think of it as wrong.

"Jonathan?"

"Yes, I'm still here." My voice sounded a little choked.

"I thought I was being clever, with Nicholls," he said in a rush. "I thought no one would pay any attention to me. That I'd be invisible."

"I thought you were—I don't know. Plotting something. Corrupting him. Not in *that* way. In a . . . subversive way."

Tarlington burst out laughing, loud and unexpected. I started to laugh too, which made him laugh harder. "Well, you know it wasn't like that," he said. "It's all out now. We met at the expedition office, and I suppose he just knew what I was. All those stories about his sweethearts! He had a girl—or a boy—in every port." The idea was shocking; sent a warmth prickling into my wrists that startled me. "I don't think it ever occurred to him to be any other way. But it was all right for him, his father wasn't James Randall." There was a catch to his voice when he mentioned him, and the aurora crept closer, as if summoned by the name. A pause. I thought of how desperate he'd seemed when I'd found them: a secret from one person in particular.

"I wouldn't have told him," I said. "Tarlington—I wouldn't. I'm sorry, I really am."

A slow, audible exhalation. "Once, on the ship, I thought you and Cooper—" He paused, as if trying to find the right way to put it. "But then—very obviously not."

I might have pretended to be shocked. But we were far past that. I'd been Harry's confessor in those hundreds of letters; had never written back to say this was inappropriate, or unwelcome, because I'd clutched so hard at any glimpse of that masculine world. Later, there had been long walks on the harbor; tearoom discussions unchaperoned; stolen meetings at the warehouse. Harry must have believed we had an understanding, and I hadn't dissuaded him. It had led us here, to these huts, to this darkened sky.

"No," I said. "He—loved me. But he wanted me to be someone very different."

I chewed the inside of my cheek, staring up at that ink-black void. The landscape around us, hushed, listening. The same landscape that had vanished everyone who'd set foot on it. "We shouldn't have come so far south."

"What?" His voice was sharp.

"Something he said." I hesitated. The veterans had always talked as if the South were alive. And if it could be alluring or cruel by turns, why shouldn't this particular place—or whatever guarded it—be vengeful?

Raised voices inside the hut made me jump. Tarlington's white face appeared, a smear of grease across his nose. "What—"

"It could be nothing—"

"When is it *ever*—" Tarlington hissed. A second noise stole all the breath from my lungs, froze me to the spot. Something scratched, scrabbled, like rats in the walls, coming from all corners of the hut at once, trying to tear its way out.

Clarke shouted. Then came a gunshot. Then silence.

IX

"Bring a light."

Clarke leaned against the pallet-board wall of the Coal Hole, breathing hard.

"What happened," I panted. "Clarke—"

He shook his head. The stove had finally gone out. I craned my neck to look past him, and in the dim light Ellis's bunk gleamed. The rifles we'd thought lost were stacked and shining like buried treasure. On the floor, a slumped figure lay in the gloom.

Clarke put his revolver down very slowly, perhaps afraid it would leap back to life.

Tarlington held up the lantern. A horrible crawling feeling climbed up my spine. The little compartment was upended, clothes and bedding strewn everywhere, as if a blizzard had suddenly blown its way through, wreaked havoc in the confined space. The boarded-up windows came into focus, and that was worse. They were covered in scrape marks. Scratches all over the walls, like someone—or something—had frantically tried to escape. I thought of Jesus, the guard dog—but he'd been lost somewhere on the plateau. And the scratches came up far too high. Something standing on two legs.

Ellis had been shot at close range; blood and white filmy pieces of brain matter spattered against the walls. The side of his head was a ruin. I shut my eyes briefly, taking a step back. Clarke was a reassuring presence behind me. Only a slight rasp to his breathing betrayed that he'd been the one doing the shooting.

"What—" Tarlington swallowed. "What did you see?"

"When," Clarke said with some effort, not answering the question, "did you last see Rees? Either of you?"

"Not since—since the crevasse," I said from behind my hand. "I've heard him coughing, but . . ."

Ellis wouldn't let anyone near Rees: an unsmiling and sinister orderly. Had been talking about whether it would be so bad—really—if Rees died. *Putting him out of his misery.*

Rees was a silent shape in the bed, a bundle of sleeping bag and blankets, and my skin crept. Tarlington shook his head. "Two days, maybe. I thought if it was pneumonia, I might take a look—"

"Look." Clarke's broad-set face was ashen. Moving slowly, he crossed the threshold and pulled back the front flap of Rees's sleeping bag.

The eyes were still open, marbled explosions of red. He looked as if he'd died shouting. His lips were pulled back to expose his teeth in a parody of his cheeky smile. Clarke pushed the bedding aside. Rees's pale, grubby neck was covered in small marks, swimming up around his chin and mouth, the little red half-moon scratches of fingernails. If it was done under a pillow, muffling the sounds of the struggle, Ellis's grip would have been inescapable. But Rees had clearly moved his head from side to side. Trying to escape it nonetheless.

As Clarke moved the covers, a faint smell reached us. Thick. Cloying. Sweet like rotting peaches.

"He's been dead for days," Clarke said quietly. "*Before* Laurence."

My stomach turned over, and I jerked my head away, pinching my nose shut.

"Then who did we hear—"

"Don't," Tarlington said. "*Don't.*"

The lantern flickered. For a moment, there was an impression of movement around Ellis, the shadows on the walls. My skin prickled. We'd been living with a murderer.

Neither of us asked Clarke what had happened. There was a discarded knife on the floor beside Ellis; I could guess easily enough from that, and the reddish swelling on Clarke's jaw. Ellis had been hoarding weapons—who knew what he'd intended for the rest of us. He must have thought he'd see out the long night alone. The last man standing. The *overwinter*.

"I heard him talking to someone," Clarke said quietly. "I thought it was Rees. So I went to see. But there was—something in the dark—"

He broke off. I looked at those horrible scratch marks, which appeared both fresh and very, very old. I remembered the scrabbling, like something had been interrupted and tried suddenly to escape. *Something in the dark*. I knew that darkness—the tall figure following us. My brothers disappearing into the night. It took many forms.

Clarke gathered himself. "The sledge?"

"It'll run," Tarlington said, a faint note of pride in his voice.

"Then we leave tonight."

I flinched. Ellis may have deserved to be left, but Rees and Laurence—I opened my mouth, and Tarlington shot me a resigned look.

"There's no time," Clarke said. "It's called us from camp, and Laurence was a steady man, not the sort to . . . do that. It's turned us on each other. It's come—inside." I shivered, wrapping my arms around myself, not asking any more. "We need to get as far from here as possible. While the weather still lets us. And pray we find something worth it on the other side."

Clarke started to lace Rees into his sleeping bag. "I'll—I don't mind," Tarlington said. "It's hardly my first dead body." He took Ellis under the armpits, dragging him back towards the bed in a smear of blood and fluids.

When they were done, I nailed the front door shut. Tarlington wanted the huts burned to the ground, and I felt the same powerful and irrational need to see them erased, ash on rock. "We don't know," Clarke said grimly, "if we'll need to come back." But the motor sledge made slow and bloody progress; we all knew a return trip was out of the question. Our one-way journey to Shore Camp was an enormous gamble against our supplies, our hauling power, the risk of starvation: that the penguin rookery Nicholls had thought he'd seen would now be repopulated. The Emperors bred in the dark.

In an empty tin can I posted up Clarke's scrawled description of our route, the last known coordinates of the *Fortitude*, and our intended destination. Finally, I tugged Francis's scarf from around my neck; admired the rich color one last time; used it to seal up the cracks, so not even the aurora could creep under. I wouldn't need it anymore.

I had the definite feeling of locking something in.

X

Winter had come to the plateau: complete darkness, wind whipping over the surface of the ice. It was past sixty degrees of frost, and the air *hurt*. The sky was coal-black, clouds blotting out the stars; we might have been six feet underground, staring up at our own coffin lids. I remembered all those nights crouching in the storage locker, safe on the *Fortitude*; rationing my candle, telling myself not to be afraid. It seemed unreal by comparison: nothing could persuade a living thing not to be afraid of this howling, murderous dark.

A knocking sound had followed us. No one knew what it was. It came and went, like a mischievous spirit, and the motor stuttered, making Tarlington swear and our little convoy—motor sledge, provisions lashed behind, dogs padding in the rear—grind to a halt. We stamped our feet and watched our breath freeze to icicles around our noses. Clarke's beard had grown tusks. With numb fingers, ropes frozen hard, it had taken hours to pitch the tent and huddle inside. Coats and Weddell had turned in circles on the snow, until only their ice-encrusted ears were visible, and promptly fallen asleep. I envied them. Getting into my sleeping bag had been torture; staying in it was worse.

"Jonathan!"

Tarlington's voice.

Outside the tent, it was a desolate morning. The constant twilight made my heart sink; the electricity in the air made my hair stand on end. The taste of metal. The moon seemed—crazily—to have waned too fast. In the distance, the aurora sat directly above Expedition Point, eddying and ebbing like tide pools, a brilliant aquamarine. It obscured the Milky Way, blocking out the stars. A little closer, Randall's grave sat in a sea of green fire.

I realized my mouth was open. Tarlington gripped my arm, pointed with his screwdriver.

I looked again. The huts sat empty: a ghost ship, abandoned by captain and crew. Through Harry's binoculars, I saw a long, dark hole in the aurora. A rippling *absence* where the flagpole grasped emptily towards the sky.

I shuddered, feeling the hairs on my arms lifting.

Tarlington drew close. "That's it, isn't it?" he said quietly.

I'd heard of the black aurora; but this was something made entirely of darkness. Although it wasn't quite man-shaped, not quite touching the ground, it appeared to be standing and watching us. Following our retreat.

This place was showing us its nightwatchman.

I'd burned the German flag, shoved it into the dying stove, as if I could convince it that we made no claim. But something told me it wouldn't be that easy. Some things couldn't be stopped once they were set in motion.

We shouldn't have come so far south.

A hurried conference. "We move on at once," Clarke said. "Get out of here."

"It'll follow us." Tarlington narrowed his eyes. "Whatever we do. Hell, it could come from anywhere. Come upon us anytime. I don't think our Adversary . . . walks."

He shot me a glance. "I think it's everywhere in this place. I think it might even *be* part of this place. Jonathan?"

"Nevertheless." Clarke strapped a knife to his boot and thrust another into Tarlington's hands. "Here. The rifle, too. Morgan—keep the Webley loaded."

"I don't know if we can hurt it," I said.

He shrugged, turning away. "I'm going to damn well try. So should you."

My traitorous mind raced through possibilities as I took a final look. Rufus, laughing at me. Randall, surveying the wasteland. Most awfully, Harry, as I'd seen him at the crevasse—on his back in the snow, watching me fumble with the service revolver. *Do it.*

I took a cold deep breath through my mouth; banished the very thought of him.

"And no one leaves the sledge, understand? We stay together. It wants to separate us."

Those shadows stretched towards us like long fingers, and it took four painful attempts to get the sledge running again. We didn't get far before a gust of wind came out of nowhere; a series of small taps, the ice grinding its teeth beneath us. Tarlington and I looked around. Clarke held up his hand. Leading by rope, he had a map tucked inside his windproofs, drawn in Nicholls's careful red ink.

"It's nothing," I said to Tarlington, although my heart thumped loudly and painfully.

We carried on. Trudging beside the motor and the sledge dragged behind, bent double, the wind set our clothing into suits of armor. I knew whenever we camped—whenever we were too tired to continue—we would have to gather around and punch one another, batter the ice out, before we could stand upright.

Then—without warning—Clarke fell.

I screamed, something in my throat tearing.

He hadn't disappeared, but had dropped nearly knee-deep, and stared up at me. With a series of explosions, the ice shifted. I screamed again.

We all went down.

It was barely a few inches, but I fell hard enough to knock the air from my lungs. The dogs barked and barked. The motor stalled and whirred until Tarlington cut the engine. All around us, the surface of the ground was settling, the sound running away for miles and miles into the stillness, like thunderstorms departing.

"What was that?" Tarlington shouted. I squeezed my eyes shut, blew air out through my mouth, crawled up onto firm land.

"A . . . depression," Clarke panted. We gathered around, shielded him from the wind as he pulled out the map. "Snow settling." The twilight was barely bright enough to read it. All the light had been sucked out of our world.

"Oh—damn to that," Tarlington said tightly. "It was a crevasse, wasn't it?"

Clarke swore. It could have been an ice stream; an invisible valley;

or nothing at all. This patch of the map was blank. I felt, for a moment, that horrible convulsive *jerk* of my harness catching me. I wrapped my arms around myself.

Tarlington looked around, guarded, his eyes drifting to the dark horizon. I wanted to tear them away. Back to us.

"This is the way we came," Clarke said. "It doesn't—"

"It must have changed," Tarlington said. "Since he drew it." I thought of what he'd said, back at the huts. *I don't think this place is real.*

"Crevasses don't come from nowhere."

"Apparently they do." A flash of the old, sarcastic Tarlington.

Clarke glared at him, then folded up the map carefully, tucked it away. "There's a weather front coming." He shut his eyes, as if listening. "We can't afford to stop."

I believed him. The air seemed to shimmer as I watched—a gas lamp coming to the end of the night. It was darker here than any place save the Pole. My feet were leaden. I tried not to think of my toes turning white, then black. The blisters. The creeping rot. "It won't be frostbite," Clarke had said, the night before. "Not yet. But don't take your boots off. Not ever. Your feet will swell, and you'll never get them back on."

Randall would have insisted on carrying an injured man on the sledge, hope against hope, no matter how much it would slow everyone down. Condemning the others to a slow march; dwindling rations; starvation.

But Clarke knew better. He would leave them.

I kicked my heels, the frozen sweat in my trousers making the fabric rasp. We didn't talk as we dug out the front end of the sledge, clipped on harnesses. No one looked back. Breath turned to ice. We needed to get moving.

The air smelled of thunderstorms. I looked around desperately. "Tarlington—"

The motor roared to life.

"We should take it in turns," Clarke called, holding up the guide rope. "Watch out for crevasses."

Whoever steered would have to walk in front, testing the snow with every step. Praying against the sudden drop, the tug on the harness tethering them to the living world. I felt violently ill. Their faces swam in front of me—Macready, Nicholls, Holmes. I could almost hear them. My heart hammered in my chest, and I didn't think I could bear it. Nicholls, and his calm determined face.

"No." I set my shoulders. "Clarke. You need to stay with the sledge. Tarlington too."

He looked at me, for the briefest of moments, then nodded. It made sense. It made damnable, perfect sense. The engineer. The navigator. And me.

"Jonathan," Tarlington put his mouth close to my ear. "Are you *sure*?"

I pushed him aside. "Let's get on with it."

I made myself walk to the front of our little procession, where deep grooves showed the recent settling of the snow, slow as a knife through syrup.

"Just take it steady, Morgan," Clarke called.

I glanced back, feeling the wind whip my face. Big billowing clouds, dark on the underside: open-water clouds, we'd once called them. Moving steadily across the sky in our direction. There was something pursuing us, and I didn't know what would happen when it caught up. My spine tingled. Again, that taste of thunderstorms.

"That's right, take it slow," said another voice, very near me, just a little overhead. Low, approving. A growl. "I won't let you be left behind."

XI

The motor sledge crawled across the snow like a tank through mud.

Harry had written to me, once, about the cheers and shouts when tanks were first deployed on the battlefield: moving fortresses, behemoths, storming the barbed wire and machine-gun emplacements. They'd thought this would surely turn the tide. But then he'd seen one grind to a halt on a dusty road in France, dying in front of him like a horse fit for the knacker's yard. The men inside were trapped as the fighting closed in around them, as unable to retreat as to advance. Although he'd kept observations on it for what seemed like days, no one ever came out.

For all he knew, they were still there.

The day slipped away into gloomy astronomical twilight. We were a wavering line in the dark: me, leading the motor; Clarke, at the rear, keeping an eye on the provisions; and Tarlington watching the engine—watching the aurora lingering over the huts, like explosions in the sky.

His father walked, invisible, beside me.

"We have all the time in the world now," Randall said. "You and me. You're off the edge of the map. You belong here, don't you, Morgan? You belong down South, with me."

It was testing us. I tried to ignore it, breathing in through my nose, out through my mouth. My ice axe sank, inches at a time, into powder snow. I scanned the whiteness, searching for the shadows of another crevasse. But no matter how much the motor coughed and spluttered, Randall was there in my ear. Just a little distance away. Muffled by my layers of helmet and ice and windproofs and balaclava. Indistinct. It made me listen more closely.

"He keeps looking back," he said, all concern. "But the real danger's ahead of you. A sudden drop! A short stop. Crevasses are the very devil, and they could be anywhere. Better return while you still can."

I shook my head. Went slower. Tried to focus on my task. Went slower still.

"All right, Morgan?" Clarke shouted. The wind was whipping around us. In the distance, I thought I saw the aurora glimmer. I gave him a thumbs-up.

In the nights after my brothers died, I'd have done anything to see them again. Harry had lived in those nights, never escaped them, and the guilt, his crushing guilt—*my punishment for what happened over there.* Tarlington was barely visible, a shrouded figure behind me. But he was doing his job, untroubled by ghosts.

I couldn't let anyone know it was trying to worm its way in.

Another patch of unbroken snow. "Not there," the voice said suddenly. "Not there!"

I swallowed. Set my shoulders square, and continued. The motor lumbered on behind me. A whistle in my ear. "Well, you were lucky."

It became harder and harder to ignore his entreaties. His voice became louder. "If you value your life. All of your lives, Morgan. A single misstep, and you've lost me my son! Sent him to his death. Down into the ground like Charlie. We came such a long way together, only for you to . . . lose . . . us . . . now."

My foot sank through the crust and down into deeper snow. I pulled back. Stopped.

Clarke called a halt. We gathered in the lantern-light, circling against the dark. "Morgan," he said, painfully calm. "We can't go this slow. There's something behind us. And if this is a—lair, a hunting ground of some kind—we need to leave it as quick and quiet as we can."

He was so close that I could see the flecks of green in his eyes, his bushy eyebrows rimed with frost. The wind whistled, and I realized those dark clouds were nearly on top of us, blotting out the stars.

Tarlington caught my unwilling gaze. "What's going on, Jonathan?"

I wouldn't say his name. Summon him further. Give this place the power to conjure him from the weather. I shook my head, mouth so dry I could have chewed on snow.

Clarke frowned. "You just need to ignore it. Do you hear me? Ignore it, turn away—stuff something in your ears if you need to."

"That's not going to work." Tarlington folded his arms. "Not if it wants to be heard. Otherwise we might as well have stayed at the huts and barred the doors."

Clarke exhaled a long, misty sigh that glimmered into ice and disappeared. "It's not real. You've told me yourself, Morgan. It's not real. Show it to me and I'll shoot it."

"It's not that easy." My mouth twisted.

"Well it bloody well should be!" he shouted. He pressed his gloves to his face, turning on the spot. "All of this! You see something, you ignore it or you shoot it. None of you have been making this easy for yourselves! It's no wonder—"

"It's no wonder *what*?" Tarlington snapped, almost shoving him.

"You've never seen anything?"

"Never!" Clarke shouted. "Because I haven't gone looking!" He took two paces towards the rope, then stopped, as if suddenly seeing how dark it had become.

My jaw hurt. My hands were locked into fists. "Go on, then. What would you do? If you saw—or heard—Randall?"

"I wouldn't bloody well follow him," Clarke said tightly, looking at the ground. "I'm not stupid. Even when he was alive, he led us to ruin."

Tarlington made a hissing noise, coming right up to him, and for a moment—just a moment—I thought he would throw a punch. Clarke stared at him, unmoving. The wind battered our backs, plucked at our clothing. The darkness outside the lantern-light was nearly absolute.

"We need to carry on," I said.

"No need," Randall's voice said in my ear.

I turned instinctively; let out a started shout when Tarlington grabbed me. He shook me roughly, fingers splayed against my collarbone, staring into my face. "What's it *saying*?" I swore at him, tried to push him off.

A beat later, he brought his hand to his mouth, making a sound like a wounded animal; turned, greatcoat billowing, and walked into the snow.

"Tarlington," I called, my heart pounding. "Stay in the light—"

"Why you?" he shouted. "Why you, and not me?"

I stamped over to him on my frozen feet. He pushed me away, not making eye contact.

"Why not your brothers, or—or bloody Cooper? That stupid vain-glorious idiot; they're *yours*—"

I exhaled a long, shaky breath, some of the fight draining out of me. "I don't know."

"He was my *father*." His smoker's voice cracked, and he gave me another, weaker shove.

"Tarlington—" Clarke said.

"It's not really him—"

"But you've been following him, haven't you—Jonathan?" he hissed, pinching the bridge of his nose. "The great Australis Randall—" Without warning, he ran to the front of the convoy. Out past my tracks, past the reach of the light, into the unbroken snow. Into the crevasse field. He was a tall, blurry shape in the darkness.

Faint red lights in the sky.

"Is it a monster, Jonathan?" His voice carried on the wind. "I thought you knew!"

I ran after him, breath coming in high-pitched little huffs, but Clarke grabbed me by the front of my coat, pushing me up against the sledge. "Stop it!" he bellowed. "*Both* of you. You bloody idiots!" He drew his revolver. "I'll go. You—stay with the dogs."

I waited. The wind screamed. The aurora had followed us. I shivered, thinking of how it had called Randall into the snow; filled him up; enraptured him. Australis Randall. He was named for the aurora, named for the South. It was trying to unnerve us—separate us. Becoming more sophisticated in its tricks. Learning how to use us against one another.

I drew the service revolver and turned around in a wide circle. The voice had gone.

Shouting came out of nowhere—*living* voices—and warmth flooded back into me. I could see Clarke towering over Tarlington, dragging him back by his collar. Tarlington wouldn't speak, but shook my hand tightly, the ice in our mittens crunching.

The sledges shuddered forwards again, the dogs on a short leash. We'd kept them against Clarke's wishes, but soon their time might come. I was exhausted, a hard, throbbing headache running around my jaw and temples. I'd have eaten anything as long as it was hot.

I led us out into unbroken snow. Perhaps there had never been any crevasses at all.

XII

Hot tea was like holding a kettle to my heart, wonderfully warm, and I gobbled my butter sledging ration straight from the greaseproof paper. Sleep was out of the question: the reindeer-skin sleeping bags that had made Randall so proud were frozen solid. But Clarke insisted on stopping to rest and eat. "We won't get anywhere if we're exhausted," he'd said, rubbing the back of his neck. "Or go running off—being foolish."

Tarlington looked guarded. "Eat." Clarke pushed another biscuit his way. He crumbled it into his tea wordlessly.

"I need to look at the sledge again."

"Not now," Clarke said. "Eat."

We'd peeled off our helmets and balaclavas, and I could see Tarlington's throat rubbed raw, as if freshly strangled. The threatened blizzard had held off, but our little tent, lit up with stove and lanterns, felt very precarious. A tiny spot of light in all that dark, as if we were showing it exactly where to find us. Cold fingers around my heart squeezed out all the warmth.

Tarlington was fiddling with Laurence's tool kit. Everything we carried was taken from dead men, and I remembered: Laurence hadn't thought the sledge would last this long. Laurence had gone willingly.

"Morgan," Clarke said quietly, putting another lump of sugar in my tea.

I nodded curtly, stretched out my shoulders. I refused to despair.

The tent billowed around us, sucked up by the wind, pulled into awful hungry angles. We shouldn't carry on with the weather so close. But—unspoken—we started to pack. It seemed a miracle the motor would still run; one that could be snatched away at any moment. The knocking sound was back.

We took off at a crawl, and I soon lost track of time. It might have been morning, afternoon, or any point in the twenty-four hours of darkness. The moon was absent, the aurora a dim glow. I couldn't see the mountains, or how far away they were, although something told me they were *reaching out* to us. That impression grew and grew, making me look around, tripping over my steps, my heart jumping, until I caught up with Clarke and made him stop.

"Where are we?"

Snow was falling.

The sledges came to a halt. Tarlington swore. "Overheated, again!" He patted the engine grudgingly, like it was some sort of very stupid animal. I stared at its tracks, thinking again of Harry; battlefields; tanks.

Warmth was just a memory. We had a routine for these breaks by now. I helped Clarke strike a lucifer to read the compass and sledge meter, and saw him scowl at the short distance we'd traveled. Tarlington looked over the motor, sometimes training his rifle on our tracks, which disappeared into nothingness at five paces. I ran short laps around them, my muscles screaming. I couldn't feel my feet. My arms were dead weights of meat on my shoulders; I remembered how Randall had smelled like spoiled meat, and ran harder and harder. The blowing snow hit my face like a thousand needles, making me release a small sound from the base of my throat, not quite a cry.

"It's getting heavier," Clarke called. "We've been going too slow—" Again, the crawling sensation. We weren't being chased; we were being *stalked*.

"If we left the motor, relayed provisions—"

"We've been over this." Clarke's voice was grim. "No."

My eyes darted around. Our patch of light was horrendously exposed, naked in the face of the darkness. There were blisters under my clothing, and I'd pricked them open by lantern-light, squeezed out the frozen matter inside, doing my best not to howl. But now it was snowing, and suddenly very hard to breathe.

"We have to." My voice grew higher. "Clarke, at this rate it'll take a month, and the weather—"

"You think I don't know?" he shot back.

"We could man-haul," Tarlington said. "We could try."

"There's hundreds of pounds of supplies on there. *No.*"

We both started to talk at once, voices rising, and he wheeled around, standing over us, blocking out the sky. "You wanted me in charge? Then I'm in charge. And leaving the motor—leaving all that behind—is madness. We might as well walk into the bloody darkness and lie down and die. How much do you think you can haul? A few days' rations each? A week, perhaps? A quarter of the fuel? And then what? There's *nothing* out there!" He was shouting now, his voice echoing around the plateau.

"Look!" he bellowed, thrusting his gloves in our faces. He'd lost several pairs; each had tied-up little stumps on the right hand, where it was just thumb and forefinger. He struggled left-handed with the matches, with the stove. This was his first expedition since the accident. "Look. It took my bloody fingers, ruined my hand, and that was one night—just one night!"

I hissed out a breath between my teeth. For a moment I thought he would hit us. But he looked over our heads, narrowed his eyes. "We carry on. Quickly, now."

Behind us, where the lantern-light ended, the drifting snow was like a sheet or a billowing curtain. And the sensation—not sight or sound but something primal, felt right down my spine and into the marrow—that there were figures beyond. Just out of reach.

"Get us moving!"

It had finally caught up with us.

I pulled out the service revolver with chattering hands, transfixed by the whispering snow. I thought of sheets; stage ghosts. Silence. Whiteness blanketed the earth, blotted out the sky, the horizon. This was what it wanted: it was trying to erase us, scrub us off the map entirely. Make us disappear like Karlmann, like anyone who landed on this shore.

It might even be part of this place. Showing us its killer-whale teeth.

Tarlington dropped a tool, hissed, "God—"

Something was gathering into sight behind the sledge. An indistinct shape. Barely more than a reflection in murky water.

At least we would die fighting. We wouldn't lie down, starve, freeze to death.

Tarlington reached, unbearably slowly, for the rifle. Keeping his eyes on the darkness. Whatever he saw, it made him suddenly stumble back, his hands shaking. Then he took the shot, eyes wild and furious.

Clarke's rifle clicked—a jam.

"Jonathan!" Tarlington yelled. "*Jonathan!*"

He turned back to the sledge; didn't look to see whether I'd heard or understood. I ran towards him, those angry knives stabbing at me, Webley at the ready. Clarke bent over, pulled on the throttle with all his might. The engine stuttered.

I stared at the void, unblinking. There was nothing there, nothing at all.

"I think I got it," Tarlington called, a thin rasp of desperation to his voice. The engine knocked. The wind whistled.

Something flickered in the shadows. Something behind a curtain. Something that wasn't really there.

"Jonathan!"

I didn't give it time to become someone I recognized. My whole world focused down to the gun, and I squeezed the trigger. The wind snatched away the sound of the shot.

But the shape was—suddenly—gone.

"Keep moving!" Clarke roared. "Just a short way—we'll come back for it!" The dogs were howling, barking, skidding around the sledge, getting underfoot. "Cut them loose!" I gathered Coats up under my arm, and he bit me so deeply I thought he'd hit bone. I stumbled. My feet were too numb to walk.

We didn't make it very far.

The wind started rising, rising, rushing around us. Blowing the snow horizontally, until it was impossible to make out Clarke or Tarlington. I could feel it *pulling* at me. Trying to lift me up, sweep me off my feet. Drag me off into the dark polar skies. I sobbed.

"Stop!" Clarke shouted. "Get back—get under cover!"

A frantic rush back to the stricken sledges. The tent thrashed like a devil, tearing itself out of our hands, dragging us across the snow. I felt every muscle in my body straining to keep myself on the ground. We lashed it to the sledge, which weighed more than five hundred pounds, but the tent seemed capable of flying away—taking us with it—at any moment. The noise of the wind and the canvas was unimaginable: an express train bearing down on us. Banging; sucking; the hammer blows of a hundred engineers. Clarke pushed me to the ground. I lay on the snow, keeping down, and crawled about until our tasks were done. We took the dogs inside the tent, where they shivered and whimpered in the corners, terrified.

Visibility had dropped, but the aurora was somehow still there; a green glow sitting right on top of us, making my head pound and ache. And always, the horrible certainty that there were more than three of us in camp. There was something outside. We huddled in the tent and waited.

I was ready.

XIII

"What did you see?" I asked Tarlington. He was prying off his balaclava, and his growing beard, like his hair, was ginger in the dim light. For once I didn't feel envy. The beard suited him: made him look older, less unfinished.

He shrugged. "Randall, I suppose. It was very fast. But I could see—his sealskin cape. His frostbitten face. Somehow his ring, even though I'm wearing it."

"You shot him."

"Of course I did."

"Clarke?"

"I didn't see anyone." My mouth twisted. He said hurriedly: "No—I don't mean that. It wasn't a person. Terrible." He rubbed a big hand over his weathered face. "Not Randall, if that's what you're asking. I don't wish for what's past."

I looked sideways at Tarlington, wondering if he'd half-hoped to see Nicholls again; laughing, creases around his eyes. I didn't know what I'd seen—what I'd shot. The darkness before the monster decided on its face.

The ice tried to punch its way through the ground cloth. The drift melted off our clothes, created marshy puddles. The dogs whined. The storm outside screamed its anger at us. We'd be drifted in. I drummed my fingers; tried to kick my legs, subtly, in the confined space.

"We need to dig out," I said.

"There's no use, Morgan," Clarke said gently. "The storm will finish when it's ready."

I'd read enough about blizzards, Antarctica, doomed expeditions. Storms that went on for weeks. I had no confidence we'd ever free the sledges. It all seemed such an awful waste. Clarke had brought in as much as the tent would hold, and we crouched amidst boxes and packs. The stove hissed, the dogs pricking up their noses at the smell of food.

"We might have made a run for it," Tarlington said, Clarke pretending not to hear. "I know it's stupid. But I don't think I can stand any more waiting."

I hushed him, and scratched Coats behind his wolfish ears, trying to draw a few degrees of warmth from his fur. Tarlington coughed, started prying open his windproofs. "At least there's room to lie down," he said in his scratchy voice. "And better food than you'd expect. I've had worse." Clarke was melting the bricks of fatty pemmican into the pan, making hoosh. We had to eat while we could.

I tried not to think about what was to come. "Smells good." It was true—my mouth was watering. "We can always dig the sledge out later."

I didn't miss the small tightening of Clarke's jaw.

"It did better than I expected." Tarlington's hands were steady—he was keeping them so—but I could hear the tremble behind his words. "And thank you for not letting me burn down those damned huts."

Somewhere over the dark horizon—we wouldn't make it to the cliffs now—they were waiting for us to return. The shiver started at the base of my neck and went all the way down to my toes. None of us looked the others in the eye.

"I'm sorry it's come to this," Clarke said, unexpectedly. He stared at Tarlington's ring, as if speaking to Randall himself. "If I'd known—"

"There's nothing to be sorry for—not yet," I said. "We'll see in the morning."

The wind struck the canvas like incoming mortars. The battlefield. France. Harry. My brothers, and where this had started.

I knew what I had to do.

We agreed to conserve fuel, and put the lantern out. The tent was darker than a coal mine. My whole body shivered convulsively, my bones knocking, my muscles clenching and contracting. I used to sit in front of the mirror, comparing myself unfavorably with that discus thrower on my old biscuit tin; wish desperately for muscles, tightness, a body I could recognize. Down South, I'd actually *grown*—could finally compare myself without flinching.

I waited for Clarke to fall asleep.

XIV

The aurora was directly overhead, rolling across the sky in jagged waves. In the green glow it was impossible to tell where drift ended and sky began. The storm's barrage had fallen silent. Perhaps we were in the eye of it. Perhaps it was simply waiting for us. I stamped my boots in the fresh snow; it was like walking on the surface of some terrible alien planet.

Tarlington hadn't asked questions. His eyes had flown open—he'd murmured, "I was waiting for you to wake me"—and started to struggle out of his frozen sleeping bag.

"You must be sure," I'd whispered, my heart pounding.

"Good God, Jonathan, of course I'm coming."

It would have been so easy to leave him sleeping. To go alone, as I'd once imagined my brothers going over the top: walking proudly at the head of the charge. But all that belonged to a different time, and a different Jonathan, who'd stood in the wardroom of the *Fortitude* and presumed to tell Randall that he knew about the South.

It would be impossible to take off our gloves outside; we'd readied the guns with numb fingers, terrified every rattle would wake Clarke. I'd once told him that the rifle was no use against ghosts. But when I'd fired on it, it had dissipated, become roiling snow.

The gun had some use. I wasn't sure what.

"Well?" Tarlington's face was pinched. "We can go as far as we like—run as far as we can—but it can reach as far as the ship, can't it? Like it did with poor bloody Cooper."

"It can." I kept my voice steady. "But I think I know why it could reach Harry. It'll keep coming until we lose hope." Harry had lost that hope at the very start. "We need to turn around and face it."

He gave me a sharp glare. "Then what?"

"I don't know. But you're right—anything's better than waiting."

"If the storm returns—"

He didn't need to finish. In a winter storm, we would be lost within moments. There'd be no way back.

I took one last look at the small red tent, dwarfed by the endless snow, knowing I was unlikely to see it again. I cupped my hands over my mouth and fixed it in mind: warmth; the smell of cooked meat; Clarke, sound asleep; the dogs, yawning widely and happily. I tried to tell myself they'd be safe for a while. But Harry must have told himself the same thing—that he might draw it off, keep it busy—and the thought made me shudder, blow steam through my fingers.

"Come on, then," Tarlington said, taking hold of my wrist. It took a few moments for my feet to move.

We walked out together.

It was so quiet. The winds played the fresh snow around us like smoke. The tent soon vanished into the gloom.

I could feel myself being watched. "Is it—following?"

Tarlington glanced back. "More than one." His voice shook. "God, this is a terrible place."

It had grown stronger with every death—with every surrender. Now we were so few, and it had become legion.

"Don't look."

We trudged on, our footfalls soft on the snow.

Shhh.

The voices started on the very verge of silence; hushed and intimate, like the hum of conversation in another room. Once again I was reminded of the corridor at home; the glow of candlelight under my brothers' door; my ear pressed to the keyhole.

They dumped us on stretchers, in the mud outside the clearing station—

The voices formed into speech.

Lying in our own waste. The smell of our rotting wounds. The nurses hurrying past, always hurrying, no time to stop, we were too far gone. Their dresses swishing over our faces. The groans and sighs as men bled out, and still more stretchers came—

I bit my lip hard, distracting myself with the metallic taste. It froze to my balaclava, and I could hear the rasp of my own breath in my ears. "Don't listen," I whispered.

The voice was unmistakably Francis, melancholy. As if he were telling me a bedtime story from the shadows, one that would not end well. Sitting on the end of my bed, in the dark, while rain pattered on the glass outside; he smelled of gunshots and dirt.

"Tarlington—don't listen." Because I could also hear snatches of another voice. Low, confidential. As if holding forth in the wardroom, telling his own stories of the South.

At least we went—

Rufus. Scornful. Talking about Tarlington.

At least we went—

And Randall, echoing it, just out of reach.

I thought he'd rot in gaol, get pneumonia with the rest of them, cough himself to death, spit like red currant jelly—and that would be the end of it—

"I can't!" Tarlington cried. His living voice made the others sound hollow. "God, Jonathan, I can't."

We stopped. I took out the service revolver. Tarlington unstrapped his rifle, straightened up: captain of his school's shooting society. He'd fought a war I'd never know.

"They're not real," he said, grabbing my arm. "You know it. You know it, Jonathan."

I drew in a long breath.

The aurora flashed like a gunshot, lighting up the sky, static electricity crackling in the air. My hair rose; I tasted metal. For a moment, there were shapes in the darkness, crowding all around us. Flutters of movement in the void, the beating of dark wings. The shadows resolving themselves into two humanlike forms. One was a faceless dark figure—at least to me.

The other circled like a tiger, silent on the snow.

"Rufus." There was no longer any harm in naming it.

His uniform was neat as deployment day; his smile handsome as the photograph in our hallway. The peaked cap made his wide green eyes very dark. "Jonathan," he said. "I've been waiting for you." The disapproval was gone from his face. He looked at me like we were children again, as if there'd never been a war. As if I'd never been an embarrassment, never stepped out of line. A deep, tender expression, reserved for guns and maps and Francis. My heart sobbed.

"What on earth are you doing here? In this lonely place." Supremely confident, as always. "Come on." He offered me his hand. Reflexively, I reached out. "We've got a long way to go together, and we must hurry."

"No—" I snatched my hand back. It was trying to trick me. Trying to get me to agree to my own vanishing.

"Come on," Rufus said patiently. "You can let him go—the conchie. We're not here for him."

"No." I raised my voice. "You were *never* going to take me with you." The wind was picking up around us, swirling and flurrying the snow, little whirlwinds and whirlpools. Veils; curtains; windows into nothingness. He came closer—I stumbled back.

I told myself it couldn't touch me.

"Thank goodness I found you. It's terrible out here, isn't it? A fellow could wander until cold and exhaustion take him." He nodded to the Webley in my twitching hand. "It's lucky you have that." His voice became intimate. Man-to-man. "There were times in the lines, you know, when I thought about it myself."

"Stay back—"

He came closer, until we were inches apart. Part of me didn't want the illusion to break; I couldn't bear the thought of seeing it dissipating, dissolving. The last sight of my brother blowing away into the snow. I held my breath, chest tightening and tightening until I could feel my ribs straining to collapse.

"Francis and I made a pact." He nodded behind him, where something was coalescing out of the air: something made from diamond dust and the flickering aurora. "I'd take care of him, if that day ever came. A clean, quick death. There's no shame in it. I thought Harry would do it for you—you're a lot like Francis, you know. You wouldn't have the stomach for it. But Harry—I trusted him to do that much, at least."

The revolver felt heavy in my hands, and I found myself thumbing back the hammer, checking the heft of it. He was right. It was a long, cold death. In the green half-light, we would never find the tent again. And even if we did, we'd only be drawing it out.

We shouldn't have come so far south.

"You know you've been thinking about it. Harry was right, you'll see—" and Rufus looked off to the side, as if he saw something I couldn't. Harry Cooper, perhaps, in the darkened snow—dead and perfected, the wind refusing to touch him. I shuddered. "There's no escaping this place. There's no escaping us."

He smiled, rare dimples appearing in the corner of his mouth. He was too young to have lines on his face, and would never grow old, not now. Peaked cap, endless green eyes. Nearly a perfect imitation.

But my brother had died a long time ago.

"No." I took a step back.

"You came here," it said, and its voice echoed as if several people were speaking at once—Rufus's diffident tones, the awful whistle of the wind behind. I realized, with a lurch of perspective, that I was speaking to something a lot larger than my eldest brother. "You came here looking for us. And now you're ours."

"You're a monster."

The smile slid off its face. "I'm your brother," it hissed, closing the distance between us. "Jonathan—"

That name didn't belong in its mouth: it was mine, and I'd claimed it on my own terms. Rufus had never seen me as I really was, but I was *Jonathan*—all that it meant—with or without him. I felt myself breaking, the pressure in my chest coming to a boil, something terrible erupting out of me at last.

I brought the revolver up, hand steady as anything, finally ready.

Suddenly it was Francis in front of me. He raised his hands; took a step back. The aurora flashed in his frightened eyes. I hesitated. My gentle brother, who loved books and flowers and sunlight. Then I fired hopelessly wide—three shots in a row—as the thing that wore Francis's face *snarled*, taking me to the ground in one deft movement, like a hawk swooping to earth.

I screamed, high and panicked. The *shock*. It was touching me at last. It was real, inhuman, ghastly. Crushing me like a tank. A mountain. A continent. Impossibly heavy. We were chest-to-chest. Not a single breath of human warmth.

Cold and heavy as a crevasse fall.

I kicked and struggled, but it was strong. Far stronger than Francis had been in life, and we'd only been making it stronger. With every death—every murder—every set of footprints wandering off into the snow. And then we'd gone to find it—to confront it. Acknowledging its might. Humans pitting themselves against the wild desolate landscape. How it must have laughed.

"It's time, Jonathan."

It had all led to this: my brother was crushing the life out of me.

I thrashed. My frozen arms felt like lead. Its cold hands went around my throat, and I screamed again. Tried to bring the Webley to bear.

Fired it—wide—as we rolled. The monster batted it away like a toy. As I fought for breath, I thought of home: the biscuit tin under my bed, my treasures—snatched away and lost forever when my mother had finally unearthed it. *Unbecoming*. I'd been right to treat it like a grenade, like a bomb in that house waiting to go off. I could understand now—it had been a weapon.

I was meant to *fight* for Jonathan Morgan.

"It's for the best. Come with us now."

It was dark, so dark, and I didn't think I could.

Starbursts exploded behind my eyes. Rufus flickered into existence. I was going to die looking at my brothers, I realized, as I'd wished and begged and prayed: anything to see them one last time. Anything to see Antarctica. The bones ground in my neck, my heels dug into the snow. I felt myself weightless.

A shout: Tarlington, too, was pinned down. *A Randall belongs on the ice*. Bulky and crouching, a half-realized shape in the darkness pressed the rifle across his neck. Powder snow sped across the scene, drawing a veil over it, as if he were receding from me. Or maybe I was getting farther away.

"Tarlington!" I screamed. "Tarlington!"

Francis put one hand on my cheek. It burned. His eyes were the green of the aurora. "Give in," he said. "Give in. It won't hurt."

It would be like going to sleep.

"Jonathan!"

Tarlington's voice brought a *thud* of recognition to my chest. I came back from where I'd been soaring, high above the scene, with the jerk of a harness snapping taut. Without thinking, I smashed the revolver into its face.

It hissed at me: a horrible long, sibilant sound, utterly inhuman.

I had to hurt it—kill it. Make it stop, stop, finally stop. I kicked and swore and struggled against it, and it became heavier—even more insistent—

But it was no longer hiding behind the aurora or weather.

Crack.

A rifle shot, the sound piercing straight through me. My ears stung. I could see, dimly, Tarlington staggering to his feet alone.

Francis—my cold, dead, impossible Francis—suddenly became insubstantial, as though we'd been plunged underwater still locked together. I kicked frantically. He was everywhere and nowhere, dissolving. Becoming the wind. The darkness. I gasped, air pumping back through my windpipe, and retched into the snow.

I struggled to my feet. "It's gone!" Tarlington shouted.

He'd shot his Adversary, and Francis had disappeared: it was all connected. We were seeing the jagged edges of the iceberg poking out of the waves. Some parts looked human. Some parts were the weather. Or whispers, a scratching noise in a pitch-dark room. Some parts—now—could wrap their cold hands around our necks. But something larger still lurked beneath the surface.

"I don't think I hurt it. I don't think we *can*." Tarlington wiped his mouth, looking around. "But it's—retreated."

He made his way over to me, pulled my muffler down to inspect the damage, and the wind on my throat was like a knife. I broke away, staring into the darkness. The moon danced across the landscape, teasing me with shadows, little ripples and eddies of movement. The snow was swirling up to our knees.

Silence.

My heart pounded. Something was out there—holding back, marshaling its forces, getting ready for another assault. I could still feel that sense of giant *presence*, very close and very angry, as if the mountains were right on top of us. And Francis had felt utterly invincible—they'd always been stronger than me.

My chest tightened; I'd faced it before. I'd face it again.

Zero hour.

Tarlington raised his rifle, arms shaking. "Can you see anything?"

"No," I said. "Did you see—"

A harsh laugh. "Yes. But he's gone. He's *gone*, Jonathan."

Gone. My mind raced back to the plateau: the billowing veil of snow where my own gunshot had prevented it from taking shape. I hadn't waited to see my brothers. Hadn't looked—hadn't yearned. Hadn't let them in.

And Clarke. He'd shoot a ghost—to show it he didn't believe in it.

I don't wish for what's past.

Tarlington met my gaze, briefly, as if he could tell what I was thinking;

he'd put a bullet in his father's memory. A twitch of his lips. The ghost of a smile.

The wind buffeted me, caught me off balance. It made the sound of people screaming in the distance; screaming as they were being crushed or maimed, screaming under the surgeon's saw.

It was trying to frighten us.

Then—the sound of a footstep on snow. Quiet. Deliberate. Just a little out of sight.

"Don't shoot!"

Hoarse. Cracking. The familiar voice grabbed at my heart.

"Stay back!" Tarlington yelled.

Out of nowhere—I had it in my sights. A clean shot. A good clean shot. I took aim. Then had to look away, because I couldn't stand it. A sob burst out of me. My arms and legs stopped working, and I dropped the revolver with shaking hands.

I was right—it hadn't gone far. It had only changed its tactics, and these were the most horrible of all.

"Don't shoot!" The figure stumbled closer, reaching out its unsteady hand. "Please, Jonathan—"

But there was no grace in him, no horrible allure. Bare face blown red raw. Nose blackened with frost. The charred edge of his coat—singed in the fire—flapping ragged. He could hardly walk.

His feet left dragging tracks in the snow.

"No." I clutched my throat. "It's him. It's really him. I'd recognize him anywhere."

"Hell, Jonathan," Tarlington hissed, not lowering his rifle. "It's a *trick*. It's been—over a week. No one could have survived that long."

"A week?" the apparition said. His wide coppery eyes were rimmed with ice crystals. A slow blink. A swallow. Absurdly, I noticed his beard had grown in; no more officer's mustache. He looked like a polar explorer at last. "No, no—it can't have been that long—"

"You were—dead," I said.

Harry laughed, a small choking sound that went straight to my heart. "I thought so, too. But they came for me. Eventually."

And in that *eventually*, I heard all the horror of a night alone at the crevasse's edge, before he was . . . taken away. Taken to wherever that nightwatchman made its rounds. This landscape was hollow. *I don't think this place is real.*

"Don't listen." The lights glinted green off Tarlington's rifle. "It's a trick—even if it *is* him—"

Harry had been followed. I thought of Randall, returned to us broken; dropped back to die.

Harry was right, you'll see.

Hovering on the edge of human sight, I caught the faint glimmering impression of Rufus's smile. *Teeth.*

Harry removed his hood; the cold didn't matter anymore. I could see he'd lose his nose. Lips. Ears. He coughed. Breath had frozen in his beard, and he was shivering slowly, like a toy soldier winding down. There was no way he'd survive this.

I made a small abortive movement forwards, then stopped myself. It *wanted* me to go to him.

"I'm sorry." Harry's voice broke. "For the ship, and—and for bringing you here. I left them. Over there. I knew they were going to die. Hundreds of men. And I left them to it. That's why they're here. Rufus and Francis. It's my *fault.*"

Their horrible unseen presence pressed down on me. "They're not real!"

"They're real." His mouth twisted. "Your brothers. My friends. And now they're—whole again. Not on stretchers, not dying. Not blown to pieces, because I—"

"Don't be stupid!" I felt my throat tear. "It's not them. You're only seeing what you want."

And how Harry had *wanted*—more than anyone. I stuttered past his awful confession: *I left them to it.* No wonder he'd expected them to come for him. A lighthouse fueled by his guilt and grief and desperation: it must have been visible for miles.

But whatever he'd done—it didn't matter.

"We're not leaving without you."

"I belong with them." He coughed again. "Maybe I'm already dead."

I did grasp his arm, then, and he stumbled. He was burning up with the cold, an unearthly fever. There was something terribly wrong with his feet. "I'm not leaving you behind," I said fiercely. "Not again." I shouted to Tarlington: "He's real. You think I wouldn't know him? This is *Harry Cooper*."

Expectancy in the air. It was waiting—eager, fascinated—to see what I'd do. Harry would slow us down. We'd have to watch him die.

He, too, had been made into a weapon.

Behind him, I caught the impression of something tall—a shadow looming up in the night air. Shimmering green light dissolving into darkness. The hole in the aurora. The *absence*.

"He's made his choice—bloody well leave him!" Tarlington hissed, gesturing with the rifle. From the darkness, massed figures were watching, too many for me to count. It could be anyone. Anything.

The iceberg of this place was indescribably large.

Harry turned. His eyes widened. Then he squeezed them shut, shaking his head, his mouth twisting painfully. He opened them again. Those figures were still there. I waited for him to insist they were my brothers; to insist we should go with them. He seemed to hesitate.

"If you're not coming—" Every word sounded like a torment. "I'll—hold them back."

"No!"

"Jonathan, *please*!"

"We can't," I said. "Harry. There's nowhere to go. We've lost the motor, we'll never make it. We've got to go back to the huts."

"No," Harry said urgently. "Listen to me. The other sledge. The deserters. It's not far off. Two days, maybe. A straight line from here towards Shore Camp, north-northwest. You'll see it—"

A thunderclap in the still air made us duck as if to avoid incoming fire. Something shifted; the wind was starting to scream towards us, picking up the drift, vanishing the horizon. The figures were even less convincing, more terrible, far taller than a human could possibly be.

"You'll see it." He was talking fast, raising his garbled voice to be heard. "Trust me. I've walked up there. Imagine a map, crumpled up. Distance means nothing. And the ship. The *ship*, Jonathan—"

The ship. The freezing air reached every part of me at once. The

Fortitude. I could see her scrubbed timbers, her masts reaching up into a pale blue sky. There was no human way he could have walked that far.

A shadow: Francis was back, suddenly present, awfully close. Mere inches away—so close I might have touched his chest, felt the lack of a pulse in his graceful wrists—he held out his hand towards Harry.

"That's enough, isn't it?" he said. There was something dreadful about his smile. No dimples. Thin lips. His gentle face had curdled.

Maybe we'll take you with us.

Another thunderclap. Rufus stood a little way off, his arms folded. "Hurry up, Cooper, or we'll leave you." That look was even plainer on his face. An inhuman—bestial—fury.

Harry had been meant to make us despair; to convince me that I should walk into the snow. But he'd seen the ship. And there was a lot it hadn't understood about Harry and me.

"Now go." Harry reached out, his movements leaden, his eyes filling up with the aurora. Under the gloves, his hands must have been white, or black. Dying by inches, because no one could have survived that journey. But what he was reaching out to wasn't Rufus—seven feet tall, in the half-light—it was his death.

And Harry was still worth saving. I took a step towards them, and it smiled.

"No," Tarlington said, horrified. "Jonathan, *don't.*"

Maybe we'll take you with us. It had always been a lie. I crouched down to retrieve the revolver, stood up tall. I was going to end this.

"I loved you," I said, too quiet to be heard over all that sobbing wind. But it was the work of a moment, the space of a breath: Lift. Sight. Fire.

I shot Rufus in the heart.

The mask slipped. Snow whirled and spun around us, screaming up over our heads, blotting out the sky. Visibility plummeted and the world disappeared. Half-glimpsed—*felt*, by senses I didn't know I had—something as vast as the ice beneath us, as empty, unknowable. The swish of a coat in the darkness. Something standing *watch*. The wind was everywhere, sixty below, a hundred degrees of frost. I couldn't breathe. I couldn't speak. I couldn't move. I would die here: we would all die here.

But I wouldn't see my brothers again. I wouldn't follow that call.

And then it resolved itself, like a bubble bursting. Like a final magic lantern slide coming into focus even as its corners smoked and caught fire, making the image buckle and warp. Francis was dying in the snow, blood everywhere, his wide green eyes blinking. He choked. He struggled. He looked at me, mute with horror. I'd shot him in the stomach.

Harry had told me about gut wounds; if Francis had been real, he would have taken a horribly long time to die.

Harry staggered over to him, sank to his knees. But Francis's blood didn't quite touch the snow. The solid thing that had strangled me had gone. Francis shimmered, just another Fata Morgana.

The disguise was pitiful.

"It's not him," I said. "Harry, come away. It's not him."

He gave me a long, unknowable look, and I saw him struggle with all the choices he'd made. "Jonathan. I'm sorry. But I have to."

"Let him go." Tarlington grabbed me, not lowering his rifle.

For one slow moment under the night sky, all three of them were there: Francis, on the ice, coughing, pressing his hands to the spreading wound; Harry, kneeling by his side; Rufus, walking out of the darkness of that landscape—its *nightwatchman*—his long shadowy trench coat swishing across the snow.

"I'll kill you," I shouted at it, my blood roaring. "You hear me? You come again, and I'll shoot you again! I'll never go with you! Don't you ever come back! It's over!"

The aurora hissed its response.

"Either let me shoot him, or let him go," Tarlington said, and I realized he was talking to me. "We have to get to that sledge."

I threw the Webley across the ice to Harry. One bullet left. He might need it, when the time came.

We ran.

XV

The aftermath was a blur. The settling snow crunched under our boots. I fell, several times, Tarlington dragging me along. We ran from the weather. We ran from Harry, and my brothers, and the monsters in the snow. We didn't look back. It seemed awfully important not to look back.

"Hell," Tarlington kept saying, scanning the horizon desperately. "Hell, hell, we went too far—"

Our tracks were hopelessly faint, covered by blanket upon blanket of soft white snow, falling around us like a benediction. At times there were no tracks at all. A single set of footprints appeared from nowhere. But they made no sense at all: starting in unbroken snow, as if Harry had dropped in from the sky.

Clarke also came out of nowhere. The astronomical twilight played tricks, and he appeared as a giant. Holding my breath, about to pass out, I'd wrestled the rifle out of Tarlington's grasp and pointed it at him.

But I was tired, so tired. It was like being hit by a train. There was a struggle, shouting, the snow muffling our voices. Clarke was gentle with me, at least: he'd nearly broken Tarlington's nose. "Do you *mind*," Tarlington hissed, but I could see his eyes wide, thankful, as he pressed a mitten to stop the bleeding.

"Did you kill it?"

The storm had vanished. The air was crisp. The moon glimmered into three false satellites, like three great eyes watching us from the sky. We were small on the face of the earth. I hugged myself, looking up at it.

"I don't know. But it's not following now."

"Then we need to take advantage." Clarke shaded his eyes and looked up. "And get as far away from here as we can."

He helped us through the drifts, back to the tent; recovered our frozen feet and numb hands. He was silent and practical, even as I screamed with the pain of coming back to life. The bullets hadn't hurt it: maybe nothing could ever hurt it. But the Jonathan that might have followed his brothers, might have heard their voices in the white spaces, might have *wished*—

He was gone with the gunshot.

In the morning we abandoned the motor sledge, iced firmly into the landscape like a mausoleum. One final act of faith. We could haul only the bare minimum, and it wouldn't be enough to get us to Shore Camp; Clarke counted and recounted, obsessively, watched us wolf our food as he tugged the icicles off his beard. I flashed him a smile, tried to shield the dogs from his gaze, even though I was starving. We were very desperate, but no matter how often we stopped in the dark Antarctic twilight, Coats and Weddell whining at shadows—there was nothing.

Nothing followed.

XVI

It felt as if we'd become the ghosts. The light had left us entirely, the stars hanging overhead twenty-four hours a day. The icy plateau—its hunting grounds—stretched from the mountains to the sea, and we fled across it. After the roar of the engine, the sound of our small sledge over the snow was nothing. Panting and footsteps and dogs. An eerie silence.

I listened for voices, then stopped myself. I knew now. I knew you had to allow some small treacherous part of your heart to beckon it—whatever it was. Like leaving a light on for sailors lost at sea. Showing it the way in.

Harry had been telling the truth. It was three desperate days; we'd had to leave so much behind, and every evening we sat looking at the tiny hissing flame of the stove, wondering whether we'd made the worst mistake in the world. But on the third day we reached a hulking shape hidden in a depression, black against the surrounding whiteness. Without the moon and clear sky, we'd have walked straight by it.

Again—the sense that we were not really there.

I struggled breathlessly to take off my harness, frozen into chain mail around me.

"God." Tarlington laughed. "God, I didn't really think—"

I could understand the impulse to laugh. The deserters had built a cave, tarpaulin roof collapsing under the weight of snow. And on the other side, forming the wall against the wind, the sledge looked like an artefact of some long-lost civilization. The stenciled oilcloth, covered by ice: *1920 British Coats Land Expedition, James Australis Randall.*

It was so showy. So futile. It was so real it almost hurt my eyes.

"Cooper was right, for once," Tarlington said. Clarke snorted, a small smile behind his eyes. We looked at one another; a glimmer of hope.

Cooper was right. I could hardly bear to think about what that meant. What that might still mean. I looked up at the sky and gave a silent prayer of thanks to Harry, wherever—and *whatever*—he was now.

I tied Coats and Weddell to our sledge. They wagged their tails at me, clearly hoping for food, although I'd given them all my pemmican. One of the deserters' crates had blown off and broken open. We approached through sugar or oats, white and powdery, crunching underfoot with the snow.

"Wait." Clarke's outstretched arm held me back. There was someone lying on the other side of the sledge.

I shook my head and pushed past; I'd seen enough death by now. Clarke gave a small shrug, and our shadows loomed together over the corpse. It was Archer, although I struggled to recognize him as someone who'd once been alive, shared our mess hall, kicked a football around deck, played cards with the night watch. He must have died while there was still daylight. His face was tanned—turned to leather, as if he had stared at the sun and gone blind. He was naked, quite naked; his limbs black as tree bark in winter.

"Here, too," Tarlington called.

"Poor bugger," Clarke said finally.

I exhaled a deep plume of frost-smoke, and left Archer behind. The deserters had made barely any progress towards the water. The winds must have forced them to take shelter. Or perhaps they'd been looking over their shoulders, afraid we might come after them.

"Help me with this." Tarlington started to dig out the provisions, not even looking at the tent or the second body inside. Jones was still holding his revolver, fingers frozen fast around it. His head was a bloody ruin.

Clarke shook his head. "What a waste. He was better than this." He leaned down to check that the photograph of Jones's wife and daughters was still safe in his front pocket. I bowed my head for a moment.

We hauled out the body and took a detailed inventory in the moonlight. This would see us as far as Shore Camp. Mortimer remained missing, though the dogs sniffed around the sledge in ever-increasing circles. The silence made me wary. There were no tracks. There was no sign of him, as if the snow had simply swallowed him whole.

I looked back at the bobbing lanterns that were Tarlington and Clarke. With a small shiver, I remembered the night of the desertion, those gunshots in the dark.

"Anything?" Clarke said.

"Nothing." I bit my lip. "I thought it was you. I thought you'd—"

"You thought I'd do something like this?" He gave me a hard look. Then snorted, and bent to wrap Archer in tarpaulin, limbs stiff and angular as a board. "I went to try to convince them—they shot at me. Disappeared into the snow like they had an appointment to keep. I didn't follow. I'm not an executioner. Neither was Randall. He was a good man, for his faults."

All those months ago, I hadn't thought of it as an execution. I'd thought it was rather heroic: dreadful, yet heroic. Utterly in keeping with the world I'd expected. But what had happened to these men, I knew, was something darker still.

I looked up at the endless sky, remembering what Clarke had said while we were still at South Georgia. We'd been sitting around the fire: the warm weight of Harry on my left side; Tarlington trying to read, and being mocked for it by the stokers until Randall's glare had silenced them. "Sometimes the South just takes a man," Clarke had said, looking thoughtfully at the bottle of whisky. "And there's no explanation. He can be a few miles from home. He can be safe at base camp, with no reason to go outside. But sometimes, the South just wants him. And the South will have him, one way or another."

He wasn't the sort for long speeches. It had run shivers down my spine, made me wrap my borrowed coat more tightly around myself, wonder whether I was equal to the frozen world below us.

Sometimes the South just takes a man.

I helped him dig. The dogs wouldn't go near the corpses.

XVII

The laden sledge was heavy, but the plateau was flat, the snow set into a smooth surface. *Good hauling*, the old Antarctic hands would have said.

Coats and Weddell pulled beside us, and I scratched under their chins and pointed out to Clarke how useful they'd become.

The ground sloped long and inexorable towards the coast ahead. When the wind came from the west, I could almost taste the salt, and pulled down my balaclava to take a deeper breath.

"Anything?" I called to Tarlington.

"Nothing." He raised his hand in salute.

There had been nothing for several nights. Just the weather, grim and gray and incapable of reason. Once or twice the throbbing wind made me jump, because I could swear someone was there: a thousand eyes in the night, unblinking. But it always disappeared as quickly as it came, like ripples on the surface of still water as something withdrew, nosing its way back under the pack. The swish of a killer's fin, cruising away out of sight. The binoculars stayed under my clothing, until the strap froze to my undershirt.

I'd hesitated before reading Harry's journal, but we'd have no more secrets. And if it was Harry watching me—somewhere in that unbroken sky—I felt sure he wouldn't want me to join him.

He was a terrible narrator, and his journal was muddled and rambling, full of contradictions, justifications. Some things I knew to be utterly untrue. But he returned, again and again, to what he'd done to my brothers.

The last year in France. They'd all ended up somehow in the same dead-end loop of the Front, battalions being stocked and restocked as they were mowed down in turn. Still, things appeared to be going well. Harry was based in the bombed-out shell of a farming village; on the other side of the lines, a short distance away, barbed wire covered the riverbank. Deadly. Impassable. The trees made it invisible to reconnaissance flights, and they'd wasted a handful of scouts, who could be seen dancing on the wire when the wind blew, scarecrows in sodden khaki rags. Plans had been made. It was near the end, everyone had become a little inured to death. Randall would have liked the attitude: failure wasn't an option. It was an article of faith that the barbed wire would be destroyed by the artillery barrage, as planned. No one wanted to think about the alternative.

But Harry had wondered. A morbid, creeping sickness, taking him at night, forcing him to look, crawl to the observation post, look again, *keep looking*. The barbed wire was still there. It remained. It persisted despite the crashing and whistle of his guns, that thunderstorm playing night after night.

Binoculars. Mud. Binoculars. Barbed wire. He was sure it was real. He was sure it was there.

His superiors shouted him down, so he didn't press it. He was jumpy, he was nervy: he was seeing things. An officer should know better. The assault would go ahead, the wheels were turning, the machine set in motion. My brothers took their rightful positions in the vanguard.

Harry said nothing.

Before: a day on leave at Southsea Beach, a hundred miles from the mud and stench and horror of the trenches. Harry had moved mountains to get leave at the same time as Rufus and Francis; Rufus had pretended—I wondered whether it was pretending—not to care one way or another. Salt spray in the air. Ice cream, to celebrate Harry's promotion at last, after slogging up through the ranks, proving himself, growing from a boy into a young man—a *temporary gentleman*, that was what they called him. I'd sat in the shade, resentful, while the three of them rolled up their trousers and splashed through the surf. Rufus, turning to Harry with a sneer: "I don't know how you did it, Cooper. You artillery boys have been useless, just useless—it's the rest of us who've been doing the work."

Francis smiled, and squeezed Harry's shoulder, saying as sincerely as he could: "Oh, they're doing their best."

Harry looked up at Francis and shrugged off his hand.

He said nothing.

Back in France, the barbed wire was still there, and still Harry said nothing. He wrote about the horrible sweeping moment when the scale of the disaster became apparent: when the guns fell silent, hundreds dead or dying, trapped by that wire. Slashing with bayonets, they had no hope of cutting it while the attack screamed on; the German guns had turned on them, and the wire was where they'd *stay*. He'd made all sorts of bargains in that moment. With fate, with the Almighty. And he'd taken it on himself, long before he'd ever seen my brothers' ruined faces. Hugged the guilt to his chest, made it his and his alone.

It was all his fault. He had killed my brothers. He had done this. It was no one's fault.

But we all have our own accounts of the South, and what brought us here.

When we finally hit the coast, it was a cold starry night. We could hear the Emperors calling from the shore ice beyond. It was like being shocked back to life.

Tarlington and I unclipped our harnesses, leaving the sledge behind, running the last hundred yards. Breath freezing, panting, boots kicking up snow, the dogs howling and yapping, eyes shining with delight. He skidded to a halt, clapping his hand over his wide mouth, then let out a whoop.

My heart soared. The boat was still there, mounded over with snow. A line of flags, dark as blood in the moonlight, fluttered in the wind. Pointed the way—over a shifting and crackling walkway of solid ice—to the wreck of our ship.

THE *DEVASTATION*, AUSTRAL SPRING 1920

"Well, she's something, all right," Clarke had said. Then smiled, slowly, as if he couldn't quite believe it.

"She's the *Devastation* now," Tarlington replied. I'd reached out to touch her hull, expecting my gloves to come away filthy with soot.

"Good girl." Clarke looked up at her with an air of adoration. "Good girl."

The great warren of the belowdecks had become less claustrophobic: from the gutted ruin of the Nursery I might have seen right through to the mess hall. The fire had taken the interior walls, hollowing the ship out, until she was sketched in angular beams and orphaned panels. Hatches led to nothing. Floorboards crumbled underfoot. But Randall's construction had been sound. The fire had failed to penetrate the greenheart hull; Wild must have opened all her inlet valves, scuttled the water tanks, soaking her from the inside as the snow had whirled outside. My heart ached for those sailors, wondering how long they'd worked in that deadly confusion of fire and wind. There was no way of knowing.

Mortimer and the sailors had been right: the *Fortitude* had been waiting for us all along.

Her hull was frozen into the shore ice like an almond in a bar of nougat, and the Weddell Sea pack had closed in around her sides, hoisting her up and sideways precisely as designed. We'd done our best to determine the extent of the damage, but there was no visibility in that midnight water, where cutlery and sleeping bags and the bodies of the lost seamen must have lurked, unreachable, below the surface. We lived precariously in the deck lockers and sledging stores, our world tilted at an angle, all the metal fixtures warped and the ruined rigging hanging like spider's silk. The wardroom clock had continued ticking, which gave me the shivers, and eventually I waded through—heart hammering, waiting for a hand to reach up from the freezing dark water and grab me—to stop the mechanism.

In each direction around her, the ice was an endless white carpet dusted with snow. It was possible to walk across the frozen landscape, floe to floe, to the rookeries tucked under the cliffs, returning with a brace of penguins. We stank of blubber and grease. The dogs ate well, too, and we became sick of the taste, the smutty thick smoke of the stove. It was barbaric. It was almost cozy at times.

Randall was as good as his word: no one would die of frostbite or exposure on his ship.

When the aurora was out, we stayed inside, telling stories and playing cards. No voices came. Nothing else walked the slanted decks. I could feel, sometimes, a *pull* from something on the shore, as if it were trying desperately hard to get my attention. But we were miles away from Expedition Point and the emptiness surrounding it. Where its *nightwatchman* walked; where cold fingers of the aurora crept over the sky; where no human flag should ever fly. A place that wasn't meant to be found.

And if it was beckoning to me, trying desperately to reach as far as the ship—as it had with Harry—I wouldn't be leaving that light on.

It could drown in its own darkness.

Austral spring crept up on us. Every day the sun came up a little farther, and we made our way out of that forever-night, the *overwinter*. I lay on the deck feeling the light on my face.

I wept openly.

The *Fortitude* would never leave Antarctica; she would barely drift back into the Weddell Sea without being swallowed up. As the ice started to twang and creak and groan under pressure, Clarke hauled himself daily over the side in harness, trying to anticipate the awful moment when she would settle; give out a low moan of distress; start to slide. Then the sea would come rushing in like the Flood, and we would have to abandon ship for a second—final—time. Take to the boats.

Live one day at a time, for however long we could.

My binoculars were trained on the horizon, and I patrolled with a flare gun rather than a rifle. Any ship would have to come this way through the pack to reach Vahsel Bay or Karlmann's huts, where we had posted our tin-can mayday on the door, painted in bold strokes: "DANGER. DO NOT OCCUPY." Clarke had bullied Randall into leaving his route with the whalers; Captain Hvalfangeri had thought a relief ship *might* be organized by the battered German nation for a hero two years missing. Randall had known Karlmann well enough to think it likely.

We didn't discuss it much, or speculate—but when it was an open-water sky, we were outside from dawn until nightfall, hanging over the railings, watching the dark sea reflect itself in the dark clouds. Weddell and Coats would howl at the sky and race around, jumping over the holes in the deck, all enthusiasm and glossy fur, making me laugh.

Closing my eyes, I could imagine the *Fortitude* still golden-tinted, warm, home. The sound of the dogs conjured up Harry, holding them scuffling and quarreling as the mongrels and the huskies fought for superiority. Duncan, exasperated, yelling at him to keep them quiet. Boyd, on the bridge, rolling his eyes and turning to Nicholls, charts shielded from the wind, accepting a cup of steaming coffee from Macready. Randall standing with his hands clasped behind his back, looking out with approval over his little kingdom.

But they were gone. I opened my eyes.

Clarke shouted, "There's something—a flash!" and scrambled along the deck, snatching up the flare guns. I ran to the side, my heart hammering, breath coming unsteady in my chest, straining to search the horizon.

Through the binoculars, I thought I could see a small speck of darkness, like grit on the lens. It shimmered, too far away, then winked out again. Perhaps a Fata Morgana. But with a flutter in my stomach, I saw that it had been northeasterly in the pack, towards Coats Land—the Sandwich Islands—South Georgia.

My smile widened.

"What do you see?" Tarlington grabbed my hand, warm and sure.

I squared my shoulders, breathing in the ice. Behind us, the frozen sea stretched to the cliffs, and the mountains were angular dark slashes of ink on a white-and-blue page. The world was wide, so wide. It would be autumn in France. Leaves would be falling on my brothers' graves, resting side by side. Here it was spring, and open-water skies. An unmapped plateau, vast and unknowable, led from the sea to the huts. They would stand empty for the next expedition that dared to come this way; perhaps they were not empty at all. In front of them, the lonely grave of Australis Randall. And Harry Cooper, good soldier, loyal friend: somewhere between Antarctica and No Man's Land.

And there were monsters in the corners of the map. Hiding in all the white spaces.

But they were gone, and I wouldn't wish to see them again.

ACKNOWLEDGMENTS

Thanks go first and foremost to my agent, Oli Munson, who picked this novel—and me—off the slush pile in early 2020 and showed tremendous fortitude in the eventful year that followed.

I'd like to thank Lara Jones, my editor at Atria: this project has benefited immensely from her passion and editorial insight. Thanks also to the entire team at Atria, particularly Chelsea McGuckin and James Iacobelli for the gorgeous cover design, so reminiscent of Frank Hurley's *Endurance* photographs; Hope Herr-Cardillo for their beautiful interior design and much appreciated attention to detail; and the eagle-eyed copyeditors and proofreaders who have certainly saved my skin more times than I can count.

I'd also like to thank Cat Camacho, my editor at Titan, whose interest in polar survival stories—and attention to detail—has been evident throughout. (I've also enjoyed the knitting chat.) Both my editors had a wealth of thoughtful comments and queries about the characters and their relationships: without Lara's and Cat's input, this novel's host of sad young men would have remained half-made, half-realized, and I owe them a considerable debt.

More gratitude than I can possibly express goes to my incredible friends and first readers, Lucy Apps and Dan Jones, whose criticism knocked the book into shape and whose continuing support has kept me sane. I'm sorry (not sorry) that we've often discussed horrible things over vegan junk food. I'm sorry (not sorry) there'll probably be frostbite in the next one too.

Thank you to everyone at Curtis Brown Creative, particularly the one and only Simon Wroe, whose tuition was encouraging, inspiring, sympathetic, and funny by turns. From my fellow students I received helpful critique (the "reaving of souls") and an inexhaustible well of camaraderie: I owe the Black's group—and Efford House set—many bottles of Picpoul when this makes it into print. You gave me the confidence I needed to keep going, and the gentle but firm prompting to send *All the White Spaces* out into the world. Thank you—not least for the title.

Thank you to the supportive and often hilarious UK 2022 debuts group, particularly Emilia Hart, for helping me through a thorny period between book deal and publication. You're all amazing.

Thanks to my generous and kind friend Sophie Wing, who has been a tireless cheerleader for this and every writing project: one day our books will sit side by side and whisper to each other when the bookshop lights go out. Thanks also to Freya Crawford, who listened to many early ideas about "the frosty gays," and to Claire Baillie for her nautical knowledge—any errors made here are entirely mine, and one day we'll go and touch the *James Caird* together.

Thanks to those quoted in the book: the poem read by Randall is "Crossing the Bar" by Alfred, Lord Tennyson, and the poem quoted by Tarlington is "Epilogue" by Robert Browning.

It goes without saying that I'm deeply indebted to my wonderful sensitivity readers (you know who you are). Without your generous and thoughtful input, *All the White Spaces* simply wouldn't exist: Jonathan and I are forever grateful.

Finally, love to my wonderful parents—this is the natural end point of all those books about ghosts—and to Alex, who always believed.

A WORD ABOUT HISTORY AND GEOGRAPHY

All the White Spaces takes place in a timeline in which Ernest Shackleton (and some other giants of early twentieth-century polar exploration) did not exist, although keen-eyed readers will recognize some common elements between Shackleton's *Endurance* expedition and Randall's *Fortitude*; this book is set in an imagined tail-end to the Heroic Age of Antarctic Exploration.

I am not a historian, nor is this—strictly speaking—historical fiction. I hope readers will forgive me for any liberties taken in the name of storytelling with the details of the War, Antarctic exploration, or indeed anything else.

Similarly, both then and now, Expedition Point—and the precise geography and weather conditions surrounding it—can't be found on any map of Antarctica.

SUGGESTED FURTHER READING

THE FIRST WORLD WAR

- *Men of War: Masculinity and the First World War in Britain*—Jessica Meyer
- *Breakdown: The Crisis of Shell Shock on the Somme, 1916*—Taylor Downing
- *Wounded: The Long Journey Home from the Great War*—Emily Mayhew
- *To End All Wars: A Story of Loyalty and Rebellion, 1914–1918*—Adam Hochschild
- *We Will Not Fight: The Untold Story of World War One's Conscientious Objectors*—Will Ellsworth-Jones

- *Boy Soldiers of the Great War*—Richard van Emden
- *Forgotten Voices of the Great War*—Max Arthur

FICTION

- *The Regeneration Trilogy*—Pat Barker

THE HEROIC AGE OF ANTARCTIC EXPLORATION

- *I May Be Some Time: Ice and the English Imagination*—Francis Spufford
- *The Heart of the Antarctic*—Ernest Shackleton
- *South: The* Endurance *Expedition*—Ernest Shackleton
- *The Lost Men: The Harrowing Saga of Shackleton's Ross Sea Party*—Kelly Tyler-Lewis
- *Endurance: Shackleton's Incredible Voyage*—Alfred Lansing
- *The Endurance: Shackleton's Legendary Antarctic Expedition*—Caroline Alexander
- *The Worst Journey in the World*—Apsley Cherry-Garrard
- *Still Life: Inside the Antarctic Huts of Scott and Shackleton*—Jane Ussher

FICTION

- *A Victim of the Aurora*—Thomas Keneally

TRANS AND QUEER HISTORY

- *Fighting Proud: The Untold Story of the Gay Men Who Served in Two World Wars*—Stephen Bourne
- *Trans Britain: Our Journey from the Shadows*—Christine Burns, ed.
- *True Sex: The Lives of Trans Men at the Turn of the 20th Century*—Emily Skidmore

Turn the page for an exclusive look at
Ally Wilkes's spine-tingling new novel,

WHERE
THE DEAD
WAIT

THEN

CAMP HOPE, THE ARCTIC ARCHIPELAGO, 31ST AUGUST 1869

Who can bring a clean thing out of an unclean? No one.

The smell hits Day in the face.

Crouching in the hut's narrow entrance, he tries not to heave. He can't afford to bring anything up: his last meal was boiled boots and lichen, supplementing the last of their rations. He presses a hand against his mouth. Grimy, his skin shriveled and yellowed, it looks more like a claw. All the fat has melted off him; even kneeling hurts. He's only twenty-four, but might as well be four-and-seventy. He knows he won't see another summer.

Day takes a deep breath. With his mouth covered, the smell is stronger, separates out into its component parts. Blubber, clinging to his nostrils. Urine, from the rusting can next to him—a latrine for those men too weak to make it outside. Sweat, layered deeper and deeper until it's something meaty. He pinches his nose, but now the smell comes in over his dry tongue and swollen gums, and he can almost taste it, like chewing on a week-old piece of liver. *It's cold,* he thinks dully, *it shouldn't smell.*

Late summer in the Arctic, the temperature hovering below freezing, today's noonday sun staring perpetually down at them like a hole cut out of the sky.

This is a terrible place.

He squints. His eyes adjust to the gloom as his knees continue screaming. They all crawl around in here; there isn't enough space to stand. Nine faces look at him, pale and ghostly, eyes too large, huddled in their sleeping bags. The stillness is awful.

"What is it, captain?"

William Day, now leader of the *Reckoning* expedition—not that he wanted it—crouches in the entrance to Camp Hope, and surveys his meager kingdom. The ceiling is the overturned hull of an eighteen-foot whaleboat, greenish and damp with condensation, and the walls are oars packed tight with boulders, moss, anything they could prize from the frozen ground with fingers and nails. Their sleeping bags are stacked in two lines facing each other, like galley slaves. A quiet sucking sound as someone wriggles their feet, disturbing the muddy surface, and their neighbor curses as the cold soup trickles slowly down the incline towards him.

It almost makes Day long for a good hard frost.

Almost.

"Captain?"

The speaker is young Tom Sheppard, and his concern sounds perfectly genuine. When Day finds him in the dark, Sheppard's got his journal clutched to his chest; he'd nursed it under his clothing all the way from the ship, taking it out each evening to cross the pages with a dense tight hand, leaving nothing out. There's a stubby pencil tucked behind his ear: Sheppard sometimes licks the tip with a pink tongue, not particularly caring where it's been. He's younger even than Day, barely into his twenties, all long lean legs, and had begged by post for a place on this expedition. Day can imagine him on the deck of an ironclad warship, the air redolent with gunpowder, sun on his face. Scribbling his appeal, touchingly expressing his faith in *The Open Polar C.*

Day stares at him. Wonders how he could have been so wrong: about a man, about the Open Polar Sea. About everything.

There's a shuffling in the entrance tunnel. Bent double, like a bear rooting out its prey, First Lieutenant Jesse Stevens pushes his way into the stinking warmth. Day can smell the cold on him, the unrelenting dark chill of the ice, and the men in the nearest sleeping bag sniff the air like bloodhounds. They're all animals here.

"You have to tell them," Stevens says. He has a very pointed nose, and the cupid's bow of his lips has never been disturbed by swelling gums. Scurvy tore through their party back on the ship: now starvation is the most common cause of death, though it's truthfully hard to distinguish the two. But Stevens's mouth has never bled, and in the dim light of the single blubber lamp he still looks handsome: golden hair and thick red-tinged beard. The angel on Day's shoulder.

Day finds himself shaking his head.

There's a murmur from the men; a small sound of interest, at the two of them in disagreement, and Stevens gives him a look. He doesn't say it out loud, but Day can hear as easy as if he'd shouted. They don't need words, the two of them.

If you won't do it, I will.

"What is it?" Sheppard says again, in his lilting Southern accent. His eyes are wide and apparently guileless, but then, they all have wide eyes, now. Skin retreats, hollows out, as their bodies consume themselves. Sheppard looks between Day and Stevens, then back again. A mute look of horror as he appreciates the danger he's in.

Day puts down the bundle he carries. He notices, with some interest, that he's trembling. "Second Lieutenant Tom Sheppard. You're under arrest."

A sharp intake of breath.

"What?"

"You heard him," Stevens says softly, from his position just behind Day.

Day's hands shake as he pulls back the cloth, displays the contents of the bundle they'd found concealed by the creek. A few pieces of hard-tack, dried to the texture of a raisin and the hardness of a cannonball; Day estimates—as dispassionately as possible, trying to swallow down the rush of saliva—that this represents the daily ration for four or five men, depending on how carefully it's broken up. A Virginia tobacco tin which sloshes with fuel alcohol. The sealskin cloth itself, when they've been chewing anything they can get their hands on, anything that will keep mouth and teeth busy, when the rations are so meager as not to be worth the name.

Men crane their necks to look at these treasures, because that's what they are: treasures. It's been nearly a year since they left the ship.

If Sheppard were merely *hoarding*, Day might have been able to find a way to show mercy. He could maybe have confined him to his sleeping-bag, like poor Blackman near his end, lashed in tight as the delirium of scurvy made him babble, sing snatches of hymns, and bend his wrists back at the joints, crab-like and pained.

But that kindly narrative is no longer possible. In the dim light of Camp Hope, the gleaming handful of copper cartridges tells all. They make a chinking sound in Day's shaking hands.

"You're under arrest for theft and attempted desertion—"

"You dirty little—" one of the men bellows, and tries to climb from his sleeping bag and launch himself at Sheppard. Kicking and thrashing, he has to crawl over several men, and there's a shriek of pain, a horrible stink, as he crosses Campbell, whose feet are badly frostbitten. A hubbub of raised voices. Coughs and splutters. Shadows dancing around the walls.

Sheppard doesn't move, his mouth hanging open in a perfect circle of surprise, making him look almost unbearably young. His attacker bares his remaining teeth, clenches his fist laboriously. Day doubts he has the strength to do any real damage, but it's the principle of the thing. Now, more than ever—*today*, more than ever, with what Day knows is up on that grave-ridge—discipline is important.

There's a sharp taste in his throat when he thinks of the grave-ridge, and once again he has to fight down the urge to heave.

"Have Sheppard separated," Day says to Stevens.

His second-in-command nods.

They go out to execute young Tom Sheppard later in the evening, well before civil twilight falls. It's nearly all the same in the Arctic summer, where daylight never truly relents, but Day wanted to give Sheppard time to make peace with his god.

He doesn't see how such a thing would be possible, himself: there's no god at Cape Verdant. Ewing, sensitive Ewing, sometimes leads them in bleating prayer, but they only have one Bible left. All the others have long since been torn up for kindling. Nearly every single verse in that Bible has been underlined, pages thumbed translucent with greasy fingers, and someone has ripped out the Book of Job, so beloved by their dead Captain Talbot. Sheppard leaves the Bible behind when Day and the other officers come to fetch him; places his hand flat on its cover for a moment, as if trying to absorb some—comfort? Absolution? Day doesn't know.

The grave-ridge looms, watchful, above their camp: the overturned boat and little red tent sit in its long horseshoe shadow, protected from the worst gales blowing in across the frozen water. The signal flag flaps in the hollow breeze.

They haven't bothered to tie up their prisoner—there's nowhere to go from this rocky little semi-circle of land. Miles of featureless gravel cliffs to the west; ice to the north, east and south, shining like a shattered mirror. It seems to rotate like a puzzle-box whenever you turn your back. Look, to the east: a berg shaped like a bear. Now it's turned to face south. Now it's crept back on itself. Now it's sunk out of existence. You can make it into anything, anything the mind can conjure.

Visibility in the channel ends after a few feet, and the haze never seems to lift entirely, not for pounding sun nor howling winds. Day thinks there's never been anywhere more cut off, more profoundly distant from all human civilization, than Cape Verdant. Even the name is a lie. The ground is hard black rock, sharp enough to cut their hands.

This land is savage. Here all savagery dwells.

Perhaps Sheppard hasn't run because he hopes Day will relent; hopes his inexperienced acting commander will stumble over the limits of his own authority (*can* he have a man executed?) or, more likely, can't bring himself to bury yet another body. Day isn't a hard man, after all. But *hope*—the word has become something they spit, sneer, imbue with all the irony of dying men.

Day swallows. The exertion of climbing the shallow ridge has him bent nearly double. Up here, the peaceless wind tugs at his tattered clothing, scours the dirt and shrapnel away from the row of graves. He steers the party until they're out of sight. He *feels*, rather than sees, Penn's brass buttons winking through their thin covering of gravel. The dead are always watching him; reminding him of their presence. As if he could forget.

He didn't want this. He didn't want any of this.

"I will—" He coughs. "I will read the order." He pulls it out. His own handwriting looks like a swarm of ants, barely recognizable.

"Second Lieutenant Thomas Sheppard, trusted with our only firearm, has been found stealing food and ammunition. Those taken together show he intends to abandon his colleagues to their deaths . . ." Day moistens his wind-chapped lips. "Abandon his colleagues to their deaths by starvation. These actions display a wickedness"—his voice drops—"and treachery that cannot be tolerated. Sheppard is therefore to be shot today, as we have no sure means to confine him."

Sheppard continues to stare up at him, trusting. Day wishes he'd look away. Sees, in his mind's eye, Sheppard's hand lingering on that Bible, fingertips pressed lightly on the cover.

"This is necessary for the expedition to survive. After the death of Captain Nicholas Talbot, I, William Day, give this order as acting captain."

It's the day after their rations finally ran out. He'd consulted with the doctor, with their scratched-off calendar, to get the date as accurate as possible. Keeping a record is the bread-and-butter of any officer; this scrap of paper will explain what happened here, will go into the official log—whether or not it will ever be read by another living being. It shows he had good reason, legitimate reason, to execute Sheppard. The paper feels commensurately heavy. It's precious.

Day looks around. They only have one working rifle, the one Sheppard usually bears. Normally there'd be some anonymity for executions: several guns, one loaded, allowing each man to comfort himself with the thought that the fatal bullet came from another. But what are they going to do—get out knives, up here in the open air, and take him to ground like prey?

"Stand still," Stevens says, gently. Stevens is a good shot, good at everything to which he turns his hand. He'd volunteered. Day had noted, with leaden humor, that it wasn't as if there were any chance of missing. Stevens had shrugged, pale eyes narrowing.

Day realizes now that Stevens thinks Sheppard might run. The sun shines down on them, makes the back of Day's neck itch.

"I didn't do it," Sheppard says suddenly. He seems to come to his senses, recognize where he is: out on the grave-ridge, surrounded by the emaciated officers who'd survived the *Reckoning*.

They shouldn't have left the ship, Day thinks, with a clarity that startles him.

Sheppard must be freezing, because he hadn't put his mittens on after relinquishing that Bible, but it hardly matters now. He turns around, looks Day in the eye. "Please! I didn't. You have to believe me!"

Day won't look away. He won't. Sheppard deserves this much.

"Did *you* find it, Captain?" Sheppard says urgently. "Captain—the things they're saying I stole—it wasn't you, was it? I've been set up—*Stevens*—"

Stevens steps forward, rifle raised. The expression on his face is almost unreadable.

But Day knows him better than anyone.

Their grim duty complete, the execution party crawls back inside the overturned boat of Camp Hope. They'll have to bury Sheppard in the morning; he's been left to freeze up where the clouds are starting to blow out sleet. He's just a body now.

"Camp No-Hope," Campbell mutters, his gaze feverish. "I'm going to die in here. Or get *murdered*, like poor Sheppard."

Campbell hasn't been out of his sleeping bag in nearly a week, not even to use the latrine tin, his system torpid on their diet of mostly inedible things. The smell from his bag tells them his legs are likely lost; the doctor says operating in these conditions will kill him from lockjaw.

"They're gonna murder me," Campbell mutters. "Kill me and eat me. Dead weight, I've heard them saying it. I've *heard* 'em."

He doesn't specify who—but conversations are broken off as the execution party returns. Sheppard had been very popular amongst the men, sometimes conducting careful "interviews," which seemed to consist largely of noting down their favorite songs, meals, girls. Any distraction was welcome. He'd also trained with their Native hunters, now long-gone and much-missed, along with all the larger game. An Arctic fox here, a hare there: Day had joined the others in insisting Sheppard must have the largest portions, their chewy little hearts. Still, barely a mouthful. But they had to keep his strength up, so he'd be able to catch more.

"I won't let you down," Sheppard had said quietly to Day, with all the earnestness of youth. Day feels ancient by comparison, warped and stretched like refractions in ice. "I won't let us starve."

But now James, who used to share Sheppard's sleeping bag, is bartering his way out of that sodden sheepskin and into the relative comfort of buffalo. Sheppard's possessions have become the camp's new currency. Every man for himself.

Stevens nudges Day. He doesn't need to speak.

Day knows he should insist Sheppard's diary is located and turned over. It's expedition property, and should be surrendered. But Sheppard lies unburied, and Day's heart squeezes. He can't bring himself to do it.

Stevens gives him a look that's a whisker from insubordination, and sighs. Day's thought of sharing his sleeping bag, *yearned* for it—curling in beside him for the heat, their bodies together making a semi-colon, two separate but closely connected ideas. They'd done so back on the *Reckoning*, when it was so cold below-decks that the thermometers froze, but now he doesn't know how it would look to the men.

"Captain," the doctor says urgently, emerging from the canvas flap at the rear of the hut. The horrible ruin of his face, criss-crossed with scars, makes him look like a gargoyle half-eaten by weather.

Day crawls down the small gangway. Behind the flap, beside their stove, Paver lies dying, his eyelids sometimes fluttering as if struggling to wake from a dream. Day hopes he's somewhere else entirely. He's been given the liquid from the soup they made yesterday, lichen and the last of the crumbled biscuit, the consistency of thin snot.

It's the day after their rations finally ran out.

"How long?"

"Tomorrow, maybe," Doctor Nye says, taking off his broken glasses to polish them. It would be humorous—an affectation, they're all so grubby—if it weren't so pitiful. "His organs are shutting down."

Paver feels boiling hot to the touch when Day loosens his collar, presses a hand to his throat. It's probably an illusion.

"The others will *die*," Nye says, and Day reads accusation in his tone. "We will all *die*."

There's still no sign of night, not even past suppertime, and the sky crowds in on them.

Day sends Stevens up onto the grave-ridge with Jackson; now, he supposes, Second Lieutenant Jackson. Normally no one leaves the hut after dinner—which tonight is just tea-dust, they can hardly spare the fuel to boil water—and they settle down to discuss food, maddeningly, right down to the drinks and desserts, conjuring five-course meals from the air. Raisin pudding with condensed milk. Hot rum and lemon punch. There's a hallucinatory realness to it. But this evening, trying not to listen, trying not to let it gnaw at him, Day had caught snatches of whispered conversation.

"Someone will be held responsible—"

"Another few weeks, and then, and then, if no one comes—"

They suspect that this is a closed season: Lancaster Sound is blocked to the whaling fleets by the same ice they can see off Cape Verdant. And so rescue is unlikely to come, and they will continue to dwindle, far from civilization, in a state of pure savagery. Not even the Bible can save them now.

When Stevens returns from the grave-ridge, he has a glint to his sharp eyes. Jackson, on the other hand, looks sick; pale, greenish. Day meets them outside, where he's been pacing and looking up at that teeming sky, whispering curses.

"Is it done?"

Stevens gives a single nod. Day knows, in this moment, he'd rather have Stevens than a thousand other men. He's golden, from his hair to his hard-edged glitter; his value. He couldn't have done this without him.

"It wasn't hard to cut," Stevens says quietly.

Sheppard hadn't yet grown cold.

Someone will be held responsible.

NOW

I: LOST

London, 5th January 1882

The relentless symmetry of the Admiralty building had always given Day a headache. Columns rose regularly, disappeared in orderly and predictable lines like soldiers, and square ceilings pressed down on him, a stone sky, like being buried under the earth. Looking to his right, he saw a set of mirrors marching off into the distance, reflecting him into eternity—unbroken, undistorted. A hundred perfect William Days, as if he'd come back from the Arctic shining and whole. He looked away quickly. He almost preferred the spitting, hissing rain outside, although this wasn't proper weather, merely the suggestion of it.

They'd been expecting him. He didn't dare hope this was a good thing. Some Admiralty man might have guffawed, slapped his thigh with mean glee: "Do you know who's come forward about the Stevens rescue? Do you *know*? Who does he think he is?"

Day rubbed his forehead, surreptitiously tried to get some of the rain out of his hat. Water pooled around his uncomfortable chair, his coat dripping like a shipwrecked mariner. Fitting, because—on his return from America all those years before—he had indeed been marooned, not on a distant island or some foreign shore, but in his family's three-story town house in Russell Square. Although he had cause to be grateful that his father and supercilious older brother had somehow managed to pass on without him, and he'd never *want* for anything—although that idea almost made him laugh—it meant he'd live alone until the end of his days. Alone, but not quite forgotten.

And now he'd washed up back at the Admiralty again.

Sitting even more upright, Day fixed his eyes on the green door leading to the private offices. Change came creakingly slow, and everything was still as he remembered it from that rather cursory "investigation" years ago. The *Reckoning* expedition had never quite been under conventional Admiralty command, hence no real court martial, and no one had wanted indecent things to be made public; he supposed he was one of those indecent things.

Turning his hands over, he inspected them for cleanliness. Neat fingernails. His hands were soft. He would be forty in a few years, and his mid-brown hair was streaked firmly with licks of gray at his temples. His face was an honest one, people said, when they wanted to be kind. An ugly scar on the back of his left hand made him self-conscious; there were only so many situations one could wear gloves indoors. People always assumed it was something dramatic. He was quick to disabuse them: told them it was an accident in the rigging as a midshipman, and they looked disappointed.

He wasn't—quite—the monster people said he was.

But he'd always known, even back then, that William Day could never be fully exonerated. Not in the eyes of the public, or the press, or God. It would be madness to try. He could see them now, just as clear as before: all those whisperers in uniform, elbowing one another when they saw him, falling silent as he passed them in these echoing halls.

Murderer. Cannibal.

The green door opened, and a man left in high temper; he was very pale, with high, well-bred cheekbones, a swoop of mahogany hair and a face like curdled milk. Another, older, followed him by walking stick and determination, upper lip and chin covered with badgery whiskers. "It's hardly to be borne," the younger hissed. "*Him?* Hopkins has over-stepped himself this time, the Arctic Council will—"

"Oh, the Council will, will it?" the old man said with coolness. "The Council has nothing to do with it. Let them sort this new disaster out themselves."

They broke off, abruptly, when they saw Day sitting there, back pressed against the wall as if he were trying to disappear. "Excuse me," he said.

The pale man made a strangled noise, and grabbed his companion by the arm, ushering him quickly and roughly around the corner out of sight. Day heard them speaking to each other in low voices, and swallowed. He'd seen the widening eyes, the flicker of contemptuous recognition: the moment he was judged instantly on the basis of the worst things he might ever have done.

Lieutenant Day of the *Reckoning*.

Or, as the papers insisted on calling it, *the* Reckoning *disaster*. His likeness had been passed around the illustrated news, a monster with beard and wild hair. *Desperate and emaciated*, they said, and it was utterly true: desperation was the natural state of Cape Verdant.

Day sighed. Who did he think he was? Stevens, his former second-in-command, had left civilization and disappeared once again into the frozen North. He, at least, still believed in the Open Polar Sea. But only two years of provisions, for an expedition three years lost—despite Stevens's winking insistence that they could all fend for themselves, Day knew the idea of such a large party surviving on hunting was ludicrous. The crew of the *Arctic Fox* would by now be on short rations, shortening rations, maybe no rations at all.

Day, more than anyone, knew what that was like.

"Mr. Day." A face appeared. "Captain William Hopkins." The stranger offered his hand. He had eyes set close together, like some small carnivorous animal, all sleek fur and pointed nose. "Won't you come in? I'm sorry to have kept you waiting."

The room beyond the green door was dimly lit, a fire in the grate, rain tap-tapping half-heartedly against the windowpanes. By the fireplace, twin high-backed armchairs in olive velvet, and a low table covered with correspondence and newspaper cuttings. It looked disordered, but Day immediately had the impression that the room's occupant knew how to lay his hands on every single scrap of paper.

"Sit, please," Hopkins said. Although outside it was too lazy to snow, the room was warm; Day could feel the heat start to suffocate him. A large chart table displayed the official map of the Northwest Passage, and Hopkins bumped into it, with an air of annoyance, on his way to the liquor cabinet.

Day accepted a whiskey. Hopkins sat opposite. Up close, he was even younger than Day had first appreciated. But something about him appealed. He seemed like the rare kind of person who got things done.

"I had hoped to speak with the First Lord," Day said delicately.

Hopkins frowned. "But he's busy, busy. You know. Resources. Egypt."

Day took a sip of whiskey. He rarely drank, and it sat like acid inside him, in the tight hard knot of disappointment that had been building since he'd reached the Admiralty. Of *course* there were resource issues. Of course he'd come for nothing, and Stevens would be abandoned to his fate. Just another lost Arctic expedition, an American one at that. Whose interests would be served by saving him?

Another act of vast indifference by the machine of British bureaucracy.

"If there's another time, perhaps—"

"Not at all. I'm the one who answered you, Mr. Day. Needs must."

Needs must—and the other half of the saying, *when the devil drives*. It reminded Day so strongly of Jesse Stevens he found a prickling sensation running down his spine.

"The Stevens business is a concern of mine. Here—take a look." Hopkins leaned forward, perched on one bony buttock, and plucked something from the pile of papers between them. With a horrible creeping sense of humiliation, one that made sweat gather under his arms, Day recognized some of those newspaper cuttings.

They came back in iron caskets! shrieked the headlines. Just six caskets, sealed for repatriation, to hide decomposition and—the rest. The separation of spirit and body, played out in ruthless and gruesome detail. All those other lives extinguished in the Arctic without a trace. And the *Reckoning* lost.

Hopkins, like everyone else, had heard the very worst about him.

The velvet cushions exhaled as Hopkins handed something to Day, with arched eyebrow, and sat back again. But it wasn't what he'd expected: letters, addressed in a feminine hand to the First Lord. It felt wrong to be handling someone else's correspondence. *For the sake of the debt which at least one of your countrymen owes my husband—*

Day's wrists prickled. He tried to put it down to the heat of the room, but there was something about that scrawling hand, and its vehement message. A debt.

Shame.

"I don't suppose you ever met Mrs. Stevens?"

Day shook his head, swallowing the sour taste in his mouth. "They married after I'd left America."

After he'd fled back to England to escape the reporters and the rumors and that horrible nickname, the one that followed him everywhere. He hadn't even been invited to the wedding; there was no place for William Day at the feast. He found it hard to imagine Stevens married. Hard to imagine him anywhere but at Day's own side.

"People say, don't they, that he's a great man. But you can imagine how indifferent the Council has been, after that—Passage business."

He wouldn't say the name of Sir John Franklin out loud, and Day supposed he knew why: two ships lost, hundreds of men, nearly as many search parties, and all the Admiralty had got out of it was that line on the map showing a wavering ice-filled strait, never seen passable. Quite useless to the plans of Empire.

Hopkins refilled Day's glass. "Mrs. Stevens"—a small snort at the name, as if the title were reserved for those of a loftier character—"is determined that her husband is still alive. Tell me, Mr. Day—do you believe the same?"

That was, after all, why he was here, in the third winter of Stevens's expedition. Day couldn't believe—refused to believe—that Stevens was dead. The man would have found a way to survive. He might be chewing on frozen blubber with the Natives. He might be manning the darkness of an ice-locked ship, hunting rats in the hold, *small deer*. He might even be eating his own boots. But he was alive. The North couldn't kill that ceaseless, searching ambition.

And Day would know when Stevens died.

How could he not?

"Yes, absolutely," Day said without hesitation.

"Good." Hopkins unfolded his arms. "Good. Because you're going to find him."